Find My Way Home

MICHELE SUMMERS

sourcebooks
casablanca

Copyright © 2014 by Michele Summers
Cover and internal design © 2014 by Sourcebooks, Inc.
Cover design by John Kicksee

Sourcebooks and the colophon are registered trademarks of Sourcebooks, Inc.

All rights reserved. No part of this book may be reproduced in any form or by any electronic or mechanical means including information storage and retrieval systems—except in the case of brief quotations embodied in critical articles or reviews—without permission in writing from its publisher, Sourcebooks, Inc.

The characters and events portrayed in this book are fictitious or are used fictitiously. Any similarity to real persons, living or dead, is purely coincidental and not intended by the author.

Published by Sourcebooks Casablanca, an imprint of Sourcebooks, Inc.
P.O. Box 4410, Naperville, Illinois 60567-4410
(630) 961-3900
Fax: (630) 961-2168
www.sourcebooks.com

Printed and bound in Canada.
WC 10 9 8 7 6 5 4 3 2 1

To the best critique partner and friend, author Laura Simcox—without you, I'd still be stuck on chapter three. Your wit and insight were invaluable.

To my sisters, Carol Lynn and Nancy. Your encouragement always brightened my day, even when peppered with constructive criticism. Love you both!

Chapter 1

JUST BECAUSE A PERSON LIVED IN A SMALL SOUTHERN town didn't mean she had shit for brains. But then again, maybe she did.

"*Gary!* Where are those *damn* lamps?"

Bertie Anderson struggled with a cumbersome box of wallpaper clutched in both arms as she pushed through the heavy front door. A glossy Scalamandre shopping bag stuffed with fabric samples dangled from her numb fingers.

She cringed as she peered at her client's dining room. Half the brown-stained, mildewed wallpaper peeled from the walls as if it suffered from some contagious skin disease. She could've sworn the walls wept at their state of raw exposure.

"Gary." She stopped shuffling to listen for a response. No Gary. "Where the hell is he?"

Dumping the box of wallpaper on the dirty drop cloth that covered the polished oak floor and untangling the strings of the fabric bag, she renewed the circulation to her fingers. She surveyed the mess before her. Great. Another day lost. This couldn't be happening.

The dining room looked as though it had been abandoned by unsavory squatters. Littered with empty coffee cups and dirty, paint-smeared rags piled high in a corner, the place smelled of new paint and old mold. With hands on her hips, Bertie scowled at the half-stripped walls.

She needed to clean this mess up fast—and find a new wallpaper hanger to replace the one who'd bolted for a family emergency. And then, of course, deal with the fact that the electrician had gone AWOL.

She studied the room, reining in her frustration, which threatened to spew forth in an ear-splitting scream. She had exactly three weeks before she was expected in Atlanta to start her job as an interior design specialist at a new firm. Sure, she wouldn't be running her own business anymore. In fact, she'd be relegated to the sample room until she'd proven herself, but it'd be worth it to leave Harmony, North Carolina. Her little hometown had choked her half to death, and it was time to escape. Despite her irritation, a small smile lifted the corners of her lips.

Soon she'd be living in a big city, exposed to designer showrooms that housed all the latest in fabrics and furnishings, *and* she'd be living away from home for the first time since her college days. Excitement kept the fear lurking in her belly under control. A new chapter in her life was about to unfold. But not until she completed this renovation—hopefully before the Milners, her clients, showed up with moving van in tow.

Bertie waggled her fingers at the pitted-brass chandelier from Home Depot hanging cockeyed from the ceiling. "Bleh. You need to go." The Milners, who hated everything tacky, would skin her alive if she left it up.

She squared her shoulders and began cataloging the Herculean job ahead of her. She had designed this particular dining room using the inside of a jewelry box as inspiration, but right now the room looked ready for the wrecking ball, not two thousand dollars' worth of wall covering and tongue-and-groove wainscoting.

"Gawd. I need a vacation."

With a lengthy sigh that echoed in the cavernous room, she hiked her black pencil skirt up her thighs and climbed the ladder that was propped against the half-stripped wall, careful not to trip in her four-inch heels.

"Okay, so today I play electrician. How hard can it be?" She eyed the dusty, hideous brass sconces, which matched the travesty of a chandelier.

"Please Lord, keep me from electrocuting myself," she prayed, unscrewing the backplate to the sconce and staring at the exposed tangle of electrical wires inside the wall cutout. Crap. She had no idea what to do with it all. A familiar ringtone began playing in the pocket of her cropped chartreuse jacket. Gary. Thank God. Her best friend always came to her rescue. And it certainly didn't hurt that he had amazing talent. She couldn't ask for a better assistant. She fished for her cell and shoved it between her ear and shoulder, answering with screws in her mouth.

"He-roh…Gawy, whey are ou?"

"Sorry. Had to pick up more paint. Anyway, the new electrician should be there any minute, and I've put in a call for another wallpaper hanger," Gary explained.

"Kay. Thansh." She spit the screws out as she ended the call and dumped the phone back in her pocket.

"Hello? Anybody home?" a deep voice called from the foyer by the front door.

She eyed the coil of wires dangerously exposed like a snake ready to strike. "In the dining room," she called. Bertie juggled the sconce and the loose backplate as she heard heavy footsteps echo on the golden oak floors.

"Excuse me? I'm looking for Bert Anderson, and I was told I would find him here."

She turned toward the voice and almost dropped the sconce. She grabbed the top rung of the ladder to keep from falling. A very tall, dark, and extremely hubbalicious guy dominated her field of vision.

Her eyes narrowed as she peered harder a second time. Hmm-mmm, a little *too* hubbalicious. The guy was *perfect*—thick, dark wavy hair; hooded, dark eyes; sensuous mouth; sexy stubble; and oh yeah, killer body. Not to mention worn jeans that fit to perfection with strategic rips that screamed *fashion statement*. And Lord, his nice, broad chest was a little *too* nice and broad. He could model for Abercrombie—bare chested with his disreputable jeans riding so low, they bordered on scandalous.

"Christ on a cracker. I'm going to kill Gary," she said under her breath as she grappled with the sconce against her chest.

If this was a new friend who needed work but didn't know how to do anything but look good and make cappuccino, she was going to hurt somebody.

"Let me help you."

Before she could object, Mr. Perfect climbed the ladder, surrounding her with his electric heat and masculine scent. He smelled like a Saturday night shot of yummy. His musky, outdoorsy scent sliced through the mold and paint fumes. No heavy cologne like most gay guys she knew. Bertie had the strangest urge to lean her back against him and sigh. *He must drive the boys wild.*

"You want it down?" he rumbled close to her ear. Nice sexy, raspy voice. What a shame.

"Yeah. Great. You need to remove the other one as well and take down the chandelier." She handed him the screwdriver and pliers. The black knit sleeves of his polo shirt exposed tanned, muscled forearms, and Bertie spied rough calluses on his right palm. The sign of a man who worked with his hands. Thank goodness.

"Okaaay? Sure." Mr. Perfect maneuvered around her and made easy work of untangling the electrical wires. He climbed down the ladder with the sconce in his hand.

Nothing made her heart go pitter-patter more than a guy who knew his way around tools. She hiked her skirt up once more and started to climb down the ladder, not caring that her butt strained against the tight fabric. The beauty of working around gay guys in the design field: They never gave her a second glance except when she needed fashion advice.

"Let me help you," he offered.

"I'm fine. Do it all the time—yikes!" The ladder rattled as her foot slipped and a big warm hand slapped her butt to keep her from falling.

"Whoa there! You okay?" he asked.

Sweet sassy molassy! Heat burned her cheeks. It had been ages since a hand—any hand—had touched that part of her anatomy. "Uh, yeah. Sorry. I'm not usually this clumsy," she said as he held her elbow in a firm grip and helped her down.

"You might want to rethink those shoes and that skirt if you plan on climbing any more ladders."

She turned and detected heat behind his narrowed eyes as his gaze traveled from her butt to the dip in her black knit top where a hint of cleavage showed. *Whoa. My gaydar must be faulty, and it's usually spot-on.* "Uh, Gary sent you, right?"

"Excuse me?" His dark brows arched up over warm, coffee-colored eyes. "I'm looking for a Bert about a—"

She laughed. "Bertie. You're looking for Bertie. That would be me."

He blinked and then studied her with dark, narrowed eyes. Her face felt warm. "Uh, I think there's been a mistake," he said in his low, raspy voice.

No kidding. Bertie reached for the sconce in his hand, dumped it in one of the large plastic paint buckets used for garbage in the corner, and sighed, "You're not an electrician, are you?"

"No. But I know how to install lights."

Great. At least he had a useful skill, and that wasn't a bad thing. And he really did have that perfect, hot look that must've taken hours of mirror time to achieve. "So, Gary didn't send you, and you're not one of his special friends?" She air-quoted "special friends" with her fingers, wearing a dubious look on her face.

"No. I'm Keith Morgan, and I don't know"—suddenly disbelief lit his coffee-colored eyes and his jaw tightened—"Jesus. Lady, I'm not gay."

"Yeah, I figured as much," she said with a shrug. After the once-over he'd just given her, he couldn't have been anything but straight. She tried not to notice how he pinched the bridge of his nose as if she gave him a headache. She slapped down her impatience. He was a hot construction guy who needed work. It wasn't every day Harmony produced a hot…anybody. Those kind of characters only appeared in small towns like Harmony in the movies or romance novels. "Um, if you're here to see me about some work, your timing is actually perfect. I'm short-handed all around and could really use an extra pair of hands."

Keith scowled, ramming his hands in his jeans

pockets and then a smile began to twitch around his lips as he shook his head. "I'm here to speak with you about design, but if you really need the help, I'll be happy to remove a few lights for you and then maybe we can talk," he said.

Bertie clapped her hands as she pressed her lips together in relief. "You would do that? Help me? Even after...not that I meant to be insulting," she said in a low voice. "Quite the contrary. Every gay guy I've ever known has not only been great looking, but incredibly talented and handy as well—unlike most heterosexuals I've encountered. In my world, it was really a compliment." She smiled, hoping to gloss over her blunder as she babbled.

"So, you're implying that only gay men are good-looking and useful," he said.

She focused on the disorganized orders needing her attention, piled high on the makeshift plywood table-top balanced on two sawhorses. It was safer than staring at his chiseled features, smoky eyes, and smirking lips. "Yup. Pretty much. But what I'm really saying is there are no good-looking, useful, straight guys left in Harmony, North Carolina." Except for a few she'd known since first grade. Of course, they didn't count. Most of them had successful careers, exceptional wives, and adorable babies. Her own love life looked stark in comparison...another thing that needed fixing.

"What about all the construction workers you encounter?" he asked as he shifted the ladder over to the second sconce.

She lifted her head and gazed out the naked bay window where the morning light poured through the leaves of the ancient oak ruling the front yard. "Well…I wouldn't know for sure. They're very good at what they do." She shook her head, making her hair swing around her shoulders. "But for some reason they're married, too old, or missing teeth. Anyway, I'm sure they don't love taking orders from a woman." She returned to sorting through the paperwork.

"Sounds like you need to broaden your market. Homosexuals and old men with no teeth can be very limiting," he said, climbing the ladder.

She gave an unladylike snort. "What I need to do is get this job finished." She peered at him through the corner of her eye. Damn. Too bad she was leaving town. Something intriguing lurked behind this guy's hooded expression. But Bertie didn't have time to play sleuth to a mystery man. Besides, she didn't normally go for enigmatic men, no matter the level of hotness.

Her cell chirped from inside her jacket pocket. "Excuse me." She put the phone to her ear and listened to a barrage of questions from her drapery workroom. Her temporary electrician got right to work, removing the second sconce. She took full advantage and openly ogled him while his back was turned. He was as fine from behind as he was from the front. His long, lean legs and nice, tight butt gave new meaning to the term *guy candy*. Sigh. Too bad. But she didn't need his kind of distraction right now. She had big plans. Big. Plans.

She finished her call and said, "Thank you again. You have no idea how much I appreciate your help. I'll be in the kitchen when you're done and we can talk."

Bertie was comparing paint sample chips against the

white kitchen cabinets when Gary came through the back door, carrying two gallons of paint, looking impeccable as ever in his crisp slacks and designer sweater.

"Hey. Got more trim color, but we need to make a decision on the kitchen and the living room," he said.

"Working on it." She fanned out the strips of color, narrowing down the choices of sage green.

"Did Hal the electrician get here?" Gary dropped the buckets on the floor by the back door.

"Not yet. I thought the dreamy guy in the dining room was him, but I was sadly mistaken."

Gary's forehead crinkled as he pulled a paint can opener from his back pocket. "Hal is far from a dreamy guy. What are you talking about?" He stared at her as if she'd been sniffing wallpaper glue.

"The guy in the dining room helping with the fixtures—"

"Yo, why is Keith Morgan removing a chandelier in the dining room?" Bertie's older brother, Calvin, interrupted as he strolled into the kitchen from the front of the house, carrying a tray with three iced coffees from the Daily Grind.

"How do you know him?" she asked. Now that she thought about it, his name did ring a bell, but she couldn't figure out why.

"Who?" Gary spoke at the same time.

Calvin handed out coffees, nodding. He ran his hand through his dark hair, still damp from his morning shower. "Keith Morgan, the professional tennis player. Ranked six or seven in the world before he retired four years ago." Cal licked a mountain of whipped cream from the top of his cup. "Can't remember why. He moved to town a few days ago. I think he bought the old Victorian, the one you've always loved, Bertie, with the big wraparound porch and the huge magnolias in front." Cal relaxed his tall, lean frame against the cabinets.

Bertie could feel the color drain from her face. Not trusting her shaky hand, she placed her untouched coffee on the dark green granite countertop.

"Cal, tell me you're joking."

"Dead serious. Would know him anywhere."

She scanned his handsome face for any signs of his usual smirk. For once in his life, Calvin's laughing, light-brown eyes never looked more serious. Crap. What had she done?

"He's a professional tennis player? As in…he's been on national television? Played at Wimbledon?"

Cal nodded. "Along with every other Grand Slam tournament."

"Oh gawd. I'm such an idiot." Bertie turned wild eyes to Gary. "Okay, here's the thing…at first, I assumed he was the electrician. He came in right after you called and asked for Bert Anderson, like he was reporting in. And then he looked so perfect…you know, too perfect," she said, choking on the last sentence.

Gary groaned. "Please tell me you didn't do what I think you did."

Bertie paced in front of the large custom-made kitchen island, her high heels making an ominous clicking sound against the flagstone floor.

"*What?* I didn't come right out and say it." Exasperation colored her voice. Both Cal and Gary looked dubious.

"I may have implied…a teensy-weensy bit…that he was maybe…you know…gay."

Gary moaned as if in pain and Cal burst out laughing, spewing coffee across the island top. "He's not, if the last Victoria's Secret model he dated is any indication," Cal said between hoots of laughter.

"I know. He corrected me. But this is still sooo embarrassing." She grabbed a wad of paper towels to wipe up the splattered mess. She stopped mid-swipe as Cal's other bomb hit her.

"What do you mean, he bought the old Victorian?"

Bertie had eyed that house for years, always wanting to get her hands on it and fix it up. It had such great potential. Right now it appeared a little dated and in bad shape, but she knew with her expertise, it could be renewed to its former glory…but that was all in the past. Time to move on to a new city with new opportunities.

"Excuse me? All done with the chandelier."

Bertie froze when Mr. Perfect, aka Keith Morgan, interrupted from the doorway to the dining room. No one spoke for several beats. The air in the kitchen grew uncomfortably hot, as if both ovens were cranked up to 500 degrees with the doors wide open.

She slumped against the wood cabinets like a limp noodle dangling from a pot of boiling water. He was straight, gorgeous, famous, *and* the owner of her dream house. Bertie's chest tightened, thinking about the old Victorian inhabited by a complete stranger.

"Hey, Keith. Welcome to town," Cal said, extending his hand. "Calvin Anderson, and this is Gary Johnson. And I think you've met my sister, Bertie." Cal indicated with a jerk of his head.

Keith nodded as he stepped forward and shook hands, and to Gary he said with a straight face, "My special *friend*, I presume?"

"I…uh…I'm already seeing someone," Gary mumbled.

"Forget about it," Keith said, his voice tinged with humor, then he pinned Bertie with a questioning stare. "No way in hell could you be mistaken for a Bert."

Leaning as far back as the solid cabinets would allow, she would've crawled inside them if she thought she'd fit; her face flamed red hot.

Cal explained. "*Bertie*…it's short for—" She cut Cal off with an I'm-gonna-strangle-you look before he could further elaborate.

Keith ignored the death glare she aimed at Cal. As he drew closer, his tall frame looked out of proportion in the room, taking up more than his allotted space and all the air, if that was possible, making breathing difficult.

"I wanted to speak to you about a decorating job. You came highly recommended, but it appears you have your hands full." He continued to stare down at her, wearing a slight frown as if trying to sort the pieces of a puzzle in his mind.

Bertie stood there doing a good imitation of a guppy with her mouth, making no sound.

Her brother, the ass, snickered. "Uh, *Bert*, call you later. Gotta go. Glad to meet you, Keith."

"Yeah, need to pick up those lamps." Gary, the traitor, scurried after Cal.

Deserters. Losers. Both of them.

She moistened her dry lips with her tongue, weighing her next words. "Keith…uh, may I call you Keith?"

She didn't wait for an answer. "Okay, here's the thing," Bertie said on a nervous laugh. "I was expecting an electrician because Gary had just called and then you came in and…I…uh, well…you know the rest. I'm sorry to admit I didn't recognize you… I'm not much of a tennis fan." She stumbled over her inept explanation as his dark features went from intense to unreadable. She straightened from her position against the cabinets and squared her shoulders.

His expression remained aloof. "Forget about it. I didn't expect you to recognize me, and I didn't mind helping out with the lights."

"You didn't?" she said, her eyes widening.

"Nah. You needed help, and it wasn't a big deal. Besides, I mistook you for a man named Bert." What he didn't say spoke volumes—that no one could mistake her five-foot-two, round-hipped, rounder-boobed self for a man.

She cleared her throat and her head at the same time. "No worries, people make that mistake all the time." She jerked on the hem of her cropped jacket, wishing it was longer, to hide her expanding hips. "As I'm sure you've been mistaken for a…uh…" Bertie blinked at Keith. What made her think he was even remotely gay when he blasted such a high voltage of testosterone it practically knocked her into the next county? "…football player?"

He lifted one mocking brow. "Uh-huh, I get that a lot."

"Um, you mentioned something about a job." Not that she was the least bit interested. No, siree. She needed to finish up here, pack her car, and hit the highway for the big city seven hours southwest of Small

Town, USA. She had newer, bigger dreams to pursue before the noose of Harmony tightened around her neck even more. But she couldn't stop picturing the Victorian house and thinking that it wouldn't hurt to hear him out. Her curiosity got the best of her, plain and simple.

Keith hesitated as though he didn't quite trust her. No…more like he saw her as some hick, small-town designer who didn't know the difference between a chair and a chair rail. His obvious reluctance started to grate on her nerves. She lifted a brow at him, but before she could do something foolish, like list her impressive qualifications and sell her creative talent in order to get the job, his lips curved into what could've passed as a smile, if it had only reached his unreadable, dark eyes.

"I need help renovating the house on the corner of Main and Carver," he said slowly.

Her breath left her lungs in a whoosh. "Not the old Victorian with the wraparound porch?"

"Yeah, peeling teal blue shutters. Why?"

Damn. So it was true. She shook her head. "I'm surprised. I had no idea it was even up for sale."

He reached into his front pocket and pulled out an old key dangling from a plastic lime-green key tag, with the address printed in dark, bold letters.

"Got the key right here," he said as he wiggled it in front of her face. "Look, I came by to see if you'd be interested in helping with the design. I can do most of the work myself, but my aunt said you were talented and thought you'd welcome the challenge." He hesitated again. "This probably isn't a good idea. You seem really busy and short-handed." He shoved the key back in his pocket.

"Wait!" She lunged forward as if to grab the key from his hand before it disappeared along with her dreams. "This can't be happening."

Keith shot Bertie a look that implied *you're weirder than a tacky disco lava lamp.* "Look, lady, it's okay. This job doesn't seem to be suited for you."

"You're wrong! I'd be perfect for this job."

What had gotten into her? Certainly not this guy, who obviously thought she was nuts and couldn't handle his renovation. She *was* nuts. She had no business entertaining a design proposal on the old Victorian. She needed to focus on getting out of town as soon as possible, not find ways to make herself stay until she *had* to leave for her new job.

He shook his head in dismissal and moved to leave. Not that she blamed him, because she hadn't said anything right since meeting him.

"Give me a shot. When do you want me?" she blurted before he reached the door.

Keith slowly turned with a half smile curling his lips. She realized too late that she sounded suggestive, or even worse...*desperate.* His gaze undressed her from the tops of her peep-toe pumps to right below her chin.

She crossed her arms over her breasts, trying to smash her ample C cups into a size B. "I meant what time would you like to meet?" she said, her voice dripping with disdain.

Again, there was that darn hesitation as his smarmy smile disappeared. Okay, smarmy might be a bit harsh...maybe heart-stopping and a little sexy would be more accurate.

"Three o'clock, today."

"I'll be there," she said through tight lips.

He gave a curt nod, and as he started to head out, an old, wiry worker with thin, gray hair and a scraggly beard poked his head through the back door.

"Hey, I'm Hal. Gary sent me. You got some electrical work?"

"Wonderful. Yes, I need you desperately," she said, clapping her hands with dramatic flair. "You can start upstairs."

"My pleasure, ma'am. Let me get my tools." Hal nodded and grinned as he backed his way out.

Bertie groaned.

Keith whipped his head around with a look of disbelief and then burst out laughing, which did amazing things to his harsh features, transforming him from dark and brooding to dazzling and delicious. His laugh would've been contagious if she weren't so ticked-off. She gave him a huge-ass eye roll and held up her index finger.

"Don't *even* say it," she admonished.

Hal was missing his two front teeth.

Chapter 2

"HOLY SHIT." KEITH SLAMMED THE SCREEN DOOR TO the old house he now owned and stomped toward the back of the first floor. When he reached the bedroom where he'd dumped his belongings, he pulled the purple and green business card from his pocket and read it again. *House Dressing. Bert Anderson, Interior Designer.* Except he noticed an ink blob or scratch over the "ie" in Bertie's name, which explained why he went hunting for a Bert instead of Bertie. A mattress with rumpled sheets lay on the floor, and he flicked the card on top of it. Since he'd pulled into town a few days ago, he hadn't gotten around to unpacking or setting up house. He'd been way too busy working up a good, deep depression with a boatload of anger on top. That left no time for mundane tasks like unloading boxes or bringing in furniture.

He rummaged through a piece of luggage and pulled out Dri-FIT shorts and a faded, green Wimbledon T-shirt. Aunt Francesca had gone too far. It didn't take a PhD to figure out why she hadn't bothered to inform him that Bert was a woman. Christ. Wasn't it enough that he'd moved to Mayberry to live in this drafty, old house as he promised? And now Aunt Francesca wanted him to hire Betty Boop, the crazy interior decorator who thought he was gay!

Picturing Bertie Anderson in those ridiculous high

heels perched on that ladder made Keith want to howl like a wolf caught in a trap. She was trouble with a triple T—as in Tight skirt, Tiny waist, and big Tits. The kind of trouble he swore he'd never get involved with again. And dammit, Aunt Francesca knew that better than anyone. Bertie Anderson had *baby doll bombshell* written all over her, with big green eyes that could make any male drown in his own drool. Aunt Francesca knew his tarnished track record almost better than he did. So why in holy hell would she insist he use Betty Boop as his designer?

He threw on his running clothes, laced up his latest neon Nike sneakers, and barged out the same screen door he'd come through minutes earlier. He didn't bother warming up his muscles before he took off running as if the hounds of hell were nipping at his heels.

Keith's pace slowed after five miles. At the end of thirty-five minutes, he bent down and gripped the hem of his shorts, gulping for air, trying to fill his burning lungs. He squinted at the packed dirt and grass as sweat dripped off his face and nose. Usually exercise gave him a natural high, but lately, not so much.

He rose and moved closer to the shade provided by the surrounding pine trees and tall oaks. His home, with the peeling paint and broken shutters, came in view right past the grove of trees. *What the hell am I doing in this town again?* He wiped the sweat off his face with the bottom of his shirt. Oh yeah, turning over a new leaf. Getting his life in order so he'd quit pissing it away on cold booze and hot women. Shit. Life shouldn't be this hard.

With a couple of clicks on the keyboard, Keith Morgan's striking image popped up on the screen of Bertie's laptop. He stood with his Nike tennis hat drawn low over his dark eyes—eyes that conveyed everything from strength to fierce competitiveness to keen intelligence. Bertie studied the enigmatic figure who dominated her screen the same way he had dominated the kitchen of her client's house earlier.

She sat in one of the colorful booths in the back of the Dogwood Bar & Grill, "the Dog" to locals. Her parents, Sarah and John Anderson, had owned the restaurant when they were alive, but now Cal ran it with Bertie's help when she could spare the time. Cal bent over her shoulder and read the article on the computer as the lunch crowd began to trickle in.

"Interesting."

"What's interesting?" She scanned the caption to learn as much as possible about Keith Morgan. Why would this famous tennis player decide to grow roots in Harmony, population 11,339, of all places? The old Victorian had been in the Fleming family for decades. The parents had moved away years ago when they'd gotten too old to take care of it, and the kids had left way before that. None of them seemed interested in selling it—until now.

But why Keith Morgan? Okay, so he was a professional tennis player and probably had gobs of money and was willing to pay top dollar in this economy…but still. Bertie had always dreamed about one day living in that house. She even fantasized about converting the first floor into her very own design studio.

Cal gave a low whistle as he read. "He made it to

the semifinals at Wimbledon twice and the French Open twice. He won the U.S. Open right before he retired. He was sixth in the ATP world ranking."

She scrolled down the page with the mouse. "Why is that such a big deal? He only won one tournament."

He snorted and smacked his own forehead. "Do you have any idea how hard it is to be top ten in the world in tennis? He won plenty of tournaments. You're only reading how far he got in the Grand Slams. He was a great tennis player. One of the few Americans to watch, especially on clay," her brother spouted off. A sports fanatic, Cal knew a little bit about every sport on the planet from football to tennis to tiddledywinks.

She cocked her head. "Okay, I'll bite. Why clay?"

"Because most Americans train on hard courts and don't perform well on the clay court circuit, but apparently the Prince did." He pointed at the screen.

"Because of his training?"

He nodded. "Yeah, I think he grew up privileged, training at country clubs. They're mostly clay."

"I want to know about his personality." She clicked the mouse and more images popped up of Keith serving something called a kick serve. According to the article, he had one of the best, along with a classic one-handed backhand. His intensity poured off the screen, almost tangible.

Bertie had no clue what it took to qualify for a Grand Slam or anything about training, and she didn't pretend to care. She wanted to know what made Mr. Perfect tick. She needed to know if he had an aversion to the color red or if florals threatened his masculinity. Did he prefer hardwood or carpet? Draperies or shutters? Fabric or leather? Important information that could make or break a design proposal. None of that information appeared alongside his tennis stats. Not that she had any intentions of accepting his not-so-enthusiastic offer to work on the house. Nope. She had her car half-packed and the design mecca of the South had already sent her an engraved invitation. *Hotlanta...here I come!*

Cal tapped the screen. "Besides his incredible record, he made about thirty-six million in career prize money. That's not including endorsements."

Wow. Talk about a truckload of money. What *was* he doing in Harmony?

"The Prince retired four years ago. Apparently he was married, but his wife died a few years back. Hmmm, doesn't say why he retired though." Cal continued to scan the article.

"A wife? How did she die?" She clicked on the link that referred to Adriana Morgan. A smiling Latin beauty, with dark hair and darker eyes filled the screen. Bertie and Cal read the tragic story of her death in a fiery car accident on the MacArthur Causeway in Miami. Apparently it had happened early one Saturday morning, returning from a night of club hopping on South Beach. Alcohol and sleep deprivation were listed as causes of the accident.

"How sad." She felt sorry for him. What a terrible way to die and for someone so young. Maybe that explained why he seemed a bit grim and guarded. Bertie remembered only too well how her dad had shut down after their mom had died. He mourned her up until his own death seven years later. Bertie and Cal had practically raised themselves once their mom was gone and their dad became a shell of the man they once knew.

"Yeah, and she left behind a baby girl."

"What?" Her head snapped up and she scanned the article. "Keith Morgan has a daughter…poor baby," she murmured. "She was only four when his wife died. So that makes her about…"

"Ten."

"Why Harmony? You think he's still grieving? That would explain his hesitation in wanting to hire me."

Cal chuckled. "Sure, because his hesitation wouldn't have anything to do with you calling him gay." She knocked his arm with her elbow. "Hey!" He rubbed his forearm. "Look, I don't know. I didn't even know the Prince had a family."

"Why do you keep calling him the Prince?" She clicked on more images of Keith playing tennis.

Cal pulled a cleaning rag from the apron tied around his trim waist and started wiping down her table. "He went to Princeton for two years before turning pro. From what I've heard, he's pretty smart. I think he even finished his degree while he played. Apparently he reads a lot and handles all his own finances or something like that. He got stuck with the nickname early on." As he scrubbed the table, a brown curl fell over his forehead. Cal always wore his thick, wavy hair a little too long, allowing it to brush the top of his collar.

"Oh. I assumed it had something to do with him being a prince of a guy with the ladies." Bertie lifted her laptop so Cal could clean under it.

"Not unless you consider being a man ho a prince."

"Man ho!" She almost dropped the laptop.

He grinned, flashing his straight, white teeth. "Yeah, I don't know details, but apparently he was a pretty wild partier. You know, he got more pussy than a Kohler toilet seat."

"Gross. I could do without the visuals." She scowled up at her brother's laughing eyes. "Was he a man ho while married?" That would make him pretty close to pond scum in Bertie's book. Mr. Slimeball sounded more and more like a spoiled professional athlete.

He chuckled again. "Couldn't say. Why don't you open with that at your meeting?" Cal ruffled her hair like he'd done since the day he'd learned to walk, before sauntering over to the bar to help serve the lunch crowd.

She smoothed her thick hair back in place, casting an irritated look in his direction. As she sipped her Mason jar of iced tea, she looked out over the cramped dining area at the regulars in their usual seats, enjoying the special of the day. Bertie had eaten the turkey burger without the bun and the salad with the dressing on the side. She didn't dare grab an order of the homemade fries, knowing she could never stop with just one.

Three young gals she recognized from the law firm downtown sat at the bar, flirting with Cal, a common occurrence any day of the week. Cal, one of the few good-looking, eligible bachelors left in Harmony, did not lack for female companionship. His quick wit, movie star hair, and athletic frame helped his cause, of course.

Miss Sue Percy waved Bertie over. She sat in the middle of the bar with Shirley Douglas. Both women had been old friends of her mother and Bertie had known them her whole life. They used to cluck after her as if she was their own little chick. Still did.

She snapped her laptop shut and headed over to greet the ladies at their favorite table, where they could oversee the entire restaurant.

"You're looking real nice today, Bertie," Miss Sue chirped.

Bertie smiled and patted her wrinkled hand. "Thanks."

"Scott is coming into town this weekend, Bertha. I'm sure he will want to see you. I hope you'll be free," Shirley Douglas stated in her firm schoolteacher voice. Bertie barely refrained from cringing. First of all, Mrs. Douglas always called her by her given name, the name that had been the brunt of so many jokes growing up and was only made worse when coupled with her middle name, Mavis. Bertha Mavis, after both her grandmothers.

She loved her parents, but for the life of her she couldn't figure out why they would name their only daughter the two worst names in the English language. Thankfully, Cal shortened it to Bertie as a toddler. But ever since she'd stepped into Mrs. Douglas's first-grade class, she'd been Bertha.

Of course Shirley would bring up Scott, her only son and Bertie's first boyfriend…if you could call sharing lunch and holding hands near the back fence at Liza Palmer's tenth birthday party a sizzling romance. Because that was the last time she remembered liking Scott in that way. For some reason, Scott never got the memo. He'd been actively pursuing her ever since.

She kept her smile from faltering. "All righty then. We'll have to check our schedules. Uh, tell Scott I'll be in touch." Moving away suddenly looked better and better.

———

"Anyone home?" Bertie called out. The lead-glass front door sat ajar and she pushed it farther open. It was three o'clock on the dot.

She had sat in her battered but serviceable blue Honda CR-V across the street for a good ten minutes, trying to decide if she was going to keep this appointment. Her insatiable curiosity won, beating down her weak practical side. The heavy door creaked as it moved. Yep, only curiosity. Because she didn't want this job. Really. She didn't. She didn't want to work for a rich, ex-professional tennis player who probably sported an attitude the size of the Pacific Ocean and an ego to match.

She stepped into the large foyer of the old home.

"Hello?" Her voice echoed in the empty grand house. Finding a front door unlocked in Harmony wasn't unusual. Doors and gates were left unlocked all the time. She did have an appointment, but the house appeared deserted.

Her eyes wandered over the warm plaster walls. Her toes curled inside her pumps as she took in the old, wide-plank oak floors, which gleamed in the glow of the afternoon light filtering in from the dining room windows. She stepped into the glorious parlor to her left and froze as she spied the beautifully carved wood mantel that was clearly original to the house. Closing her eyes, she pictured ladies in ruffled, starched blouses, sipping tea on a blue velvet Victorian sofa. The scent of beeswax and vintage textiles hung in the air.

Bertie forgot all about her meeting and poked around

for the small spiral notebook she'd shoved in her handbag. She went from room to room, snapping shots with her phone, noting the original woodwork and light fixtures, and making small sketches. She became so engrossed in her space planning that she forgot the time... and the fact that she might be trespassing an itty-bitty bit.

A screen door slammed, and her head shot up from the wood floor pattern she'd been copying. For the first time, she actually saw her surroundings. She stood in the middle of the one room that looked occupied throughout the empty house. The king-sized mattress on the floor with the rumpled sheets was a dead giveaway.

Oh my gawd.

Panicked, Bertie dove for the first door to her right, in the nick of time—a closet jammed with packing boxes and men's clothes hanging in a disorderly fashion. She crouched low behind a cardboard box stuffed with books seconds before she heard Keith come through his bedroom door.

"...yeah, it's a regular Mayberry, complete with an honest-to-God barber shop on Main Street," Keith said in a low voice.

She tried not to gasp for air as extreme fear and ultimate embarrassment crept its way up from the tips of her toes to her constricted lungs. The smell of cedar and old books tickled her nose. She could hear him on his cell loud and clear as he moved about the room.

"The house is actually great, but my aunt is trying to pull a fast one with this interior decorator."

Interior designer, you dummy. She had a degree and a license to practice. Decorator implied a bored housewife who only dabbled.

"…I know…my aunt led me to believe it was a guy. Yeah, which I could've handled no problem. Uh-huh. She wants me to work with Betty Boop."

Excuse me? I am not Betty Boop.

His voiced died away as she strained to hear more. He must've stepped into another room. She needed to get out of this closet and out the front door without being discovered by Mr. Insensitive. As she attempted to uncurl her body and stand, his voice rang out.

"…hair like Jessica Rabbit, but she's short and curvy like Betty Boop, with round, green eyes and exaggerated, curly eyelashes."

Make up your mind. Betty Boop or Jessica Rabbit? There was a huge difference. And for the record, her eyelashes were not exaggerated. Sounds of him rifling through a box of clothes reached her ears. Her knees burned from crouching so low, and she stifled a yelp as her hair caught on a wire hanger.

"Yeah. The town is quaint and quiet. The perfect place for me to get away and settle down. But I don't need my aunt riding my ass and I certainly don't need her hiring my interior decorator from the cast of Looney Tunes characters that live here."

Cartoon characters? The nerve. And who the hell was his aunt? Bertie wanted nothing more than to set Keith Morgan straight on a few things, but then she remembered she was hiding out in his closet next to his assortment of designer shoes, basically trespassing or breaking and entering—both crimes. Not good.

"Betty Boop is showing up any minute…" His voice became muffled again. Bertie edged closer to the door in her stooped position, straining to see through the slight crack to determine where Keith went. She heard water from a tap, which meant he was probably in the bathroom. She fished out her cell and punched in Gary's number.

"Hey. I need your help."

"Bertie? Why are you whispering?" Gary asked.

"Because I'm hiding in Keith Morgan's closet and I need you to get me out."

"I'm sorry, but it sounded like you said you were *hiding* in Keith Morgan's closet."

"I did. Don't start. Just get me out of here. And don't tell Cal. I'll never hear the end of it," she whispered feverishly. She could've sworn she heard Gary mumble, "this time you deserve it," but she couldn't be certain and she didn't have time to argue.

"We don't have much time. Come to his house and knock real loud on the front door while I sneak out the back. When he answers, tell him I'm running late, but I'm on my way."

"This is nuts even for you. You know this is a really bad idea."

"I'm begging you. You have to help me. I can't be caught hiding in a closet. He already thinks we live in Mayberry. He'll probably have me arrested and…I'll get thrown in jail. And even worse…I'll never get out of Harmony," she wailed in a quiet voice.

"You're talking crazy. Calm down. I'm on it. But I want a raise and—"

"Shhh." She heard Keith's shower go on. "Wait…" She listened as the water ran. "I think he's taking a shower so I can sneak—" Her words lodged in her throat as the closet door swung open and she looked up at a half-naked, marble-sculpted Greek god standing with fists on his hips, looking a lot like an enraged Keith Morgan.

"Never mind," she said in a small voice as she stared up at his granite-like jaw. The icy blast of his gaze froze her to the spot. "Busted. Uh…if you don't hear back from me in exactly fifteen minutes, call the police. And be sure to check the freezer for cut-up body parts…mainly mine." She punched her cell off, her eyes never leaving his fierce face.

"What do we have here? Barney calling Goober for backup?" he said in a chilling tone.

"Uh, okay, here's the thing…" She scrambled to stand and in her haste tripped over a pair of black Gucci loafers. She felt herself falling forward, right into Keith Morgan's glorious chest of sculpted steel.

With quick reflexes, he grabbed her by the hips before she managed to plow him over. All good. Until she realized her breasts were smashed against his bare chest. *Oh my!* He smelled musky and sweaty…a tantalizing combination. She inhaled his scent deeply. Overcome by the surrounding hotness of Mr. Perfect-Please-Be-Mine, Bertie wobbled on her four-inch heels and appeared to be molding herself to his hard, warm body. Nothing could be further from the truth. Okay, well, maybe it was a little bitty close to the truth.

Whatever you do, don't look down.

She glued her gaze to the dark stubble covering his stern jaw, fearing that if she did look down she'd see his low-slung towel, hanging even lower and revealing something pretty darn spectacular, if what she felt pressed against her stomach was any indication.

Something she hadn't seen in a very long time. Or felt. Something she didn't need to see now. Or feel. Because she could almost guarantee that she'd gawk and then do something really stupid, like beg him to take her.

———— ᴡᴡ ————

Keith witnessed Bertie's expressions go from fear to shock to sexual awareness in a matter of seconds, even though she never lowered her sea-green eyes past his chin. He wasn't completely sure, but he could've sworn there was an ongoing conversation taking place inside her head. Her generous, plump breasts were pressed up against his chest, and her soft, round hips were burning holes in his hands. He wondered if it would feel as nice if he slid his hands from around her hips to her curvaceous ass. *Okay, now I'm acting nuts.*

Bertie's big eyes went from the color of the sea to dark forest green as they grew wider and more dilated. Then it hit him—*gardenias*. He'd smelled gardenias when he'd stepped into his bedroom earlier and thought it must've been a blooming bush outside or something. But no, that would be too simple. Betty Boop smelled like gardenias and it was kind of making him a little crazy.

Shit. This was bad, *real* bad. So bad it felt fucking great. Keith's knees almost buckled as he felt Bertie take an unsteady breath, making her gorgeous full breasts expand, pulling her closer. Her delectable lips parted and he didn't think. He just acted, swooping down for a crushing kiss before she could start talking crazy and break the spell.

———— ᴡᴡ ————

Bertie froze like a statue, Keith's lips rocking over hers in a kiss so mind-blowing that he literally took her breath away. She had no idea how long she leaned into him, allowing him to kiss her, before she realized she wasn't participating and was missing some really good stuff. Since she didn't want Mr. Perfect to think he was kissing a total fool, she ran her hands up his strong, defined arms and locked them around his neck as she stood on tiptoes. Not wanting to miss out on probably the best kiss she'd ever experienced, her tongue tangled with his until the kiss became hotter and deeper and more drugging.

Suddenly his large hands were everywhere. One cupped the back of her head, tilting it for better access; the other massaged her bottom until she heard a deep, throaty moan. It took a few seconds to realize it came from her. She couldn't remember the last time a kiss elicited any kind of emotion from her, much less a deep-throated moan. A thunderbolt shot clear to the soles of her feet. She pressed even closer and gave in to the sensations pouring through her.

Keith jerked back, dropping his hands and ending the best kiss in the whole universe. "Goddammit!" he growled as he retied the loose towel around his lean hips. Bertie clutched her throat with a shaky hand.

What had she done? She needed to dig her way out of this steaming heap of humiliation. She was a professional designer, not a bimbo who hid out in hunky sports celebrities' closets like a stalker.

"Uh, okay, here's the thing…your door was open and I wandered in and then I got so absorbed in the bones of the house that—"

"Enough." Keith stepped even further back, as if Bertie had leprosy, and indicated with a sweep of his arm that she should precede him out of the bedroom. Now. Bertie moved through the door on shaky legs.

"But, I need to ex—"

"Don't elaborate any further. Look, Ms. Anderson, I'm sure you're a capable decorator—"

"Designer," Bertie interrupted as her heels clicked down the hall, making a hollow sound in the vacant house.

"Whatever. This isn't going to work out," Keith said behind her in a strained voice. "Let's forget the whole thing."

She stopped in the grand foyer, blocking the door while Keith reached around, careful not to touch her as he yanked on the doorknob. "Okay, but the thing is—" Bertie attempted to explain again, her face flushed from embarrassment.

"Thank you for your time, and I'm sorry. I didn't mean to…you know…kiss you. It was a mistake." Keith held the door open for Bertie, looking not at her but at some fascinating spot over her head, standing as if he were Prince Charles and not a half-naked stud who'd been feasting on her lips only minutes ago.

"Right. A mistake. Well, good luck." Bertie bolted from the house and down the porch steps as fast as her high heels could carry her. What a hot mess, emphasis on *hot*. She couldn't reach her car fast enough. The minute she slid into her seat, she banged her forehead against the steering wheel. "Fudge. What did I just do?"

She was dazed and disoriented, not from beating her brains out, but from sharing a life-altering kiss with a guy she barely knew. She lifted her head and with a shaky hand shoved the key in the ignition. Her reaction to Keith Morgan was appalling, especially since he clearly couldn't stand the sight of her and was probably disinfecting with Listerine at this very moment to remove the taste of her from his mouth.

"I am *so* leaving in three weeks," Bertie said out loud as she started her car and peeled away from the curb. "A herd of rampaging bulls couldn't make me stay."

———

"Shit!"

Keith watched Bertie accelerate down the street like she'd reentered the Indy 500 from a pit stop. He felt the same way. He needed to get out of here, out of this town. And stay out. He couldn't do this. Stomping back to his bedroom, he retrieved his cell phone from the bed. He almost called his former coach and best friend back, whom he'd been speaking with earlier, but instead punched another number and lifted the phone to his ear, rooted to the spot where he'd been kissing Bertie Anderson like a sailor on shore leave.

His insides got prickly and hot, and his heavy groin throbbed, helpless against the onslaught of uninvited thoughts—thoughts of Bertie's lips pressed against his. He now knew she tasted a little like cinnamon and a lot like desire. He knew the texture of her thick, mahogany hair as it curled around his fingers. And the smell of gardenias still hung in the air.

No struggling or pushing him away. Her active participation had made lust burn low in his gut. He'd barely stopped before palming her perfect breasts. Thank God he remembered why he was really here.

"Hello?" Francesca Balogh, his aunt, spoke, her voice pouring through the line.

Keith unclenched his back teeth. "We need to talk. What time are you free?"

"Cocktails are always at six. Please be on time."

"Count on it." He hit the off button, tossed his phone on the unmade mattress, and headed for the shower.

———

Keith stood in Aunt Francesca's buttery yellow living room, staring at a photo in a silver frame of his aunt and his mom posing on the Ponte Vecchio in Florence. The picture had been taken about two years ago, when Aunt Francesca traveled to Italy to visit her sister. Keith's mom had lived abroad for the last twenty years, winning the prize of absentee parent year after year.

Keith moved to the antique bar supplied with ice, crystal high balls, and a brand-new bottle of Mount Gay. His favorite. The idea of downing the entire bottle was tempting. Instead, he poured himself a plain ginger ale and took a healthy gulp, hoping to ease the tension building inside his gut and working its way up to his throat.

Keith had packed up his entire life in Miami and moved to Harmony a week ago, and the culture shock couldn't have been any stronger if he had moved to a village of huts in Zimbabwe. But he hadn't done this for himself. He'd done it for his daughter, Maddie. And as Aunt Francesca had pounded into his foggy, alcohol-soaked head, she would not allow him to fuck up Maddie's life. Well, she didn't drop the f-bomb, but Keith got the message all the same.

For Maddie, he'd made the right decision. Absolutely. One hundred percent. He had moved to Mayberry, USA, to give her a better life. Sure, he'd always miss hot Miami with its loud, colorful cultures and wild nightlife. Living in Miami had been like living inside a nightclub 24/7—an expensive nightclub with warm sand, cool water, majestic palm trees, and nights as hot and steamy as the women who trolled Ocean Drive. Not an environment conducive to molding an impressionable young girl.

And yet, all that partying until the wee hours of the morning had taken its toll on Keith. One morning, he'd woken up in more ways than one. After he'd ushered the nameless woman he'd spent the night with into a waiting cab, he had stared at his hollow eyes in the bathroom mirror and hated what he saw. He couldn't remember the day of the week or even the month. The inside of his mouth had felt as dry as packed sawdust. Keith had studied the broken image of himself for what felt like hours until he'd decided that he'd had enough. He wouldn't fight Aunt Francesca any longer. If he continued down this road of self-destruction, his daughter would lose her only surviving parent to another stupid, avoidable accident.

Aunt Francesca had laid down the law. If he didn't clean up his act, she would file for custody of Maddie. She had the money, and he had stupidly supplied her with plenty of ammunition, with his playboy image plastered all over the tabloids. She had a rock-solid case and could win over the courts. As much as his aunt's ultimatum had pissed him off, she had a point. His reckless partying had become as legendary as his tennis career, maybe more—not something he was proud of.

Whenever tennis entered his mind, which happened to be almost every minute of every day, his stomach would clench and tighten into a cramped ball. He'd given up the game he'd played since he was five. The game he had turned into a career. The game where he'd inspired tons of young kids. He had walked away from millions of dollars and his ranking within the top ten players worldwide to be a better parent to Maddie, because he loved her even more than the game. It had been so fucking noble of him. Until he'd fucked up his one unselfish act by drowning in his depression, along with a shitload of Mount Gay and a bevy of nameless women. What a complete waste. What an asshole.

So, for the past four months, Keith had been celibate. He hadn't even looked at a woman, much less slept with one. Nor had he been even remotely interested. Keith had sworn off the siren of the sultry, sexy women of his past. That ship had sailed over the horizon never to be seen again. He had zero interest in that form of temptation. He'd married it once. He wasn't about to repeat the same mistake and fall for the wrong woman again.

Until he clapped eyes on Bertie Anderson.

Bertie pulled the packing tape dispenser across the top of the box of books she had closed up. Gary had his back to her as he rifled through the basket of fabric samples on her office floor. Her hands shook a little, still reeling from the kiss with Keith Morgan that had rocked her world. She couldn't decide what upset her more: the outstanding kiss with the wrong guy or the fact that she blew her chance at getting her hands on her dream house.

After Bertie had sped away from Keith's house and his dangerous lips, she'd found herself sitting in her own driveway, trying to calm her racing heart. She'd stared through the windshield at the house where she'd lived all her life. She and Cal had put new shingles on the old gabled roof and painted the wood siding celadon green with an apple-red front door. Over the years, Bertie had given her childhood home new life inside and out with refinished wood floors, fresh coats of paint, and updated lighting. She'd intended to do more, but time had run out. In three weeks, she'd be in Atlanta and her house, her hometown, and Keith Morgan would be in her rear-view mirror.

Bertie nudged the sealed box with her knee and squeezed her eyes shut. First, she'd called him a gay electrician and then she'd hid in his closet like a common thief, only to land in his arms and kiss him like there was no tomorrow. This had to go down as one of her more embarrassing days for the year.

"Do you think he'll still hire us?" Gary asked as he pulled more design magazines out from under Bertie's cluttered desk and shoved them in another cardboard box.

"Not even if a gun was pointed at his head," Bertie said as she reached inside the closet that held all her samples and furniture catalogs.

She'd changed into a pair of low-rise jeans and stood barefoot on top of an antique oriental rug in the middle of her office. The room used to be her mother's old sewing room off the back of the house. Bertie remembered watching her mom as she bent over her old Singer, sewing black stripes on bright orange fabric for matching

Halloween outfits. Cal had wanted to be a tiger that year, and Bertie had to be one too.

"I'm leaving all these samples and catalogs in this closet for you to use. Finish packing my books and magazines and the rest is yours."

Gary looked up from the box he'd been stuffing and nodded. "Uh, you wanna explain why you were hiding in his closet one more time? Because you've done some really crazy things in the past, but I think this one might top them all. Much worse than the time you fell in Mrs. Sanchez's pool at her Cinco de Mayo party and ruined her floating light show."

"That's because her lecherous husband wouldn't stop chasing me. I was wearing my hot-pink patent leather Kate Spades. I ruined those great shoes all because that dirtbag couldn't keep his hands to himself."

The Sanchezes had thrown an over-the-top party in Raleigh and had invited at least a dozen designers in hopes of selecting someone to help decorate their overly ornate, eight-thousand-square-foot home. Bertie's design business, House Dressing, had been included on the list of prospects, and she and Gary seemed to have caught the owners' attention. All had gone swimmingly until it became clear that she'd caught the owner's attention for all the *wrong* reasons.

Gary tried not to laugh as he rubbed his trim belly. "You ruined Mrs. Sanchez's evening, along with your Diane von Fürstenberg dress. After I pulled you from the pool, your darling dress had become transparent and I thought Mr. Sanchez was going to lunge for you right in front of his wife."

"Geez. What a nightmare. Although the gossip is

that the Sanchezes are on their fourth designer now. Apparently, I wasn't the only one Mr. Sanchez chased."

"Okay, we've digressed. Back to the closet escapade with Mr. Hot Bootay," Gary said, pinning Bertie with his intense blue eyes.

Bertie buried her face in her hands. "I don't want to talk about it." Her voice muffled as she shook her head. "Keith hates me, and he hates Harmony. I need to finish up the Milners' house and get the heck out of here. And I hope I never see Mr. Perfect again for as long as I live." Bertie pulled her desk drawer out and dumped its entire contents of pencils, pens, and markers into another cardboard box.

"I'd like to see him again." Gary ran the tape dispenser across the box of magazines. "I know he pitches for the other team, but he sure is easy on the eyes. You think he'll hire me after you're gone?"

"Doubt it. Anything associated with me, he'll consider toxic. Sorry." Bertie gave Gary a sad smile. "But, hey, give it a shot. Just wait until I'm two states over before you approach him," she added.

Gary stood and placed the box on a stack of packed containers in the corner of the office. "Why this sudden urge to pack? You've been acting weird ever since you left Morgan's house. You're hiding something…you might as well spill it." Gary leaned against the stacked boxes, looking like a clothing model with his crisp linen shirt under his baby-blue cashmere sweater and perfectly creased khaki pants. He'd been working all day and he still appeared flawless.

Bertie averted her gaze from Gary's all-knowing self and started pulling folders from her file cabinet. "It's nothing, really."

"Uh-huh." Gary sank into the funky orange, leopard-spotted armchair that sat in the corner of the office. "I'm not packing another box until you come clean," he said, crossing his arms.

Glaring at him she said, "Are you forgetting who signs your paychecks?"

"That threat doesn't work anymore, girlfriend. Never did. Half the time I sign my own paychecks because you forget. Come on, I'm the one who acted like your jealous lover so that carpet rep in the green leisure suit would stop dropping by. And I covered for you when the Tangeloes found you sleeping on their guest bed after you pulled an all-nighter trying to finish their installation. Need I go on?" Gary sounded reasonable while appearing smug at the same time.

Bertie sighed as she fiddled with the pink stapler on top of her desk. "Okay. He found me hiding in his closet…which I know was a dumb thing to do, but then somehow I ended up smashed against him and we… sorta…uh…kissed," she said in a faint voice. There was a long pause.

"Way to go, girlfriend. Was it good?"

Bertie's head shot up. "I *kissed* a potential client and ruined our chances of working on that house. Do you not see how inappropriate that was?"

"Let me get this straight." Gary sat forward. "After being discovered in his closet, you jumped into his arms and started kissing him like a long-lost lover?"

"No. I mean…I didn't jump. I tripped and then fell into him, and then I tried not to look down, because he was only wearing a towel and then somehow his lips were smashed against mine and you know…we kissed."

Gary sat back, steepling his lean fingers under his chin. "Hmmm, interesting."

He gave the appearance of a college professor pondering the meaning of life, except for his beautiful, thick, blond hair which looked better than any professor's she'd ever encountered. "I don't like that superior look on your face. What's so interesting?"

"Interesting that you—"

Bertie's chirping cell interrupted Gary's sage contemplation. She reached for it on her desk.

"Aunt Franny? When did you get back in town?" She felt happy for the first time that afternoon since Keith unglued his lips from hers and ushered her out of his home and life.

"A few days ago. I was visiting my adorable niece at boarding school in Virginia. But there's something of an urgent matter that I need to discuss with you. Do you think you can come by the house around six thirty?"

Bertie stopped shuffling papers on her desk. "Is everything okay? Are you sick?" she asked, trying to keep her alarm at bay.

Panic constricted the muscles around her heart, causing a tightening in her chest that bordered on painful. Aunt Franny wasn't really Bertie's aunt, but she'd been like a mother to her for many years. She had stepped into Bertie's family's life right after Bertie's mother died of pancreatic cancer, and she hadn't left. She'd been Bertie's rock. Even at twenty-eight, Bertie still sought her advice and looked for her approval.

Aunt Franny gave a low chuckle. "I'm fit as a fiddle. No one is dying…yet. Can you make it?"

Air escaped her lungs in a whoosh. "Sure. Can I bring dinner? I'll pick something up at the Dog."

"Perfect."

Bertie sank into her desk chair and shrugged at Gary's questioning gaze. "Can I bring anything else?" she asked.

"Just yourself. Oh, and Bertie, bring enough food for three. *Ciao*."

Chapter 3

KEITH PROWLED AUNT FRANCESCA'S LIVING ROOM LIKE a restless tiger in a cage until she appeared in the doorway. "You said six o'clock." He glanced at his stainless Bulgari watch. "It's six twenty. What gives?"

Aunt Francesca breezed into the room and sank into the English sofa covered in pale blue damask. She wore a classic, soft-gray Chanel suit, her signature South Sea pearls around her neck, and a slight smile on her matriarchal face.

"It's lovely to see you too, dear. Would you like to know how your daughter is faring in that school you stuck her in?"

"Christ." Keith rubbed his hand over the stubble on his jaw, since he hadn't bothered to shave. "Please don't put it in those terms. Of course I want to hear about Maddie. We've been texting back and forth, and I spoke to her yesterday. She said you took her to dinner and then to the American Girl store."

"Did you like the picture I emailed you?" Aunt Francesca asked.

Keith couldn't control the silly smile that played around his mouth. Aunt Francesca had captured Maddie hamming it up next to a large display of dolls in the store. "She looked real cute and way too sassy for her own good," he chuckled. Keith stretched out opposite his aunt in a comfortable down-filled armchair. "She told me she thinks she's getting too old for dolls. She wants some elaborate drawing kit where she can design clothes like they show on *Project Runway* and a new skateboard or rip stick...something like that. Where does she come up with this stuff?" Keith asked, always baffled by the things that came out of his sweet, ten-year-old daughter's mouth.

Aunt Francesca's hazel eyes twinkled as she smiled at him. "Yes, I heard all about that, but I wanted to check with you first, before launching her latest fad."

His aunt appeared cool as a cucumber, patting the back of her stylish bobbed haircut as if she hadn't turned his world upside down with this sudden move to Harmony and her campaign to bring Maddie home. And for kicks, she wanted to stick him with Bertie, that bombshell disguised as a decorator.

Keith had given in on the move from Miami because he had done a gut check and knew it was the right thing to do, and he'd probably cave and bring Maddie home from boarding school, because he missed her too much. But hiring Bertie, who hid in closets, called him gay, and kissed like a connoisseur? No way. Not in a million years. That was where he drew the line.

He straightened in his chair and took another fortifying gulp of his drink. "Listen, Aunt Francesca, I understand your concern about Maddie. I get that. I agreed to move here to make a better life for her. I've done everything you've asked so far, but now I need you to ease up."

Aunt Francesca rose and moved toward the Victorian sideboard. "In what way?" She poured herself a scotch from the crystal decanter.

"I can hire my own decorator. Your lead was a bust."

Her eyes narrowed over the rim of the amber liquid in her glass. "You didn't like Bertie? Hmmm, I find that strange."

Keith jumped up from his seat and started to pace across the priceless Aubusson rug. "You know what I find strange? The fact that you didn't tell me she was a woman. You led me to believe I was calling on a man named Bert."

Keith noted her lips twitching as she smothered her smile behind her drink. "That's ridiculous. I—"

"Don't try and deny it. You knew damn well what you were doing." Keith glared at his aunt as her elegant eyebrow rose in that haughty way designed to put him in his place.

"You're certainly mighty angry over an innocent mistake. I did not mislead you. Heavens, I even gave you her card. Why would you think Bertie was a man? And why do you care either way? I hope you didn't insult her."

Keith knew his aunt…really well. She'd been better to him than his own mother, and he loved her all the more for it. But he also knew when she was up to something. He waited as she rearranged some white roses in a Steuben glass vase on top of the baby grand piano.

"What didn't you like about Bertie besides the fact that she's a woman? Did she suggest painting the house purple with pink polka dots?"

Keith shoved his fingers through his hair, thinking he needed a haircut, along with a few other things—like getting laid. Four months was a long time. Couldn't a guy go blind or something from too much abstinence?

"I don't like her. She's short and pushy and she smells like gardenias. I hate gardenias." Jesus. Now he sounded like a town idiot, like this town didn't have enough already. From the stern expression marring his aunt's face, he could tell she wasn't buying it.

"*Keith Camden Morgan,* that is the most ridiculous thing I've ever heard you say." Aunt Francesca shook her head. "You love gardenias. You would always bring me some from my own garden when you were little."

"That's not the point!" he roared. "I can't work with her. She's…she's no good for me." He started to pace again. "I need plain. Plain and mousey. Someone with no style and no curves. Doesn't this town have some eighty-year-old blue hair that likes to decorate? Someone like Aunt Bee?"

"Hey, Aunt Franny. The pasta primavera's in the kitchen. What did you need—"

Keith stopped pacing and stood with his mouth hanging open, staring at the one woman he couldn't exorcise from his head. Bertie Anderson's big, green eyes grew even bigger as she spied him in the room.

"You!" they both exclaimed in unison.

Bertie scurried away from him toward his no-good, conniving little aunt and threw Keith a nervous glance. "Aunt Franny? What's going on here? How do you know him?"

Aunt Franny? What the hell? Keith smelled a rat, and she smelled a lot like Chloe perfume and looked like a meddling, older woman in designer clothes. He hated being manipulated almost as much as he hated losing at tennis.

Keith closed the paneled doors to the living room,

and then leaned back with his arms crossed, barring anyone's escape. "Yeah, *Aunt Franny*. What the hell is going on here?"

———

Francesca Balogh secretly smiled to herself as her nephew snarled and gnashed his teeth. He resented her interference in his life, but since he hadn't bothered to live his life these past few years, Francesca figured a well-planted kick in the butt wouldn't hurt.

Her sister's son had been lost as a little boy and was even more lost as a grown man. Too many times in the past she'd held her tongue or didn't intervene as his mother, Angelina, made rash decisions after the death of Keith's dad. And Francesca regretted it. She wasn't going to stand by and allow Keith to make the same mistakes…especially with Maddie.

As for Bertie, she needed a little guidance and a lot of love and support. Francesca considered Bertie her own daughter and only wanted to see her happy and fulfilling her own dreams. She needed a nudge in the right direction, which was not three hundred and fifty miles south to Atlanta, where she'd be working a menial job for practically no pay, for some overpriced snotty designers.

Francesca patted Bertie's hand. "So nice of you to come on short notice. Why don't we have our meeting here and then we'll retire to the dining room for a little supper?"

"Meeting? What meeting?" Bertie asked.

"Come." Francesca steered Bertie by the elbow. "Sit on the settee. And, Keith, stop scowling like an angry bear. You're scaring the wits out of Bertie. Have a seat." Francesca indicated a chair with a flutter of her hand.

Keith didn't move. His eyes narrowed and his scowl deepened.

If she hadn't changed his diapers and looked after him when he was just a baby, she might be a tad bit concerned. She had a feeling his expression would get a lot worse before it got better, after he'd heard what she had to say.

Francesca retrieved a legal file from the antique inlaid secretary by the French doors. She placed her reading glasses on her nose and sat in a gilded French chair across from Bertie. Keith continued to stand guard at the door like a soldier. Bertie blinked her big, green eyes as she fiddled with the buttons on her colorful bouclé jacket.

Francesca cleared her throat. "Bertie, I've called you here because I have a proposition for you that I think you'll accept." Francesca glanced in Keith's direction. "I'm sure you remember hearing me speak about Keith in the past."

"Vaguely about a nephew, but I didn't make the connection," Bertie said cautiously.

"Nevertheless, he has recently moved to Harmony, as you know, and he has a darling ten-year-old daughter, Madeline, who is unfortunately at boarding school, but who should be—"

"Cut the crap, Francesca," Keith thundered, making Bertie jump in her seat. "What do you want now, and how much is it going to cost me?"

Francesca shot the look of death at Keith. "Fine. I'll cut the crap. You want it straight? Here are my terms," she said with steel in her voice. If he couldn't stop wallowing in his own pool of self-pity, then so be it.

But he was going to do right by his daughter if it killed Francesca. And it might.

Francesca slid her gaze back to Bertie. "Bertie, I want you to design and decorate Keith's home. You have exactly three months to get the job done. At the end of three months, if the house is completed you will receive a bonus of one hundred and fifty thousand dollars."

Bertie gasped. "*What?*"

"Of course, you will be paid your usual fee for your work, and Keith will pay for the renovation," Francesca added. "But your job is to fix that house and make a comfortable, beautiful home for Maddie."

Bertie blinked as her hand flew to her mouth.

Francesca turned her full attention to her angry nephew. He might hate her after this, but it was a chance she had to take. She leveled her gaze at Keith and observed the tension cording his neck and shoulders.

"Keith, you will make timely decisions regarding the house and not prevent Bertie from doing her job. And in that same three-month period, you will put forth all your energies and charm into obtaining a wife and mother for Maddie."

"What the *fuck*!" Keith exploded from the door. "Francesca, you have gone too far. You have no right. Find a wife…really? I'm not agreeing to any of this."

Francesca tapped the folder sitting on her lap. "Keith, I will do whatever it takes to ensure that Maddie has a good, healthy, stable home. You know that I have what it takes to fight you for full custody. Are you willing to take that risk?"

"So, you'd rather I pimp myself out and get a wife

so Maddie can have a mother?" Keith snarled, towering over Francesca.

"No. I'd rather you make a conscious effort to stop drowning in self-pity and make something of yourself."

"This is bullshit. I don't have to listen to this. I've got money too, Aunt Francesca…more money than I know what to do with. You think I won't hire an entire firm of lawyers to fight you?"

Francesca tilted her head up at an angry Keith, standing rigid as a board. "Son, what I think is that you won't drag Maddie through the court system if you really love her like you claim you do."

Keith went perfectly still and then his shoulders slumped as he exhaled a ragged breath. At that moment, her nephew looked much older than his thirty-three years.

The pain of the last six years showed in his weary eyes. "Getting married is not going to make a happy home for Maddie. I've tried marriage once…it was a disaster and you know it."

"No. It ended tragically and you stopped caring. It's time to change all that…for your daughter."

—∞—

Fascinated, Bertie sat on the edge of her seat during the heated exchange between Keith and Aunt Franny. It felt like being in the middle of the live taping of a soap opera. She should leave the room and allow Aunt Franny some privacy with Keith, but she couldn't make her legs move. Too many thoughts swirled around in her head. One hundred and fifty thousand of them. One hundred and fifty thousand big ones to stay in town…for three months. She could do that. Three months of designing the old Victorian and bringing it back to life. Twelve weeks of working for Keith Morgan. Mr. Perfect Kiss with a chip on his shoulder the size of a tractor-trailer. Oh gawd.

A groan slipped past Bertie's lips. Keith turned as if he had noticed her for the first time. He approached in slow motion, like all his joints hurt to move, and slumped down onto the settee next to her. Bertie didn't dare look his way, but she could feel his hot gaze burning a laser-like hole in the side of her head.

"Bertie, what do you say?"

"Excuse me?" Francesca had asked a question, but Bertie had been distracted by Keith sitting so close that she could smell his enticing, musky scent.

"Will you stay and fix the old Victorian for the next three months?"

"Uh, well, I can certainly start the project, and then Gary can implement—"

Francesca shook her head and waved the file folder in the air. "No. That's not the deal. No farming it out to Gary and no phoning it in. This offer is only valid if *you* stay in town and complete the job in three months. You'll have to put off moving to Atlanta. Will you do it?"

"Uh…" Bertie pictured her packed bags stuffed in the back of her car, pulling out of her driveway, waving good-bye to Cal and Gary. Then she pictured sitting in bumper-to-bumper morning traffic on Interstate 285, trying to get to work in downtown Atlanta. "Can I have some time to think about it?"

Francesca gave a curt nod. "I'll need an answer tomorrow by two, before I meet with my attorneys." Francesca raised an elegant eyebrow. "Keith?"

Dread seized Bertie's lungs as she held her breath, expecting another explosion from Mr. Angry as he stiffened next to her. Keith's deep voice filled the tense silence, sounding really close to her left ear.

"So, it's come down to this. I find a wife or you'll file for custody of Maddie."

Francesca smoothed the hem of her gray skirt. "Yes. You need to make a concerted effort. It shouldn't be that hard. You're famous, good-looking, and you have *more money than you know what to do with*." She slipped her reading glasses off, folding them on top of her file. "I have all the faith in the world you can do this."

"And I suppose my true love is somewhere hidden in this *Leave It to Beaver* town," Keith drawled.

A slight fissure of alarm crept its way up Bertie's spine at his silky tone. She glanced down at her hands fisted in her lap.

Francesca nodded. "Harmony has some lovely young ladies. I suggest you get out there and meet them."

"What if I've already found one?" Keith's thigh brushed against Bertie's.

Francesca looked at both of them, lifting a skeptical brow. "Really?"

Keith's hard thigh deliberately pressed into hers as he leaned closer. "Yeah, she's talented…on many levels. I don't know about her mothering skills, but I'd bet she'd catch on real quick."

Bertie sat rigid on the settee. Heat flushed her face, and her heart slowed to a low thud. Keith's voice had become silkier, and the idea of one hundred and fifty thousand dollars was the only thing that kept her from jumping up and running from the room.

Francesca's lips thinned into a tight line. "If she's from Harmony, I have no doubt she's a nice young lady."

Bertie sneaked a sideways glance at Keith. His dark eyes burned with fury, and anger lines bracketed his firm lips.

"I wouldn't know about nice, but she's pretty hot." His gaze locked with hers.

Bertie jumped up as if she'd been poked with a cattle prod. "Aunt Franny, I'll have an answer for you tomorrow. I'm…um…going to go now. The food's in the kit—"

"I don't approve of you fooling around and breaking her heart simply to make a point with me."

Francesca and Keith both rose from their seats, boxing Bertie in between them. Francesca had interrupted Bertie as if she hadn't been speaking, never breaking eye contact with Keith, who stood too close to her back. Proprietarily close. Like boyfriend/girlfriend close.

"Are you saying she's off-limits or just fooling around is off-limits?" Keith's sexy voice rumbled above her head. Afraid to move, Bertie kept her eyes trained on the lustrous sheen of Francesca's gray pearl necklace.

"I'm saying, tread carefully. I will not have the people I know and love hurt because you're angry and want to get back at me." Francesca's voice crackled with anger.

"If I agree to your form of blackmail, then anyone is fair game. You're not exactly giving me tons of time for this miraculous courtship."

Francesca gave a regal toss of her head. "Oh, I don't know. You always seem to do your best work under pressure. I recall you being the prince of tiebreakers and winning tennis matches under pressure. Three months is more than enough time."

"Especially if she's right under my nose."

Oh my mama pajama. Bertie suspected a diabolical grin crossed Keith's face, like a pirate forcing his victim to walk the plank.

She pushed back with her elbow into Keith Morgan's rock-hard abs and sidestepped away from the dueling blackmailers. "Okay, here's the thing…I'm not really sure what or who you're talking about and"—she held her hand up like a stop sign—"I don't want to know. But I'm also not a fuzzy yellow tennis ball to be volleyed back and forth."

Bertie bent down for her handbag she'd dropped on the carpet. "Aunt Franny, I need some time to think. I'll see you tomorrow." She turned to bolt from the room when Keith snagged her elbow, pulling her to a halt.

"Hold up. I'm coming with you." He pierced Francesca with a harsh stare. "What do you want, boss… daily or weekly reports?"

"I forbid you to date her," Francesca commanded loud and clear.

"I can't make that promise," Keith said, shaking his head. He hustled Bertie from the room, and neither one looked back to see the faint smile curling Francesca's lips.

Chapter 4

KEITH PULLED BERTIE TOWARD HIS BLACK PORSCHE Cayenne. She tried stopping him, but the wedge shoes she wore didn't give good traction.

"We need to talk," he growled as he yanked open the passenger door and tried shoving her inside.

"Hold on a minute. Where do you think you're taking me? I haven't agreed to work for you. I'm not about to get in your car and head for parts unknown." Bertie crossed her arms over her impressive chest and glared up at him. Keith barely knew her, but he recognized the mulish tilt of her chin, and he figured he'd better start talking if he wanted answers.

He closed his eyes and inhaled the crisp evening air. It was mid-March, the sun had gone down and the temperatures had dropped into the fifties. The cold pierced the gray henley sweater he wore over his long-sleeve cotton T-shirt and he fought the urge to shiver. He still hadn't acclimated to the cooler climate, even though most considered the Carolinas mild. Keith had lived among the palm trees and salty breezes of the Atlantic Ocean for years. Anything in the fifties was considered freakin' cold in Miami.

He rubbed his hands together and said, "Look, can we go somewhere and maybe grab a cup of coffee? I want to sort this whole thing out. I promise I'll be on my best behavior."

Bertie's sea-green eyes narrowed. Keith fought the urge to grin. She may look like Betty Boop, but he had a feeling she was no dummy. "No more cheap shots. What do you say?"

"Well…"

"Come on. I'm freezing my ass off out here." He held the passenger door open. Bertie hesitated, peering up at him as if he bullied small children and stole their lunch money. She gave a curt nod before hiking herself up into the leather bucket seat. He caught a brief glimpse of a very fine ass encased in a pair of tight jeans. He was in hell.

Keith drove the short distance from Aunt Francesca's neighborhood, where statelier, wealthier homes graced acre lots in Harmony, to the corner of Main and Oakwood, near the center of town. He parked in the side lot to what looked to be the local watering hole. The Dogwood Bar & Grill had small-town charm, with its gabled roof and covered porch entrance. Hunter-green shutters and window boxes with blooming yellow flowers decorated the front. He strolled with Bertie up the paved walkway lined with several dogwood trees waiting for their blooms. His hand pushed the bronze handle on the wavy-glass front door, which obscured the interior, and ushered Bertie through. Once Keith stepped over the threshold, he stopped dead in his tracks.

His head snapped back in stunned surprise. The "quaint" bar was bursting with a kaleidoscope of color. Straight ahead, aqua blue and green bell jar lamps hung over the dark brown wooden bar with chrome barstools covered in zebra-striped vinyl. Diners sat at old, plank pine tables on painted, ladder-back chairs in bright orange, pink, and lavender. And people jammed the booths, sitting on green and yellow Dalmatian-spotted vinyl, drinking out of aqua-colored mason jars. Chicken wire pendant lights illuminated each booth with colorful crystals and old-timey lightbulbs. The floor created a wave-like pattern in speckled orange, green, and blue terrazzo that led to a point directly in front of a wooden stage. A small local country band played in front of a pink and silver hexagon-patterned backdrop.

"Goddamn. What blind person decorated this place? It looks like someone tripping on drugs opened a bunch of paint cans and went spider-monkey crazy," Keith said.

"Ummph," he grunted as Bertie's elbow connected hard with his ribs in a swift jab.

"I did, you big, stupid oaf!" She glared up at him then stormed off, leaving him standing in the small, purple-painted entrance all alone.

Jesus, Mary, and Joseph. Aunt Francesca wanted this color-blind, acid-dropping decorator working on his house?

Like bloody hell.

He watched Bertie and her fine ass weave her way toward the bar like she owned the place. Customers called out her name and she waved, stopping to speak with a few. Her thick, shiny hair bounced around her shoulders, and her tight jeans caught the attention of some of the guys. Keith witnessed more than a few heads swiveling in her direction. His mouth tightened into a grim line.

When she reached the end of the bar, Keith recognized her brother, the one he'd met earlier, handing her a martini with lots of olives as if he'd been expecting her. It figured everyone knew her since her brother obviously worked as a bartender. A waitress approached wearing a neon-pink, V-neck T-shirt with *The Dog* written across her chest in sequins. He refrained from rolling his eyes, figuring Bertie designed the blinding T-shirts as well.

"Table for one? Or would you like to sit at the bar?" she asked, smiling, her lips covered with matching hot-pink lipstick. A silly pink bow flopped around her blond ponytail.

"Uh, I'm with Bertie Anderson." Keith motioned in Bertie's direction. "We'll need a table for two."

The waitress's smile grew even wider. "Certainly. Bertie always sits at the owner's table toward the back. Follow me." The waitress grabbed a menu from a lime-green painted basket tacked to the wall. Keith followed her around the noisy diners to a booth tucked into an alcove that was not completely hidden but hidden enough for a little privacy.

"Why does Bertie always eat at the owner's table?" he asked as he slid across the booth and took the menu.

The waitress placed two cardboard beer coasters on the sparkly, silver laminate tabletop.

"Because she's the owner," she giggled. "With Cal. You didn't know?"

"Know what?" Bertie appeared at the waitress's side with half a martini in her hand. She still looked pissed. "Thanks, Sara Jean. I'll have my usual and get Mr. Morgan whatever he'd like." She scooted into the booth on the opposite side.

She owned a bar *and* she decorated? What else did she do? Give manicures at Floyd's barbershop?

Keith ordered a beer, figuring he'd need the extra fortification to deal with the crazier-than-bat-shit situation he currently found himself in. He glanced out over the busy bar at people eating, drinking, and singing along with the band. The bar had a comfortable atmosphere, in a psychedelic, morning-after, hangover kind of way. Fresh bread smells and the sizzling sound of grilling meat seeped from the kitchen, making his stomach growl. He turned back to Bertie and met her gaze. From the way her lips formed a definite frown, Keith knew he had some sucking up to do.

"I'm sorry for insulting your…uh…creative talents," he said, trying not to grin. Her frown deepened. He cocked his head, thinking how that expression looked all wrong on her animated face. Her plump pink lips were made for hot, wet kisses, not frowning. Keith recalled the exact texture and succulent feel of her perfect mouth pressed against his…

"Oh, forget it," she said, snapping him out of his kissing fantasy. "These loud colors and funky interiors draw a lot of people here. Cal and I wanted to do something different when we decided to renovate."

"Looks like you've cornered the market on different," Keith added, noting the crown molding painted in a black and white geometric pattern. "How long have you owned the place?"

Sara Jean appeared with their fresh drinks and took Keith's order for the house special: marinated grilled chicken breast over spicy black beans and yellow rice. Bertie ordered a salad with grilled mahimahi on top.

"We inherited it from our parents." She licked the rim of her fresh martini glass, and Keith all but guzzled his beer, trying to forget how her tongue felt tangled with his.

"Are your parents retired?" he asked.

"No. Dead." She lowered her gaze and fiddled with the drink coaster.

Fuck. He couldn't catch a break. First he insulted her design talent, and then he mentioned her dead parents. What next? "Sorry. Listen, I didn't mean—"

"We need to discuss Aunt Franny's proposal," she interrupted.

There she went again...*Aunt Franny?* He leaned forward, trying to repress the anger surging forth over Francesca's calculated blackmailing.

"How did she become your Aunt Franny? Her only sibling is my mother, and I'm an only child. Her late husband, my uncle, didn't have any siblings either." Keith couldn't hold his testiness in check. Bertie shifted in her seat, glancing up when Sara Jean reappeared with their dinners.

"Here you go," Sara Jean said in a cheery voice as she placed the red and green Fiestaware plates piled high with food in front of them. "Uh, Mr. Morgan, would you mind signing this picture for my little brother? I didn't realize who you were until Cal told me. My brother, Danny, is a big tennis fan. He plays over at the Jaycee Park, but their courts are in really bad condition and the nets are always torn—"

"Yeah, sure." Keith reached for the computer printed picture of himself, serving at some tournament a few years ago. He scribbled his signature with Sara Jean's purple Sharpie. He tried not to think about the pinnacle of his career, when he trained eight hours a day to prepare for a tournament. He shoved the autograph back to Sara Jean as he went for his beer.

"Gosh, are you going to be training here in Harmony? Imagine having the Prince right in our backyard playing tennis. Maybe you could do something about those awful courts and—"

"Thanks, Sara Jean. I think Cal needs you at the bar," Bertie said, surprising him as he gripped the Mason jar until he thought the glass would shatter in his hand. Bertie waited until Sara Jean crossed the crowded bar before continuing.

"Francesca has been like a mother to me and Cal. She was a godsend when my mother got sick and died. We've always called her Aunt Franny, but I'll stop if it makes you uncomfortable. I certainly don't mean to take your place," she said, sounding defensive as she drizzled a little dressing over her salad, moving her food around with her fork.

"Hell, I don't care if you call her Queen Elizabeth. I only wanted to know what your relationship is with her." Keith forked a bite of chicken with the black beans and rice in his mouth. The flavors surprised him as his taste buds jumped to life. The food had a definite Cuban kick that he loved.

"Look, we both know this has the makings of a huge disaster where neither one of us will be getting what we want. I don't know what Aunt…uh, Francesca was thinking, but all I have to do is say—"

"Bertie! I love those pillows with the extra row of ruffles. I want you to make a matching one for Sweet Tea's dog bed." A terrifying lady dressed in a jean skirt with red and white ruffles on the bottom clipped across the terrazzo floor to their booth wearing red, white, and blue cowboy boots. A closer inspection revealed tiny rows of ruffles outlining her denim vest. Bertie's pretty, creamy complexion turned as red as the lady's T-shirt with *Git-R-Done* written across her monstrous chest.

"Hey, Dottie. What brings you to the Dog tonight?" Bertie asked in a faint voice.

Dottie hoisted herself up into the booth forcing Bertie to move over. "I came for the music and the four-dollar pitchers of beer, but I'm staying to meet the Prince here," she said as she stuck out her right hand featuring long, fire-engine red nails and diamond and gold rings on every finger. Keith almost burst out laughing at her platinum-blond Mae West hairdo and the thick mask of makeup she wore, which probably required a jackhammer to remove every night. He guessed her age to be anywhere from fifty…to death.

He shook her bejeweled hand. "Keith Morgan. It's a pleasure to meet…"

"Dottie Duncan. She owns the Toot-N-Tell. It's a chain of drive-through convenience stores," Bertie said, pushing her plate away. She hadn't taken more than three bites of her dinner, seeming to have lost her appetite.

"That's right. I sell everything from milk to cartons of cigarettes. All you gotta do is pull up and toot your horn. Got sixteen stores throughout the state. I understand you're settin' down roots right here in Harmony. How come? Not that I'm complaining. You're mighty fine to look at and you're gonna give that rascal Cal some competition with the ladies."

Keith cut a glance at Bertie as a small smile played across his lips.

"Unless you're already spoken for," Dottie added as she looked from him to Bertie and back.

"Keith's Francesca's nephew," Bertie said with a little too much enthusiasm.

Dottie leaned back and crossed her arms over her chest, causing her breasts to look as if they might spill from the top of her shirt. It had been so long for Keith, he didn't even consider the sick implications of actually wanting to see it happen.

"So you're Franny's nephew? I'd forgotten you belong to her. She used to talk about you all the time. When are we gonna see you play some tennis, hotshot?"

Keith cocked a brow. "I'm retired. I don't play anymore."

"That mean you forgot how?" Dottie pressed. "I've got two grandkids living in Raleigh and they love to play. Sure would like to impress them by telling them they can see you in action."

"I'm going to be real busy fixing up my house, but I'll be sure to let you know when I decide to participate in an exhibition match," he said, not caring if Dottie Duncan detected the sarcasm in his tone. Bertie started to squirm in her seat, causing Dottie to narrow her gaze at both of them again.

"Umph. I think you two are going to work out fine. Bertie here is a whiz with interiors, among other things. You're lucky to have her. Don't you forget it." She pointed her scary nail at him. "And I'll talk to you more about that exhibition match. I think that's just what Harmony needs." Dottie smiled the smile of someone who knew a great secret. And Keith had a sinking feeling he was the star attraction in that secret.

"Bertie, before I forget…can you take care of Sweet Tea for the next two days? I've got to run to Charlotte to check on a couple locations," Dottie asked as she slid from the booth.

So now Bertie could add dog walker to her list of many talents? No wonder she stunk as a decorator. She over-committed herself and didn't pay enough attention to her decorating career. Forget dog walking. She needed to take Basic Colors 101.

"Sure. No problem." Bertie's smile appeared pained.

Dottie shook her head, but her lacquered blond curls never moved. "I don't know what I'm gonna do when you move to Atlanta in three weeks. It won't be the same around here. That design firm doesn't know what a prize they're getting." She patted Bertie's hand, nodded in Keith's direction, and sashayed toward the bar.

Atlanta? Great! She'd be moving in three weeks and he wouldn't have to worry about grabbing her and shoving her down on the nearest surface so he could push himself inside her. Surely he could hold himself in check for three more weeks.

Bertie's bottom lip appeared swollen where she'd been gnawing on it. Worry lines marred her smooth features. Then it hit him like an ace down the T: she wasn't going anywhere as long as one hundred and fifty thousand dollars sat on the table. Damn Francesca.

"I'll give you three hundred thousand dollars to leave town."

Chapter 5

"OF ALL THE…THE VERY IDEA…I'M SO MAD I COULD spit!" Bertie ranted behind the bar as she shoved soapy glassware under the running water.

"Whoa there, Trigger." Cal grabbed a glass from her slippery hands before she added it to the already broken collection on the floor as her temper reached the boiling point.

"Why don't you head on home before you start smashing plates? I'll finish cleaning up." Cal thrust a dry dish towel at her and turned her toward the door. The bar had closed an hour ago, but she stayed behind to help clean. She often did to distract herself from worry—if breaking glassware constituted cleaning.

"Take my car." Cal unlocked the front door and handed Bertie his keys along with her handbag.

"How will you get home?" she asked, palming the keys. Cal lived farther outside the city limits.

"Don't worry ab—"

"Cal, you almost done?"

Bertie glanced across the bar to the office door where Angie, one of the gals who worked downtown, leaned against the doorframe with a sulky look on her face. Apparently, she'd been kept waiting by Cal the Casanova.

"Geez, Cal," Bertie muttered under her breath. "Are you actually dating her?" Cal pulled the front door open. "She isn't going to go quietly when you dump her, you know."

Cal gave her an extra shove. "You're the one with the problem. Now get moving. You have a lot of ranting, raving, and hair pulling to do." He shut the door in her face and turned the deadbolt. Bertie trudged over to Cal's SUV parked in the side lot. She drove the three miles to her home on the near empty streets of Harmony, wondering what the heck she was going to do. Not that she was even considering taking Mr. Perfectly Rude's offer to leave town for three hundred thousand dollars. The nerve. As if she could be bought like that. Okay, maybe she could, but not from him and not like that. After Keith had insulted her with his outrageous offer, he apologized, glimpsing her horrified expression. Once the outrage over what he suggested had dissipated, Bertie had told him in a calm voice to enjoy the rest of his meal and then stormed away from the booth.

To stay in Harmony would be professional suicide, but to go would be suicide on a whole other personal level. She could do a lot with the money she'd make on Keith's job, like finishing renovations on her home and helping with some of the maintenance at the Dog, and that didn't include the outrageous bonus of one hundred and fifty smackers from Aunt Franny. Bertie unlocked her kitchen door, tossing her handbag on the antique bench by the back door, and retrieved a bottle of water from the refrigerator. As she pressed the refrigerator door closed, her eye caught the two pictures stuck under sparkly shoe and handbag magnets. Bertie slipped the picture down of four-year-old Jorge Bianco, smiling and clutching a rusted John Deere toy tractor to his small chest in front of a small, brand-new yellow-painted house—a home she and Gary had helped to build through the charity organization Dwelling Place. Bertie had spent endless days and nights raising money through pancake breakfasts, school carnivals, karaoke contests at the Dog, and countless other fund-raisers. They had managed to help complete two houses for the charity and give homes to families like Jorge's who couldn't afford decent housing on migrant workers' pay. Bertie enjoyed working on those two homes with their low budgets and tight spaces almost as much as the elaborate designs of her prominent clients. Dwelling Place could always use funds, especially now, when there were so many migrant families in need outside of Harmony. Bertie slid the snapshot back under the magnet and pulled out her cell phone, pressing a name under favorites.

"Do you have any idea what time it is?" a sleepy voice answered.

"I've been thinking," Bertie said, tapping her fingernails against her countertop.

"Not again," Gary moaned.

The pounding inside Keith's head caused his groggy eyes to open. As he lay on his rumpled mattress, blinking at the lazy, lopsided circles of the white ceiling fan, he realized it wasn't his head pounding. The sound was coming from outside. More specifically, the side of his house. Keith bolted out of bed and stomped to the back door in his bare feet. He flung the door open and stepped out on the porch, unmindful that he wore only pajama bottoms and a good case of bedhead.

He blinked at the sight of construction workers crawling all over his lawn. Carpenters were ripping off old, rotten shutters, and painters were sanding and stripping paint. But the biggest shocker had to be Bertie, standing in the middle of his backyard, gesturing with one hand, while the other hand held the leash to what looked to be a brown, shaggy mongrel with a floppy purple bow tied around its neck. Keith gave his head a violent shake, wondering if this was another bad dream disturbing his sleep since moving to Pleasantville. He hadn't seen Bertie in two days, since she had left him in a huff at the bar. He'd secretly hoped maybe, if he laid low for a couple days, this whole debacle would disappear…like Bertie would leave town as planned and his aunt would come to her senses and call off this ridiculous bride-in-a-bag search.

"Hey," he croaked. No one heard him over the commotion. Keith cleared his throat. "Hey!" Still, no one paid him any mind. Shoving his thumb and forefinger in his mouth, he let out a shrill whistle. Bertie's head jerked in his direction at the same time the mongrel beast tore across the yard at full speed, pulling Bertie behind him.

"*Sweeet Teeea!*" Bertie yelled, still holding the leash. Hair flying, short skirt lifted, Bertie squealed as she fell out of her colorful clogs and landed headfirst into a pile of mulch Keith had delivered the other day for ground cover. The dropped leash trailed across the grass as the barking mongrel bolted around the corner of the house.

"*Dios mio!*" One of the painters charged over to Bertie. "Ms. Bertie, are you okay?" he asked in a heavy accent, bending down to help her up.

Bertie scrambled to straighten her short, flared skirt and extended her hand to the painter to help her up. Keith ambled over to assist…hoping to get a look at the goods underneath. Even better, Bertie brushed mulch from the long sleeves of her tie-dyed lace tunic, unaware that the string closure at the top had come undone, showcasing the tops of her creamy breasts. Keith gave a sigh of pure appreciation. Bertie looked up and locked gazes with him. His lips twitched, trying to hide his smile.

"Well, isn't this a beautiful morning?" he said as he reached and picked a piece of mulch from her tangled hair.

Bertie stumbled back, and her brow furrowed, as if she couldn't understand why he'd be standing in his own backyard. She almost lost her balance again between the pile of mulch and the foolish bushy mongrel who decided to return to the scene of the crime and bump the side of her leg. Keith grabbed her elbow to keep her upright. When he was certain she was steady, he pulled her with him toward the house, scooping up her clogs along the way.

"Okay, here's the thing," Bertie said as she skipped to keep up. "Julio, please grab Sweet Tea's leash and put him back in my car. Windows are cracked," she called to one of the workers.

Keith couldn't believe that shaggy beast of a dog wearing a stupid purple bow was Sweet Tea. Poor dog. Man, Dottie Duncan of the Toot-N-Tell won serious points for small-town weirdness. Keith opened the screen door to the porch, keeping a firm grip on Bertie's elbow. Dropping her clogs on the wood floor, he led her to the kitchen. "Sit," he commanded, pointing to one of the two ladder-back chairs next to an old farm table.

"Let me explain—"

"Sit." He pushed her into a chair and headed for the

coffeemaker next to the old farm sink. He made quick work of measuring out scoops of coffee and setting the carafe on the burner. He couldn't deal with any more drama without his caffeine fix. The rich aroma permeated the not-so-still morning air. Keith pulled down two mismatched mugs from the upper cabinet and set them next to the coffeemaker. He leaned against the cabinets and crossed his arms, fixing Bertie with his famous Morgan glare, the one he used to stare down an opponent on the other side of the net. But watching Bertie squirm as she curled her pink-painted toes around the rung of the chair made him feel like laughing, not fighting.

"Explain," he said, struggling to keep the edge in his voice as he stared at her tangled hair with bits of mulch peeking through.

Bertie released a huge breath. "I've got three months to get this place looking beautiful, and there's not a minute to waste."

Keith pushed his fingers through his own unkempt hair. "Christ. So, you're taking the money." Like he didn't know. A yard full of construction workers was a pretty good sign.

The color pink infused her cheeks. "It's a lot of money," she mumbled, fiddling with the ties to her top.

The coffeemaker spit and sputtered as it finished brewing. Keith poured the steaming morning elixir in the mugs, wishing for an extra strong *cafecito* from his favorite Cuban coffee stand instead. "Cream and sugar?"

"Cream, please."

He strained to hear her soft voice as he stirred cream into both coffees.

Their fingers brushed as he handed her the mug.

Shock widened her eyes as she felt the jolt of electric current their touch created.

Keith settled back against the kitchen cabinets and lifted the mug to his lips. Bertie blew on her hot coffee, sneaking a wary look in his direction. Yep. They'd both have to deal with this insane physical attraction, one way or another. How? He had no fucking idea, especially now that she'd be all over his house 24/7, hanging pictures and fluffing stupid, useless pillows everywhere.

"You gonna let me do my job?" she asked with visible unease.

He tipped his mug in her direction in a mock salute. "Game on."

———

Bertie barely even tasted the strong coffee sliding down her throat. She needed to think, but her mind drew a blank, so distracted by his big, bare chest and his tousled, slept-on hair. When she heard him whistle, before Sweet Tea took off like a rocket, she couldn't believe it. She didn't think he could look any better than he had the other day in nothing but a towel, but she was wrong. Way wrong. His pajama pants hung low on his hips and yet he wore them as if they were custom-made formal wear.

"So, what's the plan?" Keith splashed more coffee in his mug. The irritation she sensed earlier had vanished from his features. Maybe he would jump on board and not make this a living hell for her. Maybe.

"As you can see, we need to shore up the outside with new paint and shutters, and replace all the bad boards. I thought we'd stick with the dove-gray color and the teal blue for the shutters." Bertie sipped her coffee. "I'm using the historical colors original to the house. Aunt Fran—" Keith's eyebrows rose. "Francesca thought that would be best."

Keith yanked the chair around and straddled it. With a trembling hand, Bertie lowered the mug to the table, aware of his intense scrutiny. He was another client, putting his pants on one leg at a time like everybody else. *It's the taking them off that must be spectacular... Stop it!*

"Here's how it's going to work," he said in a brisk tone. "You run everything by me from now on. My aunt is not to be involved. Understood?"

"Yes, but—"

"It's my way or the highway. I'm the client, and you answer to me if you want to finish on time and get your bonus." He made "bonus" sound like "crack pipe."

What did he know? Bertie had her reasons for staying and taking the money and Mr. Surly Athlete with the big, broad chest and sexy, dark stubble didn't intimidate her. Okay, maybe a teensy-weensy bit, but she'd be damned if she let him see it. She lifted her chin a little.

"How do you feel about the color red?"

"I hate it." He scowled down at her.

"Good. I hate it too." Bertie stood and chunks of mulch dropped to the floor from beneath her skirt. "We need to tackle the kitchen, floors, and bedrooms. I have samples and boards to show you, along with my design proposal." She smoothed her denim skirt with her palm. "In the meantime, I'm short an electrician..." Keith tilted his head up and a smirk played around his sculpted lips. "...you need to remove the sconces on the exterior so the painters can finish," she said with a toss of her head, flinging mulch as she turned to leave.

"Where are you going?" he called out with a chuckle in his voice.

Away from Mr. Drop-Dead Gorgeous before she did something stupid, like push him down on the kitchen table and have her way with him. "Taking Sweet Tea home. Don't worry. I'll be back."

"That's what I was afraid of," he mumbled.

"I heard that," Bertie said as she shoved her feet into her Dansko clogs and banged out the screen door.

———

Once inside her car, she shut the door and realized it was time to close another door. Her hand shook as she fished for her cell phone and scrolled through her contacts for the design firm in Atlanta. She'd made her decision, and it was only proper business etiquette to inform them. Sweet Tea nudged her neck from the backseat and gave her a slobbery kiss. Bertie scratched behind his ear and straightened his purple bow. "Just give me a few minutes, buddy, and I'll get you home." She put the phone to her ear.

"Bertie?" Bill Murphy the managing partner said. "It's good to hear from you. We're looking forward to your coming down."

"Hey there, Bill. Uh, about your offer." She licked her dry lips. "I'm in the middle of a very big project that won't be finished for another three months, so er, I'm afraid—"

"I see. Must be pretty important for you to pass on this offer from one of the premier design firms of the

South." Bill made it sound like she was throwing away a multimillion dollar offer to host a show on HGTV rather than an entry level position as a junior designer.

Ignoring his sanctimonious tone, she said, "It is. Big enough that I can't walk away right now. But at the end of the next three months, if there's still an opportunity…" Her voice trailed off as she gave Sweet Tea another distracted pat on the head.

"It's possible, but I can't make any promises at the moment. We have a pile of résumés from people who are eager to be here."

"Certainly. I completely understand."

"But your portfolio showed great potential, and with a little guidance and help from our top designers, you'd be gaining a wealth of experience. And I know this was your dream job…"

Not exactly. This job was her ticket out. As for her dreams, they didn't necessarily include slaving for other designers no more talented than she.

Bill continued to blather on about the great reputation of his firm. "…so, why don't you give us a call in three months and we'll see if there's another opening for you. Hmmm?"

"Sure. Sounds great. I will definitely be in touch. Thank you so much for the offer and for understanding." As she pressed End on her phone, she bit her lower lip and started counting to one hundred…and fifty thousand. By the time she finished, maybe her three months would be up.

Two hours later, Bertie stood on Keith's porch, armed with designer ammunition worthy of the old Victorian's grandeur.

"Honey, I'm home," she called as she pushed the front door open, wrestling with bulky catalogs, wood samples, and paint chips in her bright orange leather tote. No signs of life except for the workers outside. The sconces had been removed from the front of the house, and her lips curled into a knowing smile. She dumped her tote and handbag on the wood floor in the foyer and then headed back to her car for more samples.

After unloading her car, she went around back to check on the painters, not expecting to see Mr. Cocky Athlete on a ladder, hammering up new replacement wood. Bertie touched the side of her mouth to check for drool. She wasn't kidding when she said nothing made her heart pitter-patter more than a man who knew his way around tools—and this one happened to be totally hubbalicious in cargo pants held up with a tool belt. No shirt. Again. How could she expect to get any work done around here when he insisted on parading around half-naked? Where was Hal with the missing front teeth when she needed him? She inhaled a deep breath. Three months and one hundred and fifty big ones. She could do this.

She cupped her hands around her mouth. "Hey, Paul Bunyan! You wanna come down for a minute, so I can get your approval?"

Streaks of sweat trickled down Keith's bronzed back, seeking refuge inside the top of his pants. She had never wanted to be sweat before in her life…until today.

Keith glanced at her, put his hammer and nails inside his tool belt, and climbed down the ladder. "What time is it?" he asked as he grabbed his T-shirt off the porch railing and wiped his brow.

Okay, now, cover up. He hung the shirt around his neck, cocking his dark head to one side. *No. Please.* Not the sexy athlete poster pose, the one where sweat dripped down the chest and ripped abs while said athlete wore the cocky, self-assured expression that could launch millions of dollars in sales for hemorrhoid cream. Mouth dry, she tried swallowing. She could do this.

"Time?" he asked again, pointing to her wrist.

"Oh"—she checked her bright yellow Michael Kors watch—"almost noon."

"Good. I'm starved. I'll shower. You order lunch." Keith hopped back on the porch and reached for the back door.

"But...I have stuff...I wanted—"

"Over lunch. Give me ten minutes." He disappeared inside the house.

"Good grief." She fanned her overheated face with her hand and trudged back to her car parked in the driveway. She headed to the Dog, knowing she could grab lunch in less time than ordering a pizza. Besides, she needed to make sure Mr. Carmichael, her house-bound neighbor, had a meal too. She hoped she could survive another meal with Mr. Shirtless Stud.

Thirty minutes later, Bertie came through the front door with two bags of food. She pushed the swinging door to the kitchen with her hip and stopped. Keith glanced up from the beat-up farm table with Bertie's drawings spread across it. Thank goodness he'd covered his chest in a black, long-sleeve polo. Hair still damp from his shower, he looked squeaky clean and good enough to eat. All of a sudden, the chicken mandarin salad weighing heavy in her hand lost its appeal. Keith appeared much tastier.

"What? You look stunned," Bertie said, dumping the bags on the countertop.

Keith started pushing her drawings to one side to clear a space on the table. "I guess I'm pleasantly amazed." He indicated with his hand. "Your drawings are pretty good. I like some of your ideas."

"Oh? Which ideas?" She placed the containers of food on the table and Keith opened a drawer to grab silverware.

"I like the kitchen design. It's modern but still in keeping with the style of the house," he said, handing her a fork and knife. Bertie's heart did a cartwheel. He grabbed water bottles from the refrigerator. "What took you so long? I'm starving."

"I called in an order at the Dog and then I went to check on my neighbor, Mr. Carmichael. He's old and sometimes forgets to eat."

Keith paused, holding a chip. "Let me see if I've got this. First, you walk that poor mongrel, Sweet Tea, who is obviously battling issues over his dumb name, not to mention the stupid purple ribbon. And then you check on a senior citizen to make sure he's eating? And I'm assuming you also help out at the Dog. With all these extra jobs, when do you find time to design?"

Bertie pushed the mandarin oranges around with her fork. She didn't think it'd be smart to mention that she watered plants, shopped for food, and volunteered at Dwelling Place too. She knew Keith wouldn't understand her desire or need to feel useful. Ever since the death of her parents, Bertie had filled the void in her life by helping others. Not because she dreamed of sainthood, but because she hated that empty, lonely feeling that consumed her and kept her up at night. That unsettled feeling that she didn't really belong anymore. After her mom's death, Bertie had filled her role by taking over all the cooking and cleaning. She kept hoping her dad would snap out of his depression if she showed him that nothing had changed. She worked so they could still remain intact as a family. Once her dad died several years later, Bertie had gotten used to juggling jobs to bring in extra money and to keep her mind occupied. She had a real knack for multitasking.

"Um…I find the time. My office is in my home and I…uh…work late."

Keith studied her hard for a full minute. "This is a big job with a small window of time. I expect a hundred percent on your part."

Bertie pasted what she hoped appeared a confident smile on her face. "Have no fear. I'm a master multitasker, and Gary and I will make sure—"

"There's a lot of money riding on this job. Are you willing to risk losing it because you have to stop and walk Sweet Tea or mow someone's lawn?"

"Let me assure you, Mr. Morgan. I will give your job top priority and you will get the best service possible," she replied in a prim, professional voice.

Keith stabbed a piece of Bertie's chicken with his fork, shoving the entire piece in his mouth, smiling while he chewed. Once he swallowed, he said, "As long as they're *your* services and not Gary's." He winked and her stomach twisted into a delectable knot. "I still haven't gotten over the fact that you thought I was gay. I'm going to need years of therapy."

"Oh, I'm sure one session will suffice. Your monster ego seems pretty healthy to me."

He laughed—a deep, confident laugh that had Bertie's toes curling inside her clogs.

"Let's get back to your services. Your professional services," he added when Bertie narrowed her eyes at him. "Gutting the kitchen is good, and I want to add a master bath."

Bertie stopped with her fork halfway to her mouth. "Really?" Definitely doable, and it would really enhance the house, but geez, she only had three months. "What else?"

"We need to review the furniture plan and incorporate my own pieces." She raised her eyebrows. "Yeah, hard to believe I own more than a mattress on the floor," he smirked. "I haven't had the rest trucked up yet."

Bertie sipped the cool water from the bottle. "I'm going to need pictures and dimensions. I can't—"

"All under control. My guy in Miami is putting all that together for you."

"What about the upstairs? I need to get started on your daughter's room—"

"I want her to have the connecting rooms. One as her bedroom, the other as her playroom/TV room… whatever. Rip up the carpets and refinish the wood floors." Keith paused, making a dent in his roast beef sandwich. "Start fresh with Maddie. New furniture, fabrics, the works."

A softness came over him as he spoke about his daughter. A look of peace laced with a little sadness shifted across his features. Bertie wondered if he missed his wife. If he still loved her. If he'd ever love again.

Stop it. Do not go there. Just because he kissed like a god didn't make him worthy of dating. Dating? What a joke. Bertie's naughty alter ego wanted more than a date. She wanted to hula in her slinkiest lingerie and get down with his fine bootay.

Keith wiped his hands on the paper napkin. "I want her room to be special. I want her to call this home."

"I would love to meet her and find out what she really likes," she said, realizing too late she sounded wistful.

Keith sat back, pushing his container away, and gave her a small, crooked smile. Heat crept up her chest and settled on her cheeks.

"Yeah? I'll see what I can do." His voice held a sexy, raspy quality.

"Did you check the color key? I really think the combination of blues and browns adds a—"

Keith jumped up, gathering containers off the table. "I really don't care as long as it's not pink and green or some other god-awful combination. No crazy, psychedelic patterns. This isn't the Dog."

"Not even for Maddie?" she challenged, tossing paper napkins in the garbage. She turned and Keith stood mere inches in front of her. Only a sliver of air separated her lacy tunic from his black polo shirt. His musky, outdoorsy scent filled her head.

"Maybe," he said slowly. "How good are your skills of persuasion?" Keith brushed a lock of hair behind her ear, sending shivers down her spine.

Bertie cleared her throat and her head at the same time. "Well, I've made a few selections…and…the drawings…" Her voice sounded breathy. Yikes.

Keith moved back, a sexy smile played around his lips.

"I've signed your proposal with a few revisions, and there's a check on the counter for your retainer." He grabbed a set of keys from a bowl on the counter and turned to leave.

"Hey…we're not done here. You need to make some final decisions." He kept moving toward the door. "I hope you like mauve. I plan to bathe your entire bedroom in it," she said, following behind him.

Bertie let out a squeal as Keith turned suddenly and backed her against the bare dining room wall. He leaned forward, planting his hands on the wall beside her head.

"If I see any mauve anywhere in my house…including Maddie's suite, I can assure you, you will not like the consequences." He bared his teeth in a wicked grin.

Okay. Time to show him that he really didn't intimidate her—or at least, time to pretend he didn't. She plastered a bored look on her face. "I know plenty of men who like the color mauve."

Keith's hips pressed into her stomach and Bertie started from the shock. Christ on a cracker. He was hard…again.

"Do I need to prove to you that I'm not gay, Ms. Anderson?" he rumbled close to her ear, making her light-headed.

"N-n-no. I'm good," she said, as she pushed at the brick wall that made up his chest. Keith didn't budge. His gaze lowered to her mouth and remained for several long moments. He shook his head as if breaking a spell and dropped his arms.

"Another time, perhaps?" he abruptly turned to leave.

Why not now? Oh, shut up. "I need your approval… where're you going?" Bertie called to his disappearing back.

"Bride hunting. Where else?"

Chapter 6

INSIDE THE COFFEE SHOP AT THE BARNES & NOBLE IN Raleigh, Keith flipped through a book on the economic crisis of the twenty-first century. He'd read the first chapter at least two times, not because he didn't understand the theories, but because he couldn't stop thinking about Bertie. Her luscious body and her big eyes that flared whenever he got near her, or touched her—or almost kissed her. Fuck. He needed to stay away from her, not think of ways to be inside her. He had a job to do. He needed to find a wife. No. Correction: a suitable mother for Maddie who would also happen to be married to him. Someone plain, simple, and sweet. Someone who liked to clean, bake cookies, and watch Disney movies with his daughter. Someone calm who wore Keds tennis shoes and cardigan sweaters buttoned all the way up with a strand of pearls around her neck and a black velvet headband in her hair. Not someone who looked like she could salsa all night in spandex and stilettos. Flashes of his late wife, Adriana, laughing and swirling around with a mojito in her hand burned inside his head. Not that again. No fucking way.

Tension tightened every muscle in his body. After all the domestic battles and accusations with Adriana that had spewed forth as though from a broken sewer pipe, he used to think of Maddie and calm down. Knocking up Adriana may have been a mistake, but making his baby was the best thing he ever did. Whenever he was home, he'd take the tiny bundle in his arms and rock her to sleep, holding her well into the night. Calmness would flow through him and fill in all the gaping wounds. If he was on the road, he'd pull out Maddie's pink, stuffed lamb named Smiley from his overnight bag. The innocent scent would reassure him. Maddie made the ceaseless arguing and Adriana's endless affairs, careless nights, and drama-filled days all worth it. He would do anything for Maddie, which was why he was pouring money into a dilapidated old home in Harmony and speed hunting for a wife.

He needed a real, live Mother Goose. That was what his brain told him. His body had other ideas. But he could do this...for Maddie and for himself. He didn't need to entertain fantasies about Bertie and her curvaceous figure and how great her breasts felt smashed against his chest or how she always smelled of blooming gardenias. He didn't need to recall how she tasted like cinnamon and sin when he kissed her.

He needed to find someone fast, before Bertie found her hands full of more than mere fabric swatches. Keith slammed the book closed. A couple of patrons glanced up from their laptops and gave him curious stares. He leaned back in his chair, locking his hands behind his head, plotting ways to get back at Aunt Francesca for forcing him into this predicament in the first place. He hated ultimatums and hers was a doozy. How the holy hell was he supposed to find someone to marry in a slow-moving, sleepy, small town? Or even the surrounding cities? Raleigh wasn't exactly a hotbed of great entertainment and nightlife. They still rolled the sidewalks up around midnight. And finding someone to agree to marriage in the short span of three months—which would include dating, meeting the parents, and convincing Maddie it was all for the best—was beyond ludicrous. He didn't think his fucked-up life could suck any more than it already did, but he guessed he was wrong. Way wrong.

Keith fished for his cell phone and texted, Luv u Maddie Poo! and then added a goofy smiley face. He knew she didn't have her phone with her, or he *hoped* she didn't because the boarding school didn't allow access to cell phones until after dinner. But he wanted his message to be the first thing she saw when she turned on her phone. Gathering the stack of books he chose to purchase, he headed for the register when a perky Barnes & Noble employee stopped to ask if he needed help.

"Did you find everything okay?" she asked, smiling, her cornflower-blue eyes twinkling.

"Yep. A little light reading." He chuckled, indicating the heavy books on economics and stock options he held in his hands.

"Allow me." She reached for the stack of books, brushing his fingers in the process and blushing a pretty shade of pink. "Everyone has their passions. For me, it's cookbooks. I love to bake," she said as she turned toward the front of the store and the register counter.

Suddenly Keith felt as if a dark cloud had lifted and the sun's rays beamed through the roof of the store. He stopped in his tracks and stared at the perky blond. She wore blue Keds on her feet. He raised his gaze to the acoustic tile ceiling and let out a huge breath. *Thank you, Jesus!*

His long stride ate up the space between him and

the answer to his prayers. "So, Gail, is it?" he asked, checking out her nametag. "What else do you like to do besides read cookbooks? I bet you're a fantastic cook," he said, pouring on all the charm ever instilled in him from too many boarding schools. Cute, flat-chested Gail gave a light laugh.

"Oh, I wouldn't say fantastic, but I do make a mean batch of peanut butter cookies. I'm afraid I have a bit of a sweet tooth," she ended in a shy voice. Keith stared to see if a halo glowed around her head.

"Don't we all," he mumbled.

"But I really love my job." She continued to speak in a soft, well-mannered voice as the scanner pinged at the barcodes. "I'm head of the children's department, and we have story time, plays, and all kinds of fun activities to get the kids interested in reading."

Keith froze, listening for the Hallelujah chorus. "Excuse me?" He'd missed something very important, spilling from her perfect, pale-pink lips.

She gave a nervous laugh. "Nothing. I was asking if you had any children…Mr…?"

"Morgan. But call me Keith. All my friends do," he said, ramping up his famous Morgan smile. "And yes, I have a very precocious daughter. She's ten going on twenty-one," he added with a chuckle.

"Oh, well, maybe our reading program will interest her. Maybe your wife could bring her in." Adorable, cookie-baking Gail said "wife" with the right amount of hesitation topped with curiosity.

Keith handed over his credit card. "Maddie's mom died when she was four." Gail's cornflower-blue eyes flared wide with horror.

"I'm so sorry. I didn't mean—"

"Don't apologize. You didn't know." Gail handed back his card and Keith signed the receipt. "But maybe I can bring her to one of your reading circles. When are they scheduled?"

Plain vanilla Gail graced him with a beatific smile as she handed him his bag of books. "Follow me and I'll give you a schedule."

"That'd be great." Keith fell into step beside her. "Better yet, why don't I buy you a cup of coffee while we discuss it," he said to a beaming, sensible, khaki-wearing Gail. "How do you feel about Disney movies?" he asked, leading the way to the coffee bar.

"Who doesn't love Ariel in *The Little Mermaid*?" his perfect little homemaker said.

~∿~

WELCOME TO HARMONY, NORTH CAROLINA POPULATION 11,339 WHERE EVERYONE SINGS AND LIVES IN HARMONY

Liza Palmer's blue BMW idled outside the city limits of Harmony. She drummed her fingers on the leather steering wheel, contemplating her next move.

It would be easy to pull back onto the narrow highway and drive those few short miles to her parents' house. The house that Liza used to call home. But now she had no idea what *home* meant. Not since she'd been fired. *Fired.* Her. She closed her eyes as a fresh wave of pain washed over her.

She'd left home four years ago as one of Harmony's rising stars. After graduating top of her class at law school, she'd landed a very prestigious job at a law firm in Chicago, where she'd earned her stripes and made partner in only three short years. She'd always been driven to reach her goals, even if it meant stepping on a few toes along the way. However, she had no idea how much it hurt until someone stomped on hers. Now, she felt lost…and betrayed. No shiny orange carrot to chase. Just an empty, hollow feeling that settled in her chest.

Numb to the core, she'd driven away from the Windy City with no direction in mind and had been wandering for over two weeks until she found herself staring at Harmony's welcome sign. Liza lowered her window and inhaled the fresh smell of pine mixed with green grass. Something she never smelled or even saw trapped in the high rises of her big-city world. She gave a long sigh. All roads led to home. But not for long. She simply needed enough time to start the healing process and to figure out what she wanted to do next. Yes, *home*. Maybe she'd curl up on the screened porch with a good book and give her mother all kinds of smothering time. Nothing sounded better. She'd give it two weeks—infinite possibilities.

Liza pushed the familiar beat-up door to the Daily Grind and stepped inside. Not much had changed, except maybe a few more displays of packaged snacks on a rack. Flavorful coffee smells permeated the air. Earl was busy behind the counter filling some tall guy's order. Liza moved toward the cooler on the back wall where she spied slices of Annie Mae's homemade cheesecake and cups of banana pudding. Her favorite. It had been a long time since she'd indulged her sweet tooth. She opened the cooler and grabbed one of each. Maybe she'd save one for later…then again, maybe not. She moved toward the counter, hugging her loot, when the tall guy ordering coffee turned with two cups in his hands. He looked familiar. She peered at him until realization struck.

"Hey. Aren't you the Prince?" she asked, placing her goodies on the counter. He went still and his dark, hooded eyes moved over her with unhidden masculine appreciation. It happened all the time.

"Yeah, Keith Morgan. And you?" he said in a nice, raspy voice.

For once, Liza felt nothing. She hadn't driven halfway across the country to start up a fling. Not even with Keith Morgan, ex-pro tennis player, looking every bit like sex on a stick, with his wavy, dark hair and rockhard body.

Earl chuckled behind the counter. "Hey there, Liza. You just get into town?" He jerked his head toward Keith. "Our famous new resident. He bought the old Victorian over on Carver. Gonna fix it all up and guess who's helping him?"

"Hey, Earl. Can I have a skinny latte, please? Large." Then she turned back to the Prince, now leaning against the snack display, wearing a curious expression. "Liza Palmer. I'd shake your hand but looks like it's full." She indicated his coffees to go. "I followed your tennis career, hated to see you retire."

His lips curled into something resembling a smile as a look of pain flashed behind his eyes. "Thanks. You still live in Harmony?" he asked.

Earl handed Liza her coffee and she fished for her wallet inside her Louis Vuitton cross-body bag. "Not any more. Just visiting. Who's helping with your home? Some big designer from Miami, I bet," she said with a chuckle, handing Earl some bills. Liza remembered that Keith had lived and trained in Miami for years.

"No." Keith shook his head.

"Now, why would the Prince go and do something like that?" Earl interjected as he opened the register drawer. "We've got the best right here in our own backyard."

"You're kidding, right?" Harmony didn't have the best of anything, except maybe Annie Mae's home-made desserts.

Earl half hooted, half laughed. "Oh Liza, Harmony may not be like your town, Chicago, but we hold our own."

"Ah, the Windy City. Came home to thaw out?" Keith gave her a wink.

"Yeah, something like that. So who's working on your house? I can't think of any—"

"That's funny," Earl chortled. "Like you've been away that long. You know it's Bertie."

"Oh no." Liza slid her gaze to Keith. "Really?" The Prince didn't appear embarrassed, just uncomfortable. He nodded, confirming Earl's gossip. Liza couldn't stop herself. She threw her head back and laughed out loud for the first time in weeks. "This I've got to see."

<center>~~~</center>

Keith said nothing as the pretty blond with the long po-nytail had a good laugh at his expense. What strange luck today. First, sweet Gail who loved children and baking cookies, and now this big-city, edgier blond who loved to laugh…at him, and probably chewed small children up and spit them out for lunch. Plain Gail would be better mother material, hands down. Sharp Liza would be good company and maybe a good date, another distraction. And he could use all the distractions he could find. So far, he hadn't found a cure or an escape, because he still wanted Bertie Anderson in a really bad, bad way. Keith dragged his mind out of the gutter and refocused on laughing Liza.

"If you're finished doubling over with laughter, maybe you'd like to share one of those desserts. If you can manage to give one up. You're clutching that bag as if you're gonna get mugged."

"Oh no. You're not getting any of my dessert. I've waited way too long." Her head shook, making her ponytail swing across her shoulders. "Who's the other coffee for? You got some hot date waiting in the car?" she teased with a smirk on her face. Clearly she had read some of the tabloid stories.

"Nah, but I am meeting someone."

Earl leaned over the counter. "You don't know the half of it, Liza. The Prince here has to find a wife and he's only got three months. Francesca Balogh, his aunt, has apparently laid down the law."

Thanks, Earl, for spilling the beans. How the hell did he know the story? Geez, he was well aware that Harmony was small, but he didn't realize that he'd be the hot topic on everyone's tongue. Keith guessed that made him the official town idiot. Of course his affairs would be fueling the town gossip, this being Mayberry and all. Screw it. The whole town was batshit crazy.

"What?" Liza looked as if she might burst from laughing. "Surely, he jests," she said in a tone of disbelief.

Keith shot Earl a glare. "Nope. It's so *out* there, they could write a sitcom around it. Come on and I'll give you all the hilarious details." He gestured with his elbow for Liza to follow him out.

She trotted after him. "I wouldn't miss this for the world. Man, I'm glad I came home."

—⁘—

Keith climbed the stairs to the second floor of his home looking for Bertie. Liza followed close behind. They'd both finished their coffees and shared Liza's cheesecake on a park bench in the middle of town square, down the street from the Daily Grind. Keith found Liza to be funny and insightful. He only confirmed what Earl had told her. He didn't elaborate on his fucked-up life or the fact that Francesca threatened to fight for Maddie.

As angry as Francesca's high-handedness made him, Keith didn't want to fight her. Deep down, underneath all the anger and the hurt and the loss and the self-pity, he knew Francesca was right. He knew he needed to gain control of his life and the life of his daughter before it was too late—before Maddie was all grown and before he missed being a real father to her. And as repugnant as it all seemed, that meant making this insta-bride thing happen.

Liza could've been a contender, but she laughed in his face, as was her habit, and basically told him no fucking way. And yes, she'd dropped the f-bomb. So, Keith believed he met Gail today for a reason. Now, if he could only shake the feeling that pursuing the little bookworm was a terrible mistake.

In the upstairs hallway, he followed the sound of music and the unmistakable smell of vinegar. He stopped in the doorway of the room that would soon be Maddie's.

"What the hell are you doing?"

Bertie jumped at his voice and almost fell off the ladder she'd climbed to attack the ancient floral wallpaper. Keith sprinted into action just in time to slap his hand around the back of her thigh to keep her from tumbling. The ladder wobbled and then settled back in place.

"Jesus."

"You scared me half to death!" Bertie said. "Don't you know better than to sneak up on people?" She held a scoring tool in one hand and the top of the ladder with the other. Part of her hair had slipped from the claw on top of her head and was plastered to her damp neck. She no longer wore the lacy tunic but a form-fitting, pale yellow T-shirt. Keith's hand touched bare skin below her short khaki cargo shorts. Her soft thigh burned the inside of his palm, and he itched to slide his hand up to discover what kind of panties she wore. Fingers pressed into her flesh and lingered a moment too long. Bertie's indignant expression hurtled into one of heated surprise.

"Oh my. Bertie, don't you look darling?" Liza purred from the doorway, and Bertie jumped again at the sound. This time Keith grabbed her around the waist and hauled her off the ladder before she fell off. He held her against his chest for a second—or twenty—enjoying the feel of her breasts and the hint of gardenias from her warm skin. Crap. He needed to get a grip.

Bertie's sanity prevailed. "Liza. What are you doing here?" She pushed hard against his chest with one hand while regaining her balance in her funky-colored clogs.

Liza strolled forward in black cords and brown riding boots. She held the coffee he'd bought for Bertie, which minutes ago he'd nuked in the microwave before heading upstairs. "Delivering a hot cup of coffee. Looks like you're gonna need it," she said, sounding amused.

With narrowed eyes, Bertie glanced from Liza's self-assured stance to Keith's blank face. He fought to keep the mask of indifference plastered in place. These two women had history. He'd be smart to find out what it was.

"Well, you didn't have to come all the way from Chicago to deliver coffee, but I sure do appreciate it," Bertie said with thick Southern sarcasm, taking the cup from Liza's hand.

"Like what you've done with the place." Liza's gaze roamed the half-stripped walls and the plastic-covered carpeting. "Real nice…uh…homey touch," she said, pulling a strip of loose paper from the wall and dropping it on the floor.

Bertie pierced Liza with a scathing glare.

"Uh, Liza, would you give me a minute? I need to have a word with my decorator," he said.

"*Designer*," Bertie said through clenched teeth.

"Sure, sugar…anything for you." Liza trailed her fingers down his arm. "I'll see you downstairs." She sauntered from the room, taking her big smile and cocky attitude with her.

"If you're done scaring me to death, I've got work to do." Bertie placed the coffee on a card table next to the ladder and wiped her hands down her smudged T-shirt.

Keith returned his attention to Bertie. "You're not going back up that ladder," he said, punching off the music from the iPod sitting in its docking station on the card table. "What the hell are you doing anyhow? I hired you to decorate, not do manual labor."

"Stripping wallpaper. I don't have a paper hanger right now, and all my painters are busy working on the outside."

"Where's Barney? Your partner-in-crime?"

"Who?" Bertie picked up a spray bottle and started dousing the wall.

"Gary. Why isn't he here helping you? Man, that stuff stinks." Keith plucked the bottle from her hand and sniffed it.

"Excuse me, but I need that. It's vinegar and water. Helps loosen the paper."

He held the bottle out of reach. "Where's Gary?"

Bertie planted a fist on one hip. "He's working at the Milners'. I have more than one job, you know. Their house needs to be ready in less than three weeks. Now, may I have my bottle back?" she asked, extending her hand.

He shook his head. "I'll strip the paper. You start slapping up some paint samples so I can make a decision."

A mixture of alarm and relief flickered across her flushed face, then she scoffed, "Wouldn't you rather be with your girlfriend? I can't believe out of all the people in Harmony, you chose her," she ended in a mumble.

Keith cupped her stubborn chin where he glimpsed vulnerability edged with jealousy in her troubled eyes.

"She's not my girlfriend. We just met. But I do like her. She's smart and funny and—" Bertie jerked her face from his grasp.

"Spare me the details, Don Juan. I know her better than you, and believe me, she's only out for one person: herself. You two would make a perfect pair."

"Uh-huh. And you know me so well." Bertie pulled a frown and pushed a strand of hair behind her ear. "I'll be right back. Drink your coffee and do not get back on that ladder." Keith reached for a wayward piece of wallpaper stuck to the side of her shirt, brushing the plump side of her breast in the process. On purpose. A hiss of air passed from her lips, and her nipple puckered from his touch. Yep. The charged sexual current still existed for both of them. He needed to leave before he gave in to temptation. And she needed to work at warp speed on this job. The faster she worked, the sooner she could be out of his house and his life.

Bertie jerked back from his touch. "Whatever you say, boss." She looked like she wanted to take that scoring tool and run it down his face.

"By the way, Maddie is coming home in a few weeks for spring break." He moved toward the door. "This room better be done." He stopped and glanced over his shoulder. "Or you're fired."

Chapter 7

FIRED! HE WOULDN'T DO THAT. WOULD HE? BERTIE slipped down the steps and out the back door, avoiding Keith and his unreasonable orders. She needed a break from manual labor. She also needed some answers. What an arrogant jerk. No, that wasn't right. Maybe sexy, arrogant jerk. Or sexy, dangerous, arrogant jerk. Yeah, that was it. She still trembled from his blatant touch. Why couldn't she control her physical response to him? Because he was far too dangerous, and she found him far too alluring.

Bertie rubbed her hand down the recently sanded railing on the porch, coating her palm with dust. She knew why he harassed her: A, because he could; B, he didn't want her working on his house; and C, he didn't want her anywhere in his life. As if she was thrilled to be here. Well, okay, maybe she was thrilled a little bit. Bertie's heart stammered, remembering how Keith cupped her chin and blasted her with his intensity. She'd never had a famous athlete for a client. Quite a coup for a small-town designer. His bossy personality aside, he had sexual attractiveness down to an art. Not to mention the exhilarating ring of one hundred and fifty thousand big ones. Bertie needed that money. She'd made big promises to Dwelling Place, and she planned to keep them.

Bertie made a quick stop at the side of the house to answer a few questions from Julio, her head painter. Her head popped up as she saw Liza wave good-bye and skip down the front porch. Christ on a cracker. What was Liza doing back home? Of all the places in town, she had to walk in on Bertie looking her worst at a job site that didn't look much better. And of course, Liza had to witness Mr. Studly Do-Right catching Bertie from the ladder and holding on to her a little too tight. Okay, well, maybe that part was really good, because he smelled all musky…way better than vinegar and water. And he held her in full view of Liza, which gave Bertie some satisfaction. So it hadn't been all bad, but it'd be a heck of a lot better if Liza hadn't shown up. At all.

Bertie jumped in her parked car on the side street, glancing across Keith's lawn where the majestic oaks provided great shade. She'd always loved this neighborhood with the eclectic mix of homes and the winding sidewalks. Liza also lived in a nice neighborhood near Aunt Franny, where the lots were large along with the homes. Bertie lived on the other side of the tracks—literally—in a small, humble bungalow. She and Liza had competed all their lives over everything from grades to who sold the most Girl Scout cookies. But when it came to boys, Liza always won with her long legs and blond hair.

Bertie had turned the key in the ignition when an old Chevy S-10 compact truck skidded to a halt in front of Keith's house, missing the lamppost by mere inches. Oh geez. Only one person drove that pink restored 1982 pick-up truck. Jo Ellen Huggins jumped out, carrying a Bundt cake wrapped in pink cellophane with a big, pink flower on top. Bertie enjoyed a good laugh. Keith might have to install a revolving front door. Jo Ellen wouldn't be the only one showing up with baked goods. At least there'd be food in the house. She giggled to herself as she put the car in drive and pulled onto the street.

Maria, the housekeeper, opened the back door for Bertie and told her where to find Francesca.

"Aunt Franny!" Bertie called, moving through Francesca's kitchen to her office. "We need to talk. I'm already having issues with your nephew, and I'm like, only one day on the job."

Francesca looked up from the magazine in her lap. "Not Keith. He's so reasonable and even tempered," she said, lowering the glasses from her face.

Bertie flopped down on the rosy-pink damask lounge chair and propped her feet up on the matching ottoman. "You're kidding, right? Mr. Control Freak?"

Aunt Franny chuckled, folding her hands on her desk.

"Is Maddie coming home for spring break? Because he told me I had to finish her room in a few weeks or I'm fired."

"Nonsense."

"Nonsense, she's not coming, or nonsense, he can't fire me?"

"He can't fire you. I won't allow it."

Relief flooded Bertie's system. "What about Maddie's room? I can't possibly finish before she gets here."

"That won't be necessary. Maddie will be staying with me. Although she can't wait to see her new room and all your ideas."

If Maddie had the same personality as her dad, Bertie might have to hurt someone. "Uh, that would be nice."

Bertie edged forward in her seat. "Aunt Franny, please don't take this the wrong way, but is Maddie anything like her dad? I mean, I'm sure she's beautiful and talented and smart, but…"

"Oh, Bertie. Trust me. You're going to love her."

"Aunt Francesca!"

Bertie stiffened at the sound of Keith's bellow. All animation slid from Francesca's face as she listened to the sharp thud of his footsteps on the hardwood floors.

"You need to call off your dogs." Keith burst into the room. "I've got a pink cake, pigs in a blanket, and green Jell-O with tiny marshmallows shimmying in my refrigerator. And that decorator—" Keith stopped at the sight of Bertie. Relief flooded his expression, and his aggressive stance seemed to melt away. She could feel the air being sucked from the room as he hit her with his dark, fathomless eyes.

"Funny, I didn't take you for a quitter." His voice held an almost intimate quality.

Bertie scrambled to stand. "Uh, okay…here's the thing—"

"Bertie tells me you're threatening to fire her," Aunt Franny interjected, saving Bertie from coming up with an explanation.

His gaze never left her face. "Are you going to run and tattle every time we have words? Because I didn't peg you as a chicken always needing backup, either."

"Chicken?" Bertie straightened to her full five-foot-two height. "You're being an unreasonable bully because you don't like me and—"

"So, Jo Ellen dropped by? Who else?" Aunt Franny doused the flying sparks between them with her question. Keith blinked and then turned his attention back to his aunt.

"Uh, there was Jo Ellen, driving a pink truck."

"Isn't she beautiful? She sells Mary Kay cosmetics. Her skin is flawless."

Keith's clenched fist by his side told Bertie what he thought of Jo Ellen's flawless skin.

"And then someone with red hair in big curls. Mary something with the mini hotdogs."

"Mary Ann Howard. She's a nurse at Dr. Miller's office. Lovely girl. She volunteers at the first aid station at the state fair every year," Aunt Franny explained.

"Yeah? And then the one with the green Jell-O—"

"Arlene Tomlin!" Aunt Franny and Bertie said together. Bertie started to snicker but sobered up at Keith's icy glare.

"Arlene is famous for her green Jell-O. Makes it for all the festivals in Harmony. She's a real hoot. And she wins most of the karaoke contests at the Dog. Doesn't she, Bertie?"

Keith gave an aggravated sigh and crossed his arms. "Flawless skin, Florence Nightingale, and a Faith Hill wannabe? What did you do, Aunt Francesca? Take out a billboard on the interstate?"

"Don't be silly. I only mentioned you to Jo Ellen. You know how news travels. As you can see, there are plenty of lovely ladies, all ready to start dating you. You need to ask a few out to get to know them better."

Keith let out a huge breath as if all the life was being sucked out of him. "I'll do my own hunting, if you don't mind. I don't need any more eager women dropping by with hungry eyes and grandma's recipes, auditioning to be my wife," he said in a strained but calm voice.

"I'm only trying to help, dear. You need to meet these women so you can make a decision." Aunt Franny patted the back of her classic, short hair. "Now, please tell me you haven't been growling and scowling in front of all these lovely ladies because you're likely to scare everyone away."

Keith stiffened. "I've been a perfect gentleman." He locked gazes with Bertie, daring her to blow his cover. Message received. He'd been nice to everyone *but* her.

"Wonderful to hear. I expect no less from you."

Bertie jerked as Keith grabbed her hand and drew her toward the door. "Sorry to cut this visit short, but we need to get going. We have a lot of work to do." He stopped with his hand on the doorframe. "Dinner at seven?" he asked Francesca.

"Beef tenderloin. Your favorite," Francesca said, not missing a beat. She appeared to be busy shuffling papers on her desk, biting her lip, and Bertie knew she was hiding a smile.

Keith grunted as if satisfied. "Good. See you then."

"Nice visiting with you, Aunt Fra—"

Keith yanked Bertie from the room and bellowed over his shoulder at Francesca, "And stop matchmaking!"

———

Bertie tripped after Keith as he pulled on her hand. She wondered if this was the way they would always react around each other, like a push-me-pull-me toy. Wait a minute—he didn't own her, and he couldn't boss her around. Well, technically he could. But that wasn't the point. She needed to set some boundaries.

"Stop!" she said, digging in her heels before he dragged her halfway through town. Keith came to a halt only when he reached the front of his car parked in the driveway.

"Where's your car?" he asked, noticing no other cars parked in the driveway.

"Around back, next to the carriage house." Bertie tried slipping her hand free, but he squeezed tighter, sending a shiver up her arm and down her spine.

"Listen, I need you to come back to the house with me. Okay? I can't go in there alone."

Bertie snapped her gaze to his face where he appeared a little wild around the eyes. She would've laughed if she didn't think he looked close to going over the edge. She gave him an understanding nod. "We're getting to you, aren't we?"

A soft chuckle spilled from his firm lips, catching her off guard. She'd never really heard him laugh before, except at her expense. A smile lifted her lips in return.

"If you're referring to this town, then you have no idea." Keith inched her closer until only a thin slice of cool March air whispered between them.

Bertie patted his arm with her free hand. "There, there. It will get better."

He gave her a lopsided grin and his eyes crinkled in the corners from years of playing in the sun. "The thing is, I don't see how it can, not with this ridiculous deadline and ultimatum from Francesca." He mindlessly caressed her hand. "I'm sorry I yelled in there, but I had no idea I'd be facing a full-court press with all these women. Kind of took me by surprise," he admitted sheepishly.

He really seemed rattled, and it was kind of endearing.

Kind of. As he continued to play with her hand, every organ and body part inside Bertie went still. She'd have to be dead not to be aware of the sexual energy coursing between them. Her fingers were already in love. God help the rest of her.

"I need my small-town decorator." His voice held a sexy, throaty quality. Excitement prickled her nerve endings.

For what? For a clandestine meeting at a sleazy motel? Or down by the lake where everyone used to go to make out? *I'm in, just say the word.* For once, Bertie stopped herself from blurting her thoughts, because her desires were off-the-charts, insane, nutso. She needed a good, bone-rattling shake. She didn't have time for this stupid, unwanted physical attraction.

"Why? To run interference?"

"Nah." He shook his head. "This match I have to play on my own with no coaching." His laugh sounded self-deprecating. "So, I'm leaving town in a few weeks…" In a flash, disappointment replaced her unruly excitement. "To take care of some business and pick up Maddie." This did not sound like a good seduction from a frustrated, professional athlete in desperate need…of her. "I need you to go back to your other job at the Milners' and finish up," he said in a soft but firm voice. The message behind the tightening of his jaw and dark eyes didn't take a genius to decipher.

Bertie gasped in outrage. He *was* firing her. She knew it. She tugged on her hand, gaining her release.

"I'm not firing you." Keith must have read the horror in her expression. "I'd just prefer you send Gary over in your place. Until Maddie gets here."

"What? I don't understand." Bertie stepped back, away from the delicious heat of his body that had wrapped her into a false sense of lusty haze. "I can do this job. I'm a good *designer*."

Keith rubbed his forehead as if his head ached. "I know. I've looked over the drawings and your furniture specs. So far, I'm on board." He leaned against the hood of his car. "Look, things are really fucked up for me right now. I need some time to think and, uh, sort things out. And I can't with everyone auditioning to be my wife."

Heat flamed Bertie's cheeks. Did he think she was throwing herself at him? That she wanted a crack at being Mrs. Keith Morgan? Like hell! Wanting one night of hot sex did not translate into settling down and darning socks. She wanted out—as soon as she finished this job and collected her bonus. She wanted to concentrate on her design profession, not her gofer/dog-walking/waitressing career. She had a metropolitan city to explore and bigger and better houses in her future where she could really grow her talent. She would not be joining the long line of future Mrs. Morgan wannabes with a hot apple pie in her hands.

"If you think I'm auditioning to be your wife, you're sadly mistaken. I'd rather shave my head and join a religious cult than play wife and mother right now." Bertie planted her fists on her hips to keep from smashing them in his arrogant, square jaw.

Keith's harsh laughter cracked the air. This time she didn't feel any warm and fuzzies. "That's the *last* thing I want. I don't want any wife. And you are not wife or mother material," he said, pushing away from the car and invading her space. "You're my decorator only, and I'd like to keep it that way."

A rush of anger surged through her, loosening her tongue. "I'm a *designer*, you ass. With a degree and a license. And as your designer, I have a job to do. What kind of game are you playing?" Bertie gave a dismissive wave of her hand. "Either you want me or you don't."

Sudden, smoky desire lit the backs of Keith's eyes and Bertie jumped from the heat. "I meant…as a designer…not as…uh…"

"Oh, I want you. That's not the issue," Keith said, snaking an arm around her waist and turning her, until her back hit the side of his car. Bertie slapped both hands against the soft cotton of his blue Nike tennis sweater, feeling the hard surface of his chest against her fingers. Keith pressed into her, slipping his leg between hers. His fingers trailed up her sides until he brushed the sides of her neck. He spread them wide, threading them through her hair. "I can't have you…beneath me…with me inside you…filling you," he said in a low, rough whisper. His lips hovered above hers. He was so close she could smell the hint of coffee laced with peppermint on his breath. He dropped his forehead to hers and closed his eyes with a groan. He looked as tortured as she felt.

"This is bad," Bertie stammered on a sigh. But it felt so good. "You…we—"

He raised his head and she became mesmerized by his heavy-lidded gaze as she leaned into his smoldering yumminess. His lips covered hers, silencing her words and her mind. His fingers massaged her scalp, tilting her head up for better access. She opened her mouth to him. The inside of his was hot and slick and welcoming.

Bertie trembled as his tongue touched hers. Her arms twined around his neck and she clung to him. Instead of being smart and pushing him away, she rubbed against him and deepened the kiss.

But she wanted more than a kiss. She wanted it all. For once. For once, she wanted to throw responsibility and good conscience out the window and go with her feelings. With *this* guy. Someone who was all wrong for her. Keith rocked his hips into her and Bertie groaned in the back of her throat. He wrapped one arm around her waist while the other cradled the back of her head, locking her in place. Bertie didn't know where she started and he ended. She molded herself against him like thick, warm honey.

As she was about to sink into the kiss that beat all kisses and stay there for days, a pick-up truck careened down the street with music blaring and some kid yelled, "Get a room!"

Keith jumped back as if he'd stepped in a pit of poisonous snakes. "Goddammit." He raked his fingers through his hair as if he might pull it out. "This is why you need to send Gary over. Unless you want to have sex against my car while the citizens of Mayberry stroll by." His glare blasted her as harshly as his words.

Fudge. What had she done? Bertie's shaky hands pressed against the cotton T-shirt covering her belly, trying to stop the swarm of bees inside. The fire that burned only moments before, scorching her insides, died as if it at been doused with a bucket of cold water.

She stopped trembling enough to speak. "Look, I may be guilty of kissing you back, but I don't deserve your anger or all the blame. We're both guilty—"

"Bertie? You still here? I thought you and Keith left fifteen minutes ago," Francesca called from the French doors facing the front lawn. Bertie froze. Could this day get any worse?

"Shit," Keith mumbled. Without looking back, he rounded the front of his car and yanked the door open. Bertie stumbled forward on wobbly knees as Keith cranked the engine and backed out of the driveway.

"On my way. We were…uh…discussing the…bedroom. I mean living room," she said with a nervous laugh, trying to gather her wits about her. "Bye now." Bertie waved as she headed for the carriage house. Aunt Franny waved back, wearing a satisfied smile on her lips.

<center>~~~</center>

Keith snatched the bottle of water and vinegar Bertie had left behind and started spraying the walls of his daughter's bedroom with the noxious liquid. He had changed into a pair of ratty jeans, old sneakers, and a worn T-shirt. He'd already run his five miles and spent a half hour with his weights. He was tired and his muscles ached, but he still needed a mechanical activity and stripping decaying old wallpaper was the perfect fit. He would strip every wall in the house until his body was weak with exhaustion and his mind blank. He needed to forget Bertie's full breasts caressing his chest, the taste of her full, sweet lips. And the echoes of her groans when he'd rubbed his rock-hard cock against her. Bertie equaled drama. High drama. She couldn't help it. It was the way she was wired and she thrived on it. Just like fierce competition was his drug of choice. Drama and all the trappings that went along with it fed Bertie's soul. Keith recognized the signs. He'd been married to it for three years. Yep. He would strip paper until every wall was bald and then he'd start ripping out all the carpet and dragging it to the dumpster. That should kill his libido and any remaining desire he had for Bertie with her sea-green eyes; long, curly lashes; and her silky, thick hair. That and maybe a case of Mount Gay. Damn. He was screwed.

Keith reached for his cell and sent Maddie another text with silly smiley faces about when he was coming to pick her up and how he couldn't wait, informing her he'd call that night for their usual daily chat. Then he shoved earbuds in his ears, punched his iPod on, and attacked the wall with the scoring tool to the tune of "Satisfaction" by the Rolling Stones.

Bertie found Gary at the Milners', arranging furniture in the living room. The old, musty smell had been replaced by fresh paint and new wood. "You need to get over to Keith's and finish stripping the walls. Call Dan about removing the carpet and schedule Enrique to start on the wood floors," she said, avoiding his gaze as she moved a set of antique nesting tables closer to the sofa. "I'll finish up here." Silence filled the room and Bertie knew Gary gawked at her as if she had sprouted elf ears.

She had to pretend that everything was okay. How could she reveal to Gary that she'd jumped Mr. Perfect's fine frame without any regard to their business…again. She had thrown all professionalism out the window because he kissed like a sugar-coated dream and she wanted those kisses like an alcoholic craved the next drink. Bertie angled a French armchair in the corner of the room near the bookcases.

"You want to tell me what's going on?" Gary asked in a calm voice. Bertie hated that voice. It meant that Gary already knew, but he would wait until the cows came home for Bertie to confess. But being a dried-up prune in the love market didn't give her license to jump the best-looking thing to hit Harmony in forever. Especially since that best-looking thing happened to be her client and ultimately her ticket out. Even though she'd ended up turning down the entry-level job offer in Atlanta, Bill Murphy had intimated the door might be open in case she changed her mind. Her dream of leaving town could still become a reality once she finished these projects.

"Not really. I need you over at Morgan's house, and I'll finish up here. It's only for a few weeks." Bertie sneaked a quick glance at Gary as she picked up a Swiffer duster from the box of supplies and started wiping down surfaces.

He shook his head. "Whatever." He gathered up some packing materials and shoved them in an empty cardboard box. "You'll tell me soon enough because your guilty conscience will get the best of you." Bertie ducked her head and dusted with a renewed vengeance.

Gary finished taking out the packing garbage while she kept busy wiping down the bookshelves and table-tops. When he returned, they exchanged to-do lists on each project and checked their time lines.

"His daughter is coming home in a few weeks. I'm going to need to focus on her bedroom, and you'll need to handle the kitchen renovation," she said, handing him plans for Keith's house.

"And who will be handling Keith's bedroom?" Gary asked as he shoved the plans in his briefcase.

"Um, I guess we both will." Bertie turned and started pulling custom-made throw pillows out of their protective plastic bags and arranging them on the sofas.

"Something tells me I won't be doing his bedroom or doing him…but you will."

Bertie froze over one of the pillows, in mid-designer–karate-chop mode. She'd be a crazy walnut to go anywhere near Keith again. Any more physical encounters with Mr. Love Machine would make her hard-earned self-esteem plummet to an all-time low. Even worse than senior year when she had caught Liza humping Bertie's prom date behind the trophy display in the gym.

"Hey, be careful," Gary squeezed her shoulder. "I'll be at Mr. Fine Tush's if you need me."

Bertie jumped when she heard Gary's heels thud across the wood floor in the foyer. "Wait," she called, rushing for the door. Gary paused. "Find out if we can take some of the old carpet. Two of the rooms upstairs looked decent and clean."

"Sure. What for?"

"I'm going to donate it to Dwelling Place."

Chapter 8

KEITH ROLLED OUT OF HARMONY IN HIS PACKED Cayenne to pick up Maddie from boarding school in Virginia for spring break. It was a four-hour drive and he'd allowed plenty of extra time. He needed it. He'd loaded up his tennis gear, planning to stop on the way and hit with a pro in Raleigh.

Unlike the past few weeks, where his timing had sucked, he'd pulled out of his driveway in the nick of time. Crystal Walker, one of the many young women who appeared at his door daily, rounded the corner riding her beach bike—young as in not a day over eighteen. Keith knew this because the first time she'd showed up, she held a photo album decorated with yellow smiley faces and light-blue feathers. She'd chronicled her entire life by way of snapshots, while chomping on a wad of pink bubble gum.

Keith came to a full stop at the crosswalk on Main. He waited for the group called N-Purrfect-Harmony to cross with spades, shovels, and potted plants, preparing to beautify the town square for some upcoming town fair. He chuckled at their silly floppy hats and matching Crocs.

After Crystal, he'd had visits from Harmony's famous twins, Opal and Emma Ardbuckle. Keith guessed their age to be somewhere in the forties—spinsters, their term, *not* his. Opal knitted him a stocking cap out of brown wool, and Emma brought him a six-pack of homemade beer. Out of her tub if he heard correctly.

The pressure to run away had never felt more urgent than it had this morning. These constant visits did nothing to calm his fears about his future. In fact, they accomplished just the opposite.

The last few weeks, in between future-bride encounters, he had stripped every wall bare, ripped out most of the carpet, and continued to work out and bang balls as if he were still on the ATP tour, all in hopes of falling in bed at night and sleeping like a corpse. Instead, he tossed and turned, dreaming about lush breasts, full lips, and mahogany-colored hair. All belonging to a green-eyed Bertie, who he'd barely seen since that public, scalding-hot kiss. On one hand, Keith missed Miami like he missed competing on the tennis circuit, but on the other hand, if he'd kissed someone like that standing on Ocean Drive, it would've gone viral in a matter of seconds, with all the gawking tourists carrying camera phones and itching to catch a celebrity doing the dirty deed.

Kissing Bertie again had been a big mistake. No more dumb acts and behaving like an ass in front of her. She didn't deserve his anger or his rampant sexual drive. She couldn't help it if she reminded him of his hot wife, who thrived on causing public scenes and embraced drama almost more than she partied and dropped her panties. Keith gripped the steering wheel, trying to keep his guilty thoughts at bay. Adriana had been young and beautiful. She'd had a fiery Latin temper that matched her lusty sexual appetite. She was every man's dream until she became Keith's living nightmare. But now he needed to get out of town, before he gave into another stupid craving that looked, smelled, and tasted a lot like Bertie Anderson.

The parking lot at the Dog looked full from the breakfast crowd. And Keith could've sworn he spied Bertie's beat-up, blue Honda CR-V parked near the entrance. He stepped on the gas. They'd been avoiding each other like the pox since the kiss. They communicated through Gary, which suited Keith fine.

Several miles down the road, he slowed the car as he neared the entrance to the Jaycee Park, which served Harmony and the neighboring towns. He frowned at what Harmony offered in the way of tennis for kids who couldn't afford the country club. He counted eight hard tennis courts, a baseball field, and a couple of basketball courts. He pulled into the asphalt lot and parked near the low, run-down community building. Keith sat for a moment, drumming his fingers on the steering wheel. He surveyed the surrounding property. A large field with overgrown grass and weeds abutted the property—enough room for expansion if they owned the land. Keith climbed out of his car and walked over to the tennis courts, peering through the chain-link fence with torn windscreens. Two pros fed balls to a spring-break clinic for a group of ten or twelve-year-olds. Cracks the size of craters ran through the surfaces of the courts. And most of the center straps were missing, making the nets too high.

"If it isn't Mr. Big Shot. So, you decided to pay us a visit." Keith started at the sound of Dottie Duncan's booming voice. He hadn't heard her approach. He glanced down into her overly made-up face and platinum-blond hair pulled back into a stiff ponytail with a big yellow sunflower perched on top.

"Just checking out the facility."

"It's about time. Now you can see how run down the place is. This would be a good project for you and give you something to do besides chase all the young gals in Harmony." Dottie pursed her hot-pink–lipstick coated lips.

Keith narrowed his eyes, hoping to warn her off with his famous game-face glare. "Not that it's any of your business, but I'm not chasing anyone."

Dottie smacked her gooped-up lips. "Don't get your knickers all up in a bind. I know what Franny Balogh told you." Dottie tugged on her tight orange T-shirt with Toot-N-Tell in navy stretched across her massive chest. "Get married in three months…to a nice girl."

Keith kept his gaze locked on the kids on the courts and not on the annoying woman standing next to him. "Then you should also know that I'm not pursuing any of the young ladies of Harmony. They show up on their own with no encouragement from me."

"I figured you for someone with some brains. Didn't you attend Princeton?"

He shoved his hands in his jean pockets. "Yeah. For someone so smart, how did I end up in Harmony?" He hoped she wouldn't answer.

Dottie rustled through a large silver handbag and pulled out a pack of gum. She held it out. "Gum?"

"No, thanks."

She popped two pieces onto her palm. "I was gonna say, for someone so smart how come you don't know a good thing when you see one?" She dropped the gum in her mouth and chewed.

"A good thing, huh? Are you referring to eighteen-year-old Crystal or the Ardbuckle twins?"

Dottie chewed as she rustled for something else inside her bag. "Neither one. Bless their hearts. They aren't right for you." She pulled a crinkled pamphlet out and shoved it at Keith's gut. "Take this and read it over. Then come to the meeting. We're going to need all the help we can get."

Keith took the pamphlet that read "Rejuvenate the Jaycee" and gave Dottie a puzzled look.

"Read it and then we'll talk." She stomped away in blue cowboy boots and a ruffled denim skirt, her generous hips swaying.

"Hey! You never told me who was a good thing," he called out.

Dottie hesitated and then glanced back over her shoulder. "Who makes you so crazy that you can't stop thinking about her?"

Only one person fit that description. *Bertie*. Keith's face must've registered surprise before he could mask it, because Dottie Duncan gave him a sly smile.

"You ain't no dummy after all," she chuckled and then put an extra boom in her hips as she sauntered away.

Bertie stirred a dollop of whipped cream into her hot coffee—her one guilty pleasure in the mornings when she ate breakfast at the Dog. Lucy Doolan, one of her oldest friends, sat across from her in the booth. Lucy's riotous curls no longer existed, having been tamed into submission with a hot iron. And her natural dirty blond color sported streaky highlights. Only her tilty gray eyes had remained the same since grade school, observing way more than they should. The mouth-watering smells of fresh bacon and hot biscuits filled the Dog as the early morning crowd settled down to a hearty, Southern breakfast.

"You planning on staying a few days?" Bertie sipped her creamy coffee.

Lucy's fingers, with green-painted nails, wrapped around her glass of Mountain Dew. "I'm leaving tomorrow. I have a couple temp jobs I don't want to pass up."

Lucy worked in Atlanta in marketing and social media. But right now, she was in between jobs and working for a temp agency. "Aw, I wish you could stay longer. I miss you."

Lucy's eyes turned flinty. She'd left sophomore year in high school to live with her grandparents and never returned to her home in Harmony.

Bertie pulled an exaggerated pout. "You may not believe this, but I really envy you."

Lucy grunted as she sliced into her western omelet with extra cheese and a side of hash browns.

"So, you want to hear my good news?" Bertie smiled as she speared a piece of fruit and shoved it in her mouth.

"That's why I'm here. Well, that and this great omelet," Lucy said with a twinkle in her eye.

Bertie leaned forward, placing her elbows on the table. "I can make a huge difference with Dwelling Place."

Lucy's brows rose. "Really? How?"

Bertie grinned. "I've made a deal with the devil."

"The devil? Ooo, give me details."

"Hey, girls. Sharing dirty little secrets?" Liza Palmer stood next to their booth with a coffeepot in her hand and a smug expression on her face. "More coffee?"

Bertie gritted her back teeth. "No, thanks." Liza kept popping up like a painful boil that needed to be lanced.

"I take a break in five. Mind if I join you?" Liza refilled Bertie's cup, ruining the balance of whipped cream and coffee that Bertie had achieved.

"Yes." Bertie frowned at her ruined cup of coffee.

"No." Lucy spoke at the same time.

"Perfect." Liza's gaze darted from Bertie to Lucy. "Let me get rid of this pot, and I'll join you in a sec. Don't spill anything juicy until I get back." She gave a sly wink and then sauntered off in her skinny jeans. She wore the electric-blue waitress T-shirt like a second skin. Bertie had always envied her long legs, slim hips, and fat-free body. Bertie could never pull off wearing flashy turquoise cowboy boots like Liza without looking like a stumpy rodeo clown.

"What's her deal? Wasn't she practicing law in Chicago?" Lucy asked.

"Who knows? She drove back into town and doesn't seem to be leaving." Bertie played with her spoon. "I could kill Cal for hiring her. It's not like she needs the money. I'm sure she's here to irritate the heck out of me."

"Cal always needs good help. You can't continue to fill in all the time. You have a business to run."

Disgust slammed into Bertie as Liza chatted up some truckers at the counter, throwing her head back and laughing like she'd heard the funniest joke ever. If it had three legs, Liza found a way to flirt with it and make it fall under her spell.

After Bertie's mother had died, Liza started coming around the house, dropping off brownies and bringing over her favorite romance novels for Bertie to read. Bertie had thought Liza really cared, because for once Liza had been really nice to her. Bertie had only been fourteen at the time and even though she and Liza were in the same grade, Liza seemed so much older. More mature. She'd even listened to Bertie express her fears one afternoon about living without a mom and then offered to help Bertie with her makeup, showing her a trick with cold cucumber slices and tea bags to reduce the swelling around her eyes from too much crying. They had giggled and laughed that afternoon like typical teenage girls.

The very next day, Bertie had rushed home from theater practice and found Liza in the kitchen, glued to the front of Cal, kissing him. Devastated and hurt, Bertie'd been used by a master manipulator who'd stop at nothing to get her way—even befriending a lonely, heartsick classmate. From that day forward, she had never trusted Liza.

"You think she's still after Cal?" Lucy drank her Mountain Dew, tracking Liza behind the bar.

"If it breathes and can get it up, then yep." Bertie pushed her half-eaten plate of fruit away. "She's up to something. I haven't figured out what yet."

Lucy's quiet chuckle could hardly be heard over the increasingly noisy breakfast crowd. "Bertie, sometimes you tend to blow things out of proportion. Maybe she's only visiting and reconnecting with old friends."

Or new friends. Liza had been by Keith's several times, according to Gary. Not that she gave a fat Fig Newton. She did not concern herself with the comings and goings of Mr. Hard Body. No, sir. She had a house to finish. A job to complete. She would treat Keith like any other client and be as professional as possible. No more lip-locking or molding herself to him like Play-Doh. Bertie didn't know what had gotten into her lately. Well, she did know. Keith's tongue had gotten into her, but she didn't know why she allowed it. Okay, well, maybe she did. The last time her tonsils had tangoed was six months ago. No, that couldn't be right. *Hot glue guns.* Her womanly parts started to shrivel inside her body. It hadn't been six months—it was much worse. She hadn't swapped spit or any other bodily fluids in over a year.

Her latest horizontal contact with a male had been her short and lackluster fling with Dave the architect from Raleigh. They'd met one day at a licensing workshop. The affair had lasted a good three months before Dave had a moral hiccup and decided he needed to stop cheating on his *wife*. Furious didn't begin to describe how Bertie felt with herself and Dave the slimeball. Humiliated, Bertie buried herself in work and hadn't come up for air in over a year—her punishment for falling before getting all the facts. Bertie had many faults, but being a home-wrecker was not one of them.

Lucy nibbled on a buttered muffin. "So, tell me how you're going to help Dwelling Place?"

Bertie dragged her mind out of the slums of extramarital affairs and back to the present. She pulled a folder from her bag and slid it across the table to Lucy. She needed to talk fast before Liza returned. "I've pledged one hundred thousand dollars to Dwelling Place."

"What?" Lucy opened the folder and there sat Bertie's pledge card to Dwelling Place and a check for her first installment for ten thousand dollars. "How? You gambling? Turning tricks?"

Bertie laughed at Lucy's scandalized face. "Nope. It's all been legally obtained. I'm getting a huge bonus if I finish Keith Morgan's house in less than three months, and I'm giving the bulk of it to DP." Bertie tapped the top of the check with her finger. "That's my first installment. I'll give more in another month."

"So you're guaranteed this bonus?"

The skepticism in Lucy's voice miffed Bertie. "Okay, here's the thing…it's not guaranteed, but I know I'm going to finish the job, and therefore, I'll get the money."

"You can't pledge this much right now. What if you don't finish? DP is likely to start two houses with this pledge, and then what will you do if your bonus doesn't come through?" Lucy's growing alarm started to send a slight chill up Bertie's spine.

Bertie fluttered her hand, waving off Lucy's objections and her own unease. "Stop worrying. I may have to work with the devil, and no one said it was going to be easy." A scowl marred Lucy's serious face. "Besides Lulu, I can't let those kids down. I've met little Jessica Alvarez and her family. She's only four years old—"

"Bertie, your dedication is admirable. But don't you think you're putting the cart before the horse? Don't you want to keep some of this money for yourself? You do so much for everyone else and never think of yourself. You should set the money aside for your retirement or whatever."

"No worries. I'm giving a hundred to DP and splitting the remaining fifty with Gary. I'll still have an extra twenty-five thousand to save or put to good use."

"I'm back. What'd I miss?" Liza slid into the booth next to Lucy.

Bertie bit down on her bottom lip, trying to rein in her anger at Liza's annoying presence.

"Not much. Bertie was telling me"—Bertie kicked Lucy under the table—"Ow! Uh, about her new job with Keith Morgan."

"Mmm, mmm, he is *sooo* fine. I've got plans for that lean, mean tennis machine…and they don't include tennis lessons." Liza licked her lips in a seductive way. She jabbed Lucy with her elbow. "He's got the dreamiest dark eyes, and I'm sure he knows what to do in the bedroom." Liza waggled her eyebrows in Lucy's direction, ignoring Bertie altogether.

Bertie squelched the urge to grab the maple syrup pitcher and pour it over Liza's head. She had no claim on Keith, but that didn't mean she wanted Liza playing hide-the-salami with the stud so she could brag about it all over town.

"Keith Morgan? Isn't he the famous tennis player?" Lucy asked to defuse the situation, recognizing the murderous gleam in Bertie's eye.

"The one and only. Didn't Bertie tell you?"

"She knows I'm working for him. What are you getting at, Liza?" Bertie said with undisguised irritation.

"He's wife hunting. And Bertie here is apparently off the list because she's been banned from his house and—"

"That's a lie. I have not been banned." Bertie fingered the maple syrup pitcher.

Liza chuckled. "I think it has something to do with her not being able to keep her lips to herself."

"Oh, boy. You are working for the devil." Worry

crept into Lucy's voice as she pushed the folder back to Bertie. "You need to rethink this, for sure."

Bertie snatched the folder and shoved it back in her bag. "I know what I'm doing, and I'm still on the job. Don't believe Ms. Buttinsky here. She's full of crap."

"Whoa. I can name three witnesses who saw you latched on to Keith Morgan's lips in Francesca's driveway just the other week," Liza said.

"First of all, I did not latch on to him; he latched on to me." Sort of. Bertie jabbed her index finger at Liza. "Secondly, I don't have to sit in *my* restaurant and listen to you spread useless gossip. As a matter of fact, I don't have to listen to you at all. You're fired!"

Liza drew back. "Cal hired me—"

"And I'm firing you." Bertie crossed her arms over her breasts.

"Fine. Then you're up for Roller Derby tomorrow night. I can't skate anyhow."

Fudge. Bertie hated waitressing at roller derby night because she couldn't skate worth a damn either. But she'd fall flat on her ass ten times before she'd ask Liza, the town bitch, back to the Dog.

Liza had stood to leave when Bertie blurted, "And don't forget to turn in your T-shirt," making sure she had the last word.

Liza pivoted slowly. "You want my shirt?" Alarm bells should've gone off in Bertie's head as Liza's lips curled into a reptilian smile. "You can have it." Before anyone could blink, Liza whipped her T-shirt over her head, tossed it at Bertie's face, and then sauntered toward the back of the restaurant with her head held high.

Holy goose feathers. What had Bertie done? Heads

swiveled to watch Liza modeling a lacy blue push-up bra, and then everyone turned to watch Bertie with opened mouths and alarmed expressions.

Lucy, who sat frozen like a block of ice through the entire ugly exchange, started to giggle. "Oh, Bertie." She gave in to a hoot of laughter. "Liza looked pretty good, but if that had been you…it would've caused a riot. You definitely have her beat in the boob department."

Yeah, she was one big boob. Bertie slunk lower into the booth, hoping everyone would go back to eating and coffee drinking and not google-eyeing her. "Show's over, folks. You can finish your breakfasts now," Bertie called out with a dismissive wave.

Dread settled in her stomach, curdling her breakfast. Now she needed to break the news to Cal.

"*Bertie!*" Cal bellowed from across the bar in an I'm-gonna-kill-you way.

Uh-oh. For the first time, Bertie wished she drank before noon.

Chapter 9

KEITH DROVE THE TENNIS BALL DOWN THE LINE WITH a hard forehand and moved toward the net. With a split step, he angled off a backhand volley, putting the ball away. He'd been playing since ten that morning at the Raleigh Tennis Club, and it felt good to hit the ball. A crowd began to fill the stands since word spread that he was on center court, but he'd been oblivious—exorcising his demons took all his concentration.

At the changeover, he looked up over his water bottle and gave a nod to Nick Frasier, the NFL coach of the Carolina Cherokees, standing on the veranda outside the club house. Keith had known Nick when he played quarterback for the NFL and trained in Miami before he retired from the game. He'd been invited to Nick's wedding a year ago in Raleigh, but hadn't made it because he'd had a prior engagement…with self-pity and the bottom of a bottle of Mount Gay.

Keith finished the match, winning 6–3, 6–2. Not bad for a top ten, ex-tennis pro. Fuck. This used to be his life, and somehow he needed to find his way back. Tennis needed to be part of him again, even if he didn't compete on a professional level. There had to be another way.

Keith shoved his rackets in his black-and-yellow Babolat bag and scheduled several more matches with the club pro for the following weeks. He slung the tennis bag over his shoulder and headed for the veranda. He stopped to sign autographs and have his picture taken and noted Nick engaged in the same activity. When the excitement died down and the fans started to disperse, he and Nick shook hands.

"It's good to see you hitting the ball," Nick said. "You haven't lost your touch."

Keith grunted. "Tell that to my aching legs and burning lungs."

"I know the feeling." Nick chuckled and then glanced to his side at someone who caught his attention. "Marabelle, stop hiding and come over here." He motioned with his hand to someone peering behind one of the columns.

A petite, curly headed gal scowled at Nick and then stomped toward them. "You don't have to embarrass me in front of him," she said, poking Nick in the chest with her finger.

"Tinker Bell, you embarrass yourself enough for the both of us. You don't need any help from me." Nick pulled Marabelle into his side and dropped a kiss on top of her head. "Keith, this is my wife, Marabelle, your biggest and most adoring fan." Marabelle dug her elbow into Nick's gut, but he didn't even flinch. Keith observed the couple's exchange. Even though they were jabbing at each other, it was clear as glass that they loved each other.

Keith flashed his famous Morgan smile. "Nice to meet you, Marabelle. Or is it Tinker Bell? I'm confused." He held her tiny hand in his.

"I don't care if you call me Jezebel. It's so nice to finally meet you, Mr. Morgan. I have followed your career since the very beginning, and I mourned the day you retired," Marabelle gushed as she pumped his hand.

"Thank you," Keith smiled down into her eager face. Marabelle's big, brown eyes shone with pure admiration.

"Marabelle, honey, why don't you give Keith his hand back and let him hit the showers and then we'll grab some lunch. How does that sound, Morgan?" Nick asked.

Keith squeezed Marabelle's hand and gave her a wink. "That sounds great." Marabelle appeared almost forlorn as she released his palm. "Give me about fif—"

"Hold it," she said, stopping him in his tracks. She twisted her hands as her gaze darted from Nick to Keith. "Mr. Morgan, would you mind having another picture taken with me? While you're still wearing tennis clothes? I know it's silly, but…"

"No problem. And please, call me Keith." He wrapped his arm around her shoulder, gathering her close.

"Nick, take one with my phone and your phone. Take two. Make sure I have two pictures on my phone."

"Be still, honey, and smile," Nick said. "How's that?" He handed Marabelle's phone to her.

Keith peered over her shoulder. Marabelle looked like a doll standing under his arm, reminding Keith of Bertie and how perfectly she felt tucked into him.

"Great." She beamed up at Keith. "Thank you so much, Mr.…uh, Keith."

―⁓―

The sun's fractured rays shone through the green oak leaves, giving off enough warmth that Keith and the Frasiers decided to dine outside at a small Italian restaurant in a trendy shopping area in Raleigh. Keith couldn't keep from smiling as he enjoyed the banter between the couple. It appeared as if Nick had his hands full with his pint-sized wife. Marabelle had a quick wit and relished giving her famous husband a hard time. But Keith had no doubt they loved each other. He recognized the signs—the Frasiers had trouble keeping their hands to themselves.

Keith had no recollection of sharing laughs and silly stories with Adriana. His stormy marriage seemed so long ago. Six years had passed since Adriana died a useless death, alone in her car, after a long night of partying. The official cause of her fiery car accident was too much alcohol coupled with passing out behind the wheel. They'd been married three years and never managed to create lasting, pleasant memories…and yet it had felt like an eternity in hell.

Keith reached for his water, tamping down the twisted knot that swelled his stomach. Marabelle scowled over a comment Nick made about her not having enough time to cook for him as he pulled on one of her curls. And then she laughed, giving him a quick kiss and promising to cook for him tonight. Keith pictured vanilla-looking Gail acting the same way toward him, but it didn't quite gel. She was too sweet. Not sassy enough to talk back or tease.

"Marabelle has been so busy with her tennis that she barely finds time to cook anymore. Unless it's for Beau Quinton, then she rivals the Barefoot Contessa in the kitchen," Nick said.

"Well, Beau does inspire me like no one else," Marabelle responded in a thick Southern drawl, batting her eyelashes with dramatic flair.

Bertie's big, green eyes and mulish tilt to her chin popped into Keith's head. He could definitely picture her making the same comment. *Don't go there.* Back to Gail and her sensible Keds and durable khaki pants.

Nick laughed, clearly enjoying Marabelle's teasing. "Besides all her obligations to tennis, Marabelle is a personal chef. Several players are paying customers, including Beau Quinton. But Beau's a smart quarterback. He has no desire to warm the bench. He only has an interest in Marabelle's food," Nick explained to Keith.

"Tell me about your tennis," Keith said to Marabelle.

Marabelle dabbed the corners of her mouth with a napkin. "First of all, let me clarify. Beau *begs* me on a regular basis to run away with him, but I don't have the time or the energy," she said with a straight face. Nick hooked his arm around Marabelle's neck, pulling her under his chin.

"That's because I make sure you don't have the time or the energy," he growled into her hair.

Marabelle laughed. "That's true."

"Now, stop being a smart aleck and tell Keith about your tennis." Nick planted a loving kiss on her temple.

"I help with the clinics at the tennis club and give some private lessons." Marabelle shrugged as she reached for her chicken salad sandwich.

"Tell him about the after-school program you started," Nick urged, allowing his pride to show.

Keith finished chewing a bite of his spicy grilled tuna. "Yeah, I'm interested in how you went about it. I'm toying with an idea of my own."

Surprise followed by hope skittered across Marabelle's face. "If you were to start something, it would really make a difference. With your name, you could draw all kinds of kids to the game."

"Watch out. Before you know it, Marabelle will have you selling yourself off to the highest bidder in some sort of bachelor auction like she did to me," Nick said with a chuckle.

Keith's eyebrows rose as Marabelle grinned, nodding her head. "He's right. And we made tons of money. You should consider having an auct—"

"*Marabelle*, don't even think about it." Nick's warning rang loud and clear.

Keith pulled the pamphlet on rejuvenating the Jaycee that Dottie Duncan had shoved at him earlier out of his back pocket and handed it to Marabelle. "I was thinking about working on this facility right outside of Harmony. It's really run-down, but I think it can be fixed up and even expanded and—"

"And you could start an academy. The Keith Morgan Tennis Academy. That would be so awesome." Marabelle examined the pamphlet while Nick read over her shoulder.

"She's right. This area could use a great professional tennis facility. And with your name, it could really take off," Nick added.

Keith squirmed in his seat as he fiddled with his glass of iced tea. He didn't picture himself as head of any academy. He knew how to *play* tennis. He didn't know if he had the ability to teach it or even to be an administrator. "I was thinking more along the lines of having a facility for underprivileged kids or even kids that have the desire to play but whose parents can't afford a country club." Keith tugged on the collar of his blue Nike pullover. "An academy would costs kids thousands of dollars to attend."

"Not your academy," Marabelle said. "Your academy would be special because it'd be for kids who can't afford anything else. Start a foundation. Raise money for kids who can't afford lessons, much less the training that an academy provides. The foundation pays for their tuition."

Window shoppers strolled by their table and did double-takes, checking him and Nick out. Keith leaned forward in his seat, pushing his plate away. "What about kids who *can* afford the tuition? Do we accept them?" he asked.

"Yes. If they can afford it, great. But you have to make sure there are enough teaching pros and training to accommodate everyone. And there should be no special treatment for anybody."

Keith nodded. "Looks like I've got some research to do and some money to raise."

Marabelle bounced in her seat. "There're all kinds of ways to raise money, and with your high profile and good looks—"

Nick gave a bark of laughter. "Here we go again. Keith, your biggest fan has turned into your campaign director in charge of fund-raising. Be careful, or she'll plaster your face on billboards all over town." Marabelle nodded her head so hard that her curls danced around her shoulders.

She turned to Nick. "You'd help, wouldn't you, hon?"

"Of course, babe. Anything for you."

"And we'll get Beau and Ty and a bunch of the other Cherokee players too." The excitement in her voice escalated.

Maybe this wouldn't be so bad after all. Maybe he'd discovered a way to get back into the world of tennis, to give something back to a sport that had been good to him on so many levels. "Well, it looks like I've got me a director. What do you say, Marabelle?"

"Woo-hoo! I'm on it." Marabelle raised her right hand for a high five. Keith laughed, grabbed her hand, and kissed the back. Marabelle's cheeks flamed red.

Keith winked at Nick. "I'm gathering there's never a dull moment in your house."

"You have no idea," Nick said, hugging Marabelle to his side. "Damn, Morgan. Now I'm never going to get a home-cooked meal. That's the only reason I married her." Nick let out an "oomph" as Marabelle's elbow connected with one of his ribs. This time, Keith had no doubt Nick felt it.

⎯⎯⎯⎯

An hour later, Keith found himself parked in front of Barnes & Noble. His sharp mind ran through numerous scenarios. To start an academy would be a huge step for him. It would take a great deal of research and planning. But the timing couldn't be worse. Right now, he had to give Francesca what she demanded and Maddie what she needed. He had more important issues to deal with. Ulcer-causing issues like: 1) convincing sweet, unsuspecting Gail that she should fall in love with and marry him; and 2) convincing sweet, cookie-baking Gail that she'd love to become an instant mother; and 3) convincing himself that he should want sweet, turtleneck-wearing Gail and not sassy, stiletto-wearing Bertie.

Keith checked his watch. He had half an hour before

he needed to hit the road to pick up Maddie from school. His cell chirped and he read a text message with an attached selfie of Maddie mugging for the camera with her tongue hanging out: Hurry! Can't wait for no school. He chuckled as he texted: Behave. Be there soon. Luv u! He shoved a piece of gum in his mouth, brushed his fingers through his hair, and jumped out of his car. Two minutes later, he stood by the register where Gail was stationed. She looked clean and competent, wearing a green polo shirt and a blue-and-green plaid headband in her hair. She gave Keith a shy smile as she finished ringing up her last customer.

"Can you take a break and grab some coffee?" He leaned against the counter and noticed the soft nude polish on her oval-shaped nails.

"Sure. Let me close this register and I'll meet you over there," she said.

Keith ordered two cappuccinos and found an empty table. Gail approached, wearing sensible khakis and brown loafers. He stood and pulled out her chair.

"Thank you," she murmured. "What brings you back to Raleigh?"

Desperation. Fear. Marriage. "I'm on my way to pick up Maddie at school. This is her spring break." He toyed with the lid to his coffee cup. "And I wanted to see you." He slanted a glance at Gail, hoping he hadn't scared her away with his role as a single dad.

A faint blush settled on her cheeks. "Oh. I'm glad you did. I've done some research on you since I saw you last."

Christ. Just what he needed, Gail reading about his wild partying days in Miami…and all over. How could he convince her that those days were behind him now? He had turned over a new leaf. He had a new lease on life. Fuck. How could he convince her when he still needed to convince himself?

Keith yanked on his collar, rolling his neck as fear gripped the inside of his throat. Concern filled Gail's cornflower-blue eyes. "A little stuffy in here," he said on a short laugh. "Did you…uh, read anything interesting?"

She nodded. "Tons and tons."

Shit. Keith fought not to grimace as he gave his collar one last tug. "I wouldn't believe everything you read. You can't trust anything on the Inter—"

Gail gave an angelic laugh. "Goodness. I hope I can believe all the stats on your tennis and how many tournaments you won. Did you know we have three different books on you in the store?"

The vise tightening around his chest slackened. "Books? Really?" He didn't think his mug had graced any tabloids lately—at least, he prayed it hadn't.

"Sure. You're featured in our tennis section." Gail ducked her head and spoke to the table. "I play tennis on the club level, but I'm embarrassed to say I didn't know much about you, until now." She clasped her hands together. "I was wondering if you would sign a few copies so we could put an 'autographed' gold sticker on the cover," she said in a soft, shy voice.

Thank you, Jesus. The courtship was still on. Keith swallowed the remaining panic in his throat. "Sure. On one condition." He relaxed and flashed his famous Morgan smile, designed from an early age to melt female hearts.

Gail fiddled with the delicate gold cross around her neck. "Um, okay, but I may have to check with my manager."

"Do you always ask your manager permission to date?" he said in a teasing tone.

"A date? With me?" Her voice held a mixture of disbelief and doubt.

"Sure. I'd like to take you to dinner. I think it's time we graduated from the coffee bar. How about next Wednesday?"

"Wednesday? That'd be nice. I'm sure I can get the night off."

"Great. It's a date." Keith smiled as he covered Gail's hand on the table with his. No jolt. No heat. No sexual electricity. Merely one warm hand touching another. Plain, boring vanilla. Perfect.

Chapter 10

ON SATURDAY, BERTIE WALKED SWEET TEA FOR Dottie Duncan; met with the N-Purrfect-Harmony ladies about the upcoming festival to discuss tents, tables, and chairs; planted a container garden for Shirley Douglas in an old, beat-up red wagon while barely managing to escape Scott visiting for the weekend; arranged for supplies to be delivered to Dwelling Place's warehouse; and brought Mr. Carmichael lunch and dinner. All before heading to the Dog to fill in for Liza's night shift.

Gary drove Bertie to work in her SUV because he needed it first thing in the morning to pick up some plumbing supplies and deliver them to Keith's house. "You going to be okay tonight?" He gave Bertie a deliberate once over as she struggled with her stockings that bagged around her ankles.

"Sure. Piece of cake. My skating has really improved since last time."

"Dog bollocks. You suck, but that's what makes you so adorable."

"Bite me." Bertie gave her stockings a final tug and jumped from the car.

"I'll bring the car back around noon tomorrow." Gary leaned toward the open passenger door.

"No prob. The only plans I have involve my head hitting my down pillow and staying there for about twelve hours." Bertie waved and then stopped. "You sure you don't want to come in? Dinner is on me. Besides, I could use a partner for my duet."

"I'm not dressing up in one of your flashy sequined outfits. Besides, I didn't bring my stilettos."

"Funny. I'd actually pay to see that. Go. Do whatever sophisticated thing you do on Saturday nights that doesn't include me." Gary took off after Bertie shut the car door.

Bertie stomped through the back door to the Dog and threw her orange satchel on top of Cal's desk. She jerked down on the very short, black tulle skirt, hating the way it barely covered her butt, but her skater shorts had a huge rip and looked even more risqué than the skirt. Thank goodness for the coverage of the ugly purple-and-black-striped tights she wore beneath it.

Cal burst through the office door from the kitchen. "Come on, Bertie. You're late." He glared at her. "And put your skates on."

"Dammit, Cal. You know I can't skate." She stomped her black-pump-clad foot.

"You should've thought of that before you opened your big mouth and fired Liza," Cal shot back.

Bertie yanked on her short, hot-pink T-shirt that kept creeping up, revealing her belly button. "She can't skate either, you moron. I don't know why you ever hired her in the first place. You know she hates my guts." She turned toward the mirror on the wall and adjusted the silver bow on her ponytail. Cal stepped behind her and squeezed her shoulders with his hands.

"That's not true, Bert. You guys need to call a truce and stop sniping at each other. Besides, it was only temporary. She's leaving town in a couple of weeks." Cal sounded a little disappointed at that bit of news.

Good. The sooner Liza skipped town, the better. Bertie rolled her eyes at his reflection in the mirror. "She started it."

Cal laughed and yanked on her ponytail. "Real mature. Shake a leg and get out there. The place is starting to fill up."

Bertie groaned, "If I break my leg, you have to take care of all my jobs while I lie around all day and eat Godiva chocolate."

"Just hold on to the backs of all the chairs and take orders. Whatever you do, *don't* deliver any food or drinks. Leave all that to Sara Jean and the others," Cal said as he pulled the office door open.

"Yes, sir." Bertie gave him a mock salute.

Cal smiled. "You're gonna knock 'em dead."

"Don't I know it," Bertie mumbled as she sat down to lace up her skates.

Keith held his daughter's soft, small hand that no longer felt pudgy from baby fat. When did that happen? He gave her hand a squeeze as he pushed through the front door of the Dog. Tonight the Dog had advertised roller derby and karaoke, which Keith had a hard time wrapping his mind around, but Maddie seemed to love the idea.

"Wow! This is so cool!" Maddie said. Her brown eyes lit with excitement as she scanned the kaleidoscope of colors.

"Think so? You don't think it's too loud?" *Or*

obnoxious and nauseating, he wanted to add but kept quiet. Looking at the bizarre decor made him dizzy.

"No, Dad. It's really awesome. Don't you love all the colored chairs? And look at those Dalmatian spots on the back of the booths." Maddie pointed as she pulled Keith further into the foyer.

"They make my eyes hurt," he mumbled under his breath. Maddie looked at him with a wide smile, and he softened. "It's awesome, Maddie-Poo."

"Welcome back. Is this your daughter?" The blond waitress he met a few weeks back skated forward and came to a stop in front of them. Keith tried not to gawk at her short, purple knit skirt and black fishnet stockings.

"Yep. My daughter, Maddie." He stroked the top of Maddie's silky brown hair.

"Hey there, beautiful. I'm Sara Jean. Where would you like to sit?"

"Can we have the booth with the pink table?" Maddie pointed to a booth in the middle.

"Absolutely," Sara Jean said in a cheery voice.

Keith didn't know how anyone could eat on a pink tabletop, but to see Maddie so excited, he'd do it without complaining. He nodded at Sara Jean as she led the way on her skates.

"Here you go." Sara Jean indicated their table with her hand, sporting lime green–painted fingernails.

Keith and Maddie slid into the booth as she placed menus in front of them.

"What can I get you to drink?"

Keith blinked at Sara Jean's blinding bright orange T-shirt with "Roll Dog Roll" on the front in silver sequins. He didn't know if he could ever eat again. He preferred his bars to be dark and seedy or even swanky like the ones that lit Ocean Drive in the wee hours of the morning. Too many hours had been spent in those places, which explained why he now sat inside the fantastical land of Elmo's World in a tiny town in the land of Dixie.

Maddie bounced in her seat. "Do you have lemonade?"

"Sure do. It's pink and fabulous."

Maddie nodded with a grin. "Is it hard to skate and wait tables at the same time?" she asked, checking out Sara Jean's wild outfit.

"Nah. It only takes a little practice. Unless you're Bertie, and then it's hopeless," Sara Jean laughed. "What can I get you, Mr. Morgan?"

"Call me Keith. Iced tea, unsweetened."

"Be back in a jiff." Keith watched Sara Jean glide away toward the bar and glanced at the other waitresses skating in various skimpy outfits. He released a calming breath, glad he hadn't spied Bertie. Somehow picturing her curvy figure in a tight skating outfit made his mouth go dry. Where was that tea? Flashes of sweet, flat-chested Gail, wearing black pants and a white silk blouse buttoned all the way up to the collar scrolled through his head.

"Who's Bertie?" Maddie asked, and Keith turned his attention back to his daughter.

"Uh, she's one of the owners of this restaurant, and she's also—"

"Coming through! Watch out!"

Keith turned toward the commotion and was struck with horror as Bertie careened around the backs of two chairs, clearly out of control. She grabbed the edge of a table and locked her wobbly knees to stop from rolling.

The minute she let go of the table, someone accidently bumped her from behind and she came barreling forward, wind-milling her arms, heading straight for Keith.

"Jesus!" Keith scooted to the edge of his seat and reached out to break her fall.

"Help!" Bertie wailed as she crashed into Keith's arms, propelling him backward from the force of her fall. Keith stared up at Bertie's appalled expression as she lay on top of him, trying to catch her breath.

"Daddy! Are you okay?" Maddie scrambled forward over the tabletop, trying to find her dad underneath a hot-pink T-shirt and black tulle skirt.

"Sure, honey," he said in a muffled voice to reassure Maddie. Warm curves and a bare waist filled his hands. He was better than okay. Bertie's skin-tight shirt had ridden almost up to the edge of her bra. Keith tamped down the urge to ride his hands up even farther. He willed his fingers to tug the hem of her top down.

"Uh, Maddie, honey…I want you to meet Bertie," he grunted as he gently shifted Bertie and struggled to sit up. He glanced at Bertie's horrified expression as she pushed against his chest, scrambling for a more dignified position, which caused her knee to come perilously close to his crotch.

"Whoa. Hold on there," he said in a tight voice. "Let's not ruin Maddie's chances at a sibling." He lifted Bertie until she was sitting in his lap and not crushing his balls.

Bertie straightened her twisted pink shirt with the silhouette of a roller skate in black and "Roll with the Dog" in gold sequins plastered across her chest. She appeared flustered, and he could've sworn she mumbled something about driving a stake through Cal's heart.

The tension that had been contracting every muscle in his body broke, and he started to shake with laughter. Bertie's big, green eyes narrowed to mere slits, and she mumbled something about hitting him in the head with his own tennis racket. Keith's head fell back and he howled even louder.

"It's *not* that funny," she snarled close to his face. Bertie slid from his lap to the seat next to him on the bench.

"Daddy?" Maddie's confused, small voice caught Keith's attention. His laughter petered off into a chuckle.

"Sorry. Let me start again. Maddie, this is Bertie. She's our interior decorator." Maddie's gaze darted from Keith's laughing face to Bertie's exasperated expression. Her dark brown eyes shone with knowledge far greater than her ten years.

"You own this place *and* you decorate?" she asked Bertie. Keith could tell that Bertie had graduated from pretty cool to super-duper cool in Maddie's world.

"I sure do. Me and my brother Cal own the Dog." Bertie extended her hand across the table. "It's very nice to meet you. I'm sorry about my embarrassing entrance. I'm not usually this clumsy." Bertie's laugh sounded nervous as she shook Maddie's hand.

Maddie grinned from ear to ear at Bertie, as if she were watching one of her favorite teen groups sing on stage.

Sara Jean glided forward with their drinks on a tray. "So, you've witnessed Bertie's skating firsthand, huh?" she said, placing Maddie's lemonade on the table. She handed Keith his iced tea in a Mason jar. "Last time, she landed face-first in Dottie Duncan's chest with a big plate of spaghetti. It was hilarious," Sara Jean laughed.

Bertie cleared her throat. "Thanks, Sara Jean, for those highlights. Have you taken the Morgans' dinner order?"

A few minutes later, Sara Jean skated away from the table with Keith's order of grilled salmon and couscous and Maddie's chicken tenders.

"I'm so happy I'm going to be working with you on your bedroom. You'll save some time to meet with me this week, won't you?" Bertie asked Maddie.

Maddie's eyes grew wide as tennis balls and the light bounced off her round face and scattered freckles. "Just you and me?" The excitement in her voice made Keith's chest expand with warmth.

"Sure. Just you and me, cutie. But we might have to include your dad in a few decisions," Bertie said, winking at Maddie. "Would that be okay with you?"

Maddie bounced her legs back and forth, causing her small frame to shake the entire table. "That'd be great. Right, Dad?"

"Right, Maddie-Poo," Keith agreed, loving Maddie's enthusiasm.

"*Dad*, please. I'm not a baby anymore. You can stop calling me Maddie-Poo," Maddie said as if she were thirty and not ten.

"Sorry, no can do. I get to call you my Maddie-Poo no matter how old you are. Daddy privilege." Maddie rewarded him with an eye roll followed by a small giggle.

Bertie braced both hands on the table. "Nice to meet you, Maddie. I guess I better slink away and remove my skates, so I can shove them down Cal's throat," she mumbled.

"Not so fast, little speed demon. You're not exactly steady on those things," Keith said, placing his hand on Bertie's thigh.

"You're leaving?" Maddie asked, sounding disappointed.

Keith's sentiments exactly, and he didn't know why. Something about holding Bertie in his lap felt…right. He didn't want to let her go. The scent of gardenias teased his nose and took him back to their last hot kiss when she'd looped her hands around his neck and pressed her lush body into his. Keith choked back a groan and forced his mind to think of something neutral. He struggled to picture Gail but had no luck. The best he could come up with was the new mutual fund he planned to invest in.

"Daddy, hold on to her so she doesn't fall again," Maddie instructed in a concerned voice.

Keith gave his head a shake. "I won't let her fall." Bertie tried standing, but both skates slipped out from under her. Keith grabbed the back of her shirt and pulled her down on her butt. Her feet shot straight out. "See, I didn't let her fall," he said to Maddie's alarmed face. "Maybe you should sit this one out," he said low in Bertie's ear.

"Hey, Bertie! Is this the lucky fella you almost knocked out?"

"Did you drop another plate of spaghetti?"

"Whatcha gonna sing tonight?"

Patrons gave a shout-out to Bertie from various parts of the bar.

Bertie quickly waved and answered back, "Don't know yet. Need to find me a singing partner." She straightened in her seat as if this sort of thing happened all the time. Then she grinned at Maddie. "I can't wait to get started on your room. But right now, I need to get up."

Keith's hand gripped her elbow as she scooted to the edge of the seat.

"Not so fast." Keith and Bertie glanced up at Cal, weaving toward their table. "Hey, Prince. Sorry about Barreling Bertie, here. Do me a favor and hold on to her until the karaoke starts up. And by the way, your meal is comped for the evening."

Keith shook his head, thinking his meal was being comped because of his celebrity status. "That's not necessary."

Cal laughed. "It's tradition. Whoever Bertie crashes into on derby night gets their meal on the house." Cal yanked on Bertie's floppy ponytail. "Don't let her back on the floor with those skates."

Bertie swatted at Cal. "If you wouldn't make me work on derby night, you wouldn't have to comp so many meals."

"I can't afford another floor show," Cal teased. "Have dinner with your friends and relax a little until it's time to sing, okay?"

"Yeah, and people in Hades want ice water," she yelled at Cal's retreating back.

"Is he your boss?" Maddie asked, still bouncing in her seat.

"Only in his dreams," Bertie snorted. "Enough about bossy older brothers." She signaled Sara Jean over and then returned her attention to Maddie. "I want to hear all about your school and what activities you like to do."

Bertie spent the next fifteen minutes talking to Maddie about school, sports, music, Maddie's BFF Tess, and some teeny-bopper boy band all the girls worshipped. Sara Jean brought Bertie her usual salad along with their meals, and Keith ate in silence, observing his daughter talk with her hands and use words he'd never heard come out of her mouth, like *equivalent*, *optimistic*, and *collaborated*. All good, except his daughter was growing up before his very eyes, and Keith had missed huge gaps of development by not being there. A plan to change all that formed in his mind as he listened to his baby girl sound more and more like a young adult.

"Do you like to sing and dance?" Bertie asked.

"Yeah, sure. When I know the words and I've practiced," Maddie said, shoving a strand of thick brown hair behind her ear.

Bertie checked the chunky watch on her wrist. "We have about thirty minutes. How about you and I go in the back and practice a song together?"

Maddie gaped, slack-jawed. "Huh?"

"Yeah, come on. It'll be fun. We'll do a Taylor Swift song. They're easy and fun. We've got costumes and everything."

"Dad?" Maddie looked to him for approval or rescuing—he didn't know which one.

"What do you say, *Dad*?" Bertie mimicked, shooting him a saucy smile.

Keith reached for his tea as a cold rock formed in his stomach. He had to remember that this was not Adriana gyrating on a bar in some revealing outfit. They were in Harmony for chrissakes, dancing to Taylor Swift, not some lewd rap song. He leveled a hard glare at Bertie. "Don't dress her up like a hoochie mama. Nothing inappropriate."

"Dad!" Maddie wailed.

He pointed his finger at Maddie. "I mean it. Now, go.

Maybe I'll get some peace and quiet around here. All this jabbering is giving me a headache."

Maddie scooted to the end of her seat. "Right. Just because we aren't talking tennis, football, or Wall Street, you think it's silly." She gave an exaggerated sigh. "I am a girl, you know."

The knife sliced straight through Keith's heart. He gulped back his groan of pain. His baby was growing up into a pretty, intelligent young lady with acute observational skills. And Keith didn't know if he was equipped to handle it. He gave his head a shake at Bertie's hotpink T-shirt molding her curves. This was bossy Bertie who walked dogs, fed old people, and couldn't skate, not Adriana, wearing spandex with no panties underneath. Then he pictured Gail in khakis, loafers, and headbands, and the panic that threatened to close his throat receded. No comparison. Gail would bring peace and stability to their lives. The perfect solution. Now if he could only convince his randy cock.

"And girls rule!" Bertie's exclamation jerked him back to the present. She motioned for Maddie. "Come hold my hand, and whatever you do, don't let go."

Maddie giggled as she helped pull Bertie up, holding tight so Bertie wouldn't fall again.

"Make sure you have a good view of the stage. You don't want to miss this," Bertie called over her shoulder to Keith.

Keith appreciated the view of Bertie's cute ass covered in black tulle. A small smile lifted the corners of his mouth as Bertie reached a hand around her back to yank the hem of her skirt down. Unlike Adriana, who'd flaunted her wares for any guy with eyeballs, Keith sensed that Bertie would be more comfortable wearing a sandwich board.

"You here for the show?"

Keith turned his head to see Liza Palmer sliding into Maddie's vacant seat. He nodded. "Yeah, my daughter is getting ready to perform with Bertie."

Liza fiddled with the stem of her wineglass. "Cute. I can't wait to meet her. If she's with Bertie, it will be good."

"Good as in hilarious? Because I've already witnessed her skating firsthand. Or good as in she really knows how to perform?"

Liza gave a sly smile. "Wait and see."

"Hey, Keith. When did you get back in town? I stopped by your house yesterday with a homemade banana pudding." Jo Ellen Huggins stood next to his table, wearing a pink cowboy hat, the only thing on her body he could actually name and identify. The rest of her outfit was beyond words.

"Thought we could share it together." Jo Ellen batted her gooped-up eyelashes at him, looking like a half-blind raccoon.

"I got in late last night."

Aunt Francesca would rip him a new one if she knew he hadn't stood and offered Jo Ellen a seat like a gentleman, but he'd take his chances. Liza started to cough or laugh, he wasn't sure which.

"Hey, Liza. What brings you to town?" Jo Ellen gathered her wide, pink skirt with black poodles all over it and took matters into her own hands by sliding into the booth next to him. Keith stifled a whimper. He motioned for Sara Jean to bring another round of drinks. His pleasant evening was taking a definite turn for the worse.

"Mini vacation to visit my parents. Like your pink poodle cashmere sweater. Where'd you get it?" Liza smiled into her wineglass.

"This old thing?" Jo Ellen fiddled with the white pearl button on her sweater, slipping it from the hole. Keith feared any more buttons opening for his benefit.

"Did we miss anything?" Opal and Emma Ardbuckle raced over, wearing matching bright blue band outfits. Why was everyone in this loony town dressing in costume on a Saturday night? The Ardbuckle twins pushed their way into the booth, squishing Keith against the wall and Jo Ellen Huggins and her pink poodles against him.

"It's about to start!" The Arbuckle twins squealed together. Sure enough, the lights dimmed and everyone focused their attention on the stage with the pink and silver hexagon-patterned backdrop.

First, Cal took the stage and warmed everyone up with a few funny stories. "Okay, I know why you're all here. Once again, it's karaoke night at the Dog! Put your hands together for Bertie Anderson and Maddie Morgan singing 'You Belong with Me' by Taylor Swift."

Spotlights circled the room and then zeroed in on the stage and Keith's mouth fell open as Bertie and Maddie marched out in perfect rhythm, carrying cordless microphones. Pride filled Keith's chest as he gaped at Maddie's goofy flannel plaid pajama pants and oversized T-shirt covered in handwriting. A claw held her thick brown hair on top of her head and she wore huge-framed glasses that gobbled her face. But Bertie. Keith gripped his Mason jar of tea like it was a lifeline. Bertie sparkled in an electric-blue dress with long fringe that swung from her great breasts to the tops of her thighs, down to silver stilettos worthy of a centerfold. Her hair hung in thick waves past her shoulders and when she moved—or maybe shimmied would be a more apt description—the fringe caught the light and danced.

Fuck. He wanted the exact opposite influence for Maddie. His daughter didn't need to see sparkles. Or fringe. Or cleavage. And certainly not porn-star stilettos.

Keith started to grind his teeth when Liza's hand covered his and squeezed.

"Watch," she murmured low.

Keith forced his gaze back on the stage, trying not to stare at Bertie, but it was damn near impossible. He scanned the crowd and noticed all male eyes were glued on her as well. He gave his back teeth another workout.

Bertie and Maddie danced with clever choreography and sang really well together. Bertie took a few steps back to give Maddie the spotlight. He grinned like the village fool when Maddie hammed it up and had the crowd laughing. Maddie caught his eye, searching for his reaction, and Keith gave her big thumbs-up. Maddie sang the words verbatim and followed the tune while Bertie switched octaves and added some harmony. When the song ended, Bertie and Maddie gave silly bows, laughing as the crowd cheered, then skipped off stage. Keith ducked his head as heat flushed his face.

"She's really talented," Liza said, leaning forward for Keith's ears only.

"If being a ham is talent," he said.

Liza laughed. "No, your daughter is very cute and definitely a ham, but I was referring to Bertie." Liza glanced at the women jammed in the booth to make sure they weren't paying attention to their conversation. She laughed again. "If you could see your face. I know she seems like a natural disaster sometimes, but Bertie is one of the most talented people I know."

"She seems like a competent designer," he said with some hesitation.

"She can also sing and dance, not to mention fill out a tight dress like no one else I've ever seen." Liza smirked at him as if she could read his mind like a page in a book.

Keith gave her his supercilious look with one raised brow. "I wouldn't know. I only had eyes for Maddie."

"Yeah, right."

Their attention was drawn back to the stage when Cal asked who wanted to go next.

Jo Ellen Huggins in her pink poodle glory jumped up and down in her seat, squealing, "Oooo! Me! I wanna go next." She pushed Opal or Emma, he didn't know which one, out of the booth and hurried toward the stage in a pink blur.

Liza moaned, "From what I hear, this should be good."

"What?" Keith asked. But he found his answer when Jo Ellen started dancing and singing to "Rock Around the Clock" by Bill Haley & His Comets. Holy shit. Poor Bill Haley was probably turning over in his grave. The crowd cheered and clapped along. Really? They should beat a gong or extend the hook, not encourage her.

The Ardbuckle twins turned to him with bright animated faces. "Don't go anywhere. We're performing next to 'Don't Go Breaking My Heart' by Elton John and Kiki Dee."

Keith hoped his mask didn't slip and reveal the complete horror he felt as he nodded. God, this was going to be a long night. He signaled for Sara Jean and told her to hold the tea and bring him a beer instead.

Chapter 11

BERTIE STOOD BY THE OPEN OFFICE DOOR AND adjusted her pink T-shirt. Maddie took off for the booth where Keith still sat. Bertie hesitated to step back into the fray, still reeling from the humiliation of falling into Mr. Perfect's lap. The falling part she could handle no problem. She fell all the time on derby night. But landing on top of Keith and then finding herself perched on his lap—so mortifying... so unprofessional...so awesome. Why did she always end up the fool in his presence? Okay, so she had a bad habit of stepping in poo every once in a while. But lately, she had managed to step smack dab in the middle of every pile.

One good thing came from her spectacular tumble—she met Maddie and broke the ice with her. Where Keith was remote and closed off, Maddie was animated and open. Bertie liked her on the spot and hoped that she could make Maddie happy with her design choices. Bertie needed to pick up the pace on this job if she expected to get done in time.

She'd already given Dwelling Place her check for ten thousand and her pledge for the rest. She'd visited little Jessica Alvarez at their rusted-out, single-wide home and promised her family that DP would build a house for them soon. Jessica's mom had gasped and then grabbed Bertie, kissing both her cheeks, while Jessica kicked up dirt as she danced around the dusty yard. Bertie had made a promise, and she never broke her promises.

Time to focus on completing Mr. Heartthrob's house, not on ways to land in his strong arms. And when she finished, she could move on to Atlanta, as she had planned. The most thrilling thing to happen in Harmony had been Keith Morgan moving to town and going on a wife hunt. Once he married and settled down, all the single women fluttering around with extra makeup, new outfits, and homemade casseroles would go back to their ordinary lives—including Bertie. But she didn't want ordinary. She wanted exciting and new. She wanted out.

Bertie sighed, yanking on the hem of her tulle skirt. She'd better get out there and help Cal. She glanced at the Ardbuckle twins butchering Elton John in their matching outfits and tried not to cringe. She moved between some tables and tapped Hank Thompson and his brother Walt on the shoulder.

"You guys are up next. Let's hear 'Sweet Home Alabama' before the natives get restless," she said close to their ears in order to be heard. Then she signaled Julio, her painter, and a few of his crew members to do one of their fast Latin numbers. She worked her way through the crowd until she ended back at Keith's table, where Maddie was attacking a mountain of whipped cream on a hot fudge sundae, appearing unfazed by the commotion of women swarming the booth. Keith rubbed his forehead as if it ached, and Bertie noticed he had switched from iced tea to beer. Bertie rolled her eyes at the absurdity of the situation. Time to create a diversion.

"Arlene, you better get close to the stage because Hank

is getting ready to sing." Bertie nudged Arlene Tomlin with her elbow. Arlene and Hank had dated off and on since high school, and Arlene still harbored a wicked crush.

"I do love it when that man sings." Arlene gave a dreamy sigh and headed toward the stage.

"Crystal, that darling Patrick is home for spring break. He's sitting over there with three of his friends. Why don't you go chat him up? Maybe you guys can dance together."

"Patrick's home from UNC?" Crystal asked, slicking her red, jelly-glossed lips with her tongue. "Do I look okay?" Crystal adjusted her layered cotton tank tops.

"Perfect. Tell them to save a dance for me." Bertie pointed Crystal in the right direction.

"Jo Ellen, there's a table of working women who could use your expertise. They were talking about eye creams and facials. You should go introduce yourself and give them some Mary Kay pointers. Might be some new clients for you."

Jo Ellen pushed her way out of the booth. "Let me freshen up and I'll go help them," she said in a serious tone, as if she were an ER doctor instead of a cosmetic specialist.

Bertie turned her attention back to the booth and found Keith staring at her as if she glowed radioactive green. "What?" She shrugged her shoulder. "Thought you could use a little breathing room. If you want, I can call them all back."

A huge smile broke out on his face and stole Bertie's breath. Her heart flutter-kicked inside her chest. Keith should smile more often.

"No. Breathing room is good." Keith graced Maddie with his generous smile as he dug for his wallet in his back pocket. "You almost done, Poo? I need to get you home to Aunt Francesca's. She's waiting." He threw some bills on the table.

"Uh, your meal is comped, remember?" A burst of laughter erupted from the corner of the booth. *Liza.* Bertie had forgotten she still sat there.

"You mean Keith's the one you crashed into tonight?" Liza said between hoots. Bertie's fist balled at her side. Even Liza, who no longer lived here, knew about Bertie's terrible skating reputation.

"She landed on top of my dad and then she sat in his lap," Maddie the informer added around a mouthful of ice cream. "It was so funny." She giggled.

"I bet it was." Liza slipped from the booth. "It was nice meeting you, kid," Liza said to Maddie. Liza's lip curled as she glanced at Bertie. "I'll see if Cal needs any help at the bar."

"You don't work here anymore, remember?"

Liza pointed at the black pumps on Bertie's feet. "Looks like you don't either."

Anger and irritation warred inside Bertie as she glared at Liza's retreating back. Maddie stopped shoveling ice cream, and Keith's smile disappeared. Both were riveted to the tension she'd created with Liza. She guessed Keith didn't appreciate her running off Liza—most guys didn't. Bertie heaved a sigh.

"Sorry. I didn't mean to scare her off," she mumbled.

"We need to get moving." Keith pushed Maddie's empty ice cream bowl away and handed her a napkin to wipe her mouth and hands. "Let's go before Aunt Francesca starts worrying. You should be in bed by now." He gave Maddie a slight push from the booth.

"Great singing with you, Maddie," Bertie said, patting her on the back. "I'll be by on Monday to get started on your room, okay?"

Maddie's look of worry dissolved at the mention of her room. "Okay. Don't forget."

"I won't. I promise." Bertie gave Maddie a genuine smile, which faltered at Keith's tone.

"Maddie, go wait for me by the door, but stay inside," he said in a clipped voice. "I need to speak with Bertie for a moment." Maddie shoved her hands in her pockets and crossed the room toward the front entrance. Once Keith saw that she stood in the foyer, he turned his attention back to Bertie.

"We have to meet before you do any work on Maddie's room. I need to go over some ground rules first. Okay?" he said in a low, rough voice.

Ground rules? Huh? "No, I don't understand. What ground rules? This isn't a competition. I'm trying to get her room done along with the rest of your house." Frustration laced her voice.

"Listen, there are things I don't want influencing my daughter."

"Things? Or people?" Bertie cocked her head and gave him a long, hard stare. "Do you think I'm a bad influence?" She was stunned she even had to ask the question. No one had ever considered her a bad influence…ever.

Keith jammed his fists in his jean pockets. "We'll discuss it later. Monday morning. My house. Eight a.m. sharp," he rumbled close to her face.

"Oh, for Pete—"

"Bertie! I knew I'd find you here." Bertie never

finished telling Mr. Uptight how unreasonable he sounded, because she found herself wrapped in a bear hug by Scott Douglas. "Man, I've missed you," Scott said, rocking Bertie back and forth.

"Uh, hey there," she said muffled against his cotton button-down shirt. "What brings you to town?"

Bertie pushed back and Scott laughed, holding her by the shoulders. "As if you don't know," he said. "Let's dance." He grabbed Bertie's hand and dragged her on the dance floor. Over her shoulder, Bertie glimpsed Keith leaving with Maddie, and he didn't look pleased. In fact, he looked downright furious.

"Dad, what's that noise?" Maddie twisted in the front seat to face him.

It was Keith's back molars as he ground them down to nubs. "What noise?"

"Nothing. It stopped. Anyway, thanks for dinner and the sundae. The Dog is really cool, don't you think?" Maddie didn't wait for an answer. "Do you eat there, like every day? Did you really love our song? I thought Bertie and I were the best, didn't you? Bertie can really sing and dance. She taught me all those steps real fast. Didn't you love that dress she wore? I did. All that fringe and—"

Hell no. "I'm glad you liked it, honey. And yes, you were the most fantastic out of everyone...including Bertie." Keith kept his eyes on the road and his mind off Bertie shimmying in that short, fringed dress.

"Why do you look so mad?"

He erased the scowl but his features were still tight.

"What did you say to Bertie? Are you mad at Bertie because she made all those silly women leave our table? She was only trying to help and—"

"No. That was a good thing. I'm not mad. I needed to talk to Bertie about the house, that's all," he said in a neutral voice, when he really wanted to roar and pound something with his fists—preferably that doofus in the wrinkled khaki pants and penny loafers who dragged Bertie onto the dance floor. He glanced at Maddie's solemn expression as she twisted the sleeves on her purple hoodie. "Aunt Francesca is really looking forward to your stay this week, Maddie-Poo. Anything special you want to do?" he asked, trying to remove the shroud of worry that had draped over his daughter.

"Can we go to the mall? And maybe play some tennis?" she asked in a small voice. Keith had never been one of those parents who pushed his kid into sports, especially tennis. He didn't expect Maddie to live up to what he had accomplished in life.

"Okay. Or maybe we could hit a few golf balls," he suggested, in case she really didn't want to do the tennis thing.

Maddie fiddled with the zipper on her hoodie. "And can we eat at the Dog again?" She watched him as if weighing his reaction.

The draw of the Dog…what kid wouldn't want to eat there? At least they'd graduated from Chuck E. Cheese, which was pure hell for any parent. "Sure. Whatever you want to do." He pulled his Cayenne into Francesca's driveway and killed the engine.

Maddie bolted from the car. "I can't wait to tell Aunt

Francesca all about tonight," she yelled as she rushed up the walk toward the front door.

Keith banged the back of his head against the head-rest and groaned. He needed to accelerate the speed on his courtship because he needed help raising his daughter. He needed to think about sweet, practical Gail and not hot, frustrating Bertie. His mind wanted Gail, but his body screamed for Bertie. His body could use a cold shower and maybe a horsewhip.

Keith entered the kitchen where Francesca and Maddie sat on barstools at the large island. Francesca sipped a mug of tea, and Maddie held a glass of water.

"…and we both sang and danced to a Taylor Swift song. I wish you could've seen us." Maddie jiggled in her seat as she told Francesca about her night. "Bertie is really good. But she can't skate at all. You should've seen her. Her arms were swinging in the air"—Maddie demonstrated the windmill—"and she came flying toward us and landed in—"

"Um, time to hit the sack, Maddie-Poo," Keith interrupted as he kissed Maddie on the head. "I thought we'd take a ride down to the beach tomorrow. What do you say?"

"Go on up to your room, honey, and I'll be in to check on you in a few minutes," Francesca said.

Maddie jumped up and hugged Francesca around the neck and then Keith around the waist. "Yay! The beach! Thanks, Dad." She raced from the room.

Francesca sat in quiet calm and continued to sip her tea. Restless, Keith moved about the kitchen. He picked up a green apple from the ceramic bowl on the countertop and tossed it into the air. "Maddie looked real cute up there tonight," he said, catching the apple.

"I'm sure she did. But it's good you brought her home." Francesca checked her watch. "It can get wild at the Dogwood once the dancing starts. Not a place for a ten-year-old girl to be hanging out."

Wild? Keith wouldn't go that far. A "wild night in Harmony" didn't have the same ring as a "wild night on South Beach."

"That was sweet of Bertie to sing with Maddie. I hope Bertie isn't working too hard. She needs to relax and have a little fun." Francesca put her dirty mug in the dishwasher. "And Lord knows that girl can't skate a lick."

"Don't I know it," Keith muttered under his breath. A picture of Bertie slow dancing with Goofy Guy popped into his head. "She seemed okay. When I left, she was dancing with some big guy named Scott." Keith studied Aunt Francesca to gauge her reaction.

A pleasant expression came over her face as she rearranged her wooden spoons propped in a ceramic jug next to the range. "Yes, that's Shirley Douglas's boy. He lives in Charlotte and sells insurance. He's been sweet on Bertie since grade school. I'm glad he's back in town. They make such a cute couple. Shirley is dying for them to get married. I can't blame her." Aunt Francesca handed him bottled water from her beverage refrigerator. "Here. Drink this. You look a little hot around the collar." She blew out her clove-scented kitchen candle. She didn't see Keith wrenching the cap off the bottle with extra force. "Cake, dear? Maria made it fresh yesterday."

Keith grunted, "No." He chugged his water, trying to cool his unwanted jealousy over Bertie and her childhood boyfriend. Christ. He'd forgotten that people dated as infants around here and ended up married to their first puppy loves.

"Are you sure it was Scott? Because Joseph Phillips is a big guy too, and he and Bertie have dated on and off for years," Francesca said.

Keith unlocked his back molars. "She said Scott, but what the hell do I know?"

"Well, I'm going to tuck Maddie in and then turn in myself. What time would you like to pick Maddie up for the beach?"

Keith shrugged. "Ten?"

"Fine. There's an eight o'clock service at the Episcopal Church. You should join us, dear." Aunt Francesca fixed him with her imperial stare, designed to make him quake in his boots and capitulate to whatever she demanded.

"Because my dark soul could use some saving?"

"That and you should be there with your daughter."

Keith leaned down to kiss her powdery soft cheek. "You're shameless, always playing the daughter card. One of these times it's not going to work."

Francesca laughed. "Don't underestimate me, my fine Prince. I have lots of tricks up my sleeve."

"Good night, Auntie." Keith gave a brief wave as he reached the front door.

"Keith?"

He stopped with his hand on the brass doorknob.

"You need to call your mother. Maddie should speak with her grandmother," Francesca said at the bottom of the spiral stairs.

Keith groaned and dropped his forehead on the wood door. "Of course. The prodigal son reaching out to the prodigal mother."

"Nevertheless—"

"Where's she living this month? Florence? Paris?" he asked.

"Outside Florence, where's she's been for the last two years. You'd know that if you called her more often." Francesca's curt tone told Keith she didn't approve of his relationship with his mother. What relationship? He hadn't lived in the same state, much less the same house as his mother since he'd turned thirteen.

"The phone works both ways, Aunt Francesca." He unleashed a heavy, painful breath. "Maddie and I will call her on the road tomorrow." She nodded, and he closed the door behind him.

~~~

Keith found himself back in the crowded lot at the Dog, cruising for a parking space while debating whether he should go in. One more drink and then he'd head home—to his vacant house and empty bed. He drove around the lot when he spied some couple up against a car parked near the rear entrance. The guy appeared to be doing "the lean," as he came within inches of his date, going for a kiss.

Keith chuckled. "Go for it, dude. At least somebody's getting some." He almost drove past when he noticed the girl wore purple and black-striped stockings. The same stockings Bertie had been wearing earlier with her roller derby costume. Keith hit the brake and lowered his window.

"Come on, just a little sugar," the guy whined in a deep Southern drawl.

Keith listened. Did he say *sugar*?

"Absolutely not. We're just friends, and you've had too much to drink."

Keith recognized that bossy voice. "Bertie?" he called out his window.

Bertie's head popped out from around the guy's side. "Keith? Oh my." Bertie scrambled away as she pushed the guy aside and rushed toward Keith. The guy wobbled on unsteady legs. "Of course, I almost forgot… you wanted to talk to me…I shouldn't have kept you waiting." She tugged her tight T-shirt down—it looked as if this asshole had pushed it up. Not any asshole, but Scott, the grade-school flame from earlier that evening. Scott stumbled back, shaking his head.

"Hey, Bertie…where you goin'?" Scott said with a slur, appearing bemused as he looked down at his empty outstretched hands. Keith could relate, knowing how it felt to have Bertie's juicy curves teasing his palms.

"Sorry, Scott. I have a meeting with my client—"

"Now? At…ten thirty?" Scott blinked at his watch.

"Yes. He's very anal. Thinks he owns me…you know the type…like the world only revolves around him." Bertie trotted around the hood of Keith's car. She yanked the passenger door open and practically dove inside. "Scott? Go inside and find Liza," she said. The tantalizing scent of gardenias filled Keith's car. Bertie leaned over the console toward the open window. "Liza said she really misses you."

Scott stumbled forward. "Don't drive," Bertie ordered. "Cal will find you a ride or call Coco's Cab."

Scott appeared confused and bereft without Bertie. Keith almost felt sorry for the big lug until he glimpsed Bertie's grim expression.

"Aw, Bertie…you know, I only…you mean Liza Palmer?" he asked, his befuddlement clearing up.

"Yep. The one and only. Get back inside, okay?" Bertie sat back digging for something in her orange bag. "Drive away slowly…please," she said to Keith as she pulled her cell phone out and punched a number.

Keith tore his gaze away from Bertie and eased his foot off the brake. He checked Scott through the rearview mirror, standing in the middle of the parking lot.

"Cal? Listen, Scott's drunk and shouldn't drive home. Make sure someone has his back. Yeah…no, I don't think he'll show up later…uh, Keith's driving me home… Uh-huh. Thanks. Bye." Bertie punched her phone off.

Keith stopped before pulling onto the side street. "You okay? Did he hurt you? Do I need to kick his sorry ass?"

Bertie glanced over her shoulder before settling back in her seat. "No. I'm fine. His intentions are good, but I still don't like being mauled." She scrubbed her hand around her neck as if she had germs. "Phew, am I happy to see you. I didn't think he'd ever leave. He wouldn't stop following me around and I couldn't get rid of him. Turn left." Bertie pointed with her finger.

"That's because he wants to see you naked." Keith accelerated onto the empty street. "Can't say that I blame him," he muttered under his breath.

Disapproval pinched her features. "No way. I've known Scott since I was six—"

"Which only means he's been dreaming about getting you naked since he was thirteen or fourteen."

"Huh?" Bertie's jaw dropped and she gawked at Keith as if he spoke in tongues.

"Unless he already has...and now he can't get enough. Are you guys sleeping together?" For some reason, the answer to that question was very important to him.

Bertie's spectacular chest heaved under her T-shirt. "No. Scott's a childhood friend, not a boyfriend." A frown settled around her full lips.

Keith chuckled—from relief or release, he didn't know which one, but they were both good. "Something tells me Liza was not missing that big goofball," he said.

Bertie shrugged. "Liza can handle it. He won't get very far with his roving hands." She glanced at him. "Thanks for your assistance. I had everything under control, but it would've taken a lot longer to get rid of him."

Keith shifted in his seat. "Why didn't you tell him to fuck off? He deserved it."

Bertie's eyes widened. "I could nev—he's a friend... we grew up together and his mother was my first-grade teacher." Bertie bit her plump lower lip. "He doesn't mean anything by it. He's harmless."

Keith gave a bark of laughter. "Harmless? Hardly. Bertie, that guy outweighs you by at least a hundred pounds. Copping a feel indicated he wanted more than *sugar*." Keith drew out the word *sugar*, mimicking a Southern accent.

A scowl marred her face. "He'd had too much to drink and got a little frisky. The end. I don't want to talk about Scott Douglas anymore."

Frisky my ass. Keith kept silent while Bertie only spoke to give directions. The houses appeared smaller and farther apart as Keith bumped over some old, broken-down railroad tracks. After another mile down the country road, Bertie told him to turn left. Keith followed a winding, gravel driveway until he stopped his SUV next to a bungalow-style home with a gable roof and arched front door.

"You live here?" he asked.

"Yep." Bertie checked her watch. "Cal and I grew up here. Cal got the restaurant, and I got the house after my dad died."

"Looks nice. Well cared for." Potted plants lined the front steps and a light glowed from inside. Keith noticed Bertie fidgeting in her seat and felt like laughing. Maybe not comfortable bringing men home, this Bertie. Good.

"Uh, Cal asked if you wouldn't mind staying for a few minutes. He's being overly protective, but he doesn't want Scott showing up at my door."

Keith leveled a hard look at her. "Does he make a habit of showing up?"

"Not really. But sometimes when he's back in town, he stops by late at night…uh, uninvited."

Sure he does. "Do you let him in?"

"No. But I can hear him calling my name and sometimes…he sings."

Singing. Right. Mayberry.

Bertie fiddled with the keys in her hand, avoiding eye contact. "You only have to stay about thirty minutes. Long enough for Scott to forget about me. I've got beer if you're interested."

Yeah, sure. Poor Scott had been mooning over Bertie since first grade. No way was he forgetting about her. Hell, Keith couldn't forget about her and he'd only known her a little over a month. Keith reached for the door handle. "Okay. I could use a drink. But it might take longer than thirty minutes." For what he had in mind.

Chapter 12

LONGER THAN THIRTY MINUTES? OH MY. WHAT DID that mean? Was he a slow drinker due to a medical condition? Like waiting thirty minutes after eating before jumping in the swimming pool? Big, bad, sometimes annoying, slow drinker, but mostly delicious Keith Morgan stood in her small kitchen with the painted wood cabinets and the original green subway tile backsplash. Bertie handed him a cold beer, hoping he didn't notice her shaky hand.

Her kitchen wasn't actually small, but it felt small with Mr. Hunky standing so close. Keith ran his large hand over the scarred butcher block at the end of the old marble countertop next to the stove, checking his surroundings. Bertie had a flash of him running his hand over something smoother than the rough butcher block, like her thighs or her belly or even...*Stop it.*

"Would you like a seat? I have chairs and sofas...you know, things you can sit on in the living room. It's not really a living room, more like a family room, but I have nicer furniture in there so that makes it a living room. Or maybe a parlor. I have rattier furniture on the back porch if you'd prefer that room. It's closed in but we still call it a porch." *Shut up already,* Bertie commanded her babbling tongue.

Keith smiled and sipped his beer, making her dingy white cabinets appear even dingier. Something about him

standing on her cracked cork floors like a Ralph Lauren
model, with tousled hair, scruffy face, and classic, expensive clothes, made her old kitchen appear shabby.

Keith didn't move but studied her face, and then he
took a long, slow pull of his beer, making Bertie weak
in the knees at the sight of his strong throat.

"About that sitting…" Bertie forced her gaze from
his throat to the green split vinyl chairs around the
matching 1950s chrome-and-Formica breakfast table.
She'd been meaning to update those chairs in a killer
croc-embossed, lime-green patent leather, but she hadn't
gotten around to it. Where did she put that vinyl sample?
It must be in her office somewhere.

Keith watched her with hooded eyes as he fiddled
with his beer can. Bertie's heart slammed into her chest
so hard she almost jumped.

"Remember that kiss the other day?" The sexy note
in his voice made her senses quicken.

Remember it? It was embedded in her brain. She
wished she had a video of it. Bertie's brain stuttered,
trying to think of where she'd last seen that embossed
vinyl. Maybe she gave the sample to Gary. She made a
mental note to ask him first thing in the morning.

"Do you?" The glint in his eye clouded her head.

She cleared her throat. Oh, yeah, the kiss. "Sure. It
was a whopper."

Keith's gaze dropped to her mouth and then to her
chin and even lower. Oh gawd. He had the look that a
guy gives before he makes his move, and not in a groping, clumsy way like Scott's version, but in a totally hot
way because he knew what he was doing. The look from
a man who'd had plenty of practice.

"I want to kiss you again," he whispered mere inches from her.

She inhaled his musky scent. Bertie leaned back, her butt hitting the apron of the porcelain farm sink. She locked her knees, fearing they would give out and she'd collapse at his feet. The oath she'd taken about not kissing clients screamed in her head—along with Keith's goal to find a wife and the fact that every woman in Harmony had lined up outside his bedroom door to audition.

"Uh, bad idea," she said, trying not to concentrate on the smooth gray weave of his thin sweater covering his rock-hard chest—the chest she'd like to cover with her mouth instead.

Keith remained poised as if controlling an urge to grab her and maul her against the cabinets. Maul might be a bit harsh, but at this point, Bertie would take it. *Lose control. Do something!* Bertie bit her lower lip, waiting for his next move…hoping…praying.

Keith gave a jerky shrug and shoved his hands in his pockets. "Yeah, you're right." He stepped back and picked up his beer from the table. Bertie missed his heat, and it left her cold and lonely. She wished she could take back her words. *Bad idea.* She wanted to yell, *Great idea. The best idea ever.*

Keith took one last pull of beer and placed the empty can on the table. "I better get going."

Numb, Bertie nodded as he reached for the handle on the kitchen door.

"Thanks for the ride and all."

"No problem." Keith pulled the door open.

"Good night."

He glanced over his shoulder. "Yeah, see you soon."

"Okay. Uh, Keith?"

He turned back with eyebrows raised. Bertie didn't think—she launched herself at him and hoped he'd catch her as she attached her lips to his. Keith, being a quick study and a professional athlete, held Bertie tight and kicked the door shut with his foot, all while kissing her as if he only had one more day to live. His restless hands moved to her legs and then around her bottom as Bertie wrapped her legs around his waist. He moved blindly across the kitchen until she bumped the side of the butcher block. Keith hoisted her on top, his lips never leaving hers as he pressed his heat into her, melting her bones. The kiss turned hot and wild. He tasted like beer and raw passion. Keith sucked her tongue inside his mouth and she followed him, kissing him and indulging her craving. He was so good—so good at making her feel this way, making her want to do things she had only dreamed of doing. Mindless, Bertie fell, body and soul.

His hands skated up the sides of her thighs, and he settled more intimately between her legs. Bertie ran her fingers up his shoulders and through the silky texture of his thick hair curling around his collar. He trailed kisses around her jaw and down her neck. His hand found her breast, cupping it, and she moaned deep in her throat. Bertie panted as her nipple tightened. She felt the heat of his palm through her T-shirt and satin bra.

Keith made a guttural sound. "I need this." He pushed her T-shirt up over her breasts and unhooked her bra with a flick of his wrist. His lids lowered and his breathing turned choppy. "Fuck."

"What…"

Keith grabbed both her wrists and shoved them

behind her, holding them in place with one hand, arching her back toward him as if offering her breasts up for his pure enjoyment.

"Keith, I…" Bertie panted.

"Shhh. Let me…God, you're gorgeous." His head dipped and Bertie jolted from the pull of his hot mouth latched on to her right nipple. All coherent thought left her brain as desire took its place and burned a hole in her head. He kissed her breasts, sucking and pulling and grazing with his teeth. The scrape of his unshaved jaw made her flesh tingle. She wanted more as she struggled for him to release her hands.

"Please. Keith. I need to touch you," she begged, squirming to get closer and press against him. He dragged his lips from the feast he was making of her breasts and gave her a slow, sensual smile. Her stomach clenched into a tight ball. He released her wrists, and she ran her palms under his sweater, bunching his shirt up underneath so she could feel his hot, taut skin. It wasn't enough. Bertie pushed both his shirt and sweater up with greedy hands. Keith helped by reaching behind his head, whipping the offending clothes off, and dropping them on the floor.

Finally. His chest had played a major role in her fantasies, and she needed to touch it with her fingers, lips, and tongue. Keith watched from beneath hooded lids. Bertie's palms trembled as she covered his tight nipples and feathered kisses along his throat. She could feel his ragged breathing. Her bold hands moved across his chest, and beneath her touch, his muscles bunched. Keith growled and slanted his mouth over hers in another crushing kiss. Beneath her tulle skirt, Keith started to push her stockings down.

Bertie gripped his lean waist. "Wait. Shouldn't we…here?"

Keith had already worked her stockings halfway down her thighs. "Here. Now," he growled.

He cut off her objections with his mouth and shoved her panties down, sliding his fingers inside her slick heat. "God, you're wet," he groaned against her lips.

Bertie started to see stars as his skillful fingers pushed in and out in a slow, hypnotic rhythm. Her eyes squeezed shut and his name escaped her lips, part moan, part sigh. Keith's thumb circled above his fingers against her aroused flesh. Bertie began to shudder as a climax built with every masterful stroke.

"Come for me," he rasped, biting into her lower lip. And Bertie did. She gripped his shoulders and moaned his name as her world turned upside down. Keith crushed her to his chest as tremors shook her body and rippled across her flesh.

When the sizzling inside her body subsided, leaving her boneless, Bertie floated back down to earth. She gulped air into her lungs. Her head rested in the crook of his neck and she reveled in his musky, heated scent. Keith's breathing slowed and he pulled back enough to peer down into her relaxed face. Naked desire filled his dark, smoky eyes.

"Where's your room?" He started to lift her from the battered butcher block.

"Huh?" Bertie shifted uncomfortably, suddenly appalled at her location and what she had just done. Her stockings and panties were twisted around her knees, her shirt was wrapped around her neck like a noose, and she had no idea where her bra was. Her hair had fallen from her ponytail and hung damp against her neck. She stole a glance at Keith, and of course, he looked even more scrumptious in his rumpled state. Passion agreed with him, softening all his hard edges.

Keith cradled her face in his palms and pinned her with his intense gaze. "We're not finished. I have to—" Keith stopped and his head jerked up.

"What?"

"Shhh." He put a finger to his lips. And then Bertie heard it.

"Bye bye, Birdeee…I'm gonna miss you sooo."

"Oh gawd!" Bertie pushed at Keith's chest, hopped off the butcher block, and scrambled to pull her stockings up. She stumbled into Keith, practically knocking him over. "Crap! Crap! Crap!"

"What the fuck?" Keith hit the back of the table but managed to keep Bertie upright. She hopped away and he snatched up his shirt and sweater from the floor, shoving his arms through the sleeves as the noise outside grew louder.

"Bye bye, Birdeee, why'd you have to gooo?" Scott Douglas crooned off-key from her backyard.

Bertie gave up on the twisted stockings that wouldn't go any higher than mid-thigh and shoved her arms through the sleeves of her T-shirt without a bra.

"Bertha Mavis! I know you're in there. Get out here right now before I let him sing another verse," Liza bellowed outside the back door.

Bertie froze. Alarm bells went off. Why was Liza here? Keith pushed his fingers through his hair in irritation, which only made their groping escapade more obvious. His inside-out sweater didn't help either.

"Don't make me come in there," Liza threatened as Bertie heard her stomping up the walkway.

Bertie tugged at her T-shirt and made sure her skirt covered her ecstatic female parts that mere seconds ago had been singing and doing the boogie-woogie. "Coming. Hold your horses," she called out. "I can't believe this. What is Liza doing here?"

Shock had taken a turn for the worse and full-blown panic had set in. Bertie glanced at Keith one last time, and the look of utter disgust marring his features would be imbedded in her brain forever. What had they done? She yanked open her back door just in time to stop Scott from belting out another verse. The cool evening breeze whooshed, mocking her heated cheeks and highly sensitive kitty bits that still purred.

"What?" Bertie asked. Liza had a death grip on Scott's shirttails. "Why did you bring him here?" Bertie spoke to Liza but watched Scott as he swayed on his unsteady feet.

"Hey there, B-b-bertie. Would you like me to sing s'more?" Scott wore his goofy and usually adorable grin, except tonight Bertie wanted to stomp her feet and yell at him for ruining the best sex she'd never had.

"He wouldn't go home peacefully until I had driven him here. Next time, call a—" Liza stopped talking. She studied Bertie, noting her disheveled appearance. "What have you been up to?" She raked her gaze from Bertie's tangled hair down to her twisted stockings and zeroed in on her braless state. "If I didn't know better, I'd think—" To complete Bertie's mortification, at that moment, Keith stepped into view. Liza's eyes flared with disbelief, then she narrowed them at Bertie. "My, my, my. What have we here?" Liza waggled her fingers. "How you doing there, Prince?"

Bertie wanted to smack that silly expression right off her sanctimonious face. "It's not what you think," she said through clenched teeth. It could've been. Bertie's entire body sighed in disappointment because they'd been rudely interrupted by a bumbling fool and a know-it-all ex-prom queen.

Liza raised one eyebrow. "Oh, really?"

"Screw you," Bertie growled.

"Looks like the Prince's already taken care of that."

Keith pushed past Bertie and hurried down the back steps as if leaving a burning house. "You need any help with Frank Sinatra, here?" he asked Liza, jerking his thumb at Scott, whose head flopped around his neck like a broken daisy on its stem. Keith didn't glance at Bertie. Didn't even acknowledge her. He blew past her so fast, her skirt almost flew up around her face. Okay, he regretted what almost took place, and yeah, maybe they went a little crazy on the whole groping, making out, and giving Bertie the best orgasm she'd ever had. Ever.

But the complete brush-off. That was plain cold. It wasn't like she jumped him. Okay, well yeah, she jumped him. But he could've stopped. He didn't have to swirl his tongue in her mouth and shove half her clothes off and suck on her...*stop it!* Bertie crossed her arms over her betraying breasts, hoping Liza with the eagle eye didn't notice.

Liza's gaze darted from Keith's stony expression to Bertie's flushed face. "Nope. I got everything under control. Don't let me scare you off."

"I have to be going." Keith ducked his head and

shoved his hands in his jean pockets. His boots stirred up the gravel on the driveway as he made his way to his car parked on the side. Both Liza and Bertie watched him leave. No wave good-bye. No wink. No plans to see her later.

Bertie released a huge pent-up breath. Her professional life and personal goals had suffered a huge setback. She didn't have time to be playing a hormonal teenager lusting after the gorgeous high school jock. The ramifications from this stupid, stupid, careless act made her mind spin. She was already up to her ass in alligators and she was wearing muskrat underwear.

"Wow, Bertha. Congratulations. Didn't know you had it in you. If I'd known you were doing the dirty deed, I wouldn't have stopped by with Scott." Liza made her way up the back steps as if Bertie had invited her in.

"Stop calling me Bertha." Bertie pushed her tangled hair behind her ears. "It's late. You need help getting Scott home?" she mumbled and then frowned. "Where is Scott?"

Liza's head popped up and both she and Bertie scanned the dark night. A dim glow from the outdoor sconce reached only a few feet from the back porch to the yard. Beyond that, the ground was draped in darkness. Liza shrugged.

Bertie jumped off the steps. "Scott?" Bertie stopped. "Do you hear water?" Both she and Liza listened. The sound of water streaming hit their ears.

"Scott Douglas!" Liza yelled.

"Over here. Had to take a whiz."

Bertie smacked her forehead with her palm. Holy moly. Scott Douglas was peeing on her precious

Japanese maple. "Scott, if that tree dies, you're buying me a new one." Bertie had to yell to be heard over Liza's howling laughter.

Chapter 13

LIZA DEPOSITED SCOTT SAFELY HOME IN HIS MOTHER'S caring arms. Shirley Douglas cradled Scott's snoring head on her shoulder. Shirley's mouth said thank you, but her eyes clearly said she thought Liza was the devil incarnate and had lured her precious son over to the dark side of hell.

Earlier, Liza had been prepared to dump Scott on Bertie's doorstep. In fact, she'd been gleefully looking forward to it until she laid eyes on Bertie's disheveled clothes and swollen lips and recognized what Bertie had been up to and with whom. Liza had witnessed the obvious attraction between Bertie and Keith back when they'd argued over the ladder and wallpaper. She'd suspected then that Keith wanted to fondle more than luxurious velvets and nubby chenilles. He had looked at Bertie like he'd just been released from months of solitary confinement and she was his salvation. Liza chuckled as her Beemer zipped down the empty street. She might stick around a little longer to see how all this played out. Bertie provided more entertainment for the people of Harmony than the State Fair. Bertie was the glue that kept this town vibrant and moving forward. And the beauty of it all was that Bertie had no clue. Liza would enjoy watching her fight her attraction to the bad boy of tennis. Much better than sitting home and watching *Housewives of New Jersey* or licking her own wounds.

Liza's cell buzzed, and she grappled for it on the passenger seat. She blew out a calming breath as she recognized the number that should be making her turn her car toward the interstate instead of parking it in her driveway. She almost let the call go to voice mail…almost.

"Hey," Liza said.

"Where are you?" he asked. Liza melted a little every time she heard that deep, comforting voice.

"I dumped Scott at his mom's and was heading home." She kept her voice steady.

"Don't."

Liza gripped the blue rubber cover to her phone. His sigh sounded a lot like frustration and desire mixed together.

"Come over. I need to see you." He tempted her with his honesty and his need. She kept quiet. "Don't you think we should see where this goes instead of avoiding each other?"

"I'd gotten pretty good at avoiding you," she finally answered.

"Yeah? And how's that working out for you?"

Like crap. Terrible. More miserable now than fourteen years ago. "We decided a long time ago that this was never going to happen. What happened to that?" she asked.

"We were young and immature." He hesitated and Liza held her breath. "Come on. We owe it to ourselves. Haven't you always wondered?"

Yeah, that was what got her into trouble the first time. Heart racing, she increased her speed. This could be the biggest mistake of her life. Or…this could be what she'd been searching for. "See you in fifteen."

There was a beat of silence. "You won't regret it." He sounded relieved, and her heart kicked into high gear. "I'll be waiting." And then Cal Anderson ended the call.

—◦◦—

Keith paced over the subfloor in his gutted kitchen and checked his watch for the fifth time. He remembered ordering Bertie to be here at eight on Monday morning, but he hadn't called to confirm the day before. He hadn't spoken to her since he left her standing in her kitchen, looking thoroughly kissed and well satisfied. That night, he'd lost his head and practically done the curvy, bombshell decorator with the killer green eyes and gorgeous breasts on her own kitchen counter. He'd felt the dangerous pull of temptation as he'd drunk the tasteless beer and fought the urge to grab her. And then he'd shaken off the feeling, choosing to be noble and leave her house before he did something stupid. And he'd almost succeeded. *Damn*. He'd been so close. His foot had been out the door… and then she'd jumped him. No, maybe threw herself at him would be more accurate. Either way, she'd left him no choice. He'd had to grab her. Once he'd filled his hands with her warm body and she'd given him a kiss that almost blew his head off, he'd been a total goner.

What had he been thinking? He hadn't. Keith's palms began to sweat as he rubbed them down his cargo pants. Did he not learn anything from his past? Did his miserable, dysfunctional marriage not teach him a damn thing? He considered himself a fairly intelligent guy. He'd made good grades in school—good enough to attend Princeton. Yeah, his tennis had certainly helped, but even without tennis, Keith's grades and scores had been high enough to get in.

But somewhere, somehow, he had a screw loose. He had a masochistic tendency when it came to women and relationships. The more torturous, the more he fell— hook, line, and sinker. Show him a woman who could wreak emotional havoc like a category five hurricane or a mega tidal wave, and he'd attach himself to her like a burr under her saddle.

The same thing had happened with Adriana. He'd fallen for her sultry brown eyes, her sculpted, talented lips, and her round curves she'd wrapped in shiny spandex and sparkly Lycra. Forget the fact that she'd targeted him because he was a big tennis star. Or because she found a permanent way out of her family's one-bedroom apartment in Little Havana and into a high-rise on Ocean Drive. None of that registered with him. He had followed her lead like a drooling St. Bernard on a leash, not caring that they were drunk most of the time and playing with fire. He didn't wake up from his lust-filled haze until she shoved a stick under his nose from a pregnancy kit indicating she was knocked up. Keith remembered staring at that stick and its pink plus sign like he was looking into a crater of molten lava at the exact same moment he'd lost his balance. Terrified didn't begin to cover his emotions. That pink plus sign sobered him faster than an IRS audit. That powerful little sign marched his ass down an aisle and made him say, "I do." Not exactly an aisle. More like the courthouse steps, but it didn't change the end result. Keith had married a woman he didn't love because she carried his baby.

He'd been atoning for his sins ever since. He didn't

need a therapist to tell him that his mother had fucked him up. He knew it already, and having a therapist confirm it with a bunch of psychobabble only made him feel worse and more out of control. He felt abandoned after his dad had died and his mother flitted from house to house and then country to country. He spent more time in boarding schools than in a stable home. He reminded his mom of what she'd lost—his dad. The love of her life.

He got all that. On paper, it all made perfect sense. But it still didn't stop him from wishing he'd tried harder, showed her more affection, and listened to her talk. Even when it was hard and she rambled or, worse, cried. Instead, he sulked and hid in his room. Maybe if he'd been a better son, they could've made it work as a family.

Keith shook his head. Yeah, when birds grew lips. He needed to break his cycle of fucked-up relationships. The hard-knock lessons he learned from his mom and the drama from Adriana should be embedded in his skull. And he should be smart enough not to repeat the past. He had Maddie and this broken-down house. One was perfect and the other would be as soon as the renovations were complete. He'd been given a second chance by his interfering, domineering, but well-meaning aunt. Maddie deserved a better home and a loving family. And Keith planned to give it to her. He already had the perfect candidate picked out. He needed to stay focused and keep his eye on the ball. Even on his worst days on the tennis court, as long as he kept his eye on the ball and relied on his training, he could turn a bad match around. One point at a time. Because, like tennis, he had no intentions of losing.

Keith picked up a broom and started sweeping the dust from the construction. It would be only a matter of days before he needed to move out completely. The major overhaul had started. The kitchen and master bath had been gutted. Each day, he breathed and ate more dust. He looked up at the sound of the front door closing and waited.

Bertie entered the kitchen wearing dark jeans with a long green sweater that covered her entire torso and fell mid-thigh. The sweater did a great job of hiding her shape—but not good enough to keep him from remembering. She'd twisted her hair in some sort of knot or bun, reminding him of his third-grade teacher, but without the pinched, disapproving expression. No. Bertie wore a wary expression. No smile. Just wide, green eyes that looked as if they might pool with tears any minute.

"Thanks for coming so early," he heard himself say, clearing his throat. Bertie gave a jerky nod. "Uh, about what I said—"

"Please. Don't." She stepped farther in the kitchen, clutching her orange tote as if it held rare jewels. "I was out of line, and I'm sorry for my behavior." Her gaze darted around the room, taking in everything from the holes in the walls to the exposed plumbing pipes, but not him. "You have every right to fire me." She lifted her gaze to him finally. "I hope that you won't, but I'd understand if you did."

Keith leaned against the broom handle, thinking that this frightened gal apologizing for kissing the hell out of him and allowing him to worship at the altar of pure feminine perfection didn't resemble Adriana at all. Stress, and maybe even fear, ruled her face. She didn't look at all like the person who jumped him and pressed herself to him in fiery need and desire. Or the person who allowed him to touch her in all the right places. No. She looked as if she wished the entire episode had never happened and she'd made the biggest, stupidest mistake of her whole life. Which kind of pissed him off. He couldn't stop thinking about how close he came to being inside her and how he burned to be there. She appeared to have been beating herself up for twenty-four hours, waiting for the piano to drop.

"I wasn't referring to that, and please, don't apologize. If anybody should apologize, it should be me," he said. She bit her lower lip and listened. "I'm sorry for, uh…" He cleared his throat. "For attacking you the other night. It was wrong, and I won't let it happen again." She crossed her arms as if hugging herself and nodded. "And I'm sorry for what I said about Maddie. I don't have a problem with you working with her." Relief and a little color washed over her subdued face. "We spent the day at the beach yesterday and she was so…um…excited about her room." Bertie inched closer, her troubled eyes cleared with anticipation. "Anyway, Maddie really likes you and…" Keith leaned the broom against the wall. "I want you to fix her room and make it special."

Bertie nodded but remained silent. Keith moved close enough to catch the trace of blooming flowers that seemed to float around her as if she lived in a garden. She had dark smudges under her eyes, probably from lack of sleep or stress or fear.

"I'm still on the job?" she asked.

"Yeah. And I promise not to make it too difficult for you. I'll stay out of your way as much as possible."

Bertie inclined her head, shuffling her black wedge shoe over the dusty floor. "We can keep the same arrangement for now," he murmured. His hand reached out of its own accord, and his finger touched the line of her jaw. Bertie trembled. Keith's palm cupped the side of her face. "The one where Gary oversees the big stuff." Her throat worked as she swallowed hard. "I think it's for the best," he said as he leaned forward and inhaled. Her perfect lips parted on a sigh, and she swayed toward him. "Bertie…I need—"

"Dad! Where are you?"

Keith and Bertie jerked back as if a geyser shot straight up between them. Goddammit. He was a sick fuck. He had absolutely no control around this bewitching goddess. He needed therapy and then drugs and maybe even a frontal lobotomy, because she was like a crack pipe that stole his mind and killed his inhibitions.

Bertie fidgeted with the tote stuffed with samples and crossed the room to the demolished mudroom. Keith rubbed his hand over his face.

"In the kitchen, honey."

Maddie came flouncing in, her hair in a lopsided ponytail and wearing a big smile. Her face shone with pure exuberance mixed with the perfect amount of innocence. She wrapped her skinny arms around Keith's middle and gave him a big squeeze.

"I'm so excited. Is Bertie here yet?" she asked. Keith kissed the top of her head, breathing in her clean hair and Maddie-smell that calmed him even in the worst of times.

"Hey there," Bertie called from behind them. "I'm ready to go, girlfriend. I've got lots to show you."

Maddie bounced around Keith and smiled at Bertie, flashing her slightly crooked, but perfect all the same, teeth. "Hey! Where should we start? Do you have fabrics and colors and things like that to show me?"

"Oh yeah. And much more. Now this is serious business, so we need to focus and make smart decisions." Bertie started to sling the heavy tote over her shoulder, but Keith stopped her and grabbed it.

"I'll take that. Where do you want it?"

"Let's get started," Maddie said, unaware of the crackling connection between him and Bertie.

Bertie frowned at the dusty kitchen. "I've got a good idea." She turned Maddie toward the door. "We're going to hit a great showroom in Raleigh, about fifteen minutes away, that has all kinds of fabrics, trims, and carpets. We'll set up shop on one of their large worktables, and you and I are going to make some magic." She gave Keith a nervous glance. "If it's okay with your dad."

Keith tugged on Maddie's loose ponytail. "Sounds good. Listen up, Poo." He wrapped his arm around her shoulder and squeezed. "Bertie is the expert here, so you need to listen to her. Okay?"

Maddie nodded. "I know, Dad. She's my interior designer. I'm not an idiot."

Keith's gut tightened as he chuckled at his smart-aleck daughter. "Just so we're clear: No black walls. No boy band posters tacked up everywhere. No disco ball hanging from the ceiling."

"Dad! I don't even like black walls. And we'll talk about the posters." The imp kissed him on the cheek.

"That's settled. Let's hit the road," Bertie said.

"Maddie head on out to Bertie's car. We'll be there in a minute." Maddie skipped from the room, humming. Keith faced Bertie. "She's really looking forward to this. She talked about nothing else all day yesterday." Bertie lips twitched into a pleased smile. "I don't care what you spend, but keep it tasteful."

Oh crap. That did it. Her eyes narrowed, and she crossed her arms under the shapeless sweater, outlining her fantastic breasts. Keith could worship at those perfect mounds of flesh for years and never get tired. *Focus.* She was about to rip him a new one. And he deserved it.

For your information, I don't do 'tasteless' interiors. I'm creative and clever, and I always give the client exactly what they want—*after* I've convinced them that my way is right."

"Uh-huh." Keith chuckled at her petulant speech. "If you say so. I'll be looking forward to that convincing part that I already know you're so good at." Bertie's mouth flew open and then she blasted him with a deep scowl. "I'm kidding. Now get moving before my kid bounces her way across town from excitement." Keith gave Bertie a gentle shove toward the front door.

"Gary will be here in a few minutes to oversee the construction," Bertie said in a very businesslike tone. "Maddie and I will be working at Carlson Fabric House."

Keith opened the car door for Bertie and placed her tote in the backseat. "Good. I'll drive over to Raleigh around noon and take you guys to lunch. How does that sound?" He peered into the front seat at Maddie who was already buckled in.

"Will we be done by then?" Maddie asked Bertie.

Bertie nodded. "We should have enough to show your dad by then."

"Great. It's a date."

Bertie fiddled with the key in the ignition. Keith gave a quick wave to Maddie as Bertie backed out of the driveway. He could do this. Bertie and he could have a business relationship. He trusted her design talent and ability. She'd make his falling-down house a real home. And he had a solid, well mapped-out plan that involved marrying a sweet girl with great mothering instincts. But until then, that didn't preclude him from enjoying Bertie's company. Besides, Maddie was crazy about her, and Keith didn't want to take anything away from his daughter's happiness. Yep. He could do this. They'd work on cordial, businesslike terms…like two old friends.

Until the next time she jumped him.

Then, he would not be responsible for his actions.

Chapter 14

BERTIE SMOOTHED THE FLOWERED SHEETS OVER THE twin bed in her old bedroom. She stood and checked her surroundings: clean sheets, clean set of towels, Kleenex, night-light, tween magazines on the nightstand, and a glass for water. Bertie gave a quick nod of approval. That should do it. She checked her watch. Maddie would be arriving in fifteen minutes for their girls' night. Since Keith had plans tonight in Raleigh, Maddie had shamelessly begged to sleep over while he was out. Bertie didn't mind. Maddie had been delightful to work with, and they had forged a nice designer/client bond. Maddie showed a creative flare for bold patterns, which Bertie always enjoyed more. It beat the passé, tired plaids in burgundies and greens that most of her old lady clients preferred.

For the past weeks, Bertie had been busier than a one-armed paper hanger, placing orders for fabrics and furnishings for every room in the house. Except the master. She hadn't had the courage to approach Keith about his bedroom. It felt too personal and got her all hot and bothered. She knew his king-size platform bed with the upholstered leather headboard was being trucked up from Miami. But all Bertie could think about was being his personal Sealy Posturepedic. Even though she and Keith had fallen into a companionable working relationship, despite the sizzling current that still zapped them,

Bertie gave serious thought to dumping the master bedroom plan on Gary. Maybe he'd have better luck in the swooning department.

Keith had kept his word and allowed Bertie space to do her job. He'd even approved most of the fabrics and colors that Maddie had selected, but he ix-nayed a hot pink hair-on-hide for a bench at the foot of the bed and a bright lime-green accent fabric for pillows. So they compromised and settled on a great aqua-blue stripe and a subtle lavender animal print for the bench, which made Maddie happy and met Keith's criteria.

Gary and the construction crew continued to work on the newly designed kitchen and master bath, and Keith worked right along with them, which she had to admit was hot as hell. Of course, he continued to work without a shirt, which was causing quite a stir with the single female population. Yesterday, Bertie shooed three Mrs. Morgan wannabes out of the house and posted a Do Not Disturb sign on the front door. The three-ring-circus atmosphere was slowing down their progress.

As for her unrequited lust for His Hubbaliciousness, Bertie tamped down her inner kitty meow, going days without jumping his finely formed frame. This had been no easy feat. Every time she'd been by the house to answer questions, she would catch Keith watching her with a certain look in his eyes. A look that had nothing to do with the dark walnut stain she'd selected for the wood floors or the Venetian plaster she insisted on for the walls, but a look that had everything to do with desire, tumbled sheets, and heavy panting, all directed at her. Bertie drank lots of ice water to cool her overheated parts and stuck close to Gary, avoiding Keith as much as possible.

Besides, she didn't just fall off the cotton wagon. She knew Keith's "appointment" tonight was code for "date." She didn't need to complicate matters by throwing herself at him to satisfy her craving and end her horizontal tango drought, because it was clear as a bottle of Evian that *she* was not going to become the next Mrs. Morgan.

No need to risk losing an obscene ton of dough because she wanted Keith to ring her rusty, cracked, un-rung bell. Bertie had written her goals down and committed them to memory. One: Finish Morgan house in less than two months. Two: Collect $150,000 big ones. Three: Make $100,000 donation to Dwelling Place. Four: Get the hell out of Dodge and experience the big world of design. If she happened to meet a wonderful guy who wanted to get married and have a couple of kids along the way, she'd be open to entertaining that possibility.

Her new life hovered around the corner, where she could explore another city and reinvent herself at the same time. She stayed awake nights imagining glorious scenarios, all starring her as a fabulous designer being featured in *Veranda* magazine, standing in front of her plantation-style home with her clean-cut son and her adorable daughter in a smocked dress by her side. And her gorgeous, successful husband, wearing a sexy grin along with a tweed jacket and riding boots, looking a lot like the latest Ralph Lauren model, with his hand possessively resting on her shoulder. And the article would be chock-full of information on Bertie's remarkable design career and glossy pictures of the interiors of her spectacular home. Two more months and she could start making that dream a reality. Okay, so maybe the male model was a bit of a stretch, but since it was her dream, she was leaving him in.

The doorbell chimed and jerked Bertie out of her daydream. She adjusted her black V-neck sweater and checked her hair in the mirror before racing down the stairs in her bejeweled flip-flops.

"Hey. You're right on time," Bertie said, opening the front door to Maddie and her hunky dad. *Down, hungry alley kitty.* Maddie had a pink pillow covered with fairies smashed to her chest, and Keith held her overnight bag. "Come on in." Bertie stepped back, opening the door wider.

Maddie didn't hesitate as she bounded over the threshold, taking in her surroundings like a happy puppy. Keith followed, but he kept his gaze on Bertie.

"Where would you like her things?" he asked.

"I'll take those and put them in her room upstairs. Maddie, make yourself comfortable. In a minute, we'll watch a movie and eat dinner." Bertie reached for the small suitcase, but Keith didn't release it.

"Show me the way, and I'll take her bag."

Bertie gave Keith a long, hard look. His offer had nothing to do with being chivalrous, but everything to do with checking out her home—as if she ran a house of ill repute.

"Suit yourself." Bertie peeked her head into the living room where her flat screen TV sat on top of a painted antique chest. Maddie had already curled up on the comfy, off-white chenille sofa and was punching buttons on the remote. "Maddie, you want to see your room?" Bertie asked.

"Later. I'm checking a show on the Disney channel.

You don't mind, do you?" Maddie suddenly looked up, realizing that she'd made herself at home without being invited.

Bertie laughed. "You're fine. I'll be right down."

"Maddie, stay put. I'm going to take your bag upstairs. And don't be watching the Kardashians," Keith said in a stern tone. Maddie gave an exaggerated eye roll but kept her mouth shut. Smart child.

"Okay, concerned dad, right this way." Bertie led Keith up the stairs and down the hallway to her old bedroom on the left. "My old room." She gestured with her hand. "You can put her bag on this bench, here."

Keith moved toward the old bench with the rush seat and spindle legs that Bertie had inherited from her grandma. He studied the room as if he expected a pimp or a bunch of horny teenage boys to pop out from behind her closet or under her white wrought-iron bed with the crocheted bed skirt.

"You can check the closet and behind the chest if it'll make you feel better." Bertie opened the top drawer on her dresser. "No drugs or alcohol here. I did a clean sweep earlier."

Keith crossed his arms over his chest and frowned. "You think this is funny?"

"No. I think you're being ridiculous and even insulting," she snapped back.

"I'm sorry. But I can't be too careful. I know what kids do these days. Hell, I did it when I was a stupid teenager."

"Stupid adult too," Bertie muttered under her breath as she closed the drawer and adjusted the monogrammed linen runner on top.

"Which should make me a damn expert."

Bertie glanced in the mirror at Keith only inches behind her. She sucked in a breath, hoping he didn't notice. He was close enough that his musky aroma clouded her head. She gripped the edge of the dresser to keep herself from swaying back and relaxing into his hard, yummy chest.

"Look, I know I'm a neurotic dad. Actually, I'm a lousy dad. I haven't been there for my kid when I should've been. I guess I'm trying to make up for lost time."

Bertie whirled around, forgetting that she shouldn't be touching him. She didn't care. "You're not a lousy dad. And it's not too late." She gave Keith's forearms a squeeze. "Maddie adores you, and if you ask me, she seems like a pretty smart kid. Well-adjusted. Stop beating yourself up." Keith's dejected expression slowly vanished as he quirked his firm lips.

"Yeah? I'll try to remember that. Thanks."

He brushed her cheek with a kiss. Bertie froze at the soft contact. Her cheek tingled. Keith slowly pulled back and gazed down at her. Heat sparked in his dark chocolate eyes. The same heat she'd been sensing from him all week. Desire swamped Bertie, making her sway in his direction.

His cell beeped, causing Keith to jerk back and saving Bertie from doing something idiotic, like tying him up with her lace curtains and having her way with him.

"Sorry," he mumbled as he pulled the phone from his pocket. Bertie ingested a howl of frustration along with a litany of curse words for being so stupid. Again! Keith texted back and glanced up as if embarrassed by their actions moments before. Right. Dumb. Dumb. Dumb. He had a date to meet: possible mother to Maddie and all his future gorgeous children.

"I need to get going," he said, crossing her yellow shag carpet to the door.

"There are more rooms up here. Sure you don't want to check them out? For hoodlums and drug dealers?"

"I'm good. Maybe another time." Keith bolted from the room and bounded down the steps. "Maddie, I'm off. Please behave, and don't stay up too late." Keith leaned down to kiss her on the head. "You gonna be okay?"

"More than okay. We're going to learn a new dance routine and do each other's makeup," Maddie said.

Bertie saw Keith's jaw stiffen at the mention of dancing and makeup. What did he think? That she'd dress Maddie up like a Vegas showgirl? Bertie spoke to Maddie but locked gazes with Keith. "Uh, we'll see. First we're going to have dinner, watch a movie, and maybe make ice cream sundaes."

"Bye, Dad. Love you." Maddie had already returned her attention to the TV.

Keith hesitated, checking his watch. Bertie wanted to smack him. "Love you too, Maddie-Poo," he said as Bertie pulled him from the room and then pushed him toward the front door.

"Everything will be fine. Go. Have a good time with…" Bertie waved her hand. "Whoever."

"Yeah. Okay. Thanks again for everything. You need anything?" he suddenly asked, as if he didn't want to leave.

"Nope. We're good. I just stocked up on beer and some great pot." Bertie started at Keith's thunderous expression. "I'm kidding. I'm kidding."

"I'll be back to pick her up at eight o'clock tomorrow.

Make sure she's ready," he ordered, slapping his hand against the doorframe.

"Yes, sir. Now please leave." And she closed the door in his face.

Liza thanked the waitress for her dirty martini as she set it on a cocktail napkin. It was Wednesday night and she was having drinks with one of her old girlfriends from high school. They had chosen a quiet bar in Raleigh in an upscale shopping village. She and Jane sat in a booth across from the bar but next to a window, where they had a good view of the front door and of people strolling outside. It felt good to get away from Harmony and her conflicting emotions about Cal. She and Cal shared a strange and strained history. And after Saturday night and every night since then, Liza had been sort of floating with a silly grin on her face. She had come to the conclusion, with some very persuasive convincing on Cal's part that included great sex and even better orgasms, that being away all these years and working in Chicago hadn't changed anything. She still had feelings for Cal, strong feelings, and apparently he did too.

Getting fired from her firm over a case that she'd put tons of hours into had been a real blow to her ego as well as her career. And later, discovering she'd been viciously sabotaged iced the giant cupcake. Important documents had mysteriously been withheld, and Liza knew her jilted, pissed-off, slimy ex-boyfriend who didn't take rejection well was the culprit, but she didn't have enough evidence to prove it. So, the prom queen of Harmony High had experienced a setback. Wake-up call. Slap in the face. Her ego had taken a huge hit, and it was sobering. Until then, she hadn't believed bad things could happen to her. And after hours of self-examination, she'd realized that maybe she'd been climbing the ladder of success for all the wrong reasons. Life had more to offer than hostile takeovers, mergers and acquisitions, angry stockholders, and demanding boards of directors.

Liza sipped her drink while Jane chatted about her job with a local marketing firm in Raleigh. Liza missed being around her old friends, especially the high school crowd. She and Jane had been cheerleaders together and had served on the Student Council in high school.

"You still love your job? I think that's great." Liza smiled.

Jane flipped her straight brown hair over her shoulder. "There are days I want to shoot myself, but for the most part, I'm happy. And I like living in Raleigh. It's not as bad as it used to be."

"Hmm-mm. If you say so," Liza laughed. "Still not a whole lot of action from what I can see."

"You get used to it. We even have a pro football team now. The Carolina Cherokees. For once, Raleigh is getting the same attention as Charlotte." Jane checked her cell phone. "I asked a few friends from work to meet us tonight. I hope you don't mind."

"Great. Should be fu—" Liza left her sentence unfinished as she peered over Jane's shoulder at the party entering the bar. "Well, would you look at that?"

Jane glanced over her shoulder. "What? Oh. Do you know who that is?" Jane turned back to Liza with wide eyes.

"I sure do."

Keith Morgan…on a date with a possible prospective bride—a young, cute blond. Too young. Good Lord. Did Keith want a wife or another child to take care of? What an idiot. Liza sipped her drink as Keith and his friends arranged themselves around a table tucked in a corner.

"Damn. I can't believe it; here I am talking about our pro football team and in walks Nick Frasier. Isn't he all that? Whew. I would *not* kick that man out of bed for eating crackers, I can tell you." Jane's voice lowered a fraction.

"The tall guy with the blond hair?" Liza asked.

"Yeah, Nick Frasier. I think that's his wife, the one with curly hair. Who are you talking about?"

"Keith Morgan. Ex-professional tennis player. Harmony's newest resident. You should come home more often."

"No kidding." Jane glanced in Keith's direction again. "Is he married? Is that his wife?" Jane was referring to little Alice in Wonderland wearing the black headband.

"Not yet. But he's officially looking, and I guess he's trying her out."

"Look at them." Jane sighed. "What I wouldn't do to be one of those lucky bitches." She and Liza giggled.

"Girl, I'm telling you. You're missing some good stuff. All of Harmony is hot for this guy," Liza said, watching the waitress deliver drinks to Keith's table. His young chirpy ordered a Coke. Guess she wasn't old enough to drink.

"This sounds good. I can only imagine."

Liza slid her gaze back to Jane's animated face. "Let's see…there's Arlene of course, and Jo Ellen and

Mary Ann. And none of them stand a chance. Because guess who's decorating his house?"

"I know. Bertie." Jane clapped her hands.

"The one and only. And you know what else?" Liza leaned in so her voice didn't travel. "Keith has got the hots for her."

"No. Bertie? Really? Wow. Good for her. She deserves it."

Liza savored another sip and nodded.

"You two still sniping at each other? I never could understand why Bertie hated you so much."

Liza's martini suddenly didn't taste as good as it made a bitter path down her throat. She lowered her gaze. "She doesn't hate me. At least, I don't think she does. She's sort of been kind of mad at me for a really long time."

"Yeah, well, I guess stealing her date at senior prom probably didn't help your cause." Jane tipped her drink at Liza.

Or kissing her brother. "No. I'm sure it didn't. But you want to know something?" Liza fiddled with the silver ring on her finger. "I did Bertie a favor."

"What do you mean?"

"Remember Barton Williams? Bertie's date?" Jane nodded, and Liza continued to tell her the story she'd only leaked to one other person. "He was a real jerk. He'd been bragging about how he was doing Bertie some big favor by taking her to prom. He knew she had a crush on him, and he wanted to be the one to rid her of her virginity. He kept talking about her great boobs. It was all a stupid game to him."

"How did you know?" Jane asked.

"I overheard him talking to some guys out in the hall. They were drinking from their flasks." Liza pulled a frown as she remembered that night. "He was so cocky and full of himself. I really didn't want him to be Bertie's first time. I mean, who would want that as a memory, right?"

"No kidding," Jane said. "So how did you end up making out with him? I remember Bertie leaving the prom with this fake smile on her face, acting like everything was fine. I knew she was hurt."

Liza winced as she pictured Bertie in her taffeta green gown, all color drained from her face. "I'm not proud of what I did. I came on to him because I knew he had a thing for me. For all the cheerleaders. It didn't take much to get him to kiss me."

"Does Bertie know why you did it?"

"No. And I don't want her to. I mean, it's better if she thinks I'm a jerk. I don't want her knowing what he said about her."

"I get it. What an asshole." Jane waved the waitress over. "Let's order another round and then take turns peeking at the two most delectable guys in North Carolina. I am seriously thinking about moving back home if that gorgeous hunk is wife hunting. I'd make a good wife."

"He has a ten-year-old daughter. He's really looking for a surrogate mother."

"Shit. Forget it. I don't want an instant family."

Liza chuckled. "I didn't think so."

Jane chatted nonstop about their past and the fun times they used to have. Liza half listened while her gaze continued to dart in Keith's direction. Keith kept pulling on the collar of his brown pullover sweater as if it itched. For a smart guy, Keith Morgan sure exhibited signs of being a complete moron. Half the women in Harmony would be a better match than this timid-looking mouse. Liza couldn't believe he was going to all this trouble when the perfect solution was right under his gorgeous, scruffy chin. Keith didn't want this child bride. He wanted Bertie.

A million thoughts danced in Liza's head. Bertie and Keith would make a great couple. Bertie would keep him on his toes, and she'd be a great mom to Keith's daughter. And Keith could calm Bertie down, keep her from burning out, and give her the love that she deserved. Keith and Bertie needed to stop dodging each other. They needed a friendly push. Being a tough, corporate lawyer had its perks. Liza knew how to push people into doing what she wanted. If only her relationship with Bertie wasn't on such rocky ground, she'd be able to help those two clueless lovebirds—like giving them both a big-ass shove.

<hr />

Disbelief knocked Keith back in his chair, followed by dread as Liza Palmer sauntered over to his table wearing tight jeans, pink cowboy boots, and a shit-eating grin. Conversation came to a complete halt as she sidled up next to him.

"Hello, Prince," she purred. Keith's chair scraped the wood floor as he and Nick both stood.

"Keep your seats, boys." Liza motioned to their chairs.

Keith cleared his throat and made the introductions. Liza shook everyone's hand and introduced her friend,

Jane somebody. Keith invited them to join his party. Liza, always the opportunist, jumped at the chance, while her friend stepped out to make a call. Great. Now he had snoop-dog Liza as an audience to witness his personal bride dating game.

So far, this date held no surprises. It hovered right around mid-pleasant. No drama. No fireworks. It exceeded his expectations, not that they'd been very high. The Frasiers could be intimidating with their larger-than-life personalities, but Gail had managed to hold her own in a quiet, unassuming way. She spoke intelligently about her tennis league with Marabelle and became more animated when she discovered Marabelle had been a kindergarten teacher and they had children's books in common.

For some reason, Keith couldn't get past the difference in their ages. He felt twenty years older, when in reality only ten years separated them. The age gap felt like a massive hole the size of a canyon when Liza, with her all-knowing smirk, kicked him under the table when the barmaid asked for Gail's ID before serving her a glass of white wine. Gail gave a nervous twitter and her hands shook as she rummaged for her license through her sensible black pleather handbag covered in nifty Velcroed compartments.

Bertie's image popped into his head, and Keith knew, like he knew the grip of his own racket, that if Bertie had to show her ID, she would've laughed and made a joke about how she hoped to still be carded when she turned fifty. Jesus. Keith gave himself a mental punch. He needed to stop making Bertie comparisons and focus on his goal: finding someone safe and calm. Maddie needed a stable home with a loving and caring mother who gave her the continuity Maddie craved and he lacked. Gail was perfect for this role. She would help raise Maddie with a steady hand. So what if she was a little shy? Maddie would love her. Hell, they were practically the same age. *Fuck.*

Keith squeezed Gail's cold hand. "Having fun? Boy, I sure am. Why don't we order some food?" He waved the waitress over.

Liza whispered close to his ear, "This is pathetic. I think I'll get drunk."

Chapter 15

MADDIE SWIPED A DEEP PURPLE EYE SHADOW OVER Bertie's closed lids.

"You're gonna love this," Maddie giggled.

"You're not making me look like bridezilla, are you?" Bertie said, keeping her eyes closed while Maddie worked.

"No. More like Lady Gaga."

"Oh Lord," Bertie groaned, and Maddie giggled again, clearly having the time of her life as she rubbed more blush on Bertie's cheeks.

"Almost done." Maddie unfastened the tube of black mascara sitting on the bathroom countertop.

"Here, let me do that. I don't want you poking my eye out." Bertie took the mascara wand from Maddie and turned toward the makeup mirror. "Holy cra—I mean, wow. You weren't kidding." Bertie examined her smoky eyes, pink cheeks, and bright red lips. "I do resemble a rock star, don't I?"

"Told you. Now, put on lots of mascara. It needs to be, like, super dramatic."

Bertie squinted at Maddie through the mirror. "Where'd you learn all this? They don't let fifth graders wear makeup at your boarding school, do they?"

Maddie fluffed her thick hair teased into a poufy ponytail. "No, but sometimes I get to go home with my friend Stephanie for vacations, and we pretend to be rock stars. Her mom has all this makeup and really cool stuff we can wear. She lets us do whatever we want."

Like drink, smoke, date boys? "What falls under 'whatever you want'?" Bertie asked in a casual tone as she glopped another layer of mascara onto her lashes.

"Like we get to dress up in her cool clothes and high shoes and even wear her jewelry and then we sing with Rock Band on Stephanie's Wii. Sometimes her mom records us and we can watch ourselves. It's so funny." Maddie added more blush to her already pink cheeks. "Steph's mom is real nice. Sometimes she lets us bake in her kitchen. But we don't have to clean up our mess because she has housekeepers for that."

Housekeepers. Plural. "Sounds nice." Maddie smoothed the front of a silver, sparkly tank top and fiddled with the knot in the sheer black blouse she'd borrowed from Bertie's closet as an overlay.

"Yeah, it's nice. You know, to be around a family, like with a mom and all. I kind of don't have that." Maddie's voice lowered.

I feel your pain, kid. "I think that outfit needs shoes, don't you? Let's see what else I have in my closet." Bertie squeezed Maddie's shoulder as they headed for her favorite room in the entire house—her kingdom. A walk-in dressing area that housed her wardrobe.

Bertie had renovated what used to be her parents' room by combining both their closets into one large space, which gave her room for all her clothes, shoes, and handbags. Like any girly girl who worshipped at the shoe department of Neimans and Saks, shoes and handbags probably took up two thirds of the space, neatly stacked and categorized on open shelves.

"What do you think?" Bertie asked as Maddie touched the heels of a pair of evening shoes. "You want to try those on?" Maddie had zeroed in on the most expensive pair Bertie owned: her coveted Diors with the silver straps, four-inch heels, and sequined bows.

"Sure." Maddie's mood lightened in the presence of such fabulous blingage.

Bertie pulled the shoes from their box, giving them to Maddie. "Okay, now what should I wear?"

"Let me. I'll pick a pair for you." Maddie scanned the various shelves, lingering over the designer pairs versus the more practical pairs with no names and rubber soles. "Wear these."

Oh my. Again, she selected one of Bertie's favorites, a pair of high platforms in black suede with red rhinestone heels. Bertie remembered purchasing these in hopes of wearing them to a swanky, cool New Year's Eve party in downtown Atlanta, where she'd be rubbing elbows with her new acquaintances and maybe rubbing something else with her hot new boyfriend. Well, since that fantasy had hit the skids, she might as well take them out for a spin with a ten-year-old girl. At least Maddie appreciated them.

"Perfect. Let me get dressed, and then it's time to rock and roll." She smiled at Maddie as they crossed her bedroom to the queen-size bed where Bertie's outfit had been tossed. Bertie pulled the lacy red dress over her head and wiggled it over her breasts and hips. When had she planned to wear this little number? Bertie stopped adjusting the dress for a minute to think. Nothing came to mind. It had been that long since she'd been on a real date or out dancing with friends. Two-stepping at the

Dog didn't count. The Downtown Get Down festival was coming up, but she'd be overdressed in red lace and rhinestones. Just a teensy bit.

Maddie finished strapping on Bertie's sandals and stood up. She wobbled for a second and then settled into the shoes. "Look, they fit." Sure enough. Maddie's junior-sized feet almost fit Bertie's size seven. "I'm taller than you, now."

"Most people are, honey," Bertie laughed as she straightened the long, tight lace sleeves on her dress.

"That's a pretty dress." Maddie's heels slapped the bottom of the shoes as she covered the floor to Bertie's side. "I have a picture of my mom and she's wearing a red dress too. I don't remember when though. I only have the picture."

"It's nice to have pictures to remember our parents by. You know, my mom died when I was fourteen." Maddie's eyes widened.

"You don't have a mother either?"

Bertie shook her head. "And my dad died several years after that. I only have my brother and a few distant relatives."

"My mom died when I was four. I don't really remember her. I have a few pictures though. Dad doesn't know I have the one with the red dress. I found it in a box in his closet."

"I'm sure he wouldn't mind you having it." Bertie didn't know any such thing, but it felt like the right thing to say.

"I guess. He doesn't talk about her much. She died in a car crash." Bertie remembered reading about it online when she'd been snooping. "She was real pretty. She had dark hair like me, but Dad says I look like my Nana Morgan…my grandmother."

"Then Nana Morgan must be gorgeous because you're beautiful."

Maddie's red painted lips lifted into a faint smile. "Do you remember your mom?"

Bertie curled her hand over the rhinestone earring she'd picked up from her jewelry box, feeling the sharp edges stab her palm. "Yeah, sure. I remember certain things. Like how she always had a snack of cheese and crackers waiting for me after school and how she laughed at our silly jokes and how she used to sit with me at night and listen while I read aloud." And how she lost all her hair from chemo and smelled of drugs and pain and death. Bertie gave herself a mental shake and looped the earring in her ear. "But you know who's been like a mother to me all these years?"

Maddie gave her a puzzled look. "No," she said slowly.

"Aunt Francesca." Bertie sat on the edge of her soft-gray tufted chaise longue to slip her shoes on. "She helped a lot after my mom died. She even encouraged me to study interior design. You are so lucky to have her."

"Yeah, I love Aunt Francesca. She visits me at school and takes me out to eat. Sometimes she even lets me invite a friend." Maddie adjusted the black knit skirt by rolling it up at the waist to keep it from falling down her slim hips. "But I still wish I had a mom. Like my friends do. I wish I could live at home with my mom and dad and do things, like go on vacation or make dinner together or sit around and watch TV, like a normal kid."

Bertie stood. "You do all those things with your dad, don't you?"

"Sometimes. But he…" Maddie wobbled in her heels a little as she reached for the bedroom door. "Like, he doesn't know what to do with me. And he doesn't like all this girl stuff. I bet he wishes I'd been a boy."

Probably. "Hmmm. I don't know. I think your dad is pretty over-the-top crazy about you. Look at that great room he's letting you decorate all by yourself."

"Yeah, but I won't even get to use it. I have to go back to boarding school." She made "boarding school" sound like "homeless shelter." Maddie grabbed the handrail as she click-clacked down the stairs. "And it's not like my dad spends a ton of time with me," she said over her shoulder.

Uh-huh. Like tonight. "You guys went to the beach together, and he's taken you to lunch and to dinner at the Dog. You liked that, didn't you?" She and Maddie stood in her living room near the TV and Bertie bent down and gripped the edge of the distressed wood coffee table. "Help me move this out of the way. We need to clear the floor for our dance-a-thon." Maddie pushed as Bertie pulled. "That's good." Bertie straightened.

"It's just that he's so, like, overprotective. He never wants to talk about me getting older."

Poor Keith. Bertie almost felt sorry for him…almost. It had to be hard raising a young girl as a single dad. Bertie should know. Her own dad had sucked at it.

Maddie continued to speak in a frustrated tone. "He won't even let me get my ears pierced. Everyone at school has pierced ears. I'm like the only one. I'm a freak." Maddie flopped down on the sofa, looking like a kicked puppy.

Bertie doubted she was the only girl who didn't have pierced ears. But she remembered that odd, out-of-sorts feeling after her mom had died. "I felt the same way sometimes. And my dad and brother weren't much help to me either, especially when it came to girl things."

"So what did you do?"

"Oh, sometimes I talked to my girlfriends." *Like Liza, the snake.* "And sometimes I'd hide in my favorite spot. My mom kept a room above the Dog where Cal and I could go and do our homework or sit and read. She made us floor pillows and painted the walls a bright yellow. I used to sit in the window seat and think when something troubled me."

"Do you still go up there?"

Bertie chuckled. "Not lately. But most of the time, I used to talk to your aunt. Still do. She's a real good listener."

"Yeah, but she's kind of, you know, old. She's like my grandmother. And that's another thing. I never get to see my grandparents. Nana lives in Italy, and she's never around, and my other grandparents live in Miami, but they don't get along too well with my dad."

Hard to believe. "You know what? I think you should sit your dad down this week and tell him how you feel. And I bet he'll listen and really try to make things better." Maddie's dark eyes clouded with confusion. Bertie eased next to her on the sofa. "Your dad loves you more than anything in this whole world. He may be overprotective, but that's what parents do. That's their job." She patted Maddie's knee. "What else would you like to do with your dad this week? What other activity?"

"I want to play tennis. But he doesn't ever seem to

want to." Maddie played with the stack of shiny bangles on her wrists.

How odd. "Well, he's been working too hard on the house. How about this? I'll give him a couple days off so you guys can play some tennis and have some fun."

"You can do that?"

"Sure. Your dad doesn't know this, but technically he works for me." Bertie could picture Keith blasting her with his supercilious expression.

"That's funny. You can boss him around?" Maddie asked, warming to the topic.

That might be stretching the truth like a giant rubber band. "Yeah, I can tell him that he's in the way and I need him out of the house."

"Do that! Tell my dad he's fired." Maddie started to laugh.

Okeydoke. More likely the other way around, but at least it made Maddie laugh.

Bertie pulled Maddie up from the sofa. "Come on, girlfriend. Let's dance. I need to learn some new moves."

Keith released a breath. Relieved, he pulled out of the parking lot at Gail's apartment complex. His car clocked glowed 10:15. The last time he'd been on a date that had ended so early had been in high school. This particular date fell under the uneventful category, just the way he wanted it. *Right.*

The evening had started out fine and stayed that way. Perfectly fine. No hearts stopped beating. No embarrassing scenes. No marriage proposals…yet. A simple night out, sharing dinner and drinks with some friends.

With the exception of Liza parking her cute butt in the chair next to him and shooting daggers in his direction, the night stayed right on track. Only a few hiccups where Keith could tell Gail felt a little uncomfortable. Like when a couple of pro football players had stopped by the table to speak with Nick and flirted with Liza, Marabelle, and Gail. Gail's back stiffened in her seat. No words or smart comebacks, like Liza or even little Marabelle. Especially Marabelle. Nick had assumed a relaxed pose with his arms folded across his chest, enjoying the exchange. Gail appeared as if she'd rather be castrating farm animals than bantering with a couple of crude football jocks.

Keith reconnected with Gail when he suggested that they grab a coffee at Starbucks, just the two of them. The Frasiers had already shoved off after dinner, which left Liza, who had settled in for the evening, not budging from her seat. She'd blown off her girlfriend earlier, whispering to Keith that watching him squirm was way more entertaining.

When Gail excused herself to use the restroom, Keith told Liza to beat it and made her swear she wouldn't run through Harmony yelling at the top of her lungs about tonight. Liza gave him the classic too-stupid-to-live glare, shaking her head. She gathered her stylish tan leather Prada handbag and then stabbed her pointy index finger at his chest, poking holes. She accused him of being a fucking moron. And yes, she'd said "fucking"…more than once.

After Liza cut out, Keith finished paying the bill. Damn. He missed his life in Miami. He missed his carefree, lazy days and hot, sexy nights. He hadn't had sex in at least five fucking long months. He'd give anything to toss his racket in the air and break his abstinence with-out the noose of marriage around his neck. Francesca's ultimatum strangled him. Shit. He'd better be making the right decision.

Later that night at Starbucks, he and Gail chatted over coffee and dessert and the weight on his shoulders eased. Gail relaxed and even undid the top two buttons of her sweater. At her apartment door, Keith smiled into her clear, cornflower-blue eyes. He palmed her cheek and brushed her lips with a kiss. She didn't jump or slap his face, but she didn't participate much either. As kisses went, it was chaste. G-rated. Not even a hint of tongue. Two pairs of lips pressed together for a nanosecond. And Keith felt absolutely nothing. Just the way he wanted.

Keith stopped his car in Bertie's driveway. He had no reason to go home to his vacuous, dusty house. Besides, he wanted to see Maddie. To make sure she was okay. Make sure she hadn't forgotten anything, like her toothbrush. To assure himself that she knew the rules: no smoking, drinking, drugs, or boys. He'd give her a quick kiss before heading home. That wouldn't be out of line. Fuck it. He didn't need a reason to see his daughter. Keith slammed his car door and stomped up the front steps.

Light poured through the slitted blinds from the front window and Keith could hear music. He knocked on the front door. Nothing but loud music. He knocked again with a little more force. The music blared even louder. He gritted his teeth and pounded on the red-painted door with his fist. Still nothing. Keith grabbed the wrought-iron knob and gave it a violent twist. The door opened and Keith rushed in. What he saw made his blood run cold.

In the middle of the living room, Bertie and Maddie gyrated to some video booming from the TV, using wooden kitchen spoons as microphones and wearing skimpy outfits that would make the hookers on Biscayne Boulevard salivate with envy. Keith blinked and shook his head, hoping that his worst nightmare had not become a reality. Maddie and Bertie had their backs to him as they belted the words to some bad pop song. Keith watched in frozen horror as they rolled their shoulders, shuffled their feet, and thrust their pelvises. Unaware of his presence, Bertie gave a quick hip-hop twirl and stopped short. Maddie followed but ended up bumping into Bertie's back. Bertie's face flamed as red as the dress she wore as she scrambled for the remote on the coffee table and punched the off button.

Steam poured from Keith's ears as if his head might explode. "What in the hell is going on here?" he roared between clenched teeth.

"Dad! What are you doing here?" Maddie had the nerve to glare at him, as if he had no business checking up on her. Keith sharpened his gaze on her. His mouth began to work but no sound came out. His precious, adorable daughter wore some gauzy, black sheer blouse over a highly visible silver, slinky tank top. Slinky tank top with black short skirt and silver stilettos that belonged on a Victoria's Secret model or Adriana, *not* his innocent daughter.

Bertie jumped in front of Maddie, blocking his view. "Uh, hey there. What brings you here? I thought you were on a date...er, uh, appointment."

Maddie pushed her way around Bertie. "*Daaad!* I can't believe this. Are you spying on me?" She stood with her fists pressed into her small hips, accentuating the fact that she still had a little girl's figure. No hips and no waist. Perfection. The way it should be.

"What's with the makeup and hooker outfits?" Keith gestured at their getups, still not believing his eyes. "What happened to watching Disney movies and eating popcorn?"

"Dad! I don't watch Disney movies anymore. They're for babies. I told you we were going to dress up. Besides, you're not supposed to be here!" Maddie stomped her sparkly stiletto-clad foot, jerking Keith out of his initial shock and careening him into anger.

"Don't ever you use that tone with me, do you understand?" Keith took a huge step into the nest of iniquity disguised as Bertie's living room and shook his finger at Maddie.

"B-b-but, Dad. Bertie and I were just having some fun. You ruin everything," Maddie said on a sniffle as tears pooled in her eyes.

Bertie placed her hands on Maddie's shoulders. "Uh, Maddie, honey, your dad—"

"This is *my* daughter. Stay out of it. You've done enough," he growled.

Distress registered on Bertie's face as she took a step back. Maddie's wet gaze darted from him to Bertie. "Madeline, get your things. We're leaving," he ordered using his scary low voice.

"Nooo! I don't want to leave." Maddie sounded close to hysterics. "You leave!"

Bertie gasped as Keith made a threatening step

toward Maddie. "Madeline Amber Morgan, go to your room, *right now!*" he roared.

"I hate you!" Maddie rushed from the room sobbing.

The blast of a cannonball could not have left a bigger hole as Keith rubbed his chest with his fist. His daughter had never spoken to him like that…ever. The sound of her crying carried through the empty stairwell she'd flown up.

"Keith, I…" Stunned, he tore his gaze from the stairwell and swiveled toward Bertie. "I'm so sorry. She wanted to dance…"

Fear, frustration, and terror bombarded him, making him shake inside. He'd left his naïve ten-year-old daughter only a few short hours ago and returned to find a raging, hormonal teenager inhabiting her body. He'd barely recognized her. It was like watching the movie *Alien* all over again. Except worse.

Then he focused on Bertie and his mouth dried up. He'd never been a big fan of the color red. It had always been Adriana's favorite, from shoes to teddies. But seeing all that red lace stretched over Bertie's spectacular curves made Keith want to punch a hole in her wall and roar like a lion.

He sucked air into his starving lungs. "Would you mind explaining to me how I thought I'd left my daughter to a night of Disney movies and instead find her learning the latest titty bar dance moves?" His irrational anger grew as he formed each word.

Fury surged over Bertie's features. "You've got a lot of nerve." For the second time that night, his chest took a beating from a pointy index finger. Bertie, like Liza, jabbed his abused chest three times. "Titty bar moves?

Get your mind out of the gutter. For your information, we were dancing to One Direction, a dopey teen idol group your daughter has been listening to for years. They're about as Disneyesque as you can get with the exception of the damn Mouseketeers!"

"And I suppose this is the latest Baby Gap outfit complete with ho-training heels." Keith indicated Bertie's black shoes with red rhinestones. "And what were you guys eating and drinking? Looks like a confetti of pills and beer to me." He jerked his thumb at the coffee table where a suspicious looking ceramic bowl of colorful pills sat amongst brown beer bottles.

Bertie's mahogany color hair seemed to levitate from her head and her eyes glowed a fiery green. "Pills? Beer? Are you insane?" She marched over and grabbed a bottle along with the bowl and shoved them at Keith's gut. "Try Mike and Ike's and root beer, you moron!"

Keith grappled with the bowl as he recognized the chewy candies. Jesus. What was wrong with him? What made him lose his mind when it came to his daughter? And all rationalization when it came to Bertie? He didn't understand what kept flipping that switch in his brain. "Look, let me explain. I—"

"No. Stop talking," she cut him off. "Now, you listen to me. That daughter of yours is a great kid, and she's done remarkably well without a mother, but she's a girl and she gets lonely. She wants to be with other girls and their mothers. You're her dad and she loves you, but she doesn't feel comfortable talking to you about girly things like hair and shoes and makeup. Or her period."

Keith winced. "Don't tell me—"

"Zip it! I'm not done." Bertie crossed her arms over

her phenomenal breasts and the urge to fall to his knees and pay them homage swarmed him. "Pay attention." Keith's gaze snapped to her stormy face. "She needs someone to open up to. I suggested Francesca, and even though Maddie loves her, she thinks of her as a grandmother. She doesn't feel comfortable telling her everything. So, Mr. Perfectly Insane, quit tiptoeing through the tulips with your wild scenarios and crazy accusations and get busy finding a wife. Maddie needs a stable female influence and you…you need someone to keep you in line." Bertie snatched the bowl and bottle from his hands and plunked them back down on the table.

"Can I speak now?" He gave her a rueful smile.

"Not yet." Bertie gulped and choked on a sob. She ducked her head and pressed her palms into her stomach. Keith reached for her but she backed away. "Just… just hold her dear to your heart. She wants to spend time with you. Don't ever take that for granted. I'd give my right arm to have one more day with my parents—" she broke off in a whisper.

Keith felt the same way about his dad. Over the years, he'd managed to squash the hollow feeling that threatened to crush him. His loneliness and despair propelled him forward in his training, and he'd learned early on how to use it as fuel when he competed in tennis. But Keith didn't want Maddie to feel that she had to go it alone. He wanted to be there for her. He wanted to be her rock whenever she needed it.

Old memories must've been playing inside Bertie's head because her expression turned pensive. She looked fragile and not at all like the growling mama bear protecting her cub that she portrayed minutes before. Bertie had been exactly that. She protected Maddie as if she were her own. She protected Maddie from his colossal blundering and bad parenting. He was grateful for her being the voice of reason to his off-the-rails thoughts.

Bertie cast him a wary look as if he was squirrel-shit crazy, and Keith didn't blame her. He owed her an apology. "I apologize for everything. You're right. I'm an ass."

"And an idiot."

"That too. I don't know what comes over me, but where my daughter is concerned, I'm not rational. I promise, I'll try to work on it." Keith sighed. "Thank you for…being there for her, and thank you for taking care of her."

Bertie chuckled and patted his chest in the exact spot she'd skewered moments ago. "You're a good man, Charlie Brown. A little misguided but good nonetheless. Spend these few days with her. She wants to play tennis with you."

Keith covered her hand with his. He appreciated her advice more than she could ever know. He placed a kiss on her palm. Bertie's sparkling green eyes turned into limpid pools. Her lips parted, and Keith's head dipped. "Ah, Bertie," he whispered, touching his lips to hers.

"Daddy?"

Bertie jumped back and Keith whirled around. There stood Maddie at the bottom of the stairs in her pink flannel pj's with little white kittens. Her small toes curled around the edge of the step. Her face had been scrubbed clean. Gone was the hoochie mama with the caked-on makeup. Keith's heart clammered in his chest. His ten-year-old baby girl was back.

"Um, Daddy, I'm sorry…I'm sorry for all the bad things I said. Please don't hate me. Because I don't hate you. I love you so much."

"Aw, Maddie-Poo. Don't cry. Come here, honey."

Maddie hurled herself at Keith, tears streaming down her face, and he hugged her, never wanting to let her go. "I could never hate you, no matter what you do or what you say. You know that, don't you? I love you more than anything." Keith kissed the top of her clean hair, breathing in the best smell in the world. He heard Bertie strangle back a sob. He cocked his head and smiled at her wet face. "Now, how about we ask Bertie if she wouldn't mind letting you finish your sleepover, what do you say?"

Maddie turned her hopeful but teary face to Bertie. "Of course you can, honey." Bertie held her arms out and Maddie gave her hug. "I'd be so disappointed if you left now." She cupped Maddie's face in her hands and kissed her forehead twice. "Now, why don't you and your dad sit right here for a few minutes while I change, before these killer shoes cripple me." Bertie gestured in the direction of the kitchen. "Help yourself to more root beer and Mike and Ike's. I'll be down in a jiff." She patted Maddie's cheek and squeezed her hand. Relief washed over Keith at being given another chance with Maddie. And as for thank-yous, he owed Bertie a big one.

Chapter 16

"MADDIE, FINISH UP. I THINK YOUR DAD IS HERE," Bertie called as she answered the knock at her front door the next morning.

"Good morning." Keith stood on the other side, looking better than a body had a right to. Too bad he was twisted in the head.

Bertie stepped back. "Hey. Come on in. She's almost done with breakfast." Keith smiled and that's when Bertie noticed he held a beautiful bouquet of pink and orange gerbera daisies mixed with pink peonies. *How adorable. He brought his daughter flowers.* Bertie's heart melted a little at his thoughtfulness. There was hope for him after all.

"For you," he said in his low, smoky voice. "Thank you…for everything." He extended his arm, holding the flowers.

Unable to move, like the rusted Tin Man holding his ax in the air, Bertie's hand was stuck to the edge of the door. Flowers, for her? Bertie couldn't remember receiving flowers from an eligible, single guy…ever.

"Would you like me to put them in some water?" Keith offered since she remained rusted stiff.

Bertie blinked. "Oh. Here, let me. Thank you. You shouldn't have." She reached for the lovely bouquet, wondering where he bought them so early in the morning. Maybe he was dating a florist. "Maddie's in the… uh…um…"

"Kitchen?" he supplied.

"That's it. Kitchen. This way." Keith's soft chuckle trailed behind her. "Maddie, your dad's here. You all done? Keith, can I get you a cup of coffee?"

"That'd be great."

"Daddy!" Maddie jumped up and gave her dad a hug.

"You sleep okay, Maddie-Poo?" Keith ruffled Maddie's hair.

"Yep."

"Not up all night telling secrets?" he teased.

"Nope." Maddie pulled back, giving him a suspicious look. "Why are you dressed in tennis clothes?"

"So we can hit the courts this morning. Want to?"

"Sure. But I need my clothes and tennis shoes from Aunt Francesca's."

"Way ahead of you. Clothes are in the car. Go grab them and you can change here." Before he'd finished speaking, Maddie was racing for the front door.

Bertie still stood in the middle of her kitchen like a teenage dork, holding the bouquet of flowers. "Why don't we find a vase to put these in?" he said, taking the flowers as his warm hand brushed her stiff fingers.

"Good idea. Let me think. Where would I keep vases?" She didn't recall owning any. "Maybe over the fridge. Would you mind looking...up there?" Bertie pointed to the hard-to-reach cabinet above her refrigerator, hoping nothing fell out like an old wok from the 1970s or an old box of condoms...*cookies!* She meant cookies. Bertie's brain had taken a detour as she recalled what they did the last time he stood in her kitchen. An embarrassed flush spread over her neck and cheeks, and Keith smiled like he knew her mind had skipped the tracks and wandered into naughty land.

He pulled down a cut crystal vase that had probably belonged to her mom. "This ought to do it." He put the vase under the kitchen faucet and turned it on.

"I'm ready." Bertie jumped as Maddie reentered the kitchen dressed in a pink Nike tennis skirt with matching top and hat. Maddie stopped and gave her an odd look, like Bertie had shaved initials in the side of her head. Keith placed the vase of flowers in the center of the table.

"Ready to go, Dad?"

"Yep. As soon as I get that cup of coffee Bertie offered me."

Holy doorknockers. She had totally forgotten, so lost in her daydream of Mr. Hubbalicious and his talented mouth and fingers. "Right. Coffee. No problem. Coming right up." Bertie opened the refrigerator and then slammed it closed. That was not where she kept brewed coffee.

"Bertie, you okay?" Maddie asked, still giving her a funny look.

"Never better." Bertie pulled down two pottery mugs and filled them both from the carafe, hoping she didn't spill any with her shaky hand. "Cream or sugar?" She handed a mug to Keith who was settled in one of her kitchen chairs, struggling not to laugh.

"A little cream." His smiling, coffee-colored eyes warmed her to her toes.

"No problem."

"Would you like to join us today on the tennis courts and maybe catch a movie later?"

Bertie stopped, holding a little cow pitcher of cream. "Are you talking to me?" Keith reached for the pitcher, obviously afraid she'd drop it. Smart man. He poured cream in their mugs.

"Yes. I'm inviting you to join us. Is that okay with you, Maddie?"

"That'd be awesome!"

Keith pulled out Bertie's chair. Bertie's brow furrowed. A million reasons came to mind why she shouldn't join them today. The main one that jumped to the forefront waving a red flag was not the to-do list as long as her arm, but the fact that she didn't play tennis. And she didn't relish the idea of making a fool of herself in front of him. Keith gently pushed her into her seat, since her knees had forgotten how to bend, and Bertie murmured a thank you.

"Are you coming?" Maddie bounced in her seat like an excited chipmunk.

"Okay…here's the thing." Bertie cleared her throat. Keith winked in her direction as he sipped his coffee. "Uh, I have a ton of work to do—" Maddie groaned. "On your room, cutie, and I really—"

"I think you deserve a day off. Don't you agree, Maddie?"

"Yeah. Besides, you said you were the boss. You can give yourself a day off."

This was not going well. Bertie would like nothing better than to take some time off, but maybe for a spa day or a little retail therapy. *Not* play tennis with a professional she had wicked, X-rated fantasies about. "Okay, well, here's the thing—"

"Another 'thing'?" Keith chuckled behind his mug.

"You see, I've never played tennis." Maddie's mouth dropped open at that astonishing bit of news. Of course, in her world, where her father had ruled the courts for years, everyone knew how to play tennis. Bertie didn't dare glance in Keith's direction, afraid his eyes might've bugged out. "Never even held a racket. So, I'd be like this goofy dum-dum chasing balls, tripping over my feet, dropping my racket." Maddie started to giggle. "It would not be a pretty sight," Bertie finished.

"My dad could teach you. He's a professional, you know."

Boy did she ever. A professional pain in the arse. A professional daddy on the edge. A professional kisser. *Down, girl.*

"Hmmm, I don't know, Maddie-Poo. She may be right. We've seen her skate, remember?"

Maddie pulled a silly face. "Oh, yeah." She and Keith burst out laughing.

"Hey, I may be a lousy skater, but I can dance, right?"

Maddie nodded but kept laughing.

"Okay, here's the thing," Keith mocked her favorite expression, "today, you're going to learn how to play tennis from one of the top ten tennis players in the world. Maddie, grab your things and load up the car. Bertie, get dressed." Keith rose and placed his mug in the sink and Maddie scrambled from the room, cheering with excitement.

"Did it ever occur to you that I don't own a racket?" Bertie snapped.

"Did it ever occur to you that I have plenty of rackets? Now stop stalling and put some clothes on, preferably athletic and not that red lacy number."

Bertie jerked up from loading the dishwasher and narrowed her eyes at Keith. "What'd you say?" She could've sworn she heard something like "I want to eat off you."

"Nothing." But Keith looked at her as if she had on the red dress and he was peeling it off her with his teeth. Bertie sighed as her inner kitty chased a ball of yarn and woke up her hibernating uterus.

"I know I'm going to regret this." She grabbed her sneakers from the mud room and started to leave the kitchen. "Hey, you're retired. You can't be top ten anymore."

"No. But I've still got it." And Bertie suspected he wasn't referring to tennis. Oh gawd. This was going to be a long day.

Keith drove Maddie and Bertie to the worn-down Jaycee Park on the outskirts of Harmony to get a closer look at the facility he might consider investing in. He signed in and paid the court fee at the front desk. After last night, he wanted to make it up to Bertie and Maddie regarding his bad behavior. He felt crappy for jumping to the wrong conclusions like a psycho, and he despaired over ruining Maddie's night of fun. Flowers always went a long way in the apology arena, and he figured they could all use a day off.

Out on the court, he started with Bertie, giving her a few basic instructions on how to grip the racket and demonstrating how to swing and follow through on a forehand.

Bertie wasn't kidding when she said she couldn't play tennis. But she looked cute as hell chasing down the ball. Maddie tried to help by yelling, "Watch the ball," every time Keith fed one over the net, but it only distracted Bertie and she watched Maddie instead.

After missing six forehands in a row, meaning the strings of her racket and the ball were miles apart, Bertie stomped her foot. "Arrgh. I'll never get this. I give up. You two continue without me."

"Hold up. Maddie, come over here and feed some balls. Let me help Bertie." Keith and Maddie switched sides on the court. Keith held Bertie's racket up. "Let me check your grip." He adjusted her hand slightly. "Okay. Good. Now, remember low to high and always follow through over your shoulder."

Bertie nodded and allowed him to demonstrate the swing as he continued to grip her hand. "Do you feel that?" he asked.

"Uh, feel what?" Bertie sounded a little preoccupied. It probably had everything to do with his arm brushing over her breasts. Because it sure as hell was distracting him.

"The motion? Can you feel it? Pivot with your shoulders, take the racket back, and swing low to high, finishing over your left shoulder." Keith demonstrated the motion several more times.

"Uh, I think I've got it now," Bertie said in a husky voice. Keith released her hand with some reluctance. The faint smell of gardenias from Bertie's heated body mixed with the crisp air and made him a little light-headed.

He cleared his throat. "Maddie, feed a few forehands. Nice and easy." Keith stepped back to give Bertie room to swing. Maddie fed the first two and Bertie missed, but on the third one, she made contact, whacking the ball over the net and deep into the deuce court.

"I did it!" Bertie jumped up and down.

"Yay! Way to go," Maddie cheered.

"Did you see that one?" Bertie faced Keith, grinning from ear to ear like she'd just won the finals at Wimbledon.

"I sure did. I better give Serena Williams a call and tell her she might have a little competition."

"Mock me now, tennis god, but you wait and see. I'm going to learn how to play this game," Bertie said, her nose tilted in the air.

"You planning on taking lessons?"

"Sure. I like that pro over there." She pointed to one of the pros teaching a lesson on court one, sporting long hair pulled back in a ponytail and a Fu Manchu moustache.

"That hack?" Keith laughed. "Not while I'm still around, you won't."

"Really?"

Maddie leaned over the net. "Dad, you can teach Bertie how to play, can't you? Way better than anybody else."

"See? Even Maddie knows a hack when she sees one," he said to Bertie. "Maddie, let's hit a few while Bertie takes a break."

"She's a little brainwashed by all that daddy worship you feed her," Bertie mumbled under her breath. Keith threw his head back and laughed.

Keith drilled Maddie for another forty-five minutes while Bertie sat on the sidelines and made calls, checking up on orders. A small crowd gathered behind the fence at the Jaycee Park to watch him as word spread that he was on the court. Once he and Maddie called it quits, Keith went over and signed tennis balls and pieces of scrap paper. After handing a ball back to a young boy with hero worship in his eyes, Keith looked up to see Dottie Duncan standing right behind the boy.

"Glad to see you gracing our run-down courts with your presence," she snapped by way of a greeting. "This is my grandson Tyler. He was one of your biggest fans when you played."

"Nice to meet you, Tyler." Keith shook the kid's sweaty hand while Tyler beamed up at him with bright freckles and a mouthful of metal. Keith continued to sign a few more balls until the crowd petered off. He shook hands with a couple of pros, talked a little tennis, and then he hefted his tennis bag over his shoulder and left the court, heading for the low, run-down building that housed the lockers.

Inside, Bertie was standing at the front counter next to Dottie. And Keith spotted Maddie over in the far corner, playing an old pinball machine with Dottie's grandson.

"How old is Tyler?" Keith asked, eyeing the kid to make sure his hands stayed on the machine and didn't wander in Maddie's direction. He caught Bertie rolling her eyes as she checked her phone.

"Thirteen. He's a good student and loves tennis. He lives in Raleigh and plays over at the Raleigh Tennis Club. They got a pretty nice facility," Dottie said as she picked up a stack of papers from the counter.

Keith nodded. "Uh-huh. I've played there."

"But this area could use another nice facility. You given any thought to working on the rejuvenation of this park? There's a meeting next week. We sure could use some help."

As in money and piles of it. Keith smiled. "I might stop by." Bertie's head jerked up and she studied him.

"You should consider it your civic duty." Dottie narrowed her blue–eye shadowed eyes at him and then turned her attention to Bertie. "How about you? You going to join the committee?"

For the love of God, Bertie didn't need another activity to add to her already overflowing list. But the rest of Harmony didn't seem to agree. He tried sending Bertie a telepathic message. *Just say no. Come on, you can do it. One little word.*

"Uh, well, sure. Let me check my calendar." Bertie nodded like a maniacal pigeon bobbing its head. Keith wanted to smack his own forehead. This girl needed some serious intervention on overextending herself.

"Actually, Bertie has a massive deadline looming with my house. And I'm real hard-ass to work for." Keith thought he heard Bertie mumble, "no kidding" under her breath. "I'll come to the meeting and fill in for her. If we get desperate, we can bring in Harmony's queen of volunteering."

Bertie gaped at him, and Dottie pursed her coated hot-pink lips. "All right, Mr. Big Shot. Let's see what you've got. Bertie, you're off the hook…for now." Dottie picked up a to-go cup from the Toot-N-Tell. "Oh, would you mind taking care of Sweet Tea for the next three days? I'm taking my grandkids down to Six Flags."

"No problem." Bertie cut her eyes at him as if she could hear the grinding of his teeth. Did she not learn anything? He'd given her the perfect out.

"Good. Come on, Tyler. I need to get you home

before your mama hangs me up by my toes." Tyler trotted over to Dottie as he waved good-bye to Maddie.

After changing clothes in the worn-down, ill-equipped locker rooms, Keith left Harmony and drove the fifteen minutes to Raleigh with Bertie and Maddie to an outdoor café for lunch. Bertie checked her phone for emails and texts and made calls, apologizing profusely for being so rude, but she explained she didn't want to miss any deadlines.

Keith half listened to Maddie tell him for the thousandth time how she wanted to stay home and not return to boarding school, and half listened to Bertie's one-sided conversations into her phone. Some of the calls were related to his house, but the others were all over the place. Like she told the committee for the Downtown Get Down festival that she'd decorate the food tent. And then she talked about ordering plumbing fixtures for something called Dwelling Place, saying she'd put more money in the account. She took a couple of other calls about collecting iPads for the troops overseas, delivering meals, and recovering some barstools at the Dog.

Bertie's phone chirped again, and Keith plucked it from her hand and turned it off. "Enough. You haven't taken a bite of that grilled chicken salad. Day off. Remember?"

"Yeah. Don't work anymore." Maddie shoved some hot fries in her mouth.

Bertie stabbed at her salad with a little too much force. Around a mouthful of lettuce, she said, "May I have my phone back, please?"

Keith snatched a few fries, shaking his head. "Nope. We need to discuss which movie we want to see, and

Maddie wants to ask you some questions about the summers around here."

Bertie flashed Keith the glare of death and then smiled at Maddie. "Okay. Ask away."

Maddie shrugged her thin shoulders, her features morphed into the classic puppy dog look. "Well, I have to spend the summer in Harmony and, like, I won't even know anybody, because I don't go to school around here." Keith's expression remained neutral, waiting to see what she'd pull next. "I mean, it's unfair. Everyone will be going to camp or whatever, like I won't have anyone to hang out with."

Bertie chewed on a piece of ice. "I know lots of kids hang around for the summer. There's the community pool with a massive slide, and the theatre in the park puts on plays. Lots of kids spend time at the lake, swimming, sailing, and boating. At night they grill hotdogs and burgers and roast marshmallows. That used to be one of my favorite things about the summer. Everyone loves going to the lake. And the Jaycee runs sports camps. I'm sure they play tennis, and after what I saw today, you'd be awesome." Bertie picked at the roll on her plate. "What do you normally do in the summers?"

"Usually Aunt Francesca takes me on a trip or we go to her house in the mountains." Maddie pushed a hunk of hair behind her ear. "It's okay. But sometimes it's boring."

"Come on, Maddie. You make it sound like the penitentiary, with only bread and water for three months. You've always had a good time with Aunt Francesca. Most kids would love to take those trips." Keith didn't want to get Maddie's hopes up, but maybe this summer they'd spend time together as a family…with his new wife, Gail. Thinking of Gail while having lunch with Bertie and Maddie made him slightly queasy. But just because he found Bertie physically attractive didn't mean he wanted to be sucked under by a rip current and drown in the exhaustion that made up Bertie's life. He'd already traveled and experienced the world many times during his playing years. Bertie still had that spark and desire to go out there and conquer it with flash and sparkles and fireworks, which she deserved. Anyone with that dream should do everything in their power to make it happen. One day, he hoped to pass the dream on to Maddie, but right now, he didn't need the limelight to make a good life for him and Maddie.

Keith dragged his attention back to the present and caught the tail end of Bertie's story about cheerleading camp.

"…and then I fell off the top bleacher and broke my arm, and that ended my cheerleading career forever," Bertie laughed.

"How did you learn to be such a good dancer?" Maddie asked.

"Yeah, because you obviously can't skate, cheerlead, or play tennis."

"Dad! Bertie did awesome today. It was like her first time, and she didn't grow up around tennis like we did."

Keith chuckled at Maddie's staunch defense of Bertie. He winked at his overextended, workaholic decorator and said, "You're right. She did great for a beginner."

"And I'm only going to get better when I start taking lessons from that good-looking pro. What was his name?"

"Over my dead body," Keith heard himself growl.

"No, that wasn't it." Bertie tapped her chin with her finger. "I think it was Julian. I have his card." Bertie reached for her handbag on the back of her chair.

"You actually got his card?"

"Hm-mm. When you were signing balls for your adoring fans."

"Is this true?"

Maddie nodded. "I think so. He came over to Bertie and started talking, but then I played pinball."

Keith tossed his napkin on the table. "I don't believe this. Like I can't teach you how to play tennis. Do you have any idea how much people would pay to hit a few balls with me? You can't afford me, and I'm offering my talent and years of training for free."

"You think they'd pay a thousand dollars for an hour?" Bertie asked.

"Hell no. More like five thousand dollars."

Bertie gave Maddie a high five. "You were right."

"What's going on?"

Bertie shoved a huge bite of salad in her mouth and smiled while she chewed.

"Madeline, do you mind filling in your dear old dad, please?"

"Well, Bertie was talking to that lady with the big blond hair and the black shirt with the pink ruffles. You know the one—"

"Dottie Duncan, I know. So?"

"So, that lady was saying how they want to have an exhibition match with you, and then Bertie suggested they should have a…you know, where people bid on things?"

"Auction?" Keith supplied.

"Yeah. So people would bid to play with you for like

an hour." Bertie nodded in encouragement. "And Bertie said she bet you could bring in like a thousand dollars, but I told them that people have paid five thousand dollars to hit with you. Like that time down in Florida. Right, Dad?"

Keith sat back hard in his chair. People strolled by their table and gave them curious looks and soft music played from strategic speakers hidden in the ground cover, but he barely noticed. He was too astounded at being "handled" by his ten-year old daughter and his quirky decorator, who did more planning, shuffling, hand-holding, and babysitting than she did decorating.

He crossed his arms. "I'm almost afraid to ask. But what am I being auctioned off for?"

"The rejuvenation of the Jaycee, what else? Dottie asked me if you'd help and I said yes, of course," Bertie said with a cheeky grin. "I didn't think you'd mind."

"Of course." As if Keith agreed to this kind of thing all the time. Jesus. Bertie had an addiction to three little letters. Y. E. S. Not only did she always say yes when asked to volunteer, but now she was saying yes for *him* and volunteering his services. His own agent never assumed he'd support anything without months of calls, emails, contracts, and meetings. But little misguided Betty Boop volunteered his name as if she were bringing a covered dish to the next potluck.

"I merely suggested that it'd be a great way to raise some money. The whole town wants to come out and watch you play. It's not every day we have such a huge celebrity living in our small town midst." Bertie had the nerve to bat her eyes at him.

"Please stop. I'm not sure my huge ego can take much more."

"Come on, Dad. You can bring in so much money. You're the best." Yep. Required sucking-up from his biggest, most loyal fan. "Will you do it?"

Keith paused and gave Bertie a long look. "I need to make sure it's worth my while."

Bertie stopped chewing as her brows slammed together. "Worth *your* while? You won't do charitable work without making a profit? That's obscene!"

"Huh? I don't get it," Maddie said.

Keith picked up the bill and pulled his wallet from his back pocket. "You need to use the restroom before we go, honey?" Maddie nodded. "Go ahead while I pay the bill." Maddie pushed back her chair, and Keith made sure she entered the restaurant before focusing on Bertie's blazing green eyes and stubborn chin.

"I'm not talking about money." Keith allowed his gaze to zero in on Bertie's plump lips. "What are *you* going to do for me if I go through with this auction?" he said in his best smarmy voice. A gasp escaped her lips.

Keith chuckled. "And I don't mean free pillows or a new lampshade." He deliberately leered at her chest where soft flesh peeked out from the lavender V-neck sweater she wore.

Bertie stammered, "You can't be serious?"

"Oh, but I am." He let loose a villainous laugh.

Bertie crossed her arms over the luscious breasts he'd been ogling. "Nothing. I don't want to do anything for you."

"Oh, but you do. And so do I. Think about it. We've got plenty of time."

Keith waited, wondering how long it'd take, and then Bertie blasted him. About three seconds.

"You've got a lot of nerve, Keith Morgan. If you think I'm going to...*arugh*." Keith shoved a roll in her mouth.

"Shhh. Maddie's coming."

Bertie worked the roll around in her mouth and then gulped her water to wash it down while she glared retribution at his head.

Chapter 17

FOUR DAYS HAD PASSED SINCE BERTIE HAD SPENT THE day with Maddie and her sneaky, frustrating, totally ripped, royal-pain-in-the-butt dad. It was Sunday and Bertie was still fuming over his proposition of sex for charity work. Well, not exactly fuming. More like sighing and aching and kind of wishing she was the type of girl who'd actually go through with it. She was pretty darn sure he'd been teasing, because he thrived on having the last word like he thrived on winning tennis matches.

Later that afternoon, during the movie about kid sleuths and smart-talking dogs which was ten-year-old appropriate but not interesting enough to hold a jaded ex-pro tennis player's attention, he'd done things like dropped popcorn in her lap and then pretended like he was picking up loose kernels instead of copping a feel. When he'd danced his fingers across the tops of her legs, searching for pay dirt, Bertie had clamped her thighs together like a vise, but felt a tingling that surged from head to toe, stopping at very crucial spots along the way. She'd swatted at his hand, hoping not to attract Maddie's attention, and Keith sent her a wicked, delicious smile that promised all kinds of hot and sweaty physical activity which Bertie knew had nothing to do with a racket and a fuzzy yellow ball. All teasing aside, they'd had a pleasant day, and she'd enjoyed relaxing and not working. Keith had apologized again for being a complete ass the night of the sleepover, and she decided to let the tortured, misguided, single dad off the hook.

Bertie checked her watch to discover that she'd been working at her desk for almost two hours, writing up purchase orders and paying invoices. She'd requested express shipping for fabrics and furniture, needing to expedite the process to meet this ridiculous time frame on Keith's renovations. A familiar beep sounded from her cell and she checked the screen. Gary had texted pictures of possible lamps he'd spotted at a store in Raleigh for Keith's family room and guest rooms. The shopping was always better in Raleigh. Bertie picked her phone up and texted back: like. like. hate. maybe. Hell no.

Gary texted back: got it. C u 2nite @ dog.

Bertie clicked to check her emails one last time before shutting down her computer when she heard a loud banging coming from the direction of her front door. "Geez. Keep your shirt on." She jumped up and hurried down the hall toward the front of the house, scooping up her orange tote she'd dropped on the floor the day before.

"Bertie! Dammit, open the door!" Keith bellowed on the other side. Bertie's insides turned cold at his enraged command. Not again. What had she done now? She dropped her tote at the bottom of the steps and moved cautiously to the front door. Bertie turned the knob, and Keith pushed his way in, almost knocking her on her butt.

"Where is she?" He stormed past her and barged into her living room, wearing a frantic expression. "I know she's here." Keith bolted from the unoccupied living room and into her kitchen. He peered around the wall into the mudroom, finding no one. Then he blew past a startled Bertie and flew up her stairs two at a time.

Bertie cautiously followed a Keith gone postal up the stairs as she heard him slamming closet doors like a SWAT team member looking for a wanted fugitive.

Once she'd reached the landing on the second floor, Keith burst through the door of her old bedroom. His arm snaked out and he grabbed her by the wrist, pulling her within inches of his angry face. "This is not funny. Tell me where she is...*now*," he said between clenched teeth.

Bertie struggled to wrench her wrist free, but Keith only tightened his hold. Clearly he'd gone loco because she had no clue what he was raging about.

"*Who?* What are you talking about?" she asked. After a long, tense moment, Keith closed his eyes as if in resignation. "Tell me what's going on," she urged in a calm voice, considering he still had a death grip on her wrist and her knees felt a little weak.

"M-maddie," he choked out in a rusty voice. "I can't find her. She's run away."

"*What!*" Her knees almost buckled. If it hadn't been for his fingers clamped around her wrist, she'd have fallen for sure. "What happened?" Anguish and what looked to be self-loathing crossed behind Keith's dark eyes as he stared straight through her. Bertie cupped his cold cheek with her free hand. "Tell me," she urged in a quiet tone.

He shook his head and refocused his haunted eyes. "Today. After lunch. I...uh...told her to finish packing." His throat worked. "To take her back to school.

She complained, saying she didn't want to go back like she always does. But today was different. S-she said…I had no idea…" His voice trailed off. Keith had released Bertie's wrist, and she placed her freed hand on the side of his neck, feeling his pulse racing beneath her palm.

"Listen to me. We'll find her. Why was today different? What did Maddie say, exactly?"

Keith hit the wall with the back of his head and moved from Bertie's touch, as if he didn't deserve her comfort. "Something about growing up here, like a normal kid. Like you did. She said you grew up without a mom in Harmony and turned out fine." Bertie didn't know about that. It depended on the definition of *fine*. "You guys must've had some heart-to-heart when she'd spent the night," Keith said.

Bertie nodded, trying to remember the conversation. "I guess we did."

He pushed away from the wall. "I've got to find her."

"I'm coming with you. Let me grab my phone." She raced down the stairs and jogged back to her office for her handbag and then met Keith at the front door.

"Where's Aunt Franny?"

"Turning the house upside down and searching the grounds." He pulled her behind him to his Cayenne parked willy-nilly on her front lawn. "I don't know where else to look. She's not answering her phone, and I've searched my house. I pray to God she's not hurt."

Bertie jumped in the front seat, pulling on her seat belt. "Did she say anything else?"

He shook his head. "Just something about how you had people to talk to and places to go when you felt bad, and she doesn't have that."

"Wait." She grabbed his arm as he went to put the key in the ignition. "Say that again."

"What? You had people to talk to?"

"The other part. About how I had a place to go."

"Yeah? What does that mean?"

"It means I think I know where she is."

~~~

Keith pulled into the back parking lot at the Dog, his heart racing and mouth dry. Bertie jumped out before he'd even put the car in park. Keith jogged after her as she raced through the back entrance and up a service staircase.

"Where are you going?"

She didn't answer, scurrying down a narrow hallway. Keith stayed on her heels, berating himself for allowing this to happen. How could he not know his own daughter? The signs had been there like a blinking neon light. Maddie had practically spelled it out for him. What a clusterfuck, and it was all his fault.

At the end of the hall, Bertie pushed open a door and Keith's vision was momentarily blinded by the natural light that poured into the dark hall, making the scratches on the wood floors more visible. Keith blinked, entering the attic-sized room right behind Bertie, and stopped. The dormer windows had built-in window seats and a blue-and-white faded cushion sat in the middle, with Maddie huddled on top.

Keith's thundering heart came to a squeezing halt as Maddie peered at them with a tear-streaked face.

"Oh, thank the Lord," Bertie exhaled.

"Maddie. You okay?" Keith moved forward on

wooden legs and dropped down before her. Maddie sat with her skinny arms wrapped around her calves and her head resting on the tops of her knees. Keith kissed her forehead, hugging her close to him. He repeated the silent prayer that had been running over and over in his head like a video reel, except this one was filled with thanks and gratitude.

"Daddy, I'm sorry. I didn't mean to scare you," Maddie said in a choked voice.

"It's okay, honey. As long as you're all right. I was worried about you." Keith eased back from his tight hold on Maddie and glanced at his surroundings. "What is this room?" The bright yellow walls appeared washed out from the sunlight streaming in through the large windows. Keith was kneeling on a green, braided, oval rug covering the wood floor, and Bertie stood next to a table with a white-knuckle grip on the back of one of the three chairs.

Bertie cleared her throat. "It's where Cal and I used to come after school. When our parents were both working downstairs." Bertie stopped speaking, but Keith gave her an encouraging nod. "I came here a lot after my mom died to…think or get away."

Keith turned back to Maddie, who had dried her tears on the sleeve of her pink Princeton sweatshirt. "Is that what you were doing? Getting away…to think?" he asked, hoping that he hadn't pushed her too far out of his reach with his own stupidity and lack of foresight.

"Yeah, I thought it would help."

"Did it?"

Maddie nodded. "Sort of."

"Anything you want to share with me?"

Maddie unfolded her legs. "No. I'm ready to go now. You can take me back to school." Keith almost flinched at the dejection he heard in her voice as he stood and helped Maddie up. "Sorry I used your room without your permission," Maddie said to Bertie.

"You can use it anytime you want when you're here. But be sure to let someone know where you are." Bertie hugged Maddie close and peered at Keith, concern marring her pretty features.

"Uh, Bertie? You think Maddie could get one of those famous sundaes downstairs?"

"Sure. Would you like that, Maddie?"

Maddie nodded, a small smile lifted the corners of her lips.

"Lead the way." Keith gestured to the open door with a trembling arm. Relief and other emotions he couldn't even name coursed through his body, and his limbs felt a little shaky. They moved in single file down the hall lined with stacked wooden chairs.

While Keith called Francesca on his cell to let her know he had Maddie and she was safe, Bertie led them into the restaurant through the office door. Francesca pushed for details, but Keith knew that Maddie needed him more than Francesca needed answers. He hung up. Bertie offered Maddie a seat at the end of the bar and instructed one of the waiters to fix her a special sundae.

Keith kissed Maddie on the head, closing his eyes briefly. "I'm going to speak with Bertie for a minute in her office. You okay?"

Maddie nodded. "Go ahead. I promise I'll stay right here." Keith squeezed her shoulder. "Dad...tell her you like her hair." Keith raised both brows. "Girls like that."

Maddie smiled the smile of a much older, more mature woman and then dug into her hot fudge sundae.

Keith followed Bertie back into the office and she closed the door. "I'm so sorry. I would've never told her about that room if…I mean…she asked what I used to do and—"

"It's not your fault. I'm grateful that you knew where to find her."

Bertie avoided his gaze as she straightened a stack of catalogs on the desktop with jerky fingers.

"I need to talk to you about schools in the area." He covered her hand to stop the nervous organization of the clutter. "I can't send her back to boarding school. This stunt was a cry for attention and I can't ignore it. I need her home with me." He gripped Bertie's small hand in his. "I can't fuck up anymore."

"Stop. You didn't fu…screw up. She's a child. Not a screwed-up teenager ready to hitch a ride in the next pick-up truck. You're a good dad."

If only Keith could believe those words and Bertie's earnest expression backing them up. He gave her a self-depreciating smile. "And you know this, how?"

"A blind man can see how much you and Maddie love each other. All parents doubt their ability. Single parents even more. Go with your gut and you'll be okay. Besides, you won't be a single parent much longer."

True. And Keith hoped like hell it would help the situation and not make it worse. The pressure was mounting. It was match point on his serve, and he needed to hit an ace. Bertie slipped her hand from his and moved toward a framed photo on the wall of a man and a woman standing in front of a dated entrance to the Dog. Keith connected the dots. The photo was of Bertie's parents. He saw the resemblance right away. Bertie favored her mom in the shape of her face and the color of her eyes. Keith needed to put more stock into Bertie's insights on Maddie because Bertie also mourned the loss of her parents. But to have lost her mother at such a tender age for a girl had to be especially hard. Without the guidance of her mother, Bertie had probably stumbled through her awkward teenage years. And Maddie was fast approaching that stage.

"Raleigh has several excellent private day schools. Lots of kids from here go to them. There's even a bus that takes them from the Jaycee Park if you're interested," she said, bringing him back to his current problem. "Ask Aunt Franny...er Francesca for help."

"Your parents?" Keith asked referring to the picture. He stood close behind Bertie, allowing her gardenia scent to fill his head.

"Yeah." Bertie touched the glass on the photo with the tip of her finger.

"Nice. You look like your mom." *Except even more beautiful and vibrant*, but he kept those thoughts to himself.

She chuckled, "Thanks. My mom's hair was really red and much curlier."

Keith reached out, remembering what Maddie had suggested and touched a lock of Bertie's hair, testing the silky texture between his fingers. "Yours is pretty and perfect on you."

Bertie shot him an anxious glance. "I think the stress of the day is affecting your brain."

"Maybe." He dropped the lock of hair and it fell against her shoulder. Bertie bit her plump bottom lip, and Keith wished he was biting it instead. He owed this tiny, curvy, big-eyed bombshell for helping him with his daughter in more ways than one. "Thank you."

"Excuse me?" she whispered.

"Thank you for finding Maddie, and thank you for helping me. It means a lot."

"Well, of course. I'm glad I remembered my old hiding place."

"Not only that. You're good at"—Keith shoved his hands in his jean pockets—"talking to her. And you help me to see things…er, to calm down, I guess."

Maybe the stress of the day *was* affecting him. More like the stress of the last four years. Somewhere deep inside, underneath the band of steel that squeezed his heart, a soft velvet lining coated the hard steel, easing the constriction. Keith felt it whenever Bertie was around. Somehow, in these last couple of months, she'd become like a buffer between him and his hardened heart.

Bertie glanced at everything in the cramped office but him. She seemed on edge, and without warning, the electrical current that always seemed to hum around them jolted him as if he'd stepped on a live wire.

Keith blurted, "When do you want to stop dancing around this and do something about it?" Her eyes widened in shock and he wished he'd kept his mouth shut. He shouldn't be pressuring her about anything. He needed to stay the hell away from her so she could finish his house, collect her bonus, and move on with her life…away from Harmony.

"Dancing? You want to dance…here…now?" Bertie pulled an exaggerated face. "No thanks. I'll sit this one out."

But when had he ever done the right thing? "Funny. You know what I mean." Keith backed Bertie up against the scratched metal desk as he looked into her sea-green eyes and smiled. His warmed heart beat a slow, steady thud and blood traveled with determined purpose straight from his head to his groin. "I want to do more than dance with you," he murmured, and because he couldn't resist, he pressed his lips to her warm neck.

Bertie sighed and gripped his forearm as she felt him smile against her neck. Then she maneuvered around him. "Uh, I have to—Maddie. I need to check on her."

Right. Maddie. This was not the time or the place for a seduction. He needed to repair the broken strings to his racket and get back on stadium court with his daughter.

Bertie turned and yanked the door open and then froze. "I'm an idiot," she mumbled.

To his complete and utter amazement, she whipped back around and grabbed the front of his cotton button-down, pulling him toward her. And kissed him. Hard. With lots of tongue and just the right amount of pressure. She kissed him like he was the last man on earth, and he relished every second of it. Second, not minute, because before he could gain control and take it further, she'd let go and fled the room like a scared, hunted red fox.

Keith licked the spicy, cinnamon taste of Bertie from his lips. He felt a smile stretch from his gut to the top of his head. She'd given him the opening he'd been looking for.

~~~

On Monday morning, Keith drove Maddie to Raleigh to meet with the headmaster at Trinity Academy, a private day school where he planned to enroll her. Maddie chatted nonstop about how excited she was, and after looking the school over and meeting some of the faculty, Keith was impressed enough to pay the tuition on the spot and get Maddie settled for a day of classes.

That afternoon, he collected Maddie from her new school and stopped by Barnes & Noble to buy a few books for Maddie's English class. Gail happened to be working the afternoon shift. She looked up from the register in the children's section and smiled as she spied Keith strolling toward her, holding Maddie's hand. She combed the back of her straight blond hair with her hand and straightened her green knit polo shirt, practical as always in her creased khakis and navy blue Keds tennis shoes.

"Well, hello there." Keith greeted Gail with a smile and a wink. "We were in the neighborhood. I'd like you to meet my daughter, Maddie."

Gail bent down with palms on her knees, leveling her face with Maddie's and smiled. "Hey there. I'm Gail. Your dad has told me so much about you." Gail extended her right hand.

Caution lit Maddie's eyes and then she tilted her head toward him. Keith detected irritation mixed with anger in her upturned face. Gail waited with her hand out, and Keith nudged Maddie in the back. "Madeline." He tried not to growl his warning.

"Hi," his talkative ten-year-old said as she gave Gail's hand a hard shake.

"It's so nice to finally meet you. Would you like to browse the shelves? Some brand-new books just came in today. Do you like the *Magic Treehouse* series?" Gail said in an overly bright voice.

"No. They're for babies." Maddie crossed her arms and adopted a sullen, put-upon stance. Keith had never been so proud of his spoiled child…*not.*

"Oh. Well, why don't you tell me what you like—"

"I see the *Olympian* series by Rick Riordan over there. I'll look at those," Maddie said with the enthusiasm of someone spying an overflowing basket of dirty laundry that needed sorting. "Dad, we won't be long, will we?" she whined.

"I don't know. Go look at some books," Keith said through clenched teeth. Maddie gave him another baleful look and dragged her feet over to the bookshelves. She pretended to be flipping pages of a book but kept glancing at him as if he had banished her to scrubbing moldy grout in the bathroom with a toothbrush.

Keith sighed. "I'm sorry. She's had a rough couple days. I enrolled her in a new school"—he jammed his hands in his pant pockets—"I'm making excuses. She's usually not this rude or embarrassing," he scoffed.

"Don't worry about it." Gail glanced over her shoulder at Maddie who was pretending not to eavesdrop. "I'll bet she doesn't like sharing you with anybody, especially another girl."

Keith nodded and choked back a laugh at Maddie's exaggerated eye roll. "Yeah, that's probably it." Or not. Maddie didn't seem to mind sharing him with Bertie. "Can I buy you a cup of coffee? Do you have a few minutes free?"

"Not really. I have to finish this inventory, but we're still on for tomorrow night, right?"

"Sure. What time?"

"Come by around seven and I'll cook for you."

"Great. I'll bring the wine." Keith leaned down to peck Gail on the lips when he heard a huge snort in Maddie's vicinity. Gail's cheeks pinkened, and she brushed Keith's jaw with a quick kiss.

"Madeline, let's go." Keith squeezed Gail's hand before leaving the store with an ill-humored Maddie in tow.

They rode in silence on the twenty-minute ride back to Harmony. Keith did his best to ignore Maddie's looks of disgust she kept shooting in his direction. After about the third grunt/sigh she heaved, Keith gave in and spoke first.

"What's your problem?"

"Nothin,'" she mumbled.

"Spill it. Because I'm not putting up with your hostile attitude anymore."

Maddie straightened in her seat and uncrossed her arms. "I don't like that girl," she blurted. "She's stupid."

"Madeline," he growled. "You don't even know her. And if you keep up this rude act, you're never going to get to know her."

"Good. I don't want to get to know her." Maddie pushed out her bottom lip. "Are you like dating her or something?"

"Or something." Keith watched the road and tried not to picture his daughter's neck as he strangled the steering wheel.

"Gross, Dad. I saw you try to kiss her. Does that mean you're going to marry her?"

"Just because I kiss a girl doesn't mean I'm going to marry her." Keith came to a full stop at an intersection near the overpass. "Why don't you like her? You barely said three words."

Maddie shrugged her shoulders beneath her pink sweater with the lime-green trim. "I don't know. She's… she looks like a kindergarten teacher."

"Huh?"

"She looks…boring. Are you dating her? Like, *only* her?"

"We've gone on a few dates. She happens to be very nice and sweet. If you'd give her a chance—"

"Why don't you date Bertie? I like Bertie. She's not boring, and she doesn't wear those ugly clothes. Bertie's pretty and she has really cool shoes. And Bertie's fun. Bertie's mom died when she was like fourteen, and we have lots—"

"I know all about Bertie's mom and dad. But I'm not dating Bertie. We're just friends. Bertie is my decorator—"

"Designer," Maddie interjected. "And why not? Why can't you date your designer? Bertie's smart, and she wants to learn how to play tennis. You can teach her that. And she said she's so happy I'm living in Harmony now. She's gonna let me help her with a house she's building for this poor family. She said I can help paint walls and stuff. And she said that I could help her raise money for that Jaycee Park, the one with the messed up tennis courts. And—"

"Enough!" Keith felt like shit when he saw Maddie's head jerk back and her mouth gape open. "Bertie has other plans," he bit out like rusty razor blades. And they didn't include him and an instant family. Not that he could blame her. Her dreams included living in a big city and creating big-city designs. He got that. "I know you like her, but she's only my decorator. Nothing else."

"Bertie's more than a designer. She's my friend and she—what plans?"

"Madeline, listen to me. Bertie is a nice person, but she's nice to all her clients. She's getting paid a shi... boatload of money to do this job, and when she's done, she's moving away."

Maddie gasped. "That's not true!"

Dread and fear and a few other emotions tumbled around inside Keith's constricted chest. A part of him didn't like the idea of Bertie moving away any better than Maddie did, but another part of him wished she'd hurry up and get the hell out of town before he ruined any chance of happiness for his daughter and himself. But right now, he needed to tell a hard truth and break his daughter's heart. Keith sighed.

"Ask her if you don't believe me. Before she started our house, she was moving to Atlanta to take another job, but your Aunt Francesca convinced her to stay." By dangling a hundred and fifty G's in front of her nose. "But as soon as she's finished, she's moving. She'd like to explore other avenues with her career. And I think that's smart. She'll be much happier."

Maddie shook her head at Keith, wearing the I-can't-believe-you're-my-dad expression. "You could convince her to stay, Dad," she said in her grown-up voice.

Keith chuckled. "How do you figure?"

"Because. I just know. I can tell when you look at her."

A horn blared as Keith almost swerved into the next lane. Prickly heat flushed his neck and crept toward his face. Jesus. Was he that transparent? He prayed like hell his ten-year-old daughter didn't know what he was really thinking when he looked at Bertie. The very idea horrified him. Fifth-grade sex education would never be the same.

Keith was almost afraid to ask. "Uh, how do I look at her?"

"Like she's beautiful. Like you always want to be with her." Maddie pressed her face into the glass of the passenger window. "Not like the way you looked at Gail."

―――*――

Several weeks later, on a Friday afternoon, Francesca's ears perked up as she heard her front door slam. Maddie's and Keith's loud voices carried from the foyer to her sitting room. Francesca lowered the reading glasses from her nose and turned her head toward the door to listen.

"I can't believe you're dating her *again*. That's like your third date this week, Dad," Maddie said in a petulant voice.

"That's right and it's none of your business," Keith said.

"It sure is my business if you marry her!"

"Watch your tone, young lady," Keith snapped. "If you don't straighten up and stop riding my ass, I'm going to have your *favorite person* strip your brand-new room of all that furniture and donate it to her charity." Keith's voice grew louder as he moved closer to the sitting room. "Now go upstairs and get your things together."

Francesca could hear Maddie stomping up the stairs, adding extra noise as only a mad ten-year-old could do. Maddie's "favorite person" these days was also Francesca's favorite person...Bertie. Now if Francesca could make Keith see that Bertie was his favorite person too, then all would be right in the Morgan/Balogh household.

Francesca had been holding her tongue and biding her time as she observed Keith fight his attraction to Bertie. But ever since he'd been paying more attention to his young lady in Raleigh, Francesca could feel the tension building around him and Maddie. A week ago, upon Francesca's orders, Keith had reported in with a great deal of attitude and resentment. After much prompting on her part, he filled her in about meeting Gail and how she'd be a perfect mother to Maddie. But with everything he told her, he never mentioned if Gail would be perfect for *him*. So, Francesca had concluded that she would have to intervene to keep him from making another horrible mistake. What Francesca didn't hear from his description of sweet, young Gail was exactly what she needed to know to make her next calculated move.

Keith slipped into the sitting room and threw himself onto Francesca's love seat. "Jesus. Remind me again why it was such a good idea to have her home."

He leaned his head back and sighed. She frowned at him. "I take it you two have been arguing again."

He grunted, his eyes closed. "Thank God you're the one taking her to Virginia to pick up her things from boarding school and not me, because I've a good mind to dump her on the side of the highway and leave her there. Maybe you can talk some sense into her," Keith said, keeping his eyes closed.

Francesca studied his hard features, noticing he didn't look peaceful or even particularly happy. "Hmmm, maybe. So you have another date with"—Francesca motioned with her hand—"what's her name?"

"Gail." Keith peered at her through slitted lids.

"Yes. From Barnes & Noble. She sounds like a lovely girl." Francesca added extra emphasis to the word "girl," hoping Keith would register that he didn't want a child bride. From what Francesca could gather, this young, innocent girl would never stand a chance at reining him in or keeping his attention. Even his ten-year-old daughter sensed that this relationship was doomed, but Maddie didn't have the maturity or the right words to express her instincts.

Francesca shuddered at how quickly Keith would lose interest...sexually. She hated to think of her nephew as a cad toward women, because he wasn't. But she also knew he shared his father's sharp intellect as well as his way with women. And Keith would die of boredom within weeks if his next wife didn't challenge him mentally and physically. He'd be miserable before the ink dried on their marriage license.

Francesca placed the magazine she'd been reading on top of her gilded coffee table. She felt a twinge of guilt for Keith's rash choice when it came to finding a partner. But she couldn't sit by any longer and watch him muck up his life. She used the best weapon at her disposal to spur him into action—threatening for custody. Keith wore a cloak of grief, guilt, and pain so thick that he didn't see how it dragged him and Maddie down. Francesca never considered herself a cruel person, especially with regard to anyone she loved, but the time had come for her to play the card she held close to her chest—the mother card.

Francesca smoothed the hem of her dark brown gabardine skirt. "I spoke with your mom earlier today."

Keith sat forward, clearly alert. "Yeah?"

"She called to speak with Maddie. I'll have Maddie call her back while we're on the road."

"That all she wanted?"

Francesca spotted the tightening in Keith's broad shoulders. She remembered when his remoteness first appeared regarding his mother. Right around the time Angelina left him at boarding school and moved to Europe. "No. She also wanted to know about you. I told her all about young Gail, and how you've finally met someone nice. And how she'd make a good mother to Maddie. Of course, having never met the girl"—she shot Keith a piercing glare—"I'm only going on what you've told me. And I'm trying to ignore all the things Maddie has told me."

Keith reached for the magazine on the table. "Yeah, Gail's a real nice girl," he said with no enthusiasm, as if he were speaking about getting his tires rotated. He showed more excitement when he talked about his next stock purchase than he did when he spoke of Gail.

"Well, your mother certainly approved. She thinks this is the best thing for you." Keith gave Francesca an odd look. "You know she never liked your choices in women, and Adriana was no exception—"

"I don't want to talk about Adriana," he interrupted.

"I understand. This isn't about Adriana or your past. This is about your life moving forward with Maddie." Keith gave her a jerky nod. "But Angelina really likes the sound of Gail. She was practically overflowing with excitement. She said there's nothing wrong with a simple, sweet girl who can bake cookies and loves to read children's books."

Keith tossed the magazine back on the table and rose from the love seat. "As if she'd know anything about that. What else did she say?" he asked, peering out the French doors to the freshly mowed lawn.

"Well, I'm not sure, but I think she might make arrangements to come to your wedding."

Keith's body jolted as he turned around. "You told her I was getting married already?" his voice sounded strangled. "Jesus. I haven't even gotten past first base with this girl, and you've got my mother making wedding arrangements."

On the inside, Francesca smiled and patted herself on the back, knowing that if Keith had any feelings for Gail whatsoever, wild bulls couldn't hold him back. On the outside, she squared her shoulders and lifted her nose, giving the impression of great disappointment.

"Keith Morgan, I hope you are conducting yourself in a gentlemanly manner. From what you've told me, this young girl is not experienced in the ways of the"—Francesca fluttered her hand—"you know what I mean. I hope you don't frighten her. You could very well be her...*first*."

Color flooded Keith's cheeks as he cringed. "What else did you tell Mommy dearest about my upcoming nuptials?" he smirked.

"I didn't give her an exact date, but I did say you'd gotten rather serious and I wouldn't be surprised if it happened in the next few weeks."

Keith shoved his hands in his front pockets. "I'm guessing you left out the part where you're holding a gun to my head."

"Don't you think you're being a bit dramatic, dear? I merely gave you an incentive to get moving, because I'm concerned about Maddie, as is your mother. You may not believe this, but Angelina only wants the best for her granddaughter."

Keith gave a humorless laugh. "Evident by all the times she's actually seen Maddie and how often she stays in touch."

"I'm not making excuses for my sister. I know she's been less than an ideal grandmother, or mother for that matter." Francesca glanced away from Keith's stern expression. "All those years she chose to be…away after your father died, I always filled in."

Keith gave a harsh laugh. "Away? Is that how we're phrasing it these days? I prefer the term *abandon*. She abandoned her only child and she has never apologized for it. Never."

Francesca had definitely struck a nerve, and Keith had every right to be angry. But she had hoped that as he matured into a grown man, he'd find a way to forgive his mother. And she prayed that once this act of tough love had ended, he'd find it in his heart to forgive her as well.

Angelina wanted to make peace with her son, but she was afraid and ashamed. Keith's dad had been her life, and when he dropped dead of a heart attack in his prime, Angelina drowned herself in misery and mourning, leaving her young son bereft, without his dad and then without his mother. Much as Keith had done when Adriana died. Francesca knew that Keith had never made the comparison, because he hadn't loved Adriana the way Angelina had loved Harrison Morgan. And Francesca didn't think she needed to point it out to him…yet. But back in Miami,

Keith had come dangerously close to repeating history by shutting down and leaving Maddie the same way.

"You have every right to be angry with your mother… and me." Francesca held Keith's attention. "Maybe I shouldn't have always filled in where she left gaping holes. Angelina knew you had me and I'd always be here for you. I don't know." Francesca swallowed as she adjusted the silk Hermes scarf tied around her neck. "I probably enabled her poor behavior. For that, I'm terribly sorry."

"I'm not. I'm glad you were always there for me. You were a great mother to me when she chose not to be around and I appreciated it." Keith pushed his fingers through his hair, sighing. "I don't want her input right now. She doesn't know anything about me, or Maddie for that matter."

"I understand."

"No, I don't think you do." Keith took a deep breath. "I don't want her planning my wedding or giving her opinion on something or someone she knows nothing about." Keith began to pace across the antique Aubusson rug. "Whoever I choose to marry in the next few weeks whether it be Gail or Ber—uh, or that crazy lady with the leopard suit and green Jell-O, it's going to be *my* decision. So do me a favor and keep my mother out of it."

"As you wish, dear." Francesca said, wearing a sober expression. On the inside, she'd donned her best pale blue Chanel suit with her gray South Sea pearls and stared down an aisle of a church with tears in her eyes. And the sight before her was a bride in an original Vera Wang wedding gown, a concoction of elegant beads, tulle, and lace worn by…her favorite person.

Chapter 18

"I'M WEAK. AND STUPID. I'M A WEAK, STUPID, DESPERATE, small-town girl." Bertie dropped the large roll of fabric she'd checked-in against her purchase order on the floor of her office. It was Friday afternoon. Three weeks had passed since she'd locked lips with Keith in the back office at the Dog. Three weeks of reliving the stupidest, most impulsive moment of her life. Three weeks of avoiding him, although that hadn't been hard. Aunt Franny had informed Bertie that he had enrolled Maddie in a private school in Raleigh, which had kept him busy and away from the house.

Christ on a cracker. She'd officially lost it. She'd become one of those batty, silly, impetuous old ladies. The ones everyone talked about that lived in small towns but didn't have the sense they were born with. The ones who collected scraps of lace and rubber bands. The ones who always washed and reused tin foil and had drawers and drawers full of those twisty-tie thingies and old packets of duck sauce from the 1980s. The wacky, aimless neighbor who wore weird hats and jogging suits with appliques. Yep. All Bertie needed were a few homeless cats or twenty and a talking parakeet on her shoulder.

"So you grabbed the guy and kissed him. Who wouldn't?" Gary said as he used a box cutter to cut the plastic from another roll of fabric and inspected the contents. She and Gary had been working like dogs all week on the renovations. Bertie had only three weeks to finish and the pressure was building.

"I know. That's the problem. Everyone wants to kiss the guy or, in Jo Ellen's case, *do* him in the back of her pink pick-up. I'm his designer. I'm supposed to be working with him, not trying to find a way to work *under* him. I'm not supposed to be fantasizing about his muscular, tan arms and his rock-hard chest." Or the way he freaked over his daughter and how he tried to be a good father. That part got Bertie every time.

Of course, Keith being gorgeous and totally edible didn't hurt, but Bertie was more drawn to his human side. The side where he panicked and made rash decisions and then regretted it. The side where he didn't believe in himself or his parenting skills. The tough, competitive, professional tennis player who had it all—including gobs of money—struggled with mundane things, like how much TV he should allow his daughter to watch or at what age should she be allowed to shave her legs. Bertie found his vulnerability and uncertainty to be way sexier than his thick hair and piercing dark eyes.

"You're overanalyzing. He's a great-looking guy and he seems to be hot to trot for you. And it's not like he hasn't had plenty of other opportunities. I heard Arlene came right out and propositioned him at the Daily Grind in front of the morning-coffee crowd."

"Oh Lordy," Bertie groaned.

"Miss Sue Percy told me that Arlene marched over wearing that leopard jumpsuit with the gold zipper pulled way down, showing too much cleavage. And she backed Keith into a corner and literally purred at him like a big jungle cat—if jungle cats wore lacy pink push-up bras and spiked heels."

"Oh no." Bertie pressed her hands into her face.

"And she said something like she was a hot cupcake looking for a stud muffin—"

"No! Stop. You can't be serious." Bertie snickered, picturing Arlene poured into that outfit.

Gary laughed too. "I couldn't make this up if I tried. Apparently, Morgan lit out of there as if his ass were on fire and didn't even pick up his coffee or his change."

"That poor man. No wonder he wants out. Who can blame him? He thinks he's living in the land of Looney Tunes."

"Yeah, so maybe you should hook up with him to show him we're not so bad. Think of it is as your civic duty—saving Harmony's image."

"Really? And you think by sleeping with him, it'll change his views of Harmony? I've lived here my whole life. It will take more than a romp in my bed for anyone to change their take on Harmony."

"Maybe. But it's worth a try. Besides, you've got nothing to lose and maybe even something to gain…like some great sex. When was the last time that happened?" Gary gave Bertie his all-knowing look, which meant he knew the answer to his own question better than she did. "Loser married architect from Raleigh doesn't count."

"Well, if I'm not counting loser married guy, then I'd have to say…geez, I don't even remember."

Sad but true. Which had to explain her out-of-character behavior with Keith. She was no better than Jo Ellen or Arlene. She reached for her glass on the book-shelf and choked down some sweet iced tea. Harmony was turning her into a small-town old maid gone wild, ready for her own reality TV show. Only a few more weeks. She could last that long without becoming the town trollop. Right? Bertie chugged more tea, wishing it was laced with alcohol.

"Drinking all that tea and wishing it was spiked is not going to help your problem." Gary smirked.

Bertie slammed the glass back down and sent Gary a lethal glare. Sometimes, she hated the fact that he could read her mind. "Have you gotten those orders signed and approved for the cabinet hardware?" Bertie tried for irritated-boss mode, hoping to instill some fear into Gary—not that it ever worked in the past, but she gave it a shot.

Gary stopped loading a plastic container and peered at Bertie. "They were delivered with a note attached—"

"I need them signed ASAP—"

"Look, Miss I-need-to-get-laid"—Gary jabbed a finger at Bertie's face—"don't get your thong all in a twist. The Prince hasn't been around. So I left a folder of orders his Highness needs to sign with instructions for him to return them today at the latest…to you." Gary checked his stainless steel watch. "It's a little after three. He'll be here."

Great. She didn't need Keith showing up with orders and that toe-tingling, sexy smile. "Here? You told him to come here?"

"This is your office, isn't it?" Gary said with a touch of annoyance.

"Dammit. What are you now? Yenta, the famous gay matchmaker?" Bertie planted her fists on her hips. "In case you've been unaware, I've been doing an excellent job of avoiding him for weeks. And as you can see, it's been working." Bertie jerked her head. "Look at all this work we've gotten done. We are down to the wire. I... we don't need any more distractions." She reached for an overflowing folder on her desk and shoved it into Gary's hands. "This needs to go to the workroom along with the fabric. And you're going to be here when Mr. Perfect Prince shows up with those papers."

Gary laughed as he filed the folder in the container for the workroom. "As much as I'd like to be here for the booty call...uh, I don't think so. Unless you think Morgan would be interested in a threesome."

Bertie threw a pillow form at his head. "Spare me. *That* ain't never gonna happen. Not with me, anyway."

Gary shrugged. "Okay, so a threesome is out. You can't blame a girl for trying. But if I were you, and believe me in this situation I wish I was"—Gary waggled his eyebrows at Bertie—"I'd be jumping that gorgeous man's fine form and getting the best lay of my life."

"He's a client. I can't sleep with a client," Bertie explained as if she were speaking to a four-year-old.

"He won't be in another three weeks. But you're not going to last that long."

Bertie opened her mouth to blast Gary, but what he said next stopped her. "Because he's not going to last that long. Morgan needs to blow off some steam. Preferably with you. Who knows? Maybe you'll be the next Mrs. Keith Morgan."

Bertie gripped the back of her desk chair. Gary didn't understand; he seemed to think she and Keith were playing at some game. "No way. I'm not even on the short list, and I don't want to be." Gary flashed a dubious look. "You don't understand. He has to marry or at least be engaged within the next three weeks or Francesca is going to take custody of Maddie."

Gary pooh-poohed, "Francesca wouldn't do that. She's bluffing."

Bertie shook her head. "I was there. I've never seen her so fierce. She means business. That's why Keith is so stressed out. He goes to Raleigh *a lot*. He must've met someone there." Bertie shoved a box of small glass tiles with her foot toward Gary to add to his load. "Keith is simply my client. And you and I would be smart to remember that. I have a lot riding on this job. I can't screw it up."

"You mean you can't screw Keith, in the biblical sense."

"Yeah, in both senses. Besides, he has a ton of baggage."

"Like what?"

"Like his wife's death and the fact that he married only because he got her pregnant, and he never really loved her but feels guilty about it all the same."

"Whoa. Where did you hear that? Don't tell me you're listening to Harmony gossip."

"No. I brought dinner over to Aunt Franny's the other night and for some reason she felt compelled to spill his life story."

Gary gave Bertie a strange look. The one where he knew something but he wouldn't reveal what it was. "Interesting. What else did she say?"

"You're not going to start blabbing all over town, are you? I don't think Aunt Franny or Keith would appreciate it."

"Dang. Give me some credit, would you?" Gary gave her another funny look. "What else did Francesca tell you?"

"She said that Keith's dad died when he was young and that his mother was never the same. She basically dumped Keith in a boarding school and then moved to Europe. He rarely saw her and still doesn't, which is why Aunt Franny took such a special interest in him."

"Ah, the plot thickens," Gary said, using his dramatic voice.

"No drama and no plot," Bertie said as she stapled fabric cuttings to a stack of purchase orders with unnecessary force. "In three weeks, we'll be finished with this job and Keith will be bringing a new mom home to Maddie." Bertie accidently stapled her thumb. "Ouch! Dammit all to hell." She shoved her thumb in her mouth as tears sprang to her eyes.

"You okay?"

Bertie nodded still sucking her thumb. "Yep. Fine." She examined her sore thumb and concluded there'd be no amputation. But something tugged at her heart on the inside. Every time she pictured cute Maddie, she imagined her laughing and singing and baking cookies with her new mom which happened *not* to be Bertie. *As it should be, Bertha.* She barely knew the little girl. Therefore, she shouldn't feel any connection to her. Right? Right.

"At the end of three weeks, I get to finally move on. End of story," Bertie said with way more conviction than she felt. She glanced at Gary. "What?" She could've sworn he said, "You're kidding yourself," under his breath.

"You're still moving? After you finish the renovation?"

Bertie detected a sharp edge to his tone. Maybe. No. Yes. She didn't know. Bertie avoided the question. "The electrician needs the specs on the sconces for the living room. Have the sconces been delivered?"

"Along with the track lighting, the lanterns for the dining room, and all the bathroom lights." Gary ticked off on his fingers. "Now, stop stalling and answer my question. Don't you think I have the right to know?" Gary crossed his arms with a stern glare.

Bertie pushed a hunk of hair behind her ear and sat in front of her computer, pretending to read a spreadsheet. "I'm not sure," she murmured. "About moving. I haven't spoken with the firm in Atlanta recently. We've only exchanged a few emails, but they haven't confirmed whether they could still use me or not. And what about DP? They're going to start another house with my bonus money. I'd hate to leave in the middle of that."

"Uh-huh. You know…it's okay. You're allowed to change your mind. I'm a selfish bastard. I don't want to see you leave," he said.

Bertie swiveled in her desk chair and faced him along with her internal battle. "It probably won't be forever, but I really think DP needs me and after Keith's…uh, after this renovation is over, I can devote more time to helping them. Besides, the Milners want to redo their master suite. She called yesterday and said she hated the color blue. She wants everything in lavender."

Gary shot Bertie an incredulous look. "You have got to be joking. What do you mean she hates blue? She picked blue. She said blue was her favorite color because it matched her husband's eyes. She signed off on every blue sample we showed her. Are you sure you heard correctly?" Gary plopped down on a mound of fabric samples piled up on the only other chair in the office.

"Yep. Apparently, she and Mr. Milner are having another world war and she said she never wanted to look at the color blue again. She wants everything in lavender and pink because she knows he'll hate it and she hopes he moves to another room."

Gary leaned back and groaned. "How come all we seem to attract are crackpot clients?"

"Who cares? The way I see it, the wackier the better. We get to write up another proposal on a master suite, and you and I have another job to do together. It doesn't get much better than that."

Bertie couldn't keep her happy smile from spreading. She had reasons to stay in Harmony, and they were good reasons. Really good ones.

Gary stretched his legs out and clasped his hands behind his head. "You know, that's the best news I've heard in a long time."

"About the Milners?"

"No. About you staying in Harmony. Maybe you'll make me an aunt one day."

Bertie furrowed her brows. "Huh? How did we jump the track from me staying to you being an aunt?"

"Because I've seen Maddie Morgan in action. That ten-year-old could teach seminars on how to influence people to get what you want." Gary grinned like a sleek panther toying with his prey.

Alarm prickled down her spine at what Gary implied.

"What do you mean by that?"

"I can read her like I read *Esquire* magazine. That little girl wants a new mama and she wants her to be you."

Bertie slumped in her chair. Sweet sassy molassy.

———⚬———

"What'd you think?" Keith asked Gail as they stepped onto the sidewalk outside an old historic home converted into a restaurant and bar. He had brought Gail to downtown Raleigh for dinner and to hear a new jazz band.

"The food was great. The music will take some getting used to. I'm more of a current pop kinda girl."

Keith tried not to flinch. Sweet, syrupy songs by Taylor Swift and stupid ballads by a teen boy band from England popped into his head. Songs that Maddie went crazy over.

"Of course, I love the oldies from the '80s and '90s too," Gail said, sensing that she'd insulted him.

Oldies? God, he felt ancient. Keith squeezed her hand and smiled, trying to ease her apprehension and his feeling of doom. "I like all kinds of music. How about country?"

"Love country music!"

"You wouldn't be a true Carolina girl if you didn't love the twang of pick-up trucks, cornbread, and goin' to prison." He laughed and Gail nodded, giggling. "They seem to have lots of concerts around here. Would you like to go to one?"

"That would be totally awesome," she gushed. Keith quirked a brow at her. "What?" she asked with bright eyes.

"Just trying to picture you in jeans and cowboy

boots," he chuckled. He hadn't seen her in anything but khakis, tennis outfits, or exercise clothes. On date nights, she wore conservative clothing, like what she wore tonight: black slacks, blue silk blouse with a dark blazer, and pearls. Not big on the latest fashions, his Gail. Nothing about her wardrobe would entice a man. She remained neatly packaged and buttoned up, like a proper Sunday school teacher. Keith had never even glimpsed a hint of cleavage.

Bertie's world-class cleavage jumped to the forefront in his mind as he remembered her in some drapey green top the other day. She'd bent over to pick up a stone sample at his house and that fabulous loose top did its job by falling away from her scantily clad, lace-covered breasts. Eyes had popped and jaws dropped as half the construction crew came to a complete stop to ogle her voluptuous breasts.

"Uh, well, I don't exactly own any cowboy boots, but I could probably borrow a pair from my roommate." Gail's conversation brought him back to the present and his vanilla, tame world.

Keith smiled at the pink that colored her cheeks. "You scare up some jeans and boots, and I'll provide the cowboy hats," he said. They had reached his car in the parking garage and Keith opened her door.

Gail giggled…again. "I can't picture you in a cowboy hat."

"Really? Why not?"

"You look too…sophisticated, I guess."

Keith glanced down at his designer gray cashmere sweater, worn jeans, and scuffed-up Gucci loafers and shrugged. "Next time, I'll wear my tennis hat and sweatshirt." He winked at Gail and headed for the driver's side.

Keith stood outside Gail's apartment door and peered down. Her face had a weird green cast from the cheap lights illuminating the hallway. She waited, anticipating his kiss with her lips slightly parted. A good sign. He hadn't dared try any other moves on her, partly because he didn't want to scare her away and partly because he hadn't been…interested? Inspired?

Keith pecked Gail's soft lips and pulled back. "Maybe we can take Maddie with us to the country concert. What do you think?"

Gail leaned into him and fluttered her eyelashes. "That's a wonderful idea. I would love to get to know her better." Then she went up on tiptoes and pressed her lips to his mouth. After a couple of nibbles, she said, "We should spend more time together"—nibble, nibble—"just the three of us."

Holy crap! Sweet, innocent Gail had turned into tangy, aggressive Gail. Keith slid his hands around to the small of her back, careful not to palm her ass. He shifted a little for a better fit, molding her slender frame against him, and latched his lips to hers. She gripped his shoulders and swirled her tongue with his. And for the first time, he heard Gail moan as if she wanted more than chaste kisses from him. Keith swallowed her moans and sucked her tongue into his mouth. She gave him an awkward shove and his back hit the door as she ran jerky hands up his chest and around his neck. She was ramping up the heat, but he got the distinct impression that this was not her field of expertise. He angled his head for better access, trying to get comfortable. His sweet Gail had turned tigress as she nipped at his bottom lip and gave a low growl—or maybe a clearing of her throat. Keith wasn't sure.

Her hand skipped any foreplay of running down his chest and abdomen, and went straight for ground zero. Whoa! Keith stopped her heat-seeking, inexperienced hand in the nick of time and placed it back around his neck. As much as he needed to get laid, he didn't really want it to be like this. Not some quickie in the darkened hallway of her apartment building. Not with Gail, the future mother of Maddie and maybe more children. He wanted their first time to be romantic and meaningful. Call him sappy or old-fashioned, but he had envisioned his first time with Gail to be on their wedding night. Not in her ridiculously clean granny apartment with her two weird roommates listening at the bedroom door.

But fooling around by the front door did hold some appeal. He skated his fingers up her back, threading them through her silky, straight hair. Gail sighed with pleasure as he scattered kisses around the edge of her mouth and cheek and eyelids. He nibbled on her lips as his mind wandered, thinking about the time and if Francesca and Maddie had made it to Virginia before dark. He should call and find out. His thoughts flicked over to the Jaycee Park and his business plan for the academy and then he remembered he needed to drop off some important papers for Bertie…shit. Keith broke away as if he were kissing a hairy tarantula. Gail gasped as she stumbled from his abrupt departure and his hand shot out to steady her. Fuck.

Keith rubbed his sweaty palms down his jeans. "Uh, it's late…I should call…Maddie and Aunt Francesca are waiting to hear from me," he babbled like a half-wit while Gail gulped for air. He detected a narrowing of her eyes heading straight for pissed-off land. But she ducked her head, averting her gaze, before he could be sure. She fumbled with the key in her shaky hand. He grabbed the key and shoved it in the lock. "I'll call you, okay?" he said in a steadier voice. He cupped her chin and turned her reddened face toward him. "I had a great time tonight," he said, stroking her cheek with his thumb in his attempt to steer them back on course. "I'm sorry. I just need to make sure everything's okay with Maddie."

Gail's expression softened and she gave a wobbly smile. "I understand. I had a great time tonight too. Thank you."

Keith kissed her heated forehead, pausing as he inhaled her faint, calm, pleasant scent. "Good. I'll check online for the next concert and let you know." He turned the key and pushed her door open.

Gail nodded as she moved inside. "Good night."

"Wait...I almost forgot," he heard himself say. Gail paused. "Harmony is having some kind of festival in a week or so. The Downtown Get 'Er Done or some ridiculous name like that."

Her lips tipped up in a shy smile. "I've heard of it."

"Anyway, I would love it if you could join Maddie and me." Tension seeped from her stiff shoulders. "Lots of food, music, crafts...a good old-fashioned festival. What do you say?"

"Sure. Sounds fun."

His lungs eased, releasing a huge breath. "Great. It's a date."

———

The idea of beating his head against a brick wall held great appeal. Keith cursed aloud at his stupidity. What the hell was wrong with him? He held an attractive woman in his arms who had feelings for him, and he'd almost blown all his weeks of hard work by behaving like a thirty-three-year-old virgin who didn't know what his dick was for. God, if his friends could see him now, they'd fall over laughing their asses off. Keith gave the gas pedal an extra punch as he sped from the parking lot.

Each date with Gail had gotten better and better. So far, they'd gone on a bike ride on some nature trails through one of the state parks. They had played tennis a couple of times. Play might be a stretch, but they'd hit balls together, and he'd even coached her on her serve. Overall, Gail showed potential to be a good club-level player. At least she knew the head of the racket from the butt. Unlike Bertie, who had never held a racket in her life and didn't even own a pair of decent tennis shoes.

Other dates with Gail had consisted of a couple of chick flicks at the theater. Keith would rather have gnawed off his arm, but Gail seemed to enjoy them, and it saved him from having to come up with scintillating conversation. And she'd made him dinner in her tiny, freakishly neat apartment. The food had been very good, and she even baked a chocolate cake and wrapped it up for him to take home. With the exception of her roommates, one whose hand strayed beneath the table and found its way to his thigh, and the other, who stared at him with two different odd-colored eyes and blathered on and on about the endangered Carolina gopher frog, the evening hadn't been half bad.

And tonight, he ventured out and tried something a little

more sophisticated. He shook his head. So she wasn't a big fan of jazz; it didn't matter. She had other more important qualities for him to consider. Like her athleticism, her love of tennis and books, her way with children, and her baking abilities. The mere fact that she seemed to like his daughter despite Maddie's atrocious behavior could not be overlooked. It took guts to want to spend more time with someone else's kid—particularly when the kid in question acted like a spoiled, obnoxious brat.

Keith could feel a headache stabbing the backs of his eyes as he remembered all the past arguments with Maddie over the last few weeks. He still didn't understand her immediate dislike of Gail. Maddie had only met her twice. Once at the bookstore and then one other time when Keith had picked her up from school and took her by Gail's apartment. Gail had brought a book home that she thought Maddie might enjoy reading.

The visit couldn't have been more painful if Keith had ordered everyone to have their toenails ripped out, one by one. Maddie had been obstinate and surly, and Gail kept adjusting the silk arrangement of navy blue flowers that sat in a brass bowl on her oak coffee table. Maddie scanned the contents of Gail's apartment, taking in the surfaces covered with lacy doilies and the old spinning wheel that occupied one corner. And to Keith's horror, Maddie asked Gail if she lived with her grandmother. Gail laughed and said she understood why Maddie would ask, because most of her furniture had been handed down from her grandparents and old aunts. As Keith shuffled Maddie to the door, he had to squeeze her shoulder to prompt Maddie to thank Gail for the book and the homemade lemonade.

The entire ride home that day, Maddie had sulked. But the minute she had gotten back to Aunt Francesca's house, she had miraculously cheered up and started yammering about how excited she was about her new bedroom and how she couldn't wait to move into their new house. Which drove the conversation over to Bertie and how much Maddie loved her and how she couldn't wait to work with Bertie on some charity housing project. And Maddie would give him these sly looks or would sniff in his general direction as if he had the intelligence of a baked potato.

Images of Bertie marauded his mind, making it hard to concentrate on anything else—like getting his life in order and making a serious commitment to Gail and even to Dottie Duncan and the Jaycee Park and to the start of his tennis academy. He couldn't settle down long enough to focus on any of these issues that needed his immediate attention.

As he neared the city limits to Harmony, he made the turn that would lead him to the Jaycee Park instead of heading to his empty home. From a distance, he could see the bright lights of the tennis courts which meant the courts were open. Perfect. Scrounging up a pro or two shouldn't be too hard. Just what he needed: an opportunity to smash some balls. Playing a few sets of tennis would give his muscles a workout and clear his mind. When all else failed, he could always rely on his training to regain his focus.

The next day, Keith kept busy by cleaning construction debris from his house and yard. He had called Maddie the night before and again this morning to check on their progress. Francesca wasn't planning to return home today, instead deciding to stop and visit some friends in Richmond and stay the night. Maddie had seemed okay saying good-bye to all her friends at school and was excited to be stopping in Richmond for some shopping. Keith then managed to place a few phone calls to his agent and his coach regarding his ideas on opening an academy, trying to drum up some interest, and getting the ball rolling. After running and working out, he headed over to Raleigh for another round of tennis at the Raleigh Tennis Club and then dinner with Nick and Marabelle Frasier. But once again, he found himself driving back to Harmony without any clearer answers than he had had the day before. The clock was ticking and he needed to make a move. Francesca had made it very clear that she was planning a wedding, and he'd better show up with a blushing bride. She wasn't giving him any wiggle room since he'd disappointed her with his irresponsible behavior in the past. Doing right by Maddie was too important to her and to him.

Keith caught his grim expression in the rearview mirror. He glimpsed a bulging folder on his backseat and remembered that it needed to be delivered to Bertie. He'd been given explicit instructions by Gary to get the documents to Bertie as soon as possible. He turned down the single road that led to Bertie's little gingerbread house stuck in the boonies. He didn't know why, but for the first time that weekend, he felt a sense of calm, as if he were finally heading home—a place where he belonged.

Keith parked his SUV alongside Bertie's house and killed the engine. A light shone from the kitchen window and lights were on in the front as well. He checked the time, noting it was a little after ten. Maybe a little late to be dropping off papers. But Gary had been adamant that he return the signed orders.

He pushed his fingers through his hair and adjusted the Bulgari sports watch on his wrist. Before he could chicken out, he grabbed the folder from the back and headed for the front entrance. Dropping off important papers. Nothing else. Keith's conscience glared at him and shook its fist in his face, telling him that this was a mistake. At the same time, his dick jumped to life and banged against the zipper of his jeans, yelling for Keith to let it out before it shriveled up and died.

He listened at the door for TV noises or music, but the house remained quiet. He shuffled his feet and rolled his shoulders. He'd knock once, and if Bertie didn't answer, then he'd leave the folder in her mailbox. Simple plan. Before his knuckles hit the door, it opened. Keith glanced up. There stood Bertie, with her thick hair caught on top of her head in a claw, wearing a pair of black yoga pants and a white tank top. Keith tried not to stare, but the two best breasts on the planet were braless underneath that thin white cotton.

"Hey," Bertie said on a quick breath. "What are you doing here?"

Keith fumbled with the folder in his hand. "I…uh… wanted to make sure you got this. Gary said you needed it. I've signed all the orders."

Bertie's eyes darted from his face to the folder he held out. She reached for it, saying, "Thanks. I'll start on these tomorrow." She opened the door a little wider. "Would you like to come in?" She glanced behind her. "I don't have any food to offer, but I think I've got some wine or a beer."

Keith jumped at the chance, stepping over the threshold before she could change her mind. He crowded her space as his sweater came within inches of her chest. "Sure. Beer sounds great." But he wasn't thinking about beer. He was thinking about how green Bertie's eyes appeared—except when she was excited, and then they grew darker, like a leaf changing to its autumn color with flecks of brown. Her plump lips looked like juicy raspberries, and Keith had a crazy thought of needing more fruit in his diet. And she smelled clean and fresh, as if she'd just showered. Bertie's breath seemed to be coming in small bursts as her chest made heaving motions, bringing Keith right back to his Achilles' heel: her great breasts.

"Let me get that beer," she said, but her voice sounded faint and far away. Keith pushed the front door closed without losing eye contact. He removed the folder from her fingers and tossed it on the console table by the door. He slid his hands up her smooth, cool arms until his fingers were massaging the base of her neck. He tilted her head back as Bertie's eyes closed and her berry-colored lips parted. He'd come here for this. He pressed his lips to hers and that was all it took.

Keith hoisted Bertie up and wrapped her legs around his waist, never breaking the kiss. He backed her up against the wall in the foyer and feasted on her mouth, chin, cheeks, nose, and eyes. Bertie threaded her fingers through his hair and clung to him, giving him all the encouragement he needed with her throaty moans and whimpers. She rocked against his hips as if she hated the clothing barrier even more than he did.

Keith pulled back and examined her swollen lips and

feverish eyes. "Not here. Not the first time. We need your bedroom," he growled in a frustrated voice.

Bertie appeared dazed as if she didn't understand his simple words. "Bed. *Now*," he emphasized by giving her a little shake.

"Oh. Yeah. Good."

He released her legs and she slid them down his thighs. Keith didn't waste any time. He grabbed her hand and hauled her up the stairs behind him. He kicked the door closed and started peeling off his clothes. Bertie stood on the middle of the soft-carpeted floor with her mouth open. Keith gave her a wicked grin after shucking his pants along with his boxers and kicking them across the room.

"Now it's your turn."

Bertie blinked several times. "Oh my," she breathed. "Give me a minute to take it all in. I mean, I never fantasized about it being…your being. I mean, of course, I fantasized, but I had no idea that you—"

"Now!" he growled, interrupting her prattle and grabbing the hem of her tank top, yanking it over her head. "Jesus." Bertie's perfect, full breasts bounced back into place, appearing smooth as alabaster from the silvery moonlight that filtered through her windows. Her nipples stood erect, inviting him for a taste. Keith lowered his head as he sucked one and then the other. Bertie jumped from the heat of his wet mouth and Keith grinned against her flesh. He shoved her workout pants down and took a moment to appreciate her lacy white panties embellished with tiny black bows.

"I'm going to pretend you were expecting me and wore these for my benefit." He fingered one of the satin bows that rested against Bertie's left hip. "Because, I really appreciate the hell out of them." He grinned into Bertie's flushed face. "But…now…they have to go," he said as his fingers slipped inside the elastic band and eased them down her legs. Bertie nodded as if drugged, and Keith watched as her panties floated to the floor. Then his gaze traveled back from her small toes curled into the rug, up her slim legs to where her hips flared in pure feminine form and then narrowed to her small waist. Keith touched his hand to her curvy belly. Bertie quivered beneath his fingers, and Keith wrapped his hands around her waist, bringing her flush against him until all her glorious round curves and sweet-smelling flesh molded against him like a soft, satin blanket. Keith dipped his head, capturing her lips. He made love to her honeyed mouth, driving her with his hands until she hit the side of the mattress. He gently shoved her and then followed her down on top of her fluffy bed.

Keith felt her pulse jump to life as he trailed kisses down the column of her throat. He could feel the smoothness of her skin as he slid his palm along her chest to the tops of her breasts. Her taut nipple stabbed his palm as his fingers played with her warm, full breast. Bertie suckled his tongue with a deep moan and gripped his shoulders, pulling him even closer as she squirmed under him, causing hot friction to singe his flesh. Keith let out a groan buried deep in his chest. He pulled back and gazed into her fiery eyes that mirrored his own heat.

"Do you remember the first day I met you on that ladder?"

"Mmm-hmm." Bertie stroked his arm as she bit into her lower lip.

"I wanted to do this." He buried his face in her perfect cleavage, placing tender kisses between her breasts as her hands skated down his back.

"Is that all you wanted to do?" Bertie asked in a strangled voice.

He lifted his gaze to hers and grinned. "That's just the beginning. The best part is yet to come." Keith's hot mouth on her breast drove Bertie wild. Her skin burned and her toes curled.

"Keith?"

He stopped his phenomenal nuzzling on the sensitive skin below her ear, and Bertie cupped his cheeks with her palms.

"The night we almost made love in my kitchen—"

"One of my fondest memories."

Bertie hesitated as Keith studied her. "I thought we wanted the same thing that night"—her thumb stroked the stubble on his chin—"but you ducked out of here like you'd just robbed a bank."

"I was an idiot." His gaze locked onto hers. He entwined his fingers with hers and kissed the back of her hand. "I'm not running anymore."

"What's changed?" Bertie whispered, praying she hadn't blown it with her quest for answers.

Keith rested his forehead on hers and moaned. "Me. You. I can't deny it anymore. Staying away from you has not worked. I've wanted you ever since I found you hiding in my closet." He nibbled on her lips. "I wanted you even when you thought I was gay. And if I take one more cold shower, I'll be classified as a polar bear." Keith's smile faded and his gaze grew tender. "I need you. Now. Tonight. I won't survive another day."

All Bertie could manage was a weak nod before he swooped down and took possession of her mouth and her body. Keith's hand worked its way down her body until his fingers feathered the top of her thigh and he touched her slick flesh, caressing it exactly where she wanted him most. Every sensation pooled and intensified at the dance of his talented fingers.

"Bertie," he sighed in a husky voice. He kissed her again and Bertie wrapped her arms around his neck as his fingers toyed with the wet heat between her legs, making her moan and thrash her head against the pillow.

Keith lifted his head and said, "This has got to be uncomfortable." He unclipped the claw digging into her scalp and tossed it over his shoulder. Bertie let out a breath in pleasure. Keith loosened her hair, spreading it out over the pillowcase. "God, you're so gorgeous," he said, his tone reverent.

Bertie's heart swelled with emotion she couldn't disguise anymore as she gazed into his deep, dark eyes. She felt a pull, a connection that short-circuited her brain whenever he was near. Keith touched her more than physically. He touched her heart and wrapped his fingers around her soul.

She slid her hand down his hard chest, marveling at the muscles that tensed beneath her touch. Keith rolled to the side, propped on one arm. His fingers caressed her belly, her hip, and the back of her thigh. Bertie threaded her fingers through his thick hair and walked a teasing trail down his abdomen with her other hand until she grasped his erection. Keith jerked on a groan and his entire body tensed. He was hard as a rock all over.

"Stop." He wrapped his hand around hers as she

began to stroke. "That feels too good." She looked into his heavy-lidded eyes. "I need to grab a condom from my pants on the floor," he said in a strained voice.

"The ones you tore off as if they were on fire?" Bertie smiled, watching his eyes grow darker with passion as she pushed his hand aside and gave his cock one long, measured stroke. "Keith…I'm ready for the *best* part," she purred.

"Oh God," he groaned. "Don't move." He kissed her hard and then rolled over and off the bed with athletic grace. Bertie admired the play of his sleek muscles.

He rolled a condom on in record-breaking time and rejoined her on the bed and Bertie breathed, "Hurry." Their eyes met briefly until Keith moved over her and brought the head of his cock into place. With her help, he eased the long, hard length of him inside her. Bertie gasped. It had been a long time, and she was tight, but this felt right. Then he withdrew and buried himself even deeper, and she swallowed a scream that threatened to spill forth as he filled her.

"Don't hold back. I want to hear you." Desire shone in his eyes as Keith rocked into her.

"Oh, Keith…I feel…" Bertie half groaned, half panted.

Keith plunged his tongue into her mouth, kissing her as he thrust deeper and deeper. She wrapped a leg around his waist, adjusting to his rhythm as he pumped. His greedy kisses stole her breath and she gripped his shoulders with need and passion. With each push, he drove them closer to climax, stroking her insides until she felt she'd explode. Keith tore his mouth from hers and they both gasped for air. She arched her back and dug her nails into his back. Keith dropped his head and latched on to her stiff nipple with his hot mouth. Then he planted kisses on her chest and up her throat.

"God, Bertie, you feel amazing."

"Keith," she barely said above a whisper. "Please... don't stop." Bertie wanted to say more. She wanted to tell him how she felt. She burned to tell him that she'd never felt this way before. That he was amazing and that she was going to fly apart into a million pieces. She wanted to tell him that she loved him. But then she looked up into his intense features, and he wrapped his arm beneath her knee, spreading her wider. He penetrated deeper, increasing the friction and intensifying the sensation, each thrust building toward a climax, making her mindless with need. Her heart pounded in her chest and every miniscule bit of awareness zeroed in on where they were joined as one.

"Come for me," he rasped, and Bertie obeyed as if she'd been waiting for his command. Her muscles tightened, her legs trembled, and her head fell back as she reached the pinnacle. Stars exploded behind her eyes as her orgasm slammed into her.

Keith plunged faster and deeper until a pent-up groan burst from his heaving chest. Then he stopped. Bertie could feel the tremors as his arms shuddered from the strain. Every nerve in Bertie's body burned from the soul-sucking orgasm as Keith collapsed on top of her.

After endless moments of enjoying the sensation of him still inside her, Bertie stirred. Keith's body still covered hers. She had no idea how long they'd been in that position, stuck together like glue, but her leg had begun to fall asleep from his dead weight. Okay, maybe not dead—more like delicious weight. He lifted his head and a bead of sweat trickled down his temple and curled around his jawline.

"You okay?" he asked in a rusty voice.

Bertie nodded. "Mmm, yeah. That was…wonderful," she whispered.

Keith's sexy half smile appeared. "It was." He paused to plant a kiss on her nose. "And so are you."

Bertie's heart backflipped. He rolled on his side, taking her with him as if he couldn't bear to let her go. She smoothed her hand over the sculpted muscles on his chest. He tipped her head up and pressed a soft kiss to her lips.

"Do you mind if I don't leave?"

Her heart triple flipped and a smile played around her lips. His warm gaze reflected the same love she felt for him. But Bertie didn't want to dwell on what she saw burning in his eyes or felt in his touch. She'd think about that later…much later.

"No. I don't mind." She gave a lazy smile. "I was wondering…do you think the best could maybe get even better?"

A low, deep chuckle rumbled from his chest. "We'll never know unless we try."

Chapter 19

BERTIE SAT AT THE CHROME TABLE IN HER KITCHEN, rubbing the edge of her favorite green mug with her index finger. She marveled as the sun painted the sky a rosy orange, making the leaves on the trees wake up and greet the beautiful morning. A silly smile played around her lips as she enjoyed the smell of fresh-brewed coffee filling her kitchen. She adjusted the shirt she wore and tucked it under her bottom. The white button-down shirt that belonged to Keith. Yup. Keith. The guy she'd spent hours in bed with, making love with twice…no, make that three times. Three times! Bertie hadn't had sex three times in the last year, much less in one night.

At the moment, Mr. Studalicious was taking a shower. Bertie had a sudden thought that she'd forgotten to stock the linen closet in her bathroom with clean towels and maybe he didn't have anything to dry off with. That would be tragic. Keith standing in her bathroom in all his naked glory, dripping wet with no towel. *Oh my*. She needed to get up there and make sure she caught him before he managed to cover anything important with her dainty finger towel or her lace drapery valence. Bertie giggled at her silliness as she poured him a steaming cup of coffee, adding a dollop of cream, and carried it up the stairs.

She entered her bedroom and actually blushed as she spied the bed with its rumpled covers strewn in disarray.

Pausing, she sighed, allowing the memories from the night before to sweep over her. Being physically attached to Keith was the highlight. She loved the way his hair curled around his ears and felt like silk between her fingers and how his scruffy stubble managed to tickle her in all the right places. And she loved the intensity of his dark eyes and how he directed all that intensity her way, as if she were the most beautiful woman alive. The way his passion and force consumed her. And the way his sensuous mouth pressed into her flesh in the most tender way. And how he delighted in kissing every inch of her body until she begged him to stop, but instead, he'd laughed and pinned her to the bed, starting all over, kissing every inch again and again.

The sound of the shower shook Bertie out of her reverie. She still had time to gather some clean towels. She placed Keith's coffee mug on the bedside table next to his watch, cell phone, and her contemporary crystal lamp. She went about picking up the decorative linen pillows which littered her floor and tossing them back on her bed when Keith's cell rang. Startled, Bertie checked the clock sitting on top of her antique painted end table. Who'd be calling at seven on a Sunday morning? By the time she'd reached the bedside table, the ringing had stopped.

Bertie's feet tangled with Keith's discarded jeans and sweater so she bent and placed them on the bed when his phone rang again. This time, she picked it up and glanced at a long distance number displayed on the screen. Bertie hesitated. She didn't make a habit of answering other people's calls, but she wondered if something may be wrong with Maddie. Or maybe…

before she could talk herself out of it, she pressed the answer button.

"Hello?" Her voice sounded anxious.

"Hello…darling?"

The feminine voice on the other end sounded vaguely familiar. "Aunt Franny? Sorry. I can't hear you very well."

"This is Angelina Morgan. I'm trying to reach my son, Keith. Have I dialed the wrong number?"

Total surprise robbed Bertie speechless. "Hello? Is anyone there?" Angelina Morgan said, clear as if she stood in the room next door.

"Oh, um. Yes, I'm still here. But Keith—"

"You must be Keith's new girlfriend, or is it fiancée now?" A husky chuckle poured through the line. "I'm sorry we haven't met, but I've already heard such wonderful things about you from Francesca."

Bertie could feel the color drain from her face and her fingers felt cold. Girlfriend? Fiancée? Bertie knew the way she knew her own handwriting that Keith's mother was *not* referring to her. Because up until the incredible sex they'd shared last night, she and Keith had been ducking and dodging each other like a couple of prize fighters—not dating and certainly not engaged—for fear of what might happen if they got too close. Like a night spent in bed, making love.

"Hello? Are you still there?" Bertie jerked to attention at Angelina's cultured voice.

"Yes. I'm sorry, but—"

"What the hell are you doing with my phone?" Keith snapped over Bertie's shoulder. Bertie jumped at the sound of his harsh voice, almost dropping the phone from her stiff fingers.

"You! I'm sorry." She shoved the phone at Keith. "It's your mother."

Keith's mask of anger fell into place as he snatched the phone from her hand. He breathed several obscenities before putting it to his ear and turning his back on Bertie.

Gone was the tender man who'd held her in his arms as she'd slept and then woke her with a trail of kisses along her neck. Keith strode toward the window, wearing one of her fluffy white bath towels and nothing else. Beads of water trickled down his sleek back. He planted his feet apart in a rigid stance and gripped the edge of her window frame as he growled in a low voice into the phone. Bertie inched backward, trying to vacate the room before he turned his angry eyes on her again, but Keith's burst of outrage stopped her.

"*No.* You are not coming to the wedding."

She froze as her heart flipped and fell onto the floor. Her lungs locked up and she feared she might pass out. Her brain screamed inside her head, blocking the rest of Keith's conversation. It was true. Somehow she'd always known it was true, but she never really wanted to believe it. Somewhere deep down in the far recesses of her heart, she had thought that maybe he'd want her. He'd marry her. And after last night, after all the love they'd shared, allowing their bodies to express the words they couldn't find or had feared to say, she'd been sure that Keith was the man for her. They had a connection. She loved him and had probably loved him since that first day he'd caught her hiding in his closet. And after last night, she'd thought for sure he felt the connection too.

"No. I haven't made any plans yet. Maybe. Yeah, I'll let you know. Okay…no…I'll call. Don't call me." He gave an angry punch to the off button. He lowered his head as his broad shoulders slumped forward. This was not a picture of a man who'd just shared a wonderful night with the woman he loved. This was a picture of a man who deeply regretted his past actions, who wished he was anywhere but here—a picture of a man trying to find the words to let her down easy.

"Keith," Bertie choked on a whisper. He didn't respond. He stood with his head hanging low, memorizing every tuft and fiber of her cut-pile wool carpet. Bertie cleared her throat. "Would you like to…er, talk about it?"

He lifted his head with a glassy-eyed stare as if he were far, far away, in a world that Bertie knew nothing about. Long, agonizing moments ticked by.

"She sucked as a mother," he finally said in a rough voice. "She basically abandoned me when I was fifteen. My dad had died the year before and my mom…my mom couldn't handle it." Keith pushed a heavy hand through his wet hair and then gripped his scalp as if his head pounded from a wicked hangover. "Nothing was the same after that."

Bertie held his coffee out to him, hoping it would help. Keith didn't move to take it. "I stayed in boarding school. The only family that claimed me was Aunt Francesca. She'd come up for holidays or take me on vacations. My mom would flit over now and again, but not for very long. Our relationship was painful on the good days. I resented the hell out of her. Still do."

He untied the towel around his waist and finished

drying off, oblivious to his nakedness. Bertie blushed like a schoolgirl, as if she hadn't just spent an entire night naked with him in bed. Her legs felt like jelly. She wanted to sit down or run screaming from the room, but she didn't do either.

Keith pulled on his boxers, tossing his used towel on the bed. He continued talking, almost in a monotone, as if he knew it all by rote. "She did come to see me play at Wimbledon one year and tried to meet with me. I didn't want to have anything to do with her. I had Adriana and Maddie to worry about." His humorless laugh jolted Bertie with its hollow echo. "So, after thousands of dollars and years of therapy, I realized that having a fucked-up childhood with an emotionally stunted mother was never going to change. I still fucked up most of my twenties. Why not? I had the money, the looks, and I felt entitled."

Bertie placed his untouched coffee on top her chest of drawers. "Keith…that's the past. It doesn't have—"

"Then Adriana died and even though our marriage sucked, she was Maddie's mother. I never wanted her to die. Not like that. Not alone in a burning car."

Bertie winced and reached out to touch him. "I'm sorry. It must've been horr—"

"No more." He moved away from her. "I've changed. I'm not that person anymore. As much as Aunt Francesca's ultimatum pisses me off, I'm going through with it. I'm fixing my life so that I don't fuck up Maddie's…any more than I already have. I have to do this. I'm never going back to the way things were." He spoke as if he'd memorized a speech or had been brainwashed. Bertie's heart squeezed at the pain she witnessed around his eyes and the tightening of his jaw.

He pulled up his jeans and shoved his feet in his loafers. "I refuse to have a repeat performance of one of the world's most poisonous marriages." He stopped and looked around the room as if seeing it for the first time. "I...I can't do this."

Bertie's heart slammed into her chest. "What do you mean 'this'?"

Keith finally cut his dark eyes to her. "I can't be with you. Last night was a—"

"Don't say it!" she warned. She didn't think her heart could take it. "Don't you dare say last night was a mistake."

"Not saying it isn't going to change anything."

Bertie shook her head. "Last night was the best thing that ever happened to me. You're the best thing that has ever happened to me. You and Maddie." Her legs trembled. "I love you."

Keith flinched as if she'd thrown sand in his face. Tears streaked down Bertie's face, but she didn't wipe them away. "That's right. I love you. And you love me, but you're too afraid or chickenshit or something to admit it." He turned his back and pulled on his sweater as if he didn't want to hear what she had to say.

Bertie yanked on his arm until he faced her. "You've got it in your warped, effed-up brain that I'm the wrong kind of woman. Good enough to screw, but not good enough to marry."

"Bullshit! This has nothing to do with you."

"The hell it doesn't! So your mother abandoned you. Tough shit! My mother and my father died. And all I had was Cal, the restaurant, and Aunt Franny. I had to scrape and scrap for everything I've ever accomplished. If it weren't for Aunt Franny, I would never have gone to design school." Bertie struggled for air as she filled her lungs. "You've had a great education and a career that most people only dream about. You've got more money than you could spend in a lifetime. You can do or be whatever you want. And you're blessed with a beautiful daughter who loves you. You've got it all."

Bertie looked down at her bare toes, then back up into his pain-filled face. He talked about his past that needed to stay in the past. He had closed himself off from feeling anything. Even the connection between them.

"And if you'd stop wallowing in your self-imposed purgatory, you'd see that you could have me too," she ended on a whisper.

Keith shoved his hands in his pockets and his features turned blank. An awkward silence filled the room.

"Bertie...I...I need to do what I think is right. I'm not thinking about myself. I'm only thinking of Maddie. And she needs—"

A sob tore from Bertie's throat. She pressed a hand to her mouth.

"You don't love me. You just think you do. Like you said, I'm a self-centered, selfish bastard who's got more baggage than anyone wants to deal with. You and I got caught up in a crazy relationship that revolved around an impossible deadline and lust. It was just sex, Bertie. Don't read any more into it than that."

Devastation and anger crashed into Bertie at the same time. "That's not true! I don't have just sex. Don't tell me what I'm feeling right now. I love you, but right now I'd like to kill you."

He shook his head. "Bertie, you're confusing lust for love. There's a huge difference. In a few weeks, you're gonna see that I'm right and be glad."

She folded her arms around her middle, hugging herself in Keith's shirt. "You're wrong. I'm not confused. But when the day comes that you realize you've made a mistake, I probably won't be here."

Keith crossed the room toward the door and then stopped. "That's right. You won't be," he said, anger lacing his voice. A different kind of anger. A jealous anger. Startled, Bertie stared at him. "What about your dream of leaving this hick town and making it in a big city? You'd throw all that away to stay here? To be with me? And Maddie?" His burst of laughter sounded bitter. "I don't think so. No way am I standing in the way of your dreams so you can throw it back in my face. I live with enough guilt already. I don't need to feel guilty about you too."

Keith rubbed his hand across his left wrist. When he didn't feel his watch, he moved to the nightstand and picked it up. "Last night was a mistake." Bertie choked back a sob. "But not the way you think. I loved having sex with you, and God knows I'd do it again and again if I could, but I can't. I can't screw up like that anymore."

He strapped the watch on his wrist. "Finish the house. Don't lose the money Aunt Francesca promised you over this. And follow your dreams." He gestured toward the bed. "Let's forget all this and go back to the way things were."

His rejection of what they'd shared and what had

passed between them tore her heart. But at least Bertie knew. She knew he wouldn't fight for them. He'd shut down and closed her out.

"Fine. You're right. No way I'm losing a hundred and fifty thousand dollars over one night of sex. I'll finish on time and then I'll be out of your life forever."

Keith gave a curt nod and took a step back. "Good. You won't regret it. I'll see you…take care of yourself." He turned and walked out of her room and her life.

Bertie stood in the same spot, staring at the empty doorway until she heard her front door close. She waited, hoping and praying that he'd turn around and race back up the stairs and haul her into his arms, showering her face with kisses and declaring his love for her. In the distance, the start of his car engine and the faint sound of tires backing out of her gravel driveway reached her ears. Bertie fell to her knees and sobbed into her hands.

"Fuck!" Keith hit the gas pedal and floored it down the two-lane country road. His mind calculated how long it would take if he kept driving until he entered Miami-Dade county. He needed to get the hell out of this town before it sucked the very life from his soul. He couldn't do this anymore. He didn't know who he was or what he wanted. He should never have agreed to move here and set up house, to try and make a life for himself and Maddie. He knew from day one that everyone in this town was insane. And now, they'd made him crazy too.

Keith pulled his Cayenne into an empty parking lot of an abandoned Shell station with broken windows and rusted gas pumps from the 1950s. He killed the engine and dropped his forehead on the steering wheel. God, he hated himself. What the fuck had he done? He'd just had the best sex of his life with a beautiful woman who he hadn't been able to exorcise from his brain from the minute he caught her tottering on a ladder in ridiculous high heels. Bertie had played a major role in every one of his fantasies from the minute he met her until today. And after all these months, he finally got where he'd been dying to be and he never wanted to leave. That scared him most of all. Keith's head almost exploded the minute he pushed inside her. Bertie was hot and sexy and curved in all the right places. She was sensual and responsive, and Keith got hard again just thinking about it.

This was what got Keith in trouble in the first place. He had to move past the sex. He didn't need someone like Bertie in his life, who stirred up feelings he couldn't control. He didn't need her big personality and all the drama attached to it. He'd been down that road before and knew how twisted and winding it became, with hair-pin turns and bumps and cracks and potholes. He'd get lost again and never find his way back. He didn't want twisted anymore. He wanted straight and narrow and smooth with no hills and no turns. If he tangled himself up with Bertie, he'd never find his way out. He didn't need someone who hid in closets or climbed ladders in stilettoes, or someone who drew everyone's attention as she barreled through life on skates. He didn't want someone who was surrounded by drama. He'd had it once, and it had been a disaster.

If he allowed himself to fall for Bertie, it would only be a matter of time before he felt like he was drowning.

And she'd eventually get restless, wondering about the lost opportunities his instant family had forced her to miss. He'd be helpless and she'd be resentful. Then the arguments would escalate and the whole bitching episode would start all over again. Like his first marriage.

Keith stepped out of his car and walked to the edge of the field behind the station and looked out. A few cows grazed lazily. A circle of insects swirled in front of him and the hot sun cast a golden haze over the field. He smelled dark, damp dirt and fresh-cut grass along with something sweet. His nostrils flared. Keith knew that smell. He had breathed it in all night long, like a magic potion that made all his troubles disappear. He'd fallen asleep wearing a smile, breathing that same smell. Keith turned and spied the source. The back of the dilapidated station, with its peeling paint and blackened windows, served as the perfect backdrop to the largest blooming gardenia bush he'd ever seen. The bush crawled up the cruddy walls of the building with a plethora of blooms, all in different stages of life. Keith reached out and plucked a fresh, white flower, rubbing the velvet-like petals between his fingers. He inhaled the fragrant gardenia scent and pictured Bertie all flushed with her mahogany hair spread across her white pillowcase, a smile curving her kiss-swollen lips and her green eyes glowing with pleasure. Pleasure he put there. But more than that. They glowed with all the love she had for him. The love she'd poured over him with every kiss and touch and giving of herself.

Keith closed his eyes and crushed the flower with his fist. That was how he wanted to remember Bertie. With love in her eyes. He didn't want to wake up one day and see the accusations and the blame and the indifference that he knew would come when she realized that he'd stolen all her dreams and aspirations. And he never wanted to witness that look in her eyes when she realized that he wasn't good enough for her.

Bertie met with Gary first thing on Monday morning in her office to review the last few weeks of work on Keith's house. She'd managed to wash her face and throw on an old pair of sweats and a clean T-shirt before he arrived at her house.

"Lord almighty! What the hell happened to you?" Gary asked as soon she opened the door.

Bertie ducked her head, wishing she'd applied makeup to hide her blotchy face from twenty-four hours of streaming tears. "Nothing. I might be coming down with something." *Like a broken heart from a clueless jerk who wouldn't know a good thing if it knocked him in the head with a bolt of fabric.*

"Like what? The bubonic plague? You look like shit. You better not be contagious."

"Could be a cold. Don't get too close," Bertie lied and hoped Gary wouldn't catch on. "Grab some coffee and meet me in the office."

Gary didn't move. He examined Bertie like he could see inside her brain. Finally he brushed past her toward the kitchen, mumbling under his breath, "Cold my ass."

Bertie padded her way to her office in fuzzy socks. She could do this. Gary could handle the remaining orders for Keith's house, and she'd man headquarters in her office where no one would see her. If she stayed

hidden, there'd be fewer chances of running into anyone, especially a tall, dark, dangerous, and completely
deranged ex-professional tennis player. Bertie needed
time and space to heal, forget, and move on. And she
couldn't do that when tears threatened to spill every
five seconds—especially if she had to deal with Mr.
Perfectly Tortured and Confused.

Gary strolled in, placed his mug of coffee on the
worktable, threw himself in the one chair clear of samples, and said, "Spill it."

"What?"

"You know what. Don't play dumb with me, girlfriend.
What happened between you and the studly Prince?"

Bertie swiped a betraying tear from her cheek.
"Nothing. He came by and dropped off the papers. We
have three weeks to finish and I'm not giving up."

There was a long pause before Gary spoke. "Please
tell me that at least the sex was good before he broke
your heart."

Bertie raised watery eyes to him. "What are you,
psychic?"

"When it comes to you, yes."

"Then why didn't you warn me that he'd break my
heart?" Bertie gulped back a sob.

"Aw, Bertie." Gary gathered her in his arms and
hugged her. "Do I need to get Cal to beat him up?

"N-no," she sniffled in his crisp white sleeve.

"You sit right here." He settled Bertie in the chair
he'd vacated. "I'm going to fix you some nice hot tea
and then you're going to tell old Gary all about it."

The following week Bertie and Gary worked as if their lives hung in the balance. Gary continued to be the front person on Keith's job and protected Bertie from ever having to run into him. And Bertie burned the candle at both ends by bringing meals to Mr. Carmichael, decorating for the Downtown Get Down, and running supplies to Dwelling Place, along with a check she'd written for another ten-thousand-dollar installment. Bertie had been borrowing from her savings since she hadn't collected her bonus, but she felt confident that she had nothing to worry about.

Keith only entered her mind every ten seconds or so. And she kept slices of very cold cucumbers in her fridge for her swollen eyes. And as the days passed, she tamped down any hope from creeping back into her heart. He'd stated his plan, and it didn't include her. But a part of Bertie…an itty-bitty part still felt that he'd wake up one morning and realize what a complete fool he'd been and beg her to keep his heart…forever. Okay, so she had an overactive fantasy life, but it could happen. Right? Because so far, there'd been no wedding and no announcement of a wedding. And in a town this size, news like that would've traveled faster than a hungry kid to a candy store.

The one person who had the answers to Bertie's questions would've been Aunt Franny. But Bertie refused to ask her. How could Aunt Franny have known about Keith's fiancée and not told her? She'd obviously mentioned it to her sister in Italy. Bertie's ears still burned over that embarrassing conversation. Aunt Franny's silence hurt Bertie beyond description.

At the end of the week, all of Harmony had geared

up for the festival, and even though Bertie knew Keith would be there with Maddie, there'd be plenty of activities to keep her busy and enough people to hide behind if the need arose.

By ten o'clock on Saturday morning, the high school band was playing, the Carolina Cloggers had taken the stage, the face painters and magicians were entertaining the kids, and the food vendors had cranked their generators on full blast as the combined smells of barbecue, burgers, hot dogs, chicken, and roasting corn permeated the air.

Bertie volunteered for the morning shift and helped man the booth for Dwelling Place as she and Jo Ellen Huggins sold home-baked goods to raise money. Bertie pulled her hair back from her face in a ponytail and wore a green apron with a Dwelling Place logo over a short jean skirt, aqua-blue knit T, and her favorite pink flip-flops with tiny bejeweled peace signs.

The sun beat down. Bertie stood in the only corner of the booth that provided a sliver of shade, with cool lemonade in one hand and program fanning her face in another. "Geez, it's hot."

"Don't I know it," Jo Ellen said, leaning on her palms over the table that held cakes, brownies, and doughnuts, twitching to the strings of the banjoes. "I think we could fry an egg right here on the sidewalk and it isn't even July yet." Jo Ellen stood, untied her apron, and adjusted the pink knit skirt that crept indecently up her thighs. "I'm gonna walk around. You okay without me?"

"Sure. Have fun."

Jo Ellen smiled. "I intend to. Maybe there's someone here today who needs a makeover or who'd like to dance." Jo Ellen shimmied and her pink sequined top shimmied with her.

"Preferably not the same person," Bertie added.

"Right. But at this point, I'd take about anyone." She gave Bertie a curious look. "Haven't seen much of the Prince lately, have you?"

Bertie gulped and increased the speed of the program fanning her face. "Uh, no. Not really. Gary spends more time over—"

"Rumor has it that he's found someone, and she's not from Harmony," Jo Ellen said as she looked down and adjusted the silver belt around her waist. Bertie stopped all movement as a deep chill ran through her veins. "Oh well, you win some, you lose some. Right?" Jo Ellen didn't wait for a response as she squeezed her way out of the booth and sauntered toward the dance floor set up in the middle of the food tent.

Bertie wished she could maneuver out of the booth and away from the festival for good, but someone had stopped to check out the sweets. "Can I help you? We've got some great goodies here. All homemade."

"My mouth's watering just looking at them. Did you bake all these?"

Bertie laughed. "Hardly. I only made the coconut cupcakes. I'm not big on baking."

"Oh, I *love* to bake. It's one of my favorite pastimes."

Bertie gave her a smile. "Well, I can recommend everything here. I've tasted them all, as my hips will attest, and they're all delicious."

"Hmmm. I think I'll try these red velvet cupcakes and maybe that lemon Bundt cake. This will save me from having to make dessert for my boyfriend tonight."

"Have you been exercising?" Bertie asked, noting she wore exercise clothes instead of the usual festival ware: cowboy boots, short shorts, and tight T-shirts with logos.

"No," the girl giggled.

Bertie placed the cupcakes in a tote with Dwelling Place stamped on the front. "I only asked because I like your powder-blue outfit. It matches your eyes."

The girl ran her hand down the front of her short Nike skirt. "Thanks. I'm playing tennis later with my boyfriend and his daughter. Maybe you've heard of him…"

Bertie's mind screamed, "Don't say it, don't say it!" as her hand faltered with the Bundt cake, almost dropping it on the ground.

"Keith Morgan. He lives here now. Used to be a professional tennis player."

She said it.

Bertie's body froze, but her mind raced as she took in the young girl's straight, blond hair tied back in a sleek, clean ponytail, not one that hung lopsided because of the weight of her heavy hair. A slim figure with long, athletic legs. Not pudgy hips and short legs that needed four-inch heels to look in proportion. A porcelain complexion. Not one freckle or blemish. Rosy cheeks and lips and the clearest blue eyes she'd ever seen. Not green eyes that conjured up images of murky pond water. This…this was who Keith wanted. A young, blond, blue-eyed, athletic, innocent-looking girl who loved to bake. No kidding. Anyone would want that.

"Do you know him?" the pretty blond asked, blinking at Bertie's stunned face.

"Uh, yeah, sort of. I'm helping with the design of his house," she managed to say around her swollen tongue.

"That's you?" she said, sounding enthusiastic as she handed Bertie her money. "I love what you've done with the place. It's gorgeous. I have no talent when it comes to decorating. My only talent lies in the kitchen." She gave a self-deprecating chuckle.

Bertie tamped down the bile that threatened to overtake her throat. "Th-thanks. So, you've been by the house?" She turned her back to little Miss Perfect and pressed her hand to her chest, searching for the cash box.

"Ooo, samples. Mind if I try one?" Miss Perfect didn't wait for an answer. "Yes. Keith invited me over the other day and gave me the grand tour," she said around a mouthful of brownie. "I can't wait to see what you do with the master bedroom. I love that pale, Tiffany blue you painted the walls. It's beautiful."

Master bedroom! Bertie's heart slammed into her chest so hard that it fell out and dropped to the dirt in front of her feet. She didn't think she could turn around and finish the transaction, because she was in the process of dying as her heart sputtered on the ground. "I'm glad you...er, like—"

"Gail...where've you been? My dad has been look—"

Bertie turned in time to catch Maddie bouncing toward her booth. "Bertie! I didn't know you were here." Maddie ran to the side of the booth.

"Hey there, girlfriend. You having fun?" she managed to say in a normal voice.

"I'm gonna climb the rock wall. You wanna watch?"

"Well, I have to man this booth and—" Bertie stopped. The hairs on the back of her neck stood at attention and the air turned so thick it felt like pudding. She didn't have to turn her head to know that Keith stood behind Gail.

"Keith, I've just met your designer. Well, we haven't actually met. Hey. I'm Gail Spencer." Gail extended her hand.

"Hey." Bertie clasped Gail's well-groomed hand in hers for the briefest of moments.

"This is Bertie. She's a designer, and she owns the Dog, a really cool restaurant in town where they have skating and karaoke." Bertie's insides shriveled as Maddie listed her pathetic accomplishments. "That's Gail. She sells children's books at Barnes & Noble." Bertie jerked her gaze to Maddie at the note of disgust in her voice and caught Maddie rolling her eyes. Bertie never felt the urge to hug Maddie more. She loved that kid and wanted to high-five her in front of Gail and her stupid, gorgeous, stubborn dad.

"It's…uh…good to see you, Bertie. You look… well." Keith jammed his fists in the pockets of his white tennis shorts. "Nice booth. Er, did you make all these?" he asked, referring to the sweets.

"I asked the same thing," Gail giggled. "Bertie made the coconut cupcakes."

"I want those," Maddie said. "I love coconut."

Keith's dark, hot gaze roamed over Bertie, not in a mocking way but as if he wanted to memorize every inch, down to the freckle on the inside of her right knee. Then he locked gazes with her. And she couldn't tear her eyes away.

Bertie had no idea how much time had passed, but suddenly she heard Gail clear her throat. "Uh, why don't we head over to the rock wall, Maddie?" Keith's head jerked back as if he'd been slapped out of a trance.

"I want to stay here with Bertie," Maddie said. Gail nervously fiddled with the bag holding her purchases, and Keith's lips thinned into a grim line.

"Listen, cutie. I need to finish up my shift and then I'll be sure to come find you with a coconut cupcake. Okay?"

"Maddie, let's go," Keith ordered.

"It was nice meeting you," Gail called over her shoulder as Keith ushered her away, with one hand on the small of her perfect back and the other gripping Maddie's elbow.

"Bye…bye, Bertie." Maddie waved, twisting her head over her shoulder.

Chapter 20

"WHAT'S YOUR DECISION?" FRANCESCA ASKED KEITH as he paced the length of her sitting room. It had been three weeks since the festival and Keith had finally realized some hard truths. His deadline for finding a fiancée and getting married was up. He'd called Francesca and asked for a meeting.

"You win." He stopped and stared out the French doors, seeing nothing. "I'm forfeiting the match, dropping out of the tournament."

"What do you mean?" Alarm laced Francesca's voice.

"You heard me." Francesca sat forward in her favorite French chair, wearing a coral silk sheath dress and a concerned look on her face. Hands clenched by his side, Keith said, "I'm not getting married."

"I see." Her lips pressed together and an eyebrow quirked. Clearly she didn't.

"I'm not marrying Gail. I refuse to marry another woman I don't love. Been there, done that, and I barely survived. I don't deserve that life and neither does Maddie."

"You're giving up? Just like that?" Her words cracked between them like a whip.

Keith pushed frustrated fingers through his hair. "Yeah, I guess I am. Although, you can't say I didn't give it a valiant effort." He moved next to the piano where a shallow crystal bowl sat and his gut spasmed at the sight of gardenias floating in the water. He squeezed his eyes shut. "Go ahead with the custody proceedings." His voice sounded hollow. "I can see that Maddie will benefit from your influence, and I'm not going to fight you on it." He picked up a bloom, hesitated, and dropped it back in the bowl.

"What? Where will you go? What will you do?" Agitated, Francesca stood, crossing the antique carpet to reach the bar. With shaky hands, she decanted a bottle and poured a liberal amount of scotch into a glass.

"I'm not sure, but I'm making plans—"

She turned suddenly and pierced him with a fierce glare. "You're leaving? Abandoning your daughter?"

He flinched at her incredulous tone and then watched as she swiped a tear from her cheek. "I'm not going anywhere. I've made a home here." No. Bertie had made him a home. He sucked in a breath. "I'm not bailing on Maddie or Harmony, but I refuse to marry for the sake of marrying. I'd rather be celibate for the rest of my life than force myself to marry another woman I don't love."

Keith covered the distance between them and clasped Francesca's hand and squeezed. "I think this is for the best. *You're* the best. Maddie loves it here, and she loves you."

"This is not what I want." She fiddled with the silk Hermes scarf around her neck. "I want you to be happy. I want the best for you." Stress and tension lines creased her forehead.

"I know. But I wouldn't be happy if I married for all the wrong reasons." He tugged on her soft hand. "Come, sit down. Let me explain what my plans are."

Keith stared at the melting ice watering down his fourth Mount Gay and ginger ale for the night. Patrons at the Dog laughed and sang to some bluegrass band playing on the stage, but Keith didn't hear a thing. The voice yelling inside his head had taken over, and he couldn't seem to shut it up no matter how drunk he got.

It had been almost three months since that horrible day at the Downtown festival. The last time Keith saw Bertie. The last time anyone in town had seen Bertie. After that awkward meeting with Gail over cupcakes, Keith found out later that evening that Bertie had skipped town without leaving a forwarding address. Even her brother was clueless. Keith should know, he tried beating it out of him a few weeks ago and came away with a bloody lip and bruised ego for his efforts. Cal didn't fare much better, with a swollen eye.

Gary had shut up tighter than a clam and only spoke to Keith when absolutely necessary about decorations for the house. And even Aunt Francesca had walked around wringing her hands and calling everyone in Harmony for any news of Bertie. She could not understand why Bertie had left when only two weeks remained before collecting her bonus. She'd been so close.

Keith knew.

The horror on Bertie's face when she realized who Gail was painted a crystal-clear picture.

Keith had tried for days after the festival to forget about Bertie. He even went ring shopping in hopes of solidifying his commitment to Gail. But the only ring he could focus on was a perfect emerald cut, three-carat diamond flanked by two peridot baguettes…the color of Bertie's green eyes. Not suitable for Gail.

Keith gave dating Gail his best shot. He had doubled his efforts in trying to get Maddie to accept her, but Maddie refused to bend and had fallen into a funk that Keith couldn't shake. Finally, it took sweet, sensible Gail to read the writing on the wall. She'd called Keith and asked him to meet her for coffee and proceeded to dump him. She'd spewed the line he'd used a million times before: "It's not you; it's me." Then she lobbed another ball and told him she'd met someone else. And before she left him to flounder in his cup, she told Keith that she'd suspected all along his heart never belonged to her, but to someone else. And the more she got to know him, the more certain she was. When he feigned surprise and tried back-pedaling, she narrowed her eyes and told him to get off his dumb ass and do something about it. Speechless, Keith could only stare at the back of her blond ponytail as she walked out of the coffee shop. Sweet, young Gail had the gumption to jilt a famous ex-tennis player and yes, had used the words *dumb* and *ass*. He sat in wonder at the absurdity of his life.

After that breakup, Keith's options had hit an all-time low, and he thought it best to concede to Aunt Francesca and give in to her demands. He'd finally gotten Francesca to settle down the afternoon he met with her and explained his plans for the future. Harmony would soon be the home of the new Keith Morgan Tennis Academy. Keith had worked out a deal with the city council, pledging his support and money to rejuvenate the Jaycee Park and use the adjoining property to build his academy, which would teach tennis to all levels, including the underprivileged kids in the area. Francesca had remained quiet and listened and once he'd finished, she gave a curt nod, removed her reading glasses, and then exploded.

In a nutshell, she accused him of being a shortsighted, selfish bastard. And told him if he didn't get off his ass and go after the best thing that had ever happened to him, life was going to pass him by. And yes, she used the words *bastard* and *ass*.

Keith pulled some bills from his pocket and tossed them on the table when a feminine hand reached out and scooped them up.

"Thanks. You can buy me a drink."

He didn't disguise his groan as Liza slid in the booth opposite him. She waved Sara Jean the waitress down and ordered a dirty martini.

"You look like shit," she said.

"Don't sugarcoat it or anything."

"Oh, I don't plan to. I can see that you're dumber than a bucket of lint when it comes to your personal life, and I'm going to have to intervene."

"Fuck. Spare me. I don't need another person telling me what to do with my life. I've got the whole town coming after me with pitchforks and shotguns, or whatever you crazy Southerners carry."

Liza gave him a slow, deliberate smile. "We Southerners like to tar and feather. How do you think we got the name Tar Heel State?"

"Yeah? Well, I don't see how I'm the bad guy. I'm going to put Harmony on the map with the tennis academy. You guys should be kissing my ass for pouring money into this hick town."

Liza thanked Sara Jean for her martini and brought the chilled glass to her lips. "The only way this town is ever going to kiss your fine behind is if you bring Bertie home."

Keith pinched the bridge of his nose, hoping to ward off the beginnings of a massive hangover. "And how do you propose I do that? Hell, her brother doesn't even know where she is. How the fuck am I supposed to know?"

"Oh ye of little faith. That's where I come in."

"Last time I checked, Bertie hated you."

Liza fiddled with her cocktail napkin. "She doesn't hate me. She has simply disliked me for about fourteen years, but that's about to change." Liza signaled Sara Jean over again. "Bring the Prince a big pot of hot coffee. He's going to need it."

Keith buried his head in his hands. "Why me?" he groaned.

"Don't look so pathetic. I'm doing you a huge favor."

Keith raised his brow. "Bullshit. What's in it for you?"

Liza took a slow, deliberate sip of her martini, and then said, "Precious time for myself. I don't know how much longer I can deliver meals to Mr. Carmichael and babysit Sweet Tea. So, just sit there and look hot and sexy while I tell you a story."

"Does it have a happy ending?"

"That's up to you."

Shit.

Bertie flipped through a design magazine as she lolled on the sofa in Lucy's living room. She'd been holed up in Lucy's tiny apartment in Atlanta since she bolted from Harmony almost three months ago. The only person she'd told when she shoved all her personal belongings inside her beat-up Honda CR-V was Gary. She'd handed him the key to her house and made him swear on her most coveted Manolo Blahniks and his favorite glossy of Bradley Cooper that he wouldn't tell anyone where she was. Not even Cal. Not even Aunt Franny. And not even Keith. Especially Keith.

She had no regrets so far. Okay, well maybe a few… like one hundred and fifty thousand regrets. She'd left before she could collect her bonus, and she'd let Dwelling Place down. And she missed her volunteer work and bringing meals to old Mr. Carmichael. And she even missed babysitting Sweet Tea. But mostly, she missed working on the old Victorian and bringing it back to life. Bertie would never get to see it completely finished. She had no intentions of ever walking through the rooms of that house again as long as Keith still owned it with his perfect, blond, blue-eyed young bride. That was a hurt that just kept on hurting.

But all that was in the past. Bertie didn't think about Keith or Maddie anymore. Okay, maybe she thought about them like every thirty seconds, but hey, she'd gotten better. It used to be every ten. Bertie took her little victories where she could—like living in a new, exciting city with her good friend. And working at a new, exciting design firm. Well, exciting might be stretching it a bit—or more like stretching it ten miles.

Bertie's new responsibilities consisted of sorting through tubs and tubs of discarded fabric samples tossed aside by much busier designers. Oh, and then filing away tear sheets from thousands of furniture catalogs. But the highlight of her day had to be making sure all the paint chips were clipped back into their binders in numerical order.

Too bad if her creative juices were drying up like an old peach pit and a trained monkey could do her job; she was in a new, big city. It didn't matter that she sat in traffic for two hours commuting to and from work. And it didn't matter that her cubicle was relegated to inside the bowels of the office and she never saw the light of day. None of that mattered. Because this was where she wanted to be and this was what she'd dreamed of for years.

So why did she feel so miserable?

Lucy had been kind enough to open her home to Bertie, but Bertie knew that she needed to get off her butt and find a place of her own. Even though Lucy never complained, Bertie was sure she'd gotten tired of sharing her tiny bathroom with the pedestal sink, cramped shower, and no storage.

Bertie sighed and threw the unread magazine back on the coffee table. It was Thursday night and she had nowhere to go and no one who needed her. She had approached Lucy's old neighbor next door, Mrs. Bunkins, to help with her groceries, but Mrs. Bunkins gripped her tote full of food as if Bertie was a street thug trying to rob her. And finally, Mrs. Bunkins ordered Lucy to call off her annoying roommate. Of course, Lucy didn't put it in those exact terms, but Bertie got the message.

Lucy poked her head out from the kitchen. "You hungry for dinner? I'm heating up some leftover pizza."

Bertie's stomach growled, but not in a good way.

She didn't think she could eat another pizza for the rest of her life. She missed the food from the Dog, and she missed her kitchen with the cracked cork floors and the broken green subway tile. "Nah. I'm not hungry. You go ahead without me," she said in a lackluster voice.

Lucy gave Bertie a measured once over. "Suit yourself. But if you ask me, you're being a complete idiot."

Bertie's head jerked up. "What?"

"It's obvious you're miserable. You hate it here and you should go back home."

Bertie scrambled up from the sofa and rushed to her side. "That's not true, Lulu. I love living with you. I'm sorry I've been such a lousy roommate and I know you're probably sick of me. I promise to start looking for a place this weekend. But I've loved the time we've spent together. I've really missed you. You're one of my oldest friends."

Lucy slid Bertie a strange, almost sad look. "I've loved being with you too. I hope you still feel that way when…" Lucy mumbled the last part of her sentence.

"When what? What are you talking about?"

Lucy hesitated when the doorbell to their apartment rang. "Are we expecting anybody?" Bertie asked.

"Here, drink this." Lucy shoved a glass of red wine at Bertie. "You're going to need it."

"Huh? Lucy, you're acting weird. What's going on?"

The doorbell chimed again. Lucy pushed Bertie down into a kitchen chair. "Drink. Don't move. I'll be back."

Bertie's hand shook as she sipped her wine. Something had Lucy Doolan, Bertie's good friend since fifth grade, acting weird, and Bertie didn't know what it was. Bertie took a steadier sip of wine as she listened for voices. Lucy had been acting kind of jumpy since she'd come home from work, but Bertie had been so caught up in her personal self-pity party that she hadn't bothered to inquire. Something had put that strain around Lucy's gray eyes.

"Bertha Mavis, don't you look like shit."

Not something—someone! Bertie wheezed as her wine went down the wrong pipe, and her eyes bugged out at none other than Liza Palmer standing in the doorway. Bertie coughed and sputtered, trying to catch her breath.

Liza pounded on her back. "You okay? Because I didn't come all this way for you to die on me now."

"Wh-what are y-you doing here?" Bertie managed to choke out.

"I'm your fairy godmother and I've come to take you to the ball." Liza gave Bertie's back another whack.

"Stop beating me. I'm fine. I just need some water."

Lucy rushed to fill a glass for Bertie. "Here. Drink this."

After several fortifying gulps, Bertie glared at Liza. "How did you know how to find me?" As if Bertie didn't know. Gary. She knew he'd sing like a canary. Liza must've threatened to destroy his collection of George Michael CDs.

Liza tossed her long, blond hair over her shoulder and dropped down in a chair. "That's not important. What's important is that I'm here to help you."

"Give me a break. When have you ever helped me?"

Liza leaned back and gave Bertie a sly smile. "I'm glad you asked. It's about time I told you."

Bertie crossed her arms and glared at Lucy. "You want to tell me what's going on? Or am I going to have to wring it out of you?"

Lucy shuffled her feet, fascinated by the dirt embedded in the grout on the tile floor. "Please, don't be mad. I was only try—"

"Cut her some slack, Bertha. Lucy would never betray you unless she had a really good reason. And I gave her a really good reason," Liza interjected.

Bertie rolled her eyes. "This I've got to hear."

Liza motioned for Lucy to take a seat. Lucy grabbed the bottle of wine and two more glasses and pulled up a chair. She poured a glass for herself and Liza, and refilled Bertie's.

Lucy lifted her glass. "To old friends, new friends, and new beginnings."

Liza said, "I'll drink to that," and clinked her glass with Lucy's. Both Liza and Lucy waited for Bertie.

"Dammit, Bertie! It's time to bury the hatchet. Now raise your glass and toast before I pour the whole bottle over your obstinate head," Lucy ordered.

Bertie could tell she was outnumbered. Liza was grinning like a cat that caught the mouse and Lucy had her angry face in place, with scrunched nose and squinty eyes.

Bertie heaved a huge sigh. "Truce." She raised her glass. "Now, start from the beginning."

Liza settled back and got comfortable. "Once upon a time…" And she proceeded to tell Bertie all about the night at senior prom.

Bertie exhaled a slow breath. "Is this true?" Her gaze darted from Liza to Lucy. "Why didn't you ever tell me?"

Liza gave a noncommittal shrug. "I didn't want you to know what that asshole said about you."

"It's true. I know I wasn't there, but Liza told me the story that summer." Lucy gave Bertie's hand a squeeze. "Liza swore me to secrecy. We didn't want to see you hurt."

Bertie narrowed her eyes. "What else have you been hiding from me? I suppose you want me to believe I never caught you kissing Cal in our kitchen, right after my mom had died."

"Nope. That's all true. Except…Cal sort of started it. And I am sorry you caught us and it ruined our friendship, but I'm not sorry that it happened."

"You can't still be carrying a torch for Cal," Bertie said as she sipped her wine.

"Kinda. We've been seeing each other. Ever since I moved back to town."

Lucy and Liza jumped back as Bertie spewed red wine all over the table. "What! I don't believe you. Cal never told me. He wouldn't do…you're lying—"

"Calm down, Bertha, before you have an aneurysm," Liza chuckled.

Lucy grabbed a wad of paper towels and cleaned up the mess.

"Cal and I are dating, and we plan to keep on dating with or without your blessing. And as much as I know this is a lot to take in, this is *not* why I drove seven hours to speak to you." Liza reached into her Louis Vuitton cross-body bag and pulled out a large, creamy envelope.

Bertie blanched. "Don't tell me that's a wedding invitation. Because I'm not sure I can handle my brother marrying you…yet." Or Keith marrying *anybody*, her mind screamed.

"Nope. This is better." Liza handed Bertie an

engraved invitation to a kick-off party for the Keith Morgan Tennis Academy, being held at his newly renovated home on Saturday night. *This* Saturday night. Bertie scanned the names of listed sponsors and her hand trembled when she spied her name: *Bertie Anderson, Interior Designer.* Bertie lowered the invitation to the table. "What does this mean?"

"It means we're going to a party. This is going to be huge, Bertha. Tons of celebrities and professional tennis players are going to be there. It's for the rejuvenation of the Jaycee Park and for the new tennis academy. This academy is going to bring in a whole lot of dough and new life to Harmony."

"That's wonderful for Harmony, where I no longer live and therefore no longer care about." Bertie thought her lie rang true until she glimpsed Liza's rolling eyes.

"You're right, Lucy. She's in complete denial." Liza shook the invitation at Bertie's nose. "Let me try and spell this out for you. The press has been invited. All kinds of press. Newspapers, magazines, Internet. They'll be snooping and asking questions and taking pictures of the inside of that mangy old house that you managed to turn into a real jewel. And you need to be there. This could be the break you've been looking for. Or do you like growing old, working inside a musty sample room?"

Bertie's mouth gaped open. She never considered it that way. This could really launch her career. This could put her on the map in the world of design.

"Finally. A lightbulb. Now point me to your closet so I can pick out what you're going to wear." Liza pushed her chair back and stood. "Now. We don't have a lot of time. I want to leave first thing tomorrow morning."

No. If she went back, then she'd have to face him. "You can't be serious. If you think I'm going back to Harmony to some dumb party so that Keith can flaunt his perfect life and his perfect wife, you're insane."

Liza and Lucy grabbed Bertie by the arms and hauled her into her bedroom and into her closet.

"You're going if I have to gag and bind you. Now zip it," Liza snapped.

———~~~———

Keith knew the minute Bertie stepped into the grand foyer even before he laid eyes on her. The atmosphere in the room shifted and the hint of gardenias cut through the heavy colognes and aftershaves like a breath of fresh air. He was standing in a circle with Beau Quinton, his tennis coaches, and a few investors all dressed in suits. Wives and girlfriends swarmed the rooms along with other celebrities and all of Harmony, including Jo Ellen, Arlene, the Ardbuckle twins, and half the women that had chased him for months. Live music filtered through the French doors from the back patio, and the waitstaff, in black pants and stiff bow ties, passed hors d'oeuvres and champagne cocktails.

Keith felt Bertie staring at him a split second before their gazes locked. She looked even better than he remembered. And he had an excellent memory. He hadn't dared hope that she'd come tonight, and until she walked through the door, he hadn't noticed he'd been holding his breath.

Bertie broke eye contact first and turned her back on him. She walked away, and he felt as if someone had kicked him in the gut with a steel boot. Keith caught sight of Aunt Francesca, who had escorted Bertie to the party. She gave a little shrug and followed Bertie out of the room.

Beau Quinton gave a low whistle. "*Who* was that? Please tell me she's single."

Keith cut his narrowed eyes to Beau. They shared a professional friendship, respecting each other's talents. And Keith knew Beau's reputation. He could charm the pants off a preacher's wife. If he breathed one more word about Bertie, Keith was going to knock his perfectly straight, white teeth out of his tanned face.

"I had no idea they grew hot little chili peppers like that in this sleepy town." Beau's smile slipped as he must've seen something in Keith's face that alarmed him.

"Don't even think about it. Don't get within ten feet of her. Do you understand?" he ground out between clenched teeth.

"Chillax, dude. I'm not here to hit on your woman," Beau said in a low whisper. "Now stop clenching your teeth and straighten your face. You're liable to scare old ladies with that mug."

Keith gripped Beau's shoulder and gave it a squeeze. Then he looked up and waved someone over. "Arlene, I'd like you to meet Beau Quinton, quarterback for the Cherokees. He's a big fan of green Jell-O. Tell him all about the one you make with marshmallows." Keith was pretty sure Beau said, "fuck you" under his breath before flashing his winning smile at Arlene Tomlin.

"If you'll excuse me, I need to speak with someone." And Keith left the room, searching for Bertie.

He found her next to the bar on the outdoor patio, talking with another young tennis player. John or Jack.

Single. Good-looking guy. Keith had seen him play. He had a shitty ranking because he had a shitty attitude and he partied more than he trained. Normally Keith didn't care what other players did in their downtime or who they did it with. But the attention this guy was showing Bertie, in her low-cut, emerald-green dress that knotted in the front and hugged her breasts, irritated the hell out of him.

"Hey, Prince," the young pup said as he handed Bertie a drink. "I understand that this beautiful designer here decorated your whole house." Bertie continued to smile at Jack*ass* as the jealousy started to eat at Keith until it swarmed him and threatened to pull him under like a crocodile in a death roll.

Keith gave a curt nod and then said, "Hello, Bertie."

Bertie stiffened. "Mr. Morgan."

Keith's heart stopped. It had only been three months since he'd heard her throaty voice, but it felt like an eternity. She continued to avert her gaze as if she couldn't stand the sight of him. But when she finally looked up, her animated face appeared flat and dull, not laughing and smiling and glowing with pleasure like he remembered. Fear clenched in the pit of his stomach until he could feel himself cramping. In the past, he would always use his fear or nerves as a driving force for winning matches. But this was one match where he was down two sets and losing in the third. He had killed something in Bertie three months ago. And now he was deathly afraid that he couldn't turn this match around on sheer drive alone. But he wasn't giving up. He loved her too much not to fight for her.

"Bertie, would you like to dance?" But Keith wasn't

the one doing the talking. Jackass was still in the picture, enjoying the view of Bertie's exposed cleavage.

"No," Keith snarled. Bertie and Jackass both gawked at him as if a second nose grew on his forehead. "Ms. Anderson, may I speak with you…*now*?" Keith reached for her when Jackass blocked his arm.

"There you are! I've been searching all over." Beau Quinton pushed his way into the middle of the brewing tension. "I think you promised this dance to me." Beau winked at Bertie's shocked face and maneuvered her onto the dance floor, away from Jackass's drooling mouth.

As much as Keith wanted to rearrange Beau's face for pulling Bertie into his arms and laughing with her on the dance floor, he knew Beau did it so Keith could cool down and not make a scene by dragging his woman off like a caveman. Watching her walk away for the second time this evening almost brought him to his knees. But Keith knew from thousands of hours of training that the only way to win was always to make the last shot. He'd learned to rely on his training, to grind it out and be patient.

But he'd waited three whole months—no, make that his whole life—for someone like Bertie. He didn't want to wait anymore. He wanted Bertie in his life. Tonight. This minute. For as long as he lived. Plain, simple, boring vanilla was never going to make him happy. He thrived on competition and grit and even drama. Yes, drama. Bertie's drama. Bertie's lust for life. Bertie who couldn't hit a tennis ball for love or money. He wanted Bertie, who thought nothing of climbing ladders in four-inch heels to tackle impossible tasks. Bertie made him happy. And he hadn't been truly happy for a really long time. He loved her and she loved him. Something that fierce and strong didn't vanish in three months. Or did it?

Chapter 21

"Yes, we did our best to enhance the true integrity of the house. We strove to respect its original features," Bertie said, answering another reporter's design question on Keith's home. Bertie had fielded quite a few questions and even had her picture taken next to the original restored mantel in the living room for the *Triangle Tattler*, an online newsletter. She'd been smiling and making small talk for almost an hour, and her nerves were frayed.

Bertie still couldn't believe Liza, of all the people on earth, convinced her to come home and attend this party. She and Liza drove seven hours in the same car and didn't kill each other. They'd arrived back in Harmony yesterday afternoon. Bertie had begrudgingly come to appreciate Liza and her directness, but she hadn't fully forgiven her. She'd get there one day. Maybe. But only if Liza stopped calling her Bertha Mavis. Gawd, Bertie hated her name.

Liza had pulled into Bertie's driveway and Gary and Cal had rushed out to welcome Bertie home. Bertie forgave Gary for breaking his promise, but barely. She needed to hold on to her grudge and make him squirm a teensy bit longer. But Cal's betrayal had cut Bertie to the quick. Not because he wanted to be with Liza, but because he'd never confided in her. And he'd allowed Bertie to believe all those years that Liza had been the instigator of the infamous kitchen kiss, not him. But Cal, in his usual way, tugged on Bertie's ponytail, caught her in a headlock, and told her he loved her no matter how nutty she got.

So, here she stood, dressed in an emerald-green silk wrap dress, exposing way too much boobilage and wearing her favorite Christian Dior heels—the silver ones with the sparkly bows—all because Liza Palmer kidnapped her, dressed her, and forced her to come. It didn't help that Aunt Franny cried over the phone to Bertie and insisted that Bertie escort her to the party, or that Dottie Duncan marched over to Bertie's house in rhinestone cowboy boots and poked her long, cobalt-blue fingernail in Bertie's face, delivering a blistering lecture about how she'd broken her aunt's heart and all of Harmony's. Because none of that addressed the real reason she couldn't stay here.

The real reason stood on the other side of the living room, smiling down into some glamorous woman's face as she hung on his every word. The man who'd made her love him despite his grumpy demeanor and irrational hang-ups—and then broken her heart as if it were cheap dime-store glass. The man who couldn't open his heart because of all the pain he'd carried around like a coat of armor—impenetrable. By Bertie anyway.

Bertie handed her empty glass to a passing waiter. She needed air. She glanced at her dressy bracelet watch. She'd give this nightmare of an evening fifteen more minutes before she blew out of here. Something caught the corner of her eye and she followed the sound of a giggle. A giggle she'd heard before. Bertie froze as if her coveted shoes had stepped in wet cement. There, smiling up at Keith with her perfect blond hair pulled away with a silver headband, in her perfect midnight-blue sheath dress over her perfect slim, hipless figure, stood Gail. Keith's…what? Girlfriend? Wife? *What?* And then Bertie had her answer. Gail's left hand cupped Keith's face as she kissed his cheek. And there it sat. A Tiffany-style engagement ring on Gail's perfect finger. The catty part of Bertie that wanted to scratch Gail's eyes out with her claws thought the diamond appeared rather puny. With all his gobs of money, he chose that chip of a diamond? But then maybe perfect Gail liked small stones to match her small breasts. *Stop it.*

Keith looked up and caught Bertie staring. More like gaping with her mouth open. Bertie flinched, commanded her stiff legs to move, and fled from the room. She wove her way to the front door, knocking a waiter with a tray full of plates into Dottie Duncan's generous chest covered in flamingo-pink spandex and sequins, dousing her with her champagne and a plate of creamy tortellini.

"*Wh-what the*…sweet merciful crap!" Dottie bellowed at the wet, gooey stain on her top. "Bertie, are you wearing skates again? What's gotten into you?"

But Bertie had already made it to the front door. "Sorry," she called over her shoulder. She rushed down the front steps when someone grabbed her arm.

"Where the fuck are you going?" Liza yelled at her.

"Leave me alone." Bertie wrenched her arm free. "I've had enough. I don't need to hang around any longer and watch him make googly eyes at his perfect fiancée. I can't take it anymore," Bertie choked on a sob.

"You don't understand. That's—"

"Save it for someone who cares." Bertie glared at Liza. "I'm taking Aunt Franny's car. You take her home. I'll return her car in the morning before I go to the airport."

"You're making a big mistake, Bertha," Liza said in a warning tone. But Bertie didn't hang around to listen. She jumped in Aunt Franny's car and floored it. Away from Keith and away from the life she'd never have.

At eight o'clock the next morning, Bertie stood in Aunt Franny's sitting room, wearing a short, belted orange tank dress, wedge sandals and a sheepish expression on her face. Her packed bag was by the back door. And she had already called Coco's Cab to pick her up for the airport. Bertie could only imagine the uproar that had ensued at the kick-off party after her disastrous exit last night. Cal had called, but Bertie didn't answer. Gary banged on her door around midnight, and Liza left three messages calling Bertie all kinds of names, the least of which was *complete fucking moron*. Bertie ignored all of them. She had to leave. She needed to clear her head and her heart. And she couldn't do that stuck here in Harmony with all her memories. Seeing Keith hurt too much. She couldn't stand by and watch the man she loved marry someone else. She couldn't live with the constant reminder that he didn't love her.

"I'm sorry about last night," Bertie murmured to Aunt Franny, who perched in her antique French chair in a blue silk bathrobe with her slippered feet crossed.

She fluttered her hand. "I don't care about last

night. I'm worried about you. Where are you running off to now?"

"Back home. To Atlanta."

Aunt Franny pierced Bertie with her imperial stare. "*This* is your home. You belong here. You belong with—"

"Don't say it." Bertie crossed the room and peered out the French doors onto the pristine lawn. "This is something I have to do. Probably not forever. But at least until I forget…" Her voice trailed off. She didn't want to put into words all that she needed to forget. Bertie heard Aunt Franny rise and move toward the door.

"At least say good-bye to Maddie. She has missed you so much."

Bertie clutched her chest. "Oh. Yes. I'd love to say… good-bye." Bertie licked her dry lips.

Aunt Franny frowned and then nodded. "Let me go wake her. Give me a minute."

Bertie dropped her forehead on the glass pane of the door as she listened to Aunt Franny leave the room and then climb the stairs.

She jumped at the sound of the front door slamming and the bellow that followed.

"Aunt Francesca! She's gone! Again. You said this would work. Dammit! You were wrong—"

Keith stopped as he barged into the sitting room. Shock and then disbelief raced across his face as he spied Bertie by the French doors.

"You," they both said in unison.

He'd dressed in ratty jeans and a light-blue cotton polo shirt with the tail hanging out. His hair had that tousled, just-got-out-of-bed sexy look, which always looked like hell on her. Bertie's heart crashed inside her chest at the sight of him. Her mouth worked, but no sound came out.

"Don't." Keith held up his hand. "Don't talk, please. I don't know what happened last night, but I didn't get the chance to ex—"

Bertie's traitorous heart hammered so loud she could barely hear. "There's nothing to explain. You made everything crystal clear three months ago," she said in a surprisingly calm voice.

"No. No. I made a mess of everything. I need to apologize."

She couldn't bear to look at him and lowered her gaze to her toes. "Is that why you're here? To apologize?"

"Yes. I never meant to hurt you."

No, but he did. And he would again with his apology and his hope that they could remain friends or some other crock of baked beans. No declaration of love. Only an apology for hurting her with words spoken from his inner turmoil.

"Last night you left before I could—"

Bertie squared her shoulders. "Yes. I left before I could congratulate you on your engagement. I hope you'll both be marvelously happy together. I'll be sure to send a gift from the registry."

"Huh? What engagement?"

Bertie's fist clenched at her side. "To Gail. I'm not an idiot. I saw the ring."

"Gail? Ring?" Then Keith burst out laughing, his features melting into happiness and his eyes sparkling. "If you think I'd buy an engagement ring like that, then you don't know me very well," he said between hoots of laughter.

What? Did Gail buy her own ring? Bertie didn't find any humor in the situation.

"Apology accepted. I've got to go." She moved to brush past Keith, but he grabbed her by the arms and pulled her toward him.

"No. Please don't leave me again. I don't think I can live through it." All laughter had vanished and he stared with a fierceness that caught her attention. "I know…I hurt you the day you told me you loved me. And I left. I know…I fucked up. But, Bertie, you left me and never came back. And last night…I tried to reach you, but you didn't give me a chance. You left me again."

Bertie stopped breathing. Something in his voice grabbed her. His dark eyes memorized her face, drinking her in as if she were a tall, cool glass of water and he was dying of thirst.

"What are you trying to say?" she whispered, almost afraid of the answer.

Keith kissed the top of Bertie's head and gathered her close. "I love you. I've always loved you. Ever since I found you hiding in my closet. Please tell me it's not too late. Please tell me that you love me too."

Bertie pulled back. He smiled down at her, but worry and fear lurked behind his eyes.

"What about Gail? Does she know?"

Keith's smile grew, and he pressed kisses on Bertie's face and eyes and cheeks. "Gail knows everything. She knew even before I did."

"Wh-what?"

Keith gave her a gentle shake and her eyes popped open. "Gail's engaged, but not to me." Bertie blinked. "She's engaged to one of your most ardent admirers."

Keith kissed the tip of her nose. "I'm afraid his crooning days are over for you though, because now Scott only sings for Gail."

Bertie gasped. "*Scott Douglas* is marrying Gail? Really?"

"And they couldn't be a better match. Except for us. We're perfect. And we belong together." Keith caught a tear that trailed down Bertie's cheek with his thumb. "I love you."

Bertie couldn't speak past the lump in her throat and the thudding of her heart. She grabbed the front of Keith's shirt and planted a big kiss on his mouth. He caught her around the waist and deepened the kiss. Then he pushed back, his chest heaving. "Wait."

Keith dropped down on one knee and pulled something from his back pocket and said, "Bertha Mavis, the girl with the two worst names in the world, the girl with the brightest smile, the most beautiful eyes, and the biggest heart—will you marry me?"

Bertie looked down, and cushioned in gorgeous maroon velvet was a beautiful emerald cut diamond and peridot engagement ring. Bertie dropped to her knees. "I love you! Yes...*yes*. I'll marry you." She launched herself at Keith and they both crashed to the floor, tangled up together the way Bertie hoped their life would be forever. Keith's laughter, filled with love and promises, poured through Bertie. He cradled the back of her head and pulled Bertie in for a long, hard kiss.

"Daddy!" Maddie burst into the room like an excited puppy and fell on top of them wearing her fuzzy pj's. "Yay! Bertie's going to be my mommy!"

Aunt Franny followed but hung back and observed

the playful antics of her growing family as she wiped tears from her eyes.

Keith laughed again as he kissed Bertie and Maddie and then Bertie again.

Bertie sat up with tousled hair and well-kissed lips. "Where's that ring?"

Keith raised up on his elbow, holding it between his fingers.

"Here. Let me." Bertie snatched the most beautiful ring ever and slid it on her finger. "Now *that's* a ring," she said as she held her hand out with the large diamond. "Thank goodness you knew me better than to buy some little chip."

Maddie reached for Bertie's hand with pure awe lighting her eyes as she admired the fabulous blingage. "It's beautiful," Maddie sighed.

Keith flopped back down and groaned as if in pain. "I am so outnumbered. I'm never going to win with you three women."

Bertie patted him on the chest and her eyes sparkled with amusement. "Never a dull moment in the new Morgan household."

Keith gathered Bertie and Maddie in his arms. "Just the way I like it."

Epilogue

FOR AT LEAST THE FIFTH TIME, BERTIE ADJUSTED THE gray linen pillow shams that covered the king-size bed in the master bedroom she and Keith had shared for the past amazing fifteen months.

Keith burst through the door. "Bertie, let's go. The bed looks fine. Stop worrying."

Bertie's sharp gaze darted around the room to make sure all the lamps were dimmed and every accessory was in its proper place. "It needs to be perfect, not simply fine." She ran a hand down her new burnt-orange cropped jacket and short, brown skirt. "Do I look okay?"

Keith crossed the room and wrapped his arms around her waist. "You look perfect." He kissed her and then said, "And the whole house looks perfect. You ready?" Keith pulled on her hand.

"Wait." Bertie tugged and Keith stopped. "What about my shoes? Do they say successful designer or stumpy woman trying to look tall?"

Keith's gaze flicked to the chunky suede Prada wedges on Bertie's feet. "They say successful designer who drives her husband crazy. Now, either you move on your own accord or I'm carrying you out over my shoulder."

"Okay. Okay." Bertie patted her hair as she glanced in the mirror one last time and followed Keith from the room.

"Maddie! Shake a leg. The photographer is here," Keith bellowed up the stairwell. Bertie's heart stuttered. She still couldn't believe this day had finally come. Bertie Anderson Morgan, Interior Designer, was getting her very own spread in *Veranda* magazine. It had been three weeks since she'd gotten the call and she hadn't been able to sleep or eat since. Not eating hadn't been such a bad thing, since she still had a few baby pounds to lose.

"Where's Harry?" Maddie asked, clattering down the stairs in a green-and-blue plaid taffeta dress. "Has he been fed? It's my turn to give him a bottle," Maddie stated with all the importance of a big sister.

"Gary has him and has fed and burped him like a real pro. You'll get the next feeding. Right now, we have to look perfect for the picture."

Keith appeared in the foyer holding his son, Harrison Camden Morgan, named after his dad, with a big smile of pride tugging at his lips. Bertie's breath caught like it always did when she contemplated her husband and her beautiful baby. Love flooded her heart until she was sure it would burst. Somehow Bertie, a no-name, small-town designer, had it all: a beautiful home, a budding career, a family to hold and cherish, and a gorgeous husband who loved her more and more every day.

Keith kissed the baby, murmuring silly words, and Maddie bounced in her black ballet flats, peering at the bundle in her dad's arms. Bertie blinked as tears of joy sprang to her eyes.

"What's the holdup, people? Chop, chop." Liza appeared at the front door threshold, clapping her hands. "This natural light is not going to hold. Even for the perfect family."

Keith reached for Bertie's hand and squeezed as they arranged themselves on the wraparound porch.

Maddie glanced up at Bertie. "Are you crying?"

Bertie swiped at her eye. "No, honey."

"Good Lord." Liza brushed Bertie's hand away and dabbed at her eyes with a tissue. "Can't you stop blubbering for one second to get your picture taken?" Liza cupped Bertie's chin. "Looks good. Now smile, Bertha."

The photographer adjusted their poses with Keith resting his hand on Bertie's shoulder and Maddie standing at her side and baby Harry in Bertie's arms. "Hold it right there," he said as he fiddled with his filters.

"Mom, why does Aunt Liza always call you Bertha?" Maddie asked.

"Because she's the spawn of the devil," Bertie said between her smiling teeth.

"Do you think the baby in her belly will be a devil too?"

"Most definitely," Keith said.

"Poor Uncle Cal," Maddie said.

"Hey, I heard that," Liza called out from the front lawn. And with that, Keith, Bertie, and Maddie burst out laughing just as the camera flashed.

WATCH FOR THE NEXT IN
MICHELE SUMMERS'
HARMONY HOMECOMINGS SERIES:

*Not So New
in Town*

AVAILABLE FEBRUARY 2015

FROM SOURCEBOOKS CASABLANCA

Chapter 1

LUCY DOOLAN HATED BEING CALLED LOCO LUCY. BUT as she kicked the flat tire on old Rockin' Rhonda, her beat-up Toyota Camry, she thought she might be a little nuts. She stared down at the toe of her scuffed cowboy boot and dug her heel into the gravel on the side of the narrow two-lane highway.

"Moose muffins. This is not how I pictured the end of my day." Lucy looked at the dead cell phone in her hand. So uncool for someone who made her living with the phone. Dead cell phone. Dead back-up cell phone in trunk of car. Flat tire on side of road with no spare. Not that she'd know what to do with a spare if she had one.

And she was just outside of Harmony, North Carolina—her hometown, where everyone remembered her as Loco Lucy. Where she never wanted to live again.

Ever.

Lucy plucked at the tie-dyed T-shirt sticking to her chest and belly. It had to be ninety-nine freakin' degrees, at least. She scrubbed at her neck where sweat snaked down over her skin, making her itch in the late July heat. She had all August to swelter, and it would most likely be well into October before any cool weather would come her way.

"Looks like I'm gonna have to hoof it." She peered down the empty road, squinting behind her red-framed sunglasses. No cars had been by since she'd bumped and limped old Rhonda off to the side. Forced to walk the last ten miles in blistering heat was not how she had pictured her homecoming. Entering Main Street on foot would give everybody one more reason to call her Loco. Lucy gave the dead tire one more vicious kick for good measure.

"Ow!" She hopped on one foot. "Broken-down old bucket of bolts." She glared at the rusted-out tin can. "I've a good mind not to send a tow truck, but with my crappy luck, you'll get towed into town anyhow and I'll get a fat ticket as a welcome home gift." Lucy stopped hopping and wiggled her injured toes inside her boot. "Fine. Whatever. I could use the exercise." She bent inside the car and grabbed her purse, along with her bag of Cheetos, Red Hots, and Little Debbies, slammed the door with her hip, and headed in the direction of Harmony.

"What the hell?" Brogan Reese rounded the curve in his convertible. Even in the ninety-degree heat, he'd been riding with the top down. He squinted against the late afternoon sun. Up the road a ways, some crazy gal was kicking a tire that appeared to be very, very flat. Brogan chuckled, watching her hop on one foot after venting her frustration on the dead tire. She bent for something in the car's interior, exposing a lot of leg as her short jean skirt crept up the backs of her thighs. Nice. Brogan pushed his aviator sunglasses back up the bridge of his nose as he slowed his car.

Snap out of it, dumbass.

Probably some mother trying to get back to her

double-wide trailer, home to three sets of wailing twins. He eased off the road onto the shoulder, coming to a complete stop. His new car, an XK Jaguar, aptly named after the lethal cat, purred low. He sat for a moment as crazy Tire-Kicker shoved some purple python-patterned bag over her shoulder and started down the highway in the opposite direction. As much as he enjoyed the sway of her hips marching toward town, he couldn't let her go without offering to change the tire. Besides, he needed the distraction. The lively, one-sided conversation he'd been having with himself for the past few hours had gotten boring. Along with raising more questions than answers, he'd given himself a mother of a headache. He pushed open his door and stepped out.

"Hey, there. Need some help?" he called to her retreating back.

The swaying hips stopped as Tire-Kicker turned on her cowboy-booted heels. She didn't look old and tired from multiple births, but Brogan couldn't be too sure. Huge red-speckled Wayfarer sunglasses swallowed the upper half of her face. She didn't speak but clutched her funky bag closer to her body.

"With your flat tire?" He motioned to the rusted piece of shit posing as a car on the side of the road.

"You got a spare? Because I sure don't," she said.

Why should that surprise him? Maybe the floorboards were rusted out, too. They could pull a Fred and Barney and Flintstone it back to town. Gravel crunched beneath her boots as she inched closer, gripping the straps of her bag. He still couldn't see her eyes, but he detected wariness as lines of tension bracketed her full mouth.

"I'd offer you a ride into town, but since you don't

know me, I figured you wouldn't accept. How about I call for roadside assistance?" Brogan pulled his cell phone from his jeans pocket. "You can wait in your car and I'll wait in mine until they come. Would that help?"

Streaks of purple ran through the blond hair that flopped on her shoulder as she tilted her head, studying him.

"Better yet...you can call, if that would make you more comfortable." Brogan extended the cell. She jumped back as if he meant to strike her. "Whoa." He raised both hands cautiously to show he meant no harm. "Okay then. Maybe not," he said slowly. Tire-Kicker's head moved side to side as if hunting for a place to hide. "Look, lady, only trying to help. I'm from Harmony, which is right up the road. I'm—"

"I know who you are," she said in a flat voice, catching him off guard.

"You do?" He stared at her streaky hair and hunched shoulders as she crossed her arms and lowered her head. Who was this chick? He couldn't place her. And from her Southern accent, he knew she wasn't from up North, where he'd lived the last ten years.

"Yeah," she said to the gravel mashed beneath her boots. "Brogan Reese. Harmony High's football star, homecoming king, and heartbreaker."

Shit. Here we go again.

~~~

Not him! Lucy searched for a ditch or some kind of swamp-like hole to hurl herself into. She'd rather be bleeding out in shark-infested waters than standing on the side of the road talking to him. Brogan Reese. Her high school crush. The stud of Harmony High. Who never knew she existed until…

Lucy couldn't think about that now. She needed to figure a way out of this embarrassing mess. Damn Julia! If she weren't already seven months pregnant and bedridden, Lucy would come up with more painful ways to punish her.

Julia. The bane of Lucy's existence. Childhood nemesis. Boyfriend snatcher.

Stepsister.

Inhaling hot, muggy North Carolina air, Lucy wished she were at the beach soaking up rays or in the mountains breathing crisp air. She must've been crazy—maybe she ate some bad Cheese Whiz—because how else could she explain allowing Julia to talk her into coming back home?

"Have we met?" Brogan interrupted her mental rant. Lucy's head snapped up. He didn't recognize her…at all. No surprise there. She couldn't blame him. He'd only had eyes for one person in high school, and it wasn't the gawky, awkward freshman who had skulked in the halls, hoping for a glimpse of her crush. The girl with the wild curls who had volunteered to keep stats for the football team to be near his greatness. She guessed she should consider herself lucky that he didn't recall the way she'd ruined his homecoming date with Julia, the homecoming queen. His girlfriend. The love of his life.

At one time or other, every girl fantasized about running into an ex-boyfriend or crush—looking marvelous, with flawless skin, coiffed hair, and ample cleavage perfectly displayed for ogling. And the fantasy always included being hugely successful in some philanthropic career, flaunting great success and watching him grovel at her feet, begging for crumbs from her table. Lucy had millions of those fantasies tucked away. All starring Brogan Reese. But none of them included ugly Rockin' Rhonda, the tin can listing on the side of the road, or Lucy wearing her cut-off jean skirt and a sweaty tie-dyed T-shirt.

Acknowledgments

Thanks to my wonderful editor, Deb Werksman. I felt connected to you the minute I met you! And to the great team at Sourcebooks for your patience and taking me under your wing.

To my agent, Nicole Resciniti, your support and wealth of information are priceless.

For her friendship, cheerleading, and making me laugh until I cried, thanks to my Yankee fan/friend, Noel Higgins.

And to my special peeps in Miami, especially Elise and Jennifer for that fun girls' weekend in Naples where Michele Summers was born.

And finally to my beautiful, smart, funny kids—for always understanding when deadlines loomed and mom acted cray cray! I love you so much I can't even stop!

About the Author

Debut author Michele Summers writes about small-town life with a Southern flair. She has her own interior design business in Raleigh, North Carolina, and Miami, Florida. Both professions feed her creative appetite and provide a daily dose of humor. When she isn't writing or creating colorful interiors, she is playing tennis, cooking for family and clients, knitting, reading, and most importantly, raising her two great kids. Michele's work has won recognition from the Dixie First Chapter, Golden Palm, Fool For Love, Rebecca, and Fabulous Five contests. She is an active member of the Heart of Carolina and Florida Romance Writers chapters of RWA. You can contact Michele at her website, www.michelesummers.com, where you will also locate her other social media buttons.